A SCOTTISH DESTINY

A captivating and unforgettable Scottish romance

GWEN KIRKWOOD

Sinclair Family Saga Book 4

STRATHBERRY

JOFFE BOOKS

Revised edition 2023
Joffe Books, London
www.joffebooks.com

First published by Romaunce Books
in Great Britain in 2017

This paperback edition was first published
in Great Britain in 2023

Cover art by Jarmila Takač

ISBN: 978-1-80405-854-1

CHAPTER ONE

Seventeen-year-old Marie Sinclair listened in nervous anticipation to the chattering wheels of the train taking her to Scotland. She had never travelled far from her home at Moorend Farm in Yorkshire but she was looking forward to seeing Jamie, her eldest brother, and his young wife, Rina, not to mention her loveable young niece, Marguerite. She hoped to meet some of her Scottish cousins too, but most of all she was anxious to help Rina deal with the life-threatening problems her second pregnancy was causing. She had to change trains at Kilmarnock and she was worried she might not get herself and her luggage onto the platform in time. How would she find the local train to take her to Strathlinn?

She prayed her journey would be worthwhile. Jamie couldn't afford to pay a maid to help Rina and his fierce pride and independent nature might prove a serious obstacle and prevent him accepting her help, unless she could convince him she needed a change of scene herself. He and Rina had loved each other since their early teens but their path to happiness had been strewn with problems. It would be dreadful if anything should happen to Rina after only three blissful years of marriage. There was Marguerite to consider too. At eighteen months old she needed her mother badly. Marie's mouth firmed. She loved children and she was determined to help in any way she could.

Her mother and aunt had done a little well-meaning conniving which had resulted in Aunt Maggie inviting Marie to stay on the pretext that her niece was in need of a break after caring for Lady Hanley, then the shock of her sudden death. It was true the opportunity to visit her Scottish relatives had come at a time when Marie felt unsettled and undecided about her future. For the past eighteen months she had enjoyed caring for Lady Hanley. Amazingly they had bridged the generation gap, and even more surprisingly they had overcome the gulf of their very different backgrounds. Dr Clayton had been delighted with his patient's progress as she recovered from her stroke but Lady Hanley convinced him it was all due to Marie's help and patience. Consequently her sudden death had been an awful shock to them all. Now Marie was undecided whether to train as a nurse or accept Lord Hanley's offer of working for him in the Estate Office. Her father thought she should work for him because Lord Hanley was his landlord, and also because he had arranged and paid for her to attend classes in bookkeeping and typewriting four afternoons a week during her eighteen months at Silverbeck Hall.

The train jolted and slowed. Hastily Marie gathered her belongings as they approached Kilmarnock. Her heart was pounding with nerves but one of the porters took her big suitcase and guided her to the platform where she would catch the local train to Strathlinn. There were not many people waiting so there were plenty of empty seats. She had not noticed a young man waiting for the train until he joined her in the same carriage. He smiled pleasantly and settled down. There were only the two of them in the carriage and Marie was conscious that he kept glancing at her, although he lowered his eyes whenever she looked up. Eventually he cleared his throat and asked her which station she wanted.

'I was told to get out at Strathlinn. My uncle has promised to meet me there,' Marie added, hoping Uncle Joe would be on time. Uncle Joe was her mother's eldest brother and she had assured Marie he was the kindest of men and totally reliable. Aunt Maggie was her father's eldest sister and the two had married later in life strengthening the bond between the four of them.

'Strathlinn is my destination too,' the young man volunteered. 'You have not been before? Strange it is then, I thought I had seen you somewhere.' Marie was practical and very capable but she was inexperienced with young men. She thought he sounded genuine, not one of those she had heard about who tried various tricks to get to know a girl. He wrinkled his brow, trying to remember where he had seen that reddish blonde hair with the glints of gold and silver, and the high cheekbones, and fresh pink complexion. 'Strathlinn is small but it's our nearest town. My name is Mark Blackford. I come from a place called Stavondale.'

'I have heard of Stavondale Estate,' Marie said remembering it had belonged to Rina's family. Her Sinclair relations had been tenants for four generations until Uncle Jim had bought Bonnybrae, with Jamie and Rina as partners, after the death of Sir Roger Capel, Rina's father. 'You don't sound Scottish,' she said to the young man.

'No, I was brought up in Hereford, near the Welsh Border. We had a Welsh nanny.'

'Maybe that accounts for the lilt in your voice,' Marie said, remembering the cobbler at home in Silverbeck Village. Everyone called him Taffy. She couldn't remember hearing his proper name.

'My home is in Scotland now but I had to spend the weekend with my family to celebrate my eldest brother's engagement. I shall be glad to be back,' Mark added with a heartfelt sigh. 'And you? I cannot detect your accent.'

'I'm just me.' Marie shrugged and gave a warm chuckle. He thought it was delightful — nothing like the affected trills and giggles of the young ladies at his brother's party, especially Lucinda, the girl his mother had been at pains to force into his company. In desperation to escape he had made an excuse that he was needed back in Scotland now that he was the laird of the run-down Stavondale Estate. He had left two days earlier than expected arousing his mother's anger. He looked keenly at Marie. She blushed shyly.

'But you're not Scottish?' he persisted.

'No.' Growing up with parents who had never lost their Scottish accent, then going to school in Yorkshire, Marie had a mixture of words and pronunciations which had often resulted in teasing from her schoolfriends. During her stay at Silverbeck Hall, when she was striving to help Lady Hanley regain her speech, she had instinctively copied Lord Hanley's precise pronunciation so that his wife would understand her more easily, and when she was reading to her from the books in Lord Hanley's library to pass the sleepless hours during the night. Consequently Marie's own speech had become a mixture of accents. 'I live in Yorkshire with my family,' she said relenting. 'I am here to visit my aunt and uncle and my brother and sister-in-law.'

'I see. We are almost at Strathlinn and you have not told me your name?'

'It is Marie. Marie Sinclair . . .'

'Sinclair?' Mark echoed. His lean face broke into a smile. 'Are you Jamie Sinclair's sister?'

'One of his sisters,' Marie nodded. 'We're a large family. Do you know my brother?'

'Jamie? Of course! So that's why I thought I should know you. You are very pretty of course, whereas Jamie is just a man, albeit a handsome fellow. He has the same wavy red-gold hair and wide blue eyes, the high cheekbones. I know Jamie and his wife well, or at least as well as I know any of the local people.' Marie thought he sounded wistful. She couldn't know how much he longed to be accepted. The locals treated him with reserve because he was their new laird, even though Stavondale Estate was barely half the size it had been in the days of Rina's grandfather. Mark shuddered, trying to banish unwanted memories of the man who would always haunt him. He looked at Marie. 'I am learning to be a farmer. Jamie's uncle is very patient at answering my questions and giving me advice.' He had taken one of the smaller farms into his own hands when the tenant retired, hoping a knowledge of farming might help him understand the running of the estate. He sighed. 'I have so much to learn. I want to make a good job of it and be an example to my tenants. Mr Jim Sinclair must be your uncle too of course?'

'He is my father's eldest brother, but I have never met him.'

'I believe he does not travel far but he is never idle. Jamie and Rina are the kindest and most sincere people I know.' His expression changed. He grew sombre and his dark eyes were shadowed. 'I expect you heard I killed Rina's father?' He blurted. Marie stared at him.

'Are — are you joking?'

'I wish I was.' He muttered. 'Rina has never uttered a word of recrimination. Neither have the locals if I'm honest. Everyone has been jolly decent about it, but I still shudder whenever I remember that day. It is three years ago but I still have nightmares. I shall never carry a gun again.'

'We — we did hear Rina's father had been killed,' Marie said in confusion, trying to remember what she had heard. At fourteen she hadn't paid attention to the details. 'We had never met Rina until she and Jamie came to stay with us on their honeymoon.' She smiled remembering how shocked her mother had been when she heard they had spent the first two nights of their married life in a gypsy caravan. Rina had enjoyed it tremendously and considered it all terribly romantic. They were so much in love. Marie sighed and wondered if she would ever feel like that.

* * *

She was relieved to see Uncle Joe waiting for her on the platform. She clung to the basket which her mother had insisted on sending with provisions for her journey and for Aunt Maggie. She was grateful to her travelling companion when he lifted her suitcase onto the platform. She thanked him politely but, in her eagerness to greet Joe, she paid him no more attention. Mark hid his disappointment. His two older brothers attracted girls easily, but did he want their type of girls? No, he knew he did not, even though his mother was expecting him to marry a wealthy wife. She never allowed him to forget her disappointment because he was not the daughter she had craved.

Joe carried Marie's suitcase and guided her out of the station to his motorbike.

'Gosh, is this yours, Uncle Joe?' she laughed aloud. 'Am I to get a ride in it?'

'Aye, lassie, unless you prefer to walk the three miles and more to Braeside?'

'I don't mind walking, but I'd love a ride in this.' She stroked the yellow paint of the sidecar.

'I think we shall have to tie your case on the back,' Joe said. 'It looks as though you've brought half the contents of your mother's larder in that basket. Did she think we wouldn't feed ye?'

'You must know what Mother is like,' she grinned.

'So you call Emma mother now, eh? When Maggie and I visited you at Moorend you all called her Mam.'

'Mm. The others still call her Mam. I had to speak a bit more politely while I was helping Lady Hanley. I suppose I got used to it. Oh look, that's the young man who was on the train. He told me he lived at Stavondale. Will he have to walk the three miles?'

'He will unless he has arranged for somebody to meet him.' Joe frowned, hesitating. He liked what he had seen of Master Mark Blackford, but it was impossible to forget he was the local laird since his father purchased the remainder of Stavondale Estate for him.

'Couldn't he perch on the back?' Marie asked. He had been pleasant and helpful. 'He says he knows Jamie and Uncle Jim.'

'Run and ask him then, Marie. If he wants a lift I'll leave your suitcase with the stationmaster. That might be safer anyway. Jamie will collect it in the morning when he brings the milk to the train.'

'Would you like a lift on the back of Uncle Joe's motorbike?' Marie called, hurrying after Mark. He turned and she pointed to the motorbike and sidecar with Joe still holding her suitcase. His face creased in a boyish smile. What a difference that makes Marie thought, her own smile widening.

'I would really appreciate a lift, Mr Greig, if you're sure there is room for me.'

'Well, it's not the style ye'll be used to,' Joe said wryly, 'but I see ye don't have much luggage. We can leave Marie's here and collect it tomorrow. Can you ride on the pillion?'

'Yes indeed,' Mark said with enthusiasm. 'I have envied you travelling around in this. I thought of asking you for a ride. I would like one of these myself when I can afford it. I love my horse of course, but sometimes it's not convenient to park a horse.'

'I thought you would be wanting a motorcar like your father.' Joe said.

'It will be years before I can afford one,' he said simply. 'I'm determined not to get into debt. My parents have made it clear I shall get no more help from them,' he said seriously, 'and there are so many repairs needing done to the farms I scarcely know where to begin. I really do appreciate you giving me a lift, sir.'

'Eh laddie, you shouldna be calling me 'sir',' Joe said. He felt he should be the one addressing the local laird as sir, but Mark Blackford seemed young in spite of his twenty-five years. Joe thought he probably didn't want anybody's pity but both he and Maggie had sensed a wistfulness in him. Maggie was convinced he must have lacked a loving home life. He was not arrogant or haughty even though he was the laird. Mark perched himself on the back of Joe's motorbike and clung on. He enjoyed the ride immensely but it seemed no time before Joe was letting him off at the end of the drive leading to Stavondale Manor, Stavondale Tower, Home Farm and the cottages.

'Thank you, s . . . Thank you, Mr Greig,' he said with a grin. 'I enjoyed that. You have saved me a walk too.' He looked into the sidecar at Marie. 'Bye. I hope we meet again while you are visiting.' Marie smiled and gave him a wave.

Aunt Maggie welcomed her with a hug and her warm smile. She loved all young people but the children of her youngest brother and Joe's sister, Emma, were more special, being so closely connected to both herself and Joe. She had the table set ready with scones and homemade jam, cake and shortbread. She chattered cheerily as she showed Marie the bedroom and bathroom and suggested she freshen up then come and eat. When Marie returned to the kitchen she was pouring boiling water onto the tea leaves.

'I'm longing to hear all the news, lassie. Did you have a good journey and was Joe in time to meet the train?'

'Oh yes,' she glanced at her uncle and smiled. 'He was waiting on the platform.'

'We gave Mark Blackford a lift,' Joe said, 'so we had to leave Marie's case at the station. Remind me to ask Jamie or Jim to collect it when they take the milk to the station in the morning. I expect you can lend Marie a gounie for tonight?'

'A — a goonie?' Marie asked, wrinkling her brow.

'Aye, a nightgown,' Joe nodded. 'Surely you must have heard of a gounie?'

'I don't think so, though Mother often uses Scottish words when she's talking to Dad.'

'It will be good for you to have a spell in your native Scotland then,' Joe teased.

'I thought we could take a walk up to Bonnybrae if you're not too tired, Marie. I told them all you were coming to stay. Jamie and Rina are looking forward to seeing you again and Jim is eager to meet you. He always had a soft spot for your mother when she was a lassie. He and William were close, even though your father was the youngest of the family.' She sighed, remembering the far-off days of their youth. Their own mother had often created tension, even calling Jamie a bastard although she knew he was her own grandson. He had never forgotten or forgiven her. 'You take after your father with your blue eyes and fair skin, and such bonnie copper lights in your hair.'

'The young man on the train thought I looked like Jamie,' Marie said, flushing a little as she remembered he had said she was pretty. Maggie raised her eyebrows in question.

'That would be Master Mark Blackford,' Joe informed her. 'I told you we gave him a lift on the back of the bike.'

* * *

It was a pleasant April evening when the three of them strolled up to Bonnybrae. They saw Ernest, the main horseman, as he was now, crossing the yard. He told them Jamie and Jim were still at the milking along with Doug Lamont and his wife, Alice.

'Rina enjoyed helping Jamie with the milking when she was well,' Maggie said. 'Now she says she feels deadly tired by teatime and wee Marguerite is at her most lively then, after her afternoon nap. I expect you will want to go and see the men, Joe, but we'll go to the house. You'll see them later, Marie.' Maggie was anxious to see how Rina was faring. Rina greeted Marie warmly and enquired about her journey but Marie stifled a gasp and hid her dismay at the sight of Rina's puffy face and legs. Her hands looked like those of an old washerwoman. Marguerite came toddling across the room and Marie clutched her in her arms, holding her above her head until the wee girl giggled and began to dribble. Marie lowered her into her arms and hugged her. 'Aren't you a lovely girl then?' she crooned. She looked up at Rina, her blue eyes soft and gentle. 'She's beautiful,' Marie said.

'I know,' Rina sighed, 'but she is always finding mischief the moment I take my eyes off her. It's really time for her bath before Jamie and Uncle Jim come in for supper. They like to see her before she goes to bed but she seems to flop by then.'

'Oh, can I bathe her?' Marie pleaded. 'I'm almost sorry David and Fiona no longer need help.'

'Your mother says you love children,' Aunt Maggie remarked. 'I expect that's why your headmaster thought you should be a teacher.'

'Mmm, Mother is still disappointed I didn't stay on even though Dr Clayton asked me to leave school to help Lady Hanley. I think that's why Lord Hanley arranged for me to have classes in bookkeeping and typing so I would still have some sort of education. I enjoyed caring for her though and being needed. Lady Hanley appreciated everything I did for her. I think I might enjoy training to be a nurse when I'm eighteen. I'm hoping you will tell me about your nursing, Rina.'

'Well you can certainly bathe this wee mischief if you're sure you don't mind her splashing everywhere,' Rina said with a sigh. 'I take her upstairs to the big bath now. She enjoys a swim and it is easier for me than filling the bath in front of the fire.'

'All right. Come on little scamp. Show me the way to your bath,' Marie said as the toddler clutched her outstretched fingers and gave her a wide smile. 'She has your lovely smile, Rina,' Marie called over her shoulder.

'Her night clothes are keeping warm on the hot water cylinder in the bathroom,' Rina said with a weary sigh.

'Come and sit down my love,' Maggie said, 'and tell me all your news until Marie brings her back down. I can't believe how grown up and capable she is. Emma said Lady Hanley's death has been a shock. Lord Hanley wants her to work for him in the Estate Office and he has offered her Lady Hanley's mare to ride.'

'I didn't know Marie could ride.'

'Lord Hanley taught her himself, although he told William she didn't really need much instruction. She was a natural, and he liked the way she considers the horse.'

'I wonder if she would exercise Duke for me while she is here,' Rina said. 'He needs exercising and I'm not fit to take him out myself. Anyway I can't leave Marguerite now she's toddling everywhere. I hate to ask Ernest when I know how busy the men are with the lambing and spring sowing, as well as the milking.' She sighed. 'I ought to have set more eggs with the broody hens. We shall be short of eggs to sell next year.'

'Don't worry about that, Rina. I have set more eggs than Joe and I need. I'll rear them until we see which ones are pullets then you can have whatever you want to make up your own numbers.' To Maggie's dismay Rina's eyes filled with tears.

'I feel so useless,' she muttered, trying to dry her eyes.

'Oh lassie,' Maggie crossed to the old settle where Rina was sitting. She put a comforting arm around her shoulders and drew her close. 'You're far from useless my dear child. You have made Jamie the happiest man on earth, and Jim loves having you and wee Marguerite around. He's full of the wee one's antics whenever he calls to see me. You'd think he was her grandfather. As for the chicks, you know I've always loved my hens and seeing the chicks hatch at this time of year. Nature's a wonderful thing and there's not much else I can do these days. Joe looks after the pig himself since I twisted my ankle last winter. So you see I'm more than happy to have a few extra chicks.'

'You're so kind and generous to me,' Rina said. 'You always have been, since the first day I called at Braeside when I was ten.' She scrabbled for her handkerchief and blew her nose when she heard Marie carrying Marguerite down the stairs.

'This young lady is ready for her supper now,' Marie said. 'Isn't she adorable, Aunt Maggie? Like a little angel.' She set the child on Maggie's knee. 'She says she wants soldiers, Rina. Is it all right if I boil an egg and make her some?'

'Can you be bothered, Marie? I'm sure you must be tired after your journey.'

'I'd love to make her supper. She must be a true Sinclair already because she told me exactly what she wants.' Marie grinned fondly at her niece.

'That door leads to the pantry,' Maggie said. 'I expect you still keep the eggs in there, don't you Rina?'

'Yes, we do. We have not made many changes.'

'I've heard Mother describe Bonnybrae so often it almost seems familiar,' Marie said.

She was finishing feeding Marguerite her supper and the toddler was yawning and rubbing her sleepy eyes when Jim and Jamie came in for their evening meal.

'Why hello, Marie!' Jamie grinned. Before she could reply he had lifted her off her feet to give her a bear hug. 'It's good to see you up here. What do you think of Scotland?'

'I think the country is fine, from the little I've seen of it so far, but nothing can compare with this little angel,' she said, bending to wipe the toddler's milky mouth and lift her from her wooden highchair. Immediately Marguerite held out her chubby arms to Jamie.

'Da-da, Da-da.' He took his daughter in his arms.

'Are you all ready for bed, cherub?' he asked, smiling down at her.

'She is. Her Aunty Marie has bathed and fed her while I've been lazing here,' Rina said, getting to her feet. 'Thank you Marie. That was a great help.'

'No need to thank me. It was a delight.' She broke off as Jim came into the kitchen after washing the bottles from two pet lambs.

'So this is my niece, Marie?' he said with a warm smile. 'I'm pleased to meet you lassie.' He shook her hand in his firm clasp. 'Welcome to Bonnybrae. My, but there's no doubting William is your father. You're so like he was as a bonnie wee laddie. You're a very pretty lassie.'

'I think we should be getting home now,' Maggie said.

'Oh but . . .' Rina was about to protest but Maggie tactfully cut her short.

'I've left our supper in the oven and I don't want it to burn. I hope we haven't tired you out, Rina.'

'Of course you haven't. It is lovely to see you again Marie and I know Marguerite thinks so, even if she can't tell you yet. 'Will you carry her up and put her in her cot please,

Jamie? I can see she will soon be asleep after a lovely play in the bath.'

'I thought of inviting Marie's cousins to come to Braeside to meet her on Saturday evening — or at least as many of them as can come,' Aunt Maggie said. 'Maybe you will come down for a wee while to see them too if you're not too tired Rina?'

'We'll see,' Rina murmured. She seemed to be constantly tired these days. She knew it was the baby but she had never felt like this with Marguerite.

'I'm sure the Greig cousins will come because they all live in Locheagle, or round about. There are more of the Sinclair brood and some of them live further away now. Three of them are married.'

'It would be nice to see them, Aunt Maggie,' Jamie said, 'but as Rina says it will depend on what's going on here.' He looked at his wife and there was no doubting his anxiety.

* * *

Back at Braeside they had just finished eating and Marie was helping Aunt Maggie clear away the dishes when there was a knock at the door.

'I'll get it,' Joe called. Moments later they heard his surprise. 'Hello Master Mark. What's this then? You've been to the station to collect Marie's case? Come in laddie.'

'Hello Mark,' Maggie greeted him pleasantly, but Marie saw she was a little flustered. Later she learned this was the first time he had actually been to the house.

'Oh dear, I'm sorry if I'm interrupting your meal.'

'You're not interrupting anything,' Joe assured him.

'Of course you're not,' Maggie said quickly. 'We have finished eating but we're just going to have a drink of tea. Will you join us?'

'Thank you. Tea would be lovely.' He gave a disarming smile. 'Lord Tannahill told me you make the best shortbread he has ever tasted,' he added as Maggie opened a tin and arranged the biscuits on a pretty dish.

'Well I hope you will like it too,' Maggie said. 'I see you have brought Marie's case? That was kind of you to collect it.'

'Yes, it was. Thank you very much,' Marie said shyly.

'I took the pony and cart. I'm expecting two large trunks of my own but they have not got as far as Strathlinn yet. The stationmaster reckons they should be here tomorrow afternoon. Not that they contain anything I need urgently,' he said with a wry grimace. 'Mother was annoyed with me for leaving two days earlier than she had expected. She said I might as well clear out my room and take all my belongings to Scotland since I seemed to prefer being up here rather than entertaining her guests. So I did. Clear my room I mean — everything that belongs to me personally anyway. It took two large trunks to hold everything. I don't suppose I shall use most of it but Mother obviously wants rid of me.'

'Oh, I'm sure she wouldna mean that,' Maggie said, her compassion rising to the fore.

'I rather think she did, but my home is here now and I mean to learn all I can and make a good job of running the estate, even if it is small and neglected. The tenants all speak of the old laird, Sir Reginald Capel, with great respect. If I'm to be a laird I'd like to be as good as he was. It was Lord Tannahill who persuaded my father to set me up as a landowner, so I don't want to let him down. There's a lot to learn.'

'I see,' Maggie said slowly. 'Maybe Marie will be able to help you. She has been helping Lord Hanley, her father's landlord in Yorkshire, haven't you dear?'

'We-ell, I only helped in the Estate Office. I don't know much about estate management, although I did enjoy listening to Lord Hanley and Mr Rowbottom discussing things which needed attention,' Marie said, blushing prettily. 'I'm hoping to help Rina if she will allow me, but if there is anything I can tell you . . .'

'Even the smallest bits of information could be useful,' Mark said eagerly. He sighed. 'You see I have had no experience of running an estate. I never expected that is what I would do. Since I finished at Oxford I have spent most of my time working in an import and export business to do with parts for motorcars.' He gave a wry grimace. 'Mother considers such work beneath her family, but I enjoyed it.'

When he had gone Joe remarked, 'Mark's mother sounds a bit of a snob.'

'Maybe he will be better away from his family for a while.'

* * *

Marie had always been an early riser and she was cooking Uncle Joe's breakfast when Aunt Maggie came into the kitchen.

'Hey, lassie, you're up early. You should be enjoying a rest after your journey.'

'I'll help you first. If I go to Rina's too early she might suspect that's why I've come.'

'She seemed glad of your help with Marguerite yesterday,' Maggie said. 'Rina has never been one to sit around but she seems so tired. I'm sure it's not normal. She can't get her shoes on now her feet and ankles are so swollen. She worked all the time when she was expecting Marguerite. She even milked the evening she was born. Jim says he wouldn't be surprised if she is having more than one baby this time.'

'She does seem rather large,' Marie admitted, 'but what do I know about having babies, except seeing Mother when she had David and Fiona.'

'Emma said the only time she didn't keep well was when she was expecting the wee boy who was born dead.' She shuddered. 'I hope that will not happen to Rina.'

'I will help her as much as I can if she will let me. I do wish Jamie was not so independent.'

'They both are, that's the trouble. No amount of money is worth sacrificing good health though. Rina seems to blame herself.'

When Marie appeared at Bonnybrae later that morning Rina was pleased to see her and Marguerite came toddling towards her immediately, arms lifted, showing her tiny white teeth in a welcoming smile.

'She has your smile already, Rina,' Marie chuckled, unable to resist the plea of 'Up. Up, Ree. Ree?'

'She can't say Marie,' Rina said. 'She's been calling for you since she wakened up but we didn't know what she meant at first, then when Jamie carried her downstairs she went straight for the rag doll you brought her and said, 'Ree bwing,' and hugged the doll. It is lovely by the way.'

'A friend of Mum's makes them. She does make a good job, doesn't she? I asked her to make one for Marguerite when I knew I was coming. She always has one on the go.'

'I can see it's going to be a favourite,' Rina smiled. 'Thank goodness it's not breakable.'

'Can I peel the vegetables while you do whatever you need to do? Are they for soup? Marguerite can sit in her highchair close beside me and watch.'

'Oh Marie, are you sure? That would be a big help. I'll get on with skimming the cream. I keep adding it for three days. Tomorrow I need to churn.'

'I love churning the butter,' Marie said. 'Mother says I'm almost as good as she is. Will you let me have a go tomorrow? Marguerite can come and watch and I'll sing to her. I always sing while I'm churning. I'll sing her nursery rhymes.'

Marie's willingness to help was genuine but it was her eagerness to include Marguerite which overcame any uncertainty Rina might have had, and she was genuinely pleased to have her sister-in-law's cheerful company and another pair of hands and eyes.

'Can I stay for lunch if I make a big pot of soup?' Marie called through to the pantry where Rina was skimming cream from the large shallow pans.

'Of course you can, Marie. I'd be happy for you to stay whenever you like. I'm going to bake some fresh bread as soon as I've done this. I think Jamie and Uncle Jim are missing me baking because I don't seem to have either the time or the energy.'

'I can bake gingerbread loaves and shortbread if you don't mind me having a go, but you would need to manage the oven. I'm not so good at baking the soda scones on the girdle. Mother says I need practice, but I make good bread, and currant bread. I love having a good old pummel at the dough, don't you?'

'You're welcome to pummel mine anytime,' Rina said with feeling. 'It's another of the things which exhaust me. I can't believe I'm so useless.'

'Of course you're not useless, Rina. I'll get cracking now and if we get everything done Aunt Maggie said you might let me exercise Duke this afternoon while Marguerite is having her nap. You should take a rest as well while things are quiet.'

'I'd love you to take Duke for a good ride. Remind me to draw you a map of all the farms. I'm sure they would love to meet you. They're all very friendly and when they hear you're Jamie's sister they will be sure to make you welcome.'

'I couldn't possibly introduce myself but a map would be useful so that I don't get lost and trespass on other people's property. I met Mark Blackford on the train. He called at Braeside last night to deliver my case from the station and he asked if I would tell him whatever I've learned from Lord Hanley about estate management. He doesn't seem very confident. He says he wants to learn and to make a good job.'

'He's a nice young man, isn't he?' Rina said with a smile. 'He calls to see Uncle Jim sometimes to ask his advice about the small farm he has kept in his own hands. Glenside it's called. Uncle Jim says he would be better concentrating on the estate and letting the farm to a tenant. There were always a few tenants who didn't pay their rents until they got a reminder, even in my grandfather's time.' She pulled a face. 'Father never kept them up to date and the buildings have deteriorated badly. It will not be an easy job for Mark.'

'By the sound of things you are the one who could advise him, Rina.'

'No. I knew the tenants and what should be done to maintain the property but I have no idea about accounts and getting estimates to compare, or paying the bills and deciding what should be a priority. From the little I've heard, Mark wants to improve everything at once. Nobody could do that. Lord Tannahill could have advised him but he has not been up to Stavondale for a while.'

The two of them chatted as they worked and Marie set about kneading the bread while Rina ironed Marguerite's tiny clothes and Jim's and Jamie's shirts. The morning passed quickly and Rina was delighted when Marie turned out a batch of new bread to cool.

'What is this one? I've never seen a loaf with raisins in before.'

'Haven't you? Maybe it's a Yorkshire recipe then. Mother usually makes one with the last of the dough. She adds fruit and peel and a bit of sugar and some spice, depending on what she has in the pantry. We have it instead of scones for afternoon tea before the milking, spread with butter of course.'

'It smells delicious. I almost want to eat it now.' Rina laughed and Marie realised it was the first time she had heard the spontaneous merry laugh they had all loved from the first day they met Rina as a new bride. After lunch was cleared away and both Marguerite and Rina were taking a rest Jamie took Marie to the field gate and whistled for Duke. He came at a trot and Marie led him to the stable.

'You seem to have cheered Rina up today, Marie,' Jamie said as he showed her where the harness and brushes were stored. 'I'm glad you've come. I hope you can stay a while.'

'That depends on how long Aunt Maggie and Uncle Joe are willing to keep me,' Marie said. 'I have a healthy appetite you know, big brother.'

'Aunt Maggie enjoys feeding folks, but you could easily have your meals with us. Rina said you had made the soup and baked the bread anyway.'

'Well I do love seeing my wee niece,' Marie grinned, 'if you're sure neither Rina nor Uncle Jim would mind me being at Bonnybrae too often?'

'They will both be pleased,' Jamie assured her, 'and I'd do anything if it helps Rina. I'm terribly worried about her.' He buckled the saddle more tightly. 'There you are. Give him a good gallop and enjoy your ride.'

Apart from stolen rides on their milk pony at home Marie had never had a pony of her own to ride until Lord Hanley had taught her to ride his wife's horse, May. She had loved it. Now she gave Duke a good canter down the track, past Braeside, and down to the narrow public road. She had Rina's map in her pocket, but it was fairly simple and she remembered she turned right for most of the farms on the Stavondale Estate, and East Lowrie village. Her mind was on her unknown cousins as she trotted along so she didn't notice Mark Blackford holding his own horse. He was standing by the gate into one of the farms with another man.

He beckoned her to stop and greeted her eagerly as she drew near.

'Good afternoon, Miss Marie Sinclair, and how are you enjoying exploring the Scottish countryside?'

'It is lovely around here, especially on such a beautiful spring day. What a lot of lambs there are in the fields already. I love to see them dancing around or basking in the sunshine.' Marie said happily.

'There speaks a real country lassie,' Mark's companion said with a chuckle.

'Marie, this is Bill Massie, one of the Stavondale tenants. Bill this is Jamie Sinclair's sister from Yorkshire. She is visiting Bonnybrae and her aunt and uncle at Braeside.'

'Aah,' the man's smile faded. 'I heard Mistress Rina Sinclair isna keeping in good health. Is she better now?

'No,' Marie admitted. 'I am hoping to help a little and give her time to rest. This is Rina's pony I am exercising.'

'I thought I recognised him. She was a grand lassie young Rina. You tell her Bill Massie was asking for her and wishing her good health.'

'I will. She speaks highly of her grandfather's tenants and old friends.'

'You must be William's lassie then, if ye come frae Yorkshire?' he asked rubbing his brow. 'I remember he moved down there when he married. So ye'll be Jim's niece, aye and a niece o' Robin and Jack Sinclair?'

'I am, but I have not met them yet,' Marie said.

'They're your tenants too Mr Blackford.'

'If you will excuse me I must get on, or Marguerite will be awaken and climbing out of her cot before I have given Duke a gallop.'

'I will ride with you, if you don't mind company, Miss Sinclair?'

'Of course I don't mind, but please do call me Marie.'

'Do you think you might find time to come to the Estate Office one evening soon and give me your advice? Things are in a terrible muddle. I don't want to criticise but I'm learning the estate affairs have been neglected for a long time, according to some of the tenants. Sir Roger hadn't employed an agent for some years and he didn't do the work himself either.' He sighed heavily. 'I have been round most of the farms and made a list of the repairs which are needing done but there's so many. Will you give me your advice?'

'I'm no expert on estate management but I will come if you think I may be able to help. I must get back soon. I'm worried about Rina. She seems exhausted.'

'All right. I'll see you tonight then?'

'All right. I will ask Jamie if I can borrow his bicycle.' They parted, but Marie wheeled Duke around and called his name. 'If I don't come tonight it is not because I don't want to help, but Rina and Marguerite must come first.'

'Thank you for explaining Marie. I'm using a room in my house as the Estate Office. That's at Stavondale Manor. I'm usually around in the evenings. I shall look forward to seeing you whenever you can come.' Marie wondered if he was finding it lonely living alone and amongst strangers.

CHAPTER TWO

Marguerite and Rina had enjoyed a good rest while Marie was exercising Duke.

'I feel so much better,' Rina said, smiling. 'Please stay to share our evening meal and talk to Uncle Jim and Jamie.' Marie didn't want to refuse her invitation so she didn't mention her arrangement to meet Mark Blackford. She didn't know why she should feel sorry for a young man who owned an estate, however neglected, but she did.

On Saturday evening Maggie made a delicious buffet supper in the large kitchen at Braeside and Marie enjoyed meeting her cousins. She was younger than most of them, except Aunt Bessie's daughter, Laura. She was delighted to see that both her aunt and her cousin had similar colouring to herself. Her Greig cousins were more like her mother with their dark hair and slight build. She knew Uncle David and Aunt Julie had three children, Luke, Mark and Ruth, all names from the Bible. She remembered Aunt Julie's father had been the minister in Locheagle church and had officiated at her parents' marriage. Both Luke and Mark were enthusiastic about taking her to the local dances and introducing her to some of their friends in Locheagle, but they understood when she said she would love to join them but she had come to help Rina. She had called in briefly with Marguerite so they had seen how ill and exhausted she looked and they understood. Aunt Julie particularly seemed upset by her condition, but otherwise it was a lovely evening. It was only when they had all gone home that Uncle Joe drew Marie aside.

'Ye're a good lassie, Marie, and we know you came to help Rina, but you're young and you should be enjoying yourself on a Saturday night. You could cycle down to Locheagle when there's a band playing. They're nice laddies. They will look after you.' Marie began to protest but Aunt Maggie intervened.

'Joe's right, Marie. You shouldn't be tied to Bonnybrae all the time. You deserve a bit of pleasure. If you get Marguerite bathed and away to bed that's a big help to Rina and we're always willing to help if we can.'

'That's kind of you both,' Marie said with a smile. 'I will consider going to one of the dances but I'd like to see how Rina keeps first. She tires so easily. She puts on a brave face but I'm sure she knows something is wrong.'

Marie enjoyed exercising Duke each afternoon and she began to look forward to having Mark Blackford's company. Sometimes she accompanied him when he visited his tenants. She had mentioned meeting her cousins and the local dances.

'Oh do let me know if you decide to go, Marie. I'd like to come with you. I could take the pony and trap, or I might buy myself a bicycle like Jamie's then we could cycle together,' he said eagerly.

'I'm sure Rina would lend me her bicycle then you could borrow Jamie's. I wouldn't go often. Rina's health is really worrying and it's the reason I came.'

* * *

She managed to spend a couple of evenings at the Estate Office with Mark after she had put Marguerite to bed, but she was incredulous at the chaos.

'No wonder you feel overwhelmed. Didn't your father look at the records and the farms before he bought it?'

'My father isn't an estate man. He knows even less than I do. I have made a list of all the repairs needing done but there are so many and no spare capital.'

'I'm no expert,' Maria said, 'but I reckon the first thing is to make a list of the tenants who are behind with their rent then either call on each of them in person, or at least send them a firm letter asking them to settle their rents if they wish to keep their tenancies.'

'Some of them might quit.'

'As far as I can see there are only about six of them and two of those are only a couple of months behind. Three are more than eighteen months behind, one even more. Lord Hanley and Mr Rowbottom would say they needed a no-nonsense reminder. If any of them have real hardship you can discuss things and maybe come to an arrangement where they pay off some of their debt each month.'

'How efficient you sound,' Mark said admiringly.

'I only know what I learned from Lord Hanley and his conversations with his agent. They were quite open because I was there to help and they knew I would be discrete. They knew I would not gossip locally, even to my own family. I expect Rina knows the tenants but I wouldn't discuss your business. Most of this mess must be due to her father.'

'It is but that's why my father got the estate at a bargain price. You will help me when you can won't you, Marie?'

'I'll try, but as I said, Rina and Marguerite come first. I expect you're tired of me mentioning Lord Hanley,' she said, 'but he had a machine called a typewriter and he sent me to classes to learn to type his letters. He says they look more official than handwritten ones. He bought a kind of carbon paper so we could keep a copy.' She began to giggle. 'At first we put the paper in the wrong way round and the letter was on both sides of the first page. It was no use to send to anyone.'

'You think I should get one of these machines?'

'We-ell, the letters demanding payment, or asking tradesmen for estimates, would look more professional. They might take more notice. Could you afford a typewriter?'

'I'll make enquiries.'

'You could ask Uncle Joe. He told me they have two in the office at his mill.'

* * *

Marie was riding back to Bonnybrae on Duke when she was surprised to see a small car in the road outside Aunt Maggie's house at Braeside. She had never heard of Aunt Maggie having friends who owned a car before. She cantered on up to Bonnybrae and jumped lightly from the saddle before leading Duke into the stable to take off his harness and give him a good grooming. She was growing increasingly fond of the gentle-natured horse and she always carried a titbit for him before turning him back into his paddock. She latched the gate and turned to cross the farmyard. She was surprised to see the black car was now parked near the back door at Bonnybrae, and Aunt Maggie and a young couple were entering the house. In a panic she hurried after them. She needed to wash and change out of Rina's riding breeches before greeting any visitors but she was also afraid Rina might still be resting. It wouldn't be good if they startled her and made her jump up too quickly.

Marie ran quickly upstairs to the room Rina had told her to use whenever she wanted to change. She already felt at home and at ease at Bonnybrae. As she passed the half-open door she heard Marguerite beginning to murmur to herself, so she tapped lightly and went in. Rina was lying on her bed but her eyes were open.

'I've had a good rest, Marie. Did you and Duke enjoy your ride?'

'We did. We always do. He's a lovely natured horse.' She crossed to the bed and put a restraining hand on Rina's shoulder. 'Don't jump up. Just take your time and wash your face to freshen up. We have visitors. I don't know who they are but Aunt Maggie is with them and they arrived in a small black car.'

'Oh? I don't know who that can be in a car. Has Mark Blackford bought one?'

'No, it's not Mark. It's a couple. I'll take Marguerite with me while I change to give you a few minutes. Thank goodness we baked fresh scones this morning. There is still some gingerbread left and Aunt Maggie's fruit cake. If you think I should make them some tea, just give me a nod.'

'Oh Marie, you're so good. I don't know what I shall do when you go back to Yorkshire.'

'That's funny,' Marie smiled, 'but Mark said the same thing and I haven't done that much for either of you. Anyway, I shall stay as long as Aunt Maggie can put up with me.'

'You could move in here. We've plenty of room and Marguerite would love that. So would I.' She sighed wistfully.

'Do you mean it, Rina? I'd love to stay with you and help you look after Marguerite more. We could move her cot into my room then she wouldn't waken you so early in the mornings. But what would my big brother think? And what about Uncle Jim?'

'I'm sure they would be as pleased as I would. Uncle Jim has remarked several times how you remind him of your mother. You know what needs to be done and you get on with it.'

'When you come from a large family everyone has to pull their weight so it's second nature. Anyway you ask them, Rina. If you want me to stay here, tell me. Aunt Maggie and Uncle Joe will not mind.' Secretly, this is exactly what they had all hoped for. She scooped Marguerite up in her arms and carried her to the room where she had left her own skirt and blouse and a clean apron. It did not take her many minutes to wash her face and hands, and sponge Marguerite's, and pull on her clothes. Thank goodness for the bathroom. Marguerite rarely wet her nappies these days and Marie held her over the toilet so that there would be no accidents when they went down to greet the visitors. They were all in the large sitting room with Rina.

'Oh, Marie,' Rina cried, her face wreathed in smiles. 'Do come and meet Melissa. I told you about us nursing together. She is my very best friend.'

'I've heard a lot about you and I am pleased to meet you,' Marie said taking Melissa's outstretched hand and returning her shy smile.

'And this is Dr Frank Meadows, Melissa's husband.' Rina turned to greet the tall, slim young man with the serious face. His handshake was firm and she knew he was silently assessing her even as they greeted each other.

'Shall I make a cup of tea for all of us while you talk to your friends, Rina?'

'Yes, you do that, lassie,' Aunt Maggie said quickly. 'I'll come and help you. They wouldn't eat anything at my house and Dr Meadows has to return to the hospital tonight.' Once they were in the kitchen Maggie turned her anxious face to Marie. 'I told them what Rina was like while they were with me. Dr Meadows said if she really is as bad as I described it sounded serious and he would try to persuade her to go back to Glasgow with them and stay overnight to see one of the obstetricians — at least I think that's what he called him. Anyway, he said they would check Rina's condition. His own boss specialises in mothers and babies and he says he is one of the best. Melissa is expecting a child too, although not for some months. This Mr Chambers is keeping an eye on her.' While she talked she was busy setting out the cups and saucers. 'As soon as Rina came into the room I saw the dismay on Dr Meadows face, although he quickly hid it when Rina turned to greet him. He threw me a look later and shook his head. I'm sure he knows I was not exaggerating.'

'I doubt if he will manage to persuade Rina to go with them,' Marie said slowly. 'She will not want to leave Marguerite and Jamie. I don't blame her. She says I can move up to Bonnybrae and stay here though. She also agrees it would be a good idea to move Marguerite's cot into my bedroom to get her used to being in a different room before the new baby comes. Maybe Rina will be able to rest longer in the mornings too.'

'Oh, you're a good lassie, Marie,' Aunt Maggie said gratefully. 'You're so mature for your years. It would break my heart, and Joe's, if anything should happen to Rina.'

'Do you think we should make some ham sandwiches for tea, as an extra, in case they do persuade Rina to go with them? They wouldn't want to stop anywhere on the journey. Rina gets uncomfortable if she has to sit anywhere in one place for long.'

'Is there any ham?'

'Yes, I boiled it yesterday and made a big pot of pea soup with the stock. The bread was baked yesterday but it will slice better for sandwiches. I'll mix some mustard and put out ajar of chutney so they can add what they like.'

'How like your mother you are, lassie.' Aunt Maggie sighed. 'I thank God for that and that you have come to help us.'

They were almost ready to brew the tea in the big pot when Dr Meadows came through to the kitchen. His expression was grave and Marie suppressed a nervous quiver in the pit of her stomach.

'Rina's condition is far more serious than I expected, in spite of your description, Mrs Greig,' he said sombrely. 'I told them I was coming out to stretch my legs and to give Mel and Rina time to talk, but what I would really like is to have a word with her husband on his own. It is imperative to make both Rina and Jamie understand her condition may be serious.'

'I will show you out of the back door,' Marie said. 'Jamie and Uncle Jim are due in for their tea before they start the milking so you will meet them coming down from the field with the horses. Make it clear to Jamie that you need to speak with him urgently.'

Jamie didn't recognise Mel's husband at first but they did not know each other well and he had never seen him in casual clothes before. Frank Meadows knew they might not have much time on their own, so he seized the opportunity to impress on Jamie how serious Rina's condition seemed to him and the possible consequences if he was right.

'Thank you for coming,' Jamie said quietly. 'I know things are not normal this time. We're all worried about her but we try not to let Rina see. In her heart I'm sure she knows something is not right. Whatever it takes, I want to do what is best for Rina. I couldn't bear anything to happen to her.' Jamie's voice was rough with emotion and Frank Meadows nodded in understanding.

'Even if it means taking her back with us today? The less time she waits the better chance she will have. Do you have anyone to look after your wee girl?'

'I'm sure my sister will stay and Marguerite has got used to her now. The problem will be persuading Rina to leave her and go to Glasgow.'

'That is why I needed to know if I should have your support in persuading her. If I am right, Mr Chambers, the surgeon, will want to keep her in hospital in Glasgow.'

'You must do what is best for Rina,' Jamie said with a note of desperation. 'If it is a choice between saving Rina or the baby, you must save my wife. Do I have your word?'

'Yes, you do, Jamie. I am glad you understand we may have to make a choice. I feared I might have to persuade you too. Your help and support will make all the difference. Your aunt and sister have made us a lovely tea so we shall try to hide our feelings and hope that Rina will eat a good meal before she sets out with us.'

'I hope to God you can persuade her,' Jamie said fervently. 'She has seen our local doctor but all he advised was that she should rest as much as she can. I have been so relieved since my sister came up from Yorkshire. Marie is a great help.'

Jim suspected things were serious when he knew Dr Meadows wished to speak to Jamie alone, but he was relieved to know the young doctor had come to see Rina and he could tell by their faces that things were not good. He groomed and fed both the Clydesdale horses before turning them out to pasture for the night then he followed the two younger men into the house for tea. He knew they were putting on a cheerful front for Rina's sake but he was taken aback when they finished eating and he realised Mel and her husband wanted to take Rina back with them tonight to get the opinion of his superior.

'I couldn't possibly go and leave Jamie and my wee Marguerite,' Rina protested. 'and it will cost an enormous amount to see a specialist doctor, let alone stay at the hospital.' She was near to tears and Jim chewed his lip. He hated to see her so distressed. Jamie's face was pale with worry.

'I don't care how much it costs, Rina. You mean more to me than all the money in the world. Please, please go with Mel and at least see what this doctor has to say,' Jamie pleaded.

'B-but I c-can't leave you, Jamie.' She looked around the table. 'What sort of wife am I for a working farmer if I go and leave all this?' Her voice shook. She brushed away tears.

'You know I will do my best to look after things, Rina, until you return,' Marie said gently. 'Mother would never expect me to return home while I can be of use.'

'Y-you've been so good already.'

'Rina,' Mel said in her soft voice. 'You will like Mr Chambers. He is keeping his eye on me and our little one. In your heart you know you must seek advice. You were a good nurse and your instincts were always right. Jamie loves you. He doesn't want to lose you. You must get the best care available.'

It was Mel's gentle voice which finally persuaded Rina that she should accompany them back to Glasgow. She knew she was fortunate to have Frank's influence in getting her the best care available, but she also knew it would cost more than they could afford. She turned to look at Jim but he seemed to read her mind.

'Lassie you mean more to us than all the farms, and all the stock, in Scotland so don't worry about anything except getting well and getting back here to care for this wee lassie.'

When Rina had gone upstairs to pack an overnight bag and toiletries Marie said, 'I have a writing pad and envelopes and some postage stamps down at your house, Aunt Maggie. I could run down and get them for Mel to give to Rina. She'll want to write if she has to stay in the hospital.'

'That would be a good idea,' Dr Meadows said. 'Anything which will help to keep her calm and relaxed. It is a pity there are no telephones in this area to keep in touch. I hear they have erected a telephone for public use on a street in London. It is in a small red kiosk so anyone can use it so long as they pay their money.'

'We could telephone to my parents with any news,' Mel suggested quickly. 'Perhaps Mr Greig would call on them to hear what Mr Chambers says?'

'Oh yes, it would be a great relief to have news, Melissa. I know Joe would be happy to visit your parents on his way home,' Maggie said eagerly.

'Rina will want to write to Jamie. I remember when we were nursing she wrote every day. She was so pleased to get his letters in return.' She looked at Jamie sympathetically.

'I'll go and carry her bag down,' he said gruffly, glad to find an excuse to be alone with his wife, to be able to kiss her goodbye in private, and perhaps comfort each other if they could. His heart ached with love — but it was heavy with fear. Dr Meadows had not held back his concerns. He knew how much Rina would hate being away from home, even though she had found their lively two-year-old exhausting, at least until Marie came. Marie! He couldn't expect her to stay for the next two months and work for nothing. He gnawed his lower lip. He would have to make an appointment with the bank manager and explain what was happening and ask for a private loan to pay the hospital and doctor's fees and wages for his sister. This was not Uncle Jim's burden. This was his own responsibility.

He found Rina in tears and he drew her into his arms and kissed her tenderly, doing his best to reassure her.

'You know dearest Rina, how much I shall hate you being away from us, but,' he shuddered, 'I could never forgive myself if anything went wrong when we could have prevented it. I couldn't live without you, my love.'

'I know,' Rina sobbed quietly. 'How shall we pay the doctors and the hospital fees? I am a useless wife, Jamie. I'm a burden instead of a helper and partner as I longed to be.'

'Frank Meadows say Mr Chambers is one of the best gynaecologists in the country.'

'Yes, Mel said the same and she says he is most particular about hygiene, both in the theatre and on his wards. I remember how important that was at the fever hospital.'

'If they say it will be better for you to stay in the hospital, I will come to Glasgow to visit one way or another, I promise.'

'But it is two months before the baby is due, Jamie, or at least that's what I thought originally. I can't stay away two months.'

'Dr Meadows wonders if the dates could be wrong,' Jamie said slowly. 'You said you were never sure about them.'

'That's true, but I couldn't be more than two weeks out, three at most.'

'We both know what a difference three weeks can make with lambs and calves and I'm sure human beings must be similar. Anyway, my darling Rina, please, please accept all the care they can give you and come back to us safely.'

'I do hope I can bring you a baby son, Jamie.'

'Oh Rina, I don't care about having a son, or anything else so long as you come back to us safe and well.'

When Frank and Melissa drove away, taking a tearful Rina with them Marguerite was inconsolable, crying for her mama.

'It's because she sensed Rina was upset at going and she saw her tears,' Maggie said.

'I'll take her for a walk to see the lambs and the wee pigs,' Marie said. 'It will take her mind off seeing her mother being driven away in a motorcar.' She tucked the little girl into the low trolley which Joe had made for pushing her around the farmyard. Maggie had padded it with an old woollen blanket so she didn't get bumped. Marie pushed it to and fro as they talked. Soothed by the movement, Marguerite put three fingers in her mouth and lay quiet, except for a little hiccoughing sob every now and then.

'She has never seen a car before, has she?' Marie remarked.

'No. It must seem frightening to a wee bairn. So noisy, not like the pony and trap.'

'But she has heard Uncle Joe's motorbike . . .'

'She's seen it. She has not heard it going, and it never took away her mama,' Maggie said. 'I think I should stay and help you until Marguerite is settled and into bed. I could make the evening meal up here for all of us. Joe will soon come to find me when he gets home from work and sees I'm not there. He will want to know what's going on.'

'Yes, he will. I said I would help Mark Blackford with his letters and sending out his bills this evening but he will guess something is wrong. He understands Rina comes first.'

'I'm sure he will understand, lassie,' Maggie said. 'I thank God you're here with us for I could never have managed on my own, not with wee Marguerite.'

'Do you want me to do anything to help before we start the milking?' Jamie called from the scullery.

'What did Dr Meadows say to you?' Maggie asked. 'When he got you outside on your own?' She noticed Jamie's ruddy face looked pale and drawn. Her heart ached for him.

'He couldn't be sure about anything without a proper examination and he didn't want to embarrass Rina when she has known him as a friend. In any case he is not a specialist doctor yet. He wonders if Rina could be carrying twins when she is so large. He is seriously concerned about the swelling. He says that is not good. He is afraid it may indicate a problem with kidneys, or some other condition. He insisted she should see his boss without delay. He — he said it may be necessary to abort the baby to save Rina's life.'

'Abort it? Oh no! Surely not after all Rina has gone through . . .' Maggie gasped.

'I-I told him to do whatever is best for Rina. I insisted she must come first.' He looked at Maggie almost defiantly.

'I don't care about another baby, or anything else so long as they save Rina's life and send her back to me.' He turned and went outside. Marie suspected her brother was near to breaking down in tears, and she didn't blame him. She felt like crying herself but Marguerite demanded her attention.

'I shall need to pack my things and bring them up to Bonnybrae,' she said. 'I'll do that when Marguerite is in bed if you will stay up here until I return, Aunt Maggie?'

Later that evening, when her aunt and uncle had gone home to Braeside and Marguerite was sound asleep in her bedroom, Marie settled down to write to her parents and tell them the latest development concerning Rina's health. She knew they would be anxious when they heard Rina was in hospital but it was no use trying to hide these things. Marie knew Aunt Maggie would tell her mother anyway. They had always shared their troubles as well as their joys. She explained she had moved to Bonnybrae and she expected to remain until Rina's baby was born, whether or not they kept her in hospital. She tried to finish on a more cheerful note.

> *I think I told you I was helping Mark Blackford some evenings to sort out his Estate Office and send letters out to the tenants who are behind with their rents. He has bought a typewriter and I am showing him how to file copies. I don't know anything about estate management, except what I have learned from listening to Mr Rowbottom and Lord Hanley, but I have more idea what needs to be done than Mark has. I suspect his parents bought him a small run-down estate well away from their home and now they consider they have done their duty by him. You would almost think he was not part of the family. I just wish he had someone like Mr Rowbottom to give him an idea how to go on. Even I can see that some of the repairs are a priority, like the roofs on the barns and houses. The tenants who owe most rent are the ones who make demands. I am relieved my Sinclair uncles always pay their rent on time. Rina says it was the same in her grandfather's time but he inspected them all regularly*

and he was strict with the ones who fell behind. It was her father who neglected everything. I feel sorry for Mark. It is not how he planned to spend his life. He seems to have done well at Oxford. He wanted to train as an engineer. Since the war and the invention of tanks he believes there will be a great future in the manufacture of motorcars and machines for farming and other industries, but his mother considers such work dirty and beneath her family. She sounds very snobbish.

I gave the postage stamps you bought to Rina so she can write to Jamie from the hospital. I still have some money so I shall go down to the post office at Locheagle tomorrow. It will exercise Duke. I shall not have much time for him now but Aunt Maggie will come up and listen for Marguerite if I put her down for her afternoon nap. The Greig cousins were going to take me to the village dances but that will have to wait a while.

I will let you know as soon as we have any news, even if I only have time for a very short letter. I know you will both understand.

Marie concluded her letter with messages for her brothers and sisters. She didn't realise how much she had written about Mark Blackford or how much sympathy she had for him. Yawning she checked on Marguerite, sleeping soundly in the cot close beside her, then she tumbled into bed herself and offered a heartfelt prayer for Rina.

CHAPTER THREE

It was a worrying time waiting for news, but Dr Meadows had told Jamie that complete rest could help. After Rina's second night in hospital Joe called on Mr and Mrs MacQuade to see whether Melissa had telephoned.

'Mel phoned this afternoon,' Mrs MacQuade said. 'Mr Chambers has taken Rina under his care and he has taken blood and urine for testing but whatever the root of the trouble he emphasised complete rest is necessary for both Rina and the baby. Mel says she is worrying about how much it will cost but Mr Chambers knows she was a nurse herself under Matron Gilroy. He says if she will cooperate with some of his students and help them to learn by studying her condition then he will reduce his own fees. He said she was an ideal subject because she understood that doctors and nurses needed experience of every illness and condition and she would understand why he was so strict about hygiene. He thinks it will be of benefit to them all, but especially those who intend to go into general practice.'

'That's very good of Mr Chambers,' Joe said. 'But Rina will find it difficult to rest.'

'I know how active she was,' Mrs MacQuade agreed, 'but Mel said she was exhausted when they reached the hospital.'

'Aye, the stress will not help,' Joe agreed. 'It upset her leaving Marguerite.'

'That's understandable. My husband would have liked to talk to her in person but Mel said Mr Chambers will only allow close family at present so he has written her a letter instead. She should get it tomorrow. He hopes to reassure her about the money.'

'We'll all help find the money,' Joe said gruffly, 'if only they can send Rina home safe and well. It will upset her not having a baby at the end of it all but Jamie insisted they must put Rina's life first.'

'Oh, I do so agree with him,' Mrs MacQuade said fervently. 'I know most men crave for a son but I'm glad Jamie loves his wife more.'

'Aye, it would break his heart if she doesn't get over this,' Joe said gruffly and bid her goodbye. He told Maggie and Jamie of his visit.

'I've been thinking on the way home though,' he said, 'do you think we could go to Glasgow on my motorbike on Saturday? Maggie, could you and wee Marguerite travel in the sidecar if we wrap you up well with a blanket and a shawl? Would you ride pillion as far as that Jamie?'

'I can do anything if you're willing to give it a try, Uncle Joe.' Jamie said, his eyes shining with gratitude. 'I'm sure it would help Rina if she can see us all.'

'I'm not working this Saturday so we could aim to be there for afternoon visiting.' Joe did not mention his own fear of the city traffic with the huge drays, often heavily loaded with barrels of beer or whisky, and pulled by a pair of large Clydesdale horses, and sometimes as many as four horses. Although not many people could afford motorbikes or cars, the numbers were increasing and the city streets always seemed busy with people hurrying here and there, shopping, working, delivery boys on bikes.

Maggie was both excited and anxious at the prospect of journeying to Glasgow but all Jamie could think of was seeing his beloved Rina and hearing the surgeon's latest verdict.

Since she would not have Marguerite to watch over, Marie volunteered to help Uncle Jim and Doug Lamont with the milking. Doug's wife, Alice, also offered to help when she heard their plans, if her mother could come to look after their toddler, Freddie. She could bring the baby with her to the byre in the pram.

After their anticipation it was a dreadful disappointment when Saturday dawned pouring with rain and no sign of drying up. Jamie knew, without Joe's confirmation, that it would be foolhardy to set out, especially with Aunt Maggie and Marguerite.

'We should all be soaked before we passed through Strathlinn,' Joe said gloomily. 'I'm sorry I mentioned a visit and raised your hopes, Jamie.'

'It's not your fault Uncle Joe but I do need to see Rina,' Jamie said in desperation. 'I'll go on my own on the train next weekend. I don't think I could manage Marguerite as well, although I know from her letters that Rina is missing her terribly.'

The rain was still pouring down after lunch but Joe was restless.

'I think I'll take a ride to the MacQuades' house and enquire whether they have heard anything more from Melissa,' he said.

'Oh, but Joe,' Maggie protested, 'you'll be soaked to the skin before you get there!'

'I know but I shall not go in or linger. I'll have a hot bath as soon as I get back here. I know how disappointed Jamie is and we shall all feel better if there is any news.'

'Mel phones us regularly, but there are no developments,' Mary MacQuade said, after trying hard to persuade Joe to step inside.

'Not today, thanks,' Joe said, 'I would drip everywhere in spite of my waterproofs. 'We had intended to take Marguerite to visit if the weather had been reasonable.'

'Yes, I'm sure Rina will be missing her dreadfully. The only thing Mel did say was that Rina seemed a bit more relaxed and more resigned to staying in hospital. She told Mel she had forwarded my husband's letter to Jamie. Whatever they have decided to do you can tell him Mel thinks it must have helped.'

'I'll tell Jamie. He'll welcome any crumb of comfort. Now I'd better get back. Even the small ford by the Stavondale burn was higher than I've ever seen it.'

Fortunately Joe reached home without any mishaps and Maggie ushered him straight into the bath.

'I'll bring you a hot cup of tea as soon as you're in and I'll scrub your back and warm you up,' she promised.

'I shall enjoy that.' Joe gave her a wicked grin and a wink, but he was glad to get out of his wet clothes. 'It's more like autumn than May,' he said.

Jamie had been out in the field checking up on some of the sheep so he heard Joe's motorbike returning. He hurried to Braeside to see if there was any news.

'Joe said something about you and Rina exchanging letters from Mr MacQuade,' Maggie told him. 'Whatever they concerned, Mel thinks Rina is more resigned to staying in hospital until the baby is born as Mr Chambers has advised.'

'Yes, Mr MacQuade wrote to Rina. She forwarded his letter on to me. She had forgotten her grandfather left her his jade collection and two Chinese vases. Mr MacQuade put them in the bank for safe keeping. She doesn't know I have seen Mr Dixon, the bank manager, and arranged a personal loan to pay the hospital fees and the doctor. He was very understanding but he needs to use my share of Bonnybrae as security for the loan. He must have remembered about Sir Reginald's things being in his vault after I left.'

'I see,' Maggie said slowly, not really understanding it all.

'I think the vases and things must be fairly valuable. Both Mr Dixon and Mr MacQuade believe Rina's grandfather would have wanted her to sell them and use the money if it can help her regain her health. I suppose they're right,' Jamie said glumly, 'but I ought to be able to pay for the care of my own wife.'

'I understand how you feel, Jamie,' Maggie said gently, 'but sometimes we all have to swallow our pride, especially if it helps someone we love, as you love Rina.'

'If we feel worried sick about paying the hospital and doctor's fees, what do people do if they can't even borrow the money for a doctor?'

'I suspect many a one will die,' Maggie said. 'Good health is precious.'

'We both agree this is not Uncle Jim's burden. He's being decent about everything.'

'Of course he is, Jamie. You make all his hard work at Bonnybrae worthwhile. You're the nearest he has to a son of his own, and you're his namesake.'

'That's what he said but I still feel guilty, and so does Rina. I was afraid she might insist on coming home so I have agreed to her selling her treasures. Mr MacQuade is going to send the things to London to be sold, but it will take time. Meanwhile Mr Dixon has arranged the loan.'

'I am glad. We all know how much you love Rina. It's not as though you want the money for your own pleasure as her parents did.'

Jamie and Aunt Maggie wrote regularly about the daily trivia, trying to reassure Rina that all was well. Marie usually added a short note to enclose with Jamie's letters and she helped Marguerite hold a pencil in her tiny fist to make a big kiss and a few squiggles, or a stick man and a lamb.

* * *

When Joe arrived at work on Monday morning, Mr Courton, the man who had been his boss since he started work as a boy, and who was now his partner and a good friend, enquired about news of Rina. Joe told him what little they knew. He explained their plans to visit the hospital with Marguerite had been wrecked by the wet weather.

'I said to my wife that's exactly what would happen when it was so wet. It always worries me, Joe, in case you get a chill travelling on that machine of yours in bad weather. You know I couldn't manage this place without you now. Why don't you buy a car? I could pay you an advance on your share of the business. We have a fair amount of capital and you save us a lot of expense the way you maintain the machinery and manage the workforce.'

'No, no. I don't need an advance. I never get a chill. Anyway you would manage fine without me.' Joe grinned, but in his heart he knew they made a good team together. Bob Courton must be about six years older than himself because he was already working in the mill offices with Mr Courton senior, his uncle, when Joe started work at fourteen. Many things had changed over the years. They had more machinery than they had had before the war. It was this side of the business which Mr Courton could not become accustomed to, while Joe found the manufacturing side far more interesting than sales and accounts, although he did keep himself familiar with all aspects. Life could be unpredictable and he would never like the company to be in a position where one of their competitors could come in and take over at a rock-bottom price, if only for Mrs Courton's sake. She was a kindly woman and he had always liked her. The Courtons had only had one child, a little girl, and she had died with the fever when she was seven years old.

'Will you think about it Joe?' Mr Courton was asking.

'I'm sorry my mind was wandering,' Joe said. 'Think about what?'

'I'm just saying I have a fancy for one of the new British cars — a four-seater Morris Oxford — instead of my old Tin Lizzie.'

'You haven't had the Ford T that long,' Joe said, 'or at least you haven't driven it that many miles yet. Didn't Morris start by making bicycles before the war?'

'Aye, I think maybe he did, but he's progressed to making cars so it's time you followed his example and moved to driving a car instead of yon motorbike.'

'You think so?' Joe chuckled.

'I'm serious. I'll sell you my Ford for a hundred pounds, then I'll buy myself an all-British Morris.'

'Morris used to buy in all the components wherever he could get them before the war. They weren't made in Britain. He only assembled them and called them a Morris car.'

'Maybe he did but he's a wealthy man now. I read in the *Glasgow Herald* that he supplies fifty-one percent of the British market — even more than Ford. Anyway what about it? Ella agrees with me that you would be safer, as well as warm and dry, in a car. You could take your wife, and the wee girl, to visit whatever the weather.'

'A car would take a lot more petrol than my motorbike,' Joe said.

'You can afford two bob a gallon, Joe, so don't pretend you can't.'

'I remember you telling me you paid a hundred and seventy-five pounds for your Tin Lizzie when you bought her. I'd be robbing you if I only paid you a hundred. She's like new.'

'I offered it to you for that so you're not robbing me. Anyway, all machines lose their value when they've been used. You're always telling me that about the factory machinery. At least think about it. Discuss it with your wife and tell me tomorrow.'

On and off during the day Joe did think about Bob Courton's offer. He smiled inwardly when he considered what his mother and his father would have said at the faintest suggestion of their son owning a motorbike, even less a car. He could hear them clearly advising him to keep his money in his pocket for a rainy day. They would have considered such luxury was only for royalty. As far as he and Maggie were concerned Rina and Jamie were the nearest they would have to children of their own and Rina being so ill meant the rainy days were here now. He and Maggie had already agreed they would help Jamie pay the hospital fees. Since the day they married, Rina and Jamie had been determined never to get into debt, as Rina's father had done. It was one of the reasons they hadn't hired a maid. Joe could understand that the unexpected hospital bills had come as a blow. Jim said they were scrupulous about budgeting and repaying their share of the bank loan they had all taken out to buy Bonnybrae between the three of them. It would be a bleak day for all of them if anything were to happen to Rina. Joe and Maggie had been thrifty all their lives and their savings had accumulated beyond their expectations. As his responsibilities at the factory had increased, Mr Courton had made sure he was paid accordingly, as well as making him a partner, assuring a secure future when they were both too old to work.

If the valuation of the jade collection had been accurate, it seemed possible his and Maggie's contribution to the medical fees might not be required after all. Lady Capel had thought they were valuable because she had tried to take the jade collection for herself, without telling her husband, even though she knew it was part of Rina's inheritance. It was her deceit which had made Mr MacQuade seek a professional valuation and then take the items to be stored at the bank until Rina was ready to appreciate them. She had been too stricken with grief at her grandfather's death to pay attention to his possessions so she had completely forgotten about them. If they were worth even half the value MacQuade expected, Joe knew their own savings would not be required. A car would make regular visits to the hospital easier and seeing Marguerite would surely make Rina happier. He decided he would discuss Mr Courton's proposition with Maggie that evening.

Joe was surprised by his wife's spontaneous reaction. Maggie wholeheartedly approved of Mr Courton's suggestion.

'I've always been afraid you would have an accident on your motorbike, Joe, but you know that. Anyway, he's right. You're not getting any younger and one of these days you'll get a drenching and catch pneumonia. I couldn't bear that to happen. So if Mr Courton wants to sell you his car, and if he considers you would be safer inside it than on your motorbike, then I agree. Besides we shall still have money left to help Jamie with some of the hospital fees if Mr MacQuade's plans fail. In the meantime, Mr Dixon has arranged a loan.

'It's thanks to you being such a good and thrifty wife that we have money in the bank,' Joe said, and drew her into his arms, making her blush with the passion of his kiss.

When he released her, he told her Mr Courton had suggested he should drive the car home on Friday evening so that he could take her to the hospital to see Rina on Saturday.

'If we don't like it he says he will take it back on Monday. We'll not tell Jamie the arrangements this time. I don't want him to be disappointed again if anything goes wrong. Rina will be longing to see him and wee Marguerite.'

'Marguerite would have more room in a car,' Maggie said, 'but won't you need to learn to drive it before we can go to the hospital, Joe?'

'Oh, I can drive it already. Bob Courton knows that because I often drive if we need to go to a meeting together, or when we inspect one of the warehouses, or meet some of the buyers. He never drives if I'm there to do it for him. He says he wants to buy a Morris Cowley made in Britain but I doubt if it will make much difference. He really doesn't like any sort of machines. I understand now though why he is so good at selling our products.' He grinned. 'I couldn't do that side of the business. I suppose he's right, we make a good team.'

On Friday evening when Jamie saw Joe arriving home in a Model T Ford motorcar he couldn't believe his eyes. As soon as the milking was finished and he had eaten his evening meal he ran down to Braeside to see what it was all about. Maggie had already tried sitting in the front, then in the back, then stroking the bonnet and inspecting the wheels.

'We shall get you to the hospital tomorrow, Jamie, whatever the weather does.' She looked fondly at Joe, then reached up and gently stroked his cheek. 'You're a good man, Joe Greig. I'd love to see Mother's face if she could see us now. She would never believe Emma's big brother has done better than any of her own family.'

Jamie scowled, remembering the bitter old woman who had called him a bastard and told him he didn't belong. Meg, a year younger than himself, had thought she was a witch. Joe saw his expression and read his mind. He knew Jamie would never forget, or forgive.

'She looked down on me too,' he said with a wry grin, hoping to lighten Jamie's brooding memories. 'She never guessed I was aiming to marry her precious daughter.'

'She would never have believed what a good husband you are, dear Joe.' Maggie smiled dreamily.

'Och, Aunt Maggie! I'm going home if you and Uncle Joe are going to get all amorous,' Jamie declared. Joe winked and squeezed his wife's ample waist.

'Think we're too old for a wee bit of love, do ye laddie?'

'I suppose not, and I do like the car,' Jamie conceded. 'I shall be grateful if you can drive us to the hospital tomorrow. Rina sounds terribly homesick in her letters. I'm afraid she will insist on coming home if I don't get to see her. She can't even sew or knit to pass the time. Her fingers are too swollen. She was never idle and she's missing Marguerite.'

'I know. I wonder if we should take her some books to read.'

'Marie suggested books. She loves reading herself. She has two books for Rina to borrow by somebody called Jane Austin. She says Lady Hanley loved to hear her reading to pass the time during the nights she couldn't sleep.'

'I will lend you my book of poetry,' Joe offered. 'Your Uncle Davy gave it to me. He and Emma were the ones who loved books. Marie must take after your mother.'

'She promised to help Mark Blackford with his estate work. She's sent a note explaining that she can't get to Stavondale Manor but she has offered to type the letters in the evenings when Marguerite is in bed, if he wants to bring the typewriter and the files here.'

'It's not Marie's responsibility to work for Master Mark,' Maggie said, 'but I expect if she promised to help him, she will feel she's letting him down.'

'She does, and I feel guilty that she's spending all her time helping us at Bonnybrae. It must be bothering her because she mentioned Mark and his problems in her letter to Mother and Father. She feels sorry for him. Apparently he wanted to be an engineer. He knows almost nothing about managing an estate. But . . . I was wondering,' he glanced sheepishly at his Uncle Joe. 'While you have got a motorcar could you er . . . would you bring the typewriter and the files, and stuff here for Marie? I wouldn't feel so guilty about her working for us then and I think she'll enjoy the change.'

'If you think he'll agree to have his business papers brought to Bonnybrae I could collect them,' Joe said.

'You wouldn't . . . ? Er . . . could we go for a ride to Stavondale now, to try out the car?' Jamie said eagerly. 'I could explain to Mark then and see what he says.'

'That's not a bad idea, laddie.' Joe grinned in response. 'What about it Maggie? Will you come too? It's not far to Stavondale Manor and you can see if you will be comfortable.'

'All right,' Maggie agreed. 'Wait while I tidy my hair and put on a clean apron.'

Mark Blackford was astonished when a car drew up beside his house. He had been feeling down in spirits. He was finding it difficult to make friends. Everyone here treated him with a deference he neither wanted nor deserved. He was missing Marie's lively conversation as well as her help.

'We'll wait in the car,' Joe said, 'while you see what he says. I can understand if he prefers to keep his business affairs to himself.'

Jamie began to explain why Marie had not been to see him and diffidently passed on her suggestion about her doing the letters at Bonnybrae.'

'Marie would do that, for me?' Mark asked, 'Even though she knows I can't pay her much yet?

'It was her idea but if you . . .'

'It would be a great help. Can you wait while I gather things together? There seems to be something new needing attention every day.'

'All right. We wanted to try out Uncle Joe's car, so I thought it was a good chance to move the typewriter. Is it very heavy? I've never seen one.'

'It would be awkward on horseback, or on a bicycle,' Mark grinned. 'Marie said Lord Hanley has one. He thinks people pay more attention to official-looking letters, and even I can see it will be useful to have a copy. Will you ask Mr and Mrs Greig to come in?'

Stavondale Manor was a large house but Mark had obviously been sitting in the small room near the kitchen. Maggie noticed that everything was clean and tidy but it was almost austere. It didn't feel homely, or even lived in. Her heart went out to the young man, so far from his family and friends. For the first time she understood why Marie wanted to help him adapt to his new life.

Eventually he came through from a room across the hall which he, on Marie's advice, had turned into his office. It was near enough the door for easy admittance should any of his tenants, or other businessmen wish to call on him. He was carrying a box of files plus a thick packet of paper. He set it down on a small table.

'Would you mind if I came back with you to explain a few things to Marie? I could hold the typewriter on my knees.'

'We don't mind at all laddie but . . .'

'That's a good idea,' Jamie said. 'You could ride back here on Duke. It's bothering Marie because she promised Rina she would look after him but she hasn't had time to exercise him properly. I feel guilty because we're keeping her so busy.'

'That would suit me,' Mark beamed. 'I'll ride my own horse up to Bonnybrae tomorrow and lead Duke back.'

'That would be a great idea,' Jamie declared. 'Uncle Joe is driving Aunt Maggie and me to Glasgow. We're going to visit Rina so we're taking Marguerite with us. I will tell Marie she must make time for herself while we're away.'

'Oh good,' Mark almost clapped his hands. 'Maybe we could exercise both horses together. I've missed her company.'

'That sounds like a good idea to me,' Maggie said. 'Marie ought to get out more and meet her cousins but . . . well things are difficult now.'

'I understand Mrs Greig, and I know Marie loves looking after her young niece, so I'm sure she will not be unhappy, except for Rina's health.'

They all trooped outside to the car and Mark set down his boxes and walked all round.' His interest was genuine and Joe asked if he would like to see under the bonnet.

'Oh yes, please, if you don't mind.' Joe obligingly lifted up the side and together they discussed various parts of the engine.

'It sounds as though you understand a bit about engines,' Joe remarked in surprise. 'Maybe I shall know where to come if I have any problems with her.' Joe was a little bemused by Mark Blackford's obvious interest and understanding of the various parts.

'I would certainly help if I could,' Mark said with enthusiasm. 'If I ever bring Stavondale up to scratch and make any money for myself I shall buy a car.'

'Can you drive one?' Jamie asked, feeling more respect for the younger man who owned an estate, yet knew so little about running it, or about the farm he had kept.

'Oh yes,' Mark laughed. 'I learned to drive with my friend Rupert during our last summer at Oxford. His uncle taught both of us. Of course, I was forgetting, you know Lord Tannahill. He is a fine man. I wish I had an uncle like him.'

'He was certainly kind and helpful to Rina,' Maggie said quietly, wondering if the young man knew Lord Tannahill had hoped to marry her.

'He's always been generous to Rupert, and to me. I stayed with them often. He bought a kit with the various engine parts for us to put together. Unfortunately, we didn't have a car body to put it in,' he grinned, 'but Lord Tannahill said it would help us understand how the engine fitted and how it works. He wanted to learn more about engines himself but he has so many matters demanding his attention. For once I managed to do something better than Rupert,' he added modestly.

'I can believe that,' Joe nodded. 'You seem to have a fair grasp of this one.'

'I'm convinced we shall see more machines for transport and in farming one day. If I'd had my way I would have gone to work where they manufacture cars but my family, especially my mother, think I have feathers for a brain,' he said a little bitterly. 'Nobody believed it was possible to make a machine that could stay in the air. I'm sure there will be others now.'

'I think you're right, laddie.' Joe nodded. 'The railways and the machines we use in the mills have made great leaps forward.'

'Of course!' Mark said. 'Marie told me you have machines to drive your looms.'

'We do indeed,' Joe beamed. 'Maybe you'd like to see them some day.'

'Oh yes, I would like that,' Mark said eagerly.

'I think it is time we were getting back,' Maggie said quietly. 'Jim and Marie will wonder where you are, Jamie.'

'They will. They didn't know I was coming to see your car, Uncle Joe. I didn't expect to get a ride in it. I'd love to see the faces of Mother and Dad when I write to tell them. They'll never believe you can drive a motorcar, even less that you would buy one.'

'Your parents have had a large family to rear, Jamie. That makes all the difference. We would rather have had a family too, wouldn't we Maggie?'

'Of course we would but we're lucky to have you and Rina, Jamie. We love you both like our own, but we haven't had to feed and clothe you so now we can afford a car to get you to the hospital.'

'I never thought of it like that,' Jamie said. 'We wouldn't want to be without Marguerite for all the motors in the world.'

'Of course you wouldn't,' Maggie said warmly. 'She has found a place in Marie's heart too so don't feel too guilty about keeping her busy. I know she is happy to help when

Rina is going through such a difficult time. After all it's what families do, help each other in times of trouble.'

'Some families!' Mark said darkly. 'I doubt if mine would care if they never saw me again. We-ell, father might give me a thought or two if I'm lucky.'

'Oh Mark, you're too young to be so cynical,' Maggie chided gently. 'Anyway, I'm sure you're wrong.'

'I suppose I should be grateful he has bought me this estate — even if it will need all the income for repairs for the next five years or more. He didn't ask whether it was what I wanted to do with my life though. At the time I was too shocked and upset after shooting Rina's father to consider anything. That still gives me nightmares.'

'You should try to forget about it, laddie,' Joe said kindly. 'No one blamed you, least of all Rina. Now we'd better get back.'

CHAPTER FOUR

The following morning Mark rode up to Bonnybrae on Bali, leading Duke. Jamie and Jim were crossing the farmyard as he arrived.

'Morning, Mark,' Jamie called cheerily. 'Thanks for returning Duke. Marie will probably ride over to Stavondale this afternoon once I take Marguerite out of the way.' Jim noticed Mark's look of disappointment.

'Why don't you put both ponies in the stable and join us for a bite to eat?' he suggested kindly. 'Marie is making an early meal so Jamie can get away to the hospital.'

'You're sure that will be all right?'

'It will be fine. Marie was making a big pot of soup so there will be plenty to go round. Anyway I know she wanted to talk to you — something to do with a letter she received this morning.' He looked at Jamie's retreating back. 'All Jamie can think about is getting away to see Rina, but I canna blame him. He had a letter from her friend, the one who is married to a doctor. Apparently Mr Chambers, the chief doctor, wants to see him at two o'clock to discuss Rina's condition so he can't afford to be late.'

'No, of course not. It will not take me long to unsaddle these two and rub them down.'

When Mark entered the kitchen Marie turned to greet him with her usual smile.

'You're welcome to join us, but you'll have to make do with eating in the kitchen.'

'I eat in my own kitchen so it suits me. There's a delicious smell. It's making me hungry already.'

'I thought Mrs MacCrindle had taken you under her wing. Doesn't she set your meals in the dining room?' Marie asked. 'Rina says she was very correct with Sir Reginald Capel.'

'She cooks me an evening meal most days and I eat it in the small sitting room off the kitchen. She would have come up and cooked all my meals, including breakfast but I'm trying to keep my expenses down. I hadn't reckoned on paying a cook. She is a gem though. She has arranged for a woman to do washing and help her "clean through" as she calls it.'

'Things have changed then since Sir Roger and his wife were at Stavondale,' Jim said, pulling out a chair for Mark and one for himself.

'Probably,' Mark said drily. 'My mother would disapprove of the way I live, but she's not here. Mrs Mac understands since I explained about the money. She would work for nothing if I would let her. She tries hard to mother me. I suspect Lord Tannahill asked Mr McGill, his farm manager, to keep me supplied with milk and cheese and butter. They even brought me a side of bacon to hang in the pantry so I can slice it as I need it. I don't know how I shall ever repay Lord Tannahill. He has always been as kind to me as he is to Rupert.'

'Some people like to give,' Marie said. 'Lord Hanley gave me his wife's jewellery casket and what he called her trinkets. I'm sure some of them are quite valuable. I said I couldn't possibly accept them, but he insisted it had been Lady Hanley's wish that I should have them. I still feel overwhelmed by their kindness. Lord Tannahill, as well as Rupert's mother, probably appreciated you for being a good friend when Rupert has no father or brothers and sisters.'

'If you had been an arrogant fellow, as some young men can be,' Jim said, 'people wouldn't have wanted to help.'

'Uncle Joe and Jamie say Lord Tannahill has a fine motorcar,' Marie said. 'It's a pity he didn't teach you how to drive it because . . .'

'But he did!' Mark grinned. 'We were talking about it last night when Mr Greig showed me his new car.'

'You can drive a car? Really?' Mark nodded. Marie clapped her hands. 'That's splendid. I'll explain later, here comes Jamie and my wee angel.' She scooped Marguerite up in her arms and sat her in her highchair between herself and Jamie.

They were just finishing their meal when they heard Joe drive up. Marie carried Marguerite and put her in the back beside Maggie. She was already sucking two fingers, a sure sign she was ready for a sleep. Jim came out to see the new acquisition.

'I wonder what our mother would say now, Maggie, if she could see you riding in style.' Jim remarked with a grin. He walked round the car but Jamie was impatient to be off.

'Give Rina our love,' Marie called, 'and don't forget to hand over her clean washing and bring anymore to me. We can't expect her friend to keep doing it.' She waved them off.

'Now come on in and I'll make a fresh pot of tea then you should rest, Uncle Jim.'

'Ye're a good lassie, Marie. You go and enjoy a ride on Duke.'

'I was hoping we might ride together?' Mark said.

'All right, but I would like you to read the letter I received from Lord Hanley. Mr Rowbottom, his agent, has had a fall and broken his leg and fractured his shoulder in two places. He is unable to ride his horse to inspect the cottages and farms, as he usually does. Lord Hanley has been driving him to attend to essential matters.' She sighed as she passed Mark the letter. 'He promised to teach me to drive and I think he was hoping I would go back and help out when it is an emergency but I can't go back yet. If you could help him out instead of me, Mark, you could ask him all the questions I can't answer about managing an estate and awkward tenants. You would need to stay down there for a couple of weeks or so. I'm sure I can handle any letters until you return.'

Mark read the letter and his face lit up.

'Gosh, Marie! This is exactly what I need, someone who really knows about things, and I love motorcars.'

'Will you write to Lord Hanley then? Tell him I passed his letter on to you?'

'I'd love to go but . . .' His face fell. 'There's Glenside. I haven't many animals yet, a few sheep, two pigs, plus my horse, but I can't abandon them.'

Jim opened his mouth and closed it again without speaking.

'Come on Uncle Jim,' Marie said with a half laugh. 'You may as well tell Mark what you're thinking. He won't be offended will you Mark?'

'Of course not. I need all the advice I can get, Mr Sinclair.'

'It's not my place to tell ye what to do laddie,' Jim said awkwardly, 'but if ye really want to know what I think about you keeping Glenside I reckon ye're wasting your time and money. Ye'd be better off letting it. At least you would get an income from the rent.'

'I thought I might understand the tenants and their problems better if I learned to farm,' Mark said.

'I've been farming all my life,' Jim said with a sigh, 'and I'm still learning. No two years are the same and things are changing since the war. Jamie was telling me last night you believe they'll invent more motors and machines to make transport and farm work easier and quicker. Ye could be right, but none o' that will teach you how to manage your estate, or how to bring it back to the way it was in Sir Reginald's time.'

'I see,' Mark said slowly. He looked young and deflated.

'Of course, it's none of my business,' Jim said hastily.

'It is when you're offering me your best advice, but I would never get a tenant at short notice and Marie's friend needs help now by the sound of things.'

'I know two young men who would seize the chance to rent Glenside tomorrow.'

'You do?' Mark asked incredulously.

'Yes, so long as you understand this. I'm not trying to pull strings for my family. My brother's farm neighbours Glenside and my nephew is getting married and looking for a house. A small farm to rent would be even better. Then there's the Mitchells. They're neighbours too. They have a son who will soon be ready for a farm of his own.'

'Both tenants pay their rents,' Marie said. 'That's important.'

'Then I'll call to see your brother and nephew first,' Mark said eagerly. 'Maybe we could ride over there this afternoon, Marie? If they are interested in taking on the tenancy I will write to your friend, Lord Hanley.'

'If my brother does take it on, tell him what stock you have Mark and why you want to sell so unexpectedly. Knowing Robin I'm sure he will buy them at a fair price, but be sure it's what you want.'

'It is, if I go to Yorkshire for a few weeks. If I had dreamed Father was going to buy me a run-down estate, I would have asked Lord Tannahill for advice long ago — but none of his farms are run down and I expect his tenants all pay their rents on time.'

Mark saddled up both the ponies while Marie washed the dishes and tidied the kitchen. She never forgot her mother's teaching, but it would be good to escape for an hour or so on Duke, to gallop across the fields with the wind in her hair and the sun on her face. Both horses and riders were well matched and they arrived at the public road together, breathless, laughing and full of the joy of youth and good health.

'I never thought I would find another companion to match Rupert,' Mark said admiring Marie's escaping curls, more golden than copper in the sunlight, her flushed cheeks and sparkling eyes, 'especially not one as interesting and intelligent, and pretty in addition.' He thought of his brother's simpering fiancée with distaste and shuddered when he remembered the girl his mother had singled out for him.

'I would never have believed I would enjoy riding as much as I do,' Marie confessed, blushing a little at Mark's compliment. Although she was practical and capable beyond her years, she had little experience of boyfriends. It had been Mark's diffidence which had made her feel at ease with him when they met on the train. No one could say he was brash. 'Lord Hanley will probably let you ride May. She's a lovely horse. She belonged to Lady Hanley. I will try to exercise Bali if you do go to Yorkshire. It would be more convenient for me if you ask Uncle Jim if you can bring him to Bonnybrae to graze.'

'I understand how busy you must be, Marie. You're a fine person to help your family as you are doing, and you're a good friend to me.' He smiled at her. 'I suppose we had better ride up the track to your uncle's farm at a more sedate pace.'

'I suppose so. This is your business though Mark so I shall escape and talk to Aunt Evelyn if I can while you tell Uncle Robin about Glenside.'

Jim Sinclair had been right. Robin accepted the opportunity to take over the Glenside tenancy without hesitation. He also agreed to take over the animals at a fair price.

'We shall need more stock to graze the extra acres anyway and bring in more income now Billy will soon have a wife to keep. He'll be over the moon with the news,' Robin grinned at his youthful landlord. 'He will be in for tea before we start milking. 'Will ye stay and take a cup with us?'

'I am here with your niece, Marie, so it will depend whether she has time to stay,' Mark said. 'In fact it was your brother's suggestion that I should offer you the tenancy.'

Marie had only met her aunt and cousins once, at Aunt Maggie's, but they welcomed her warmly and tea was already on the table when the men joined them.

'Marie has been telling me Maggie and Joe have bought a motorcar and taken Jamie and his wee girl to visit Rina in hospital,' Evelyn said. 'The tea is ready. Marie wants to get back to help Jim with the milking in place of Jamie.' Before Mark could speak Billy came into the kitchen, already drying his hands.

'Why, hello Marie, it's good to see you again. I wondered who the horses belonged to . . .' He stopped short when he caught sight of Mark.

'We have some good news for you, laddie,' his father said. 'Mr Blackford is offering us the tenancy of Glenside with immediate occupation at the same rent per acre as we pay here. The house is empty so you will have your own wee palace to start married life.'

'Is it true?' Billy turned to Mark, his blue eyes alight with hope.

'Yes, your Uncle Jim advised me, but I wouldn't have offered it to you if your father was one of the tenants who are always behind with the rent.'

'I should hope not,' Robin Sinclair said soberly. 'We were brought up never to owe anybody, least of all the laird. Sir Reginald Capel would have put out tenants who didn't pay their rent. His son neglected the estate shamefully.'

'Yes, so Rina says, even though he was her father. Marie thinks I should be firmer with the tenants who are in arrears but I am going to spend a few weeks in Yorkshire with her father's landlord, Lord Hanley. He needs someone to drive his motorcar and take his injured land agent around the estate. In return she says he will advise me on estate management.'

'Aah, that will be William's landlord, eh, Marie?' He eyed his niece shrewdly. 'I heard you had been helping Mr Blackford in the Estate Office. Some of the tenants had received letters to pay up or quit?'

'We didn't put it as bluntly as that!' Marie protested. 'It would serve some of them right though. According to the records they were owing rent long before the estate was sold. I do understand things may get more difficult in future. Dad says the government has already forgotten about the country being near to starving when our ships were sunk. They have repealed the 1920s Act, so there is free trade again. Lord Hanley believes thousands of tons of grain will come in from America now there are binders for harvesting the cereals.'

'My, ye're a chip off the old block, lassie, but ye seem to understand what's happening in the world, even though ye're so young. William always had fire in his blood but he expected men to be fair and honest too. I reckon ye take after him. We all felt he and Emma had a raw deal from our mother. I hear he's still bitter although they have made a success.'

'Mother and Father both work hard. Lord Hanley says Dad is the best farmer on his estate. Mr Rowbottom, his agent, doesn't allow tenants to get behind with rents.'

'I expect the disgruntled ones on the Stavondale Estate will accuse you of favouritism when they hear we're getting the tenancy of Glenside,' Robin said to Mark.

'You can tell them you got it because you make a good job and you pay your rent on time. There's no favouritism about that,' Mark said firmly. 'I am glad to have your brother's advice. I don't know all the tenants and their families yet.'

As they rode back to Bonnybrae, Marie turned to Mark with a smile.

'That's one place you will always be welcome to a cup of tea.'

'Yes, I'm getting to know people gradually,' Mark said. 'If I can help you with any of the work I will come back to Bonnybrae with you, but I would be no use at milking cows.'

'You could feed and groom the horses if you want? There's the young calves to feed, not to mention looking round the sheep to make sure the lambs are all paired up with their mothers, and check the few late ones which have not lambed yet.' She grinned. 'Even if you do check them I expect Uncle Jim will still go round again this evening.'

'I would like to help. I owe you both.'

'Of course you don't owe us, Mark,'

'I would like to come back with you anyway. I promise to help if I can. If I'm lucky your uncle might invite me to join you for your evening meal.' He winked at Marie, bringing the ready colour to her cheeks, but she laughed at his pleading, hangdog expression.

'That will be up to me but you can stay if you're good.' She chuckled. 'I have made two big steak pies and lots of vegetables. It's apple sponge for afters, but I shall need to make some custard — not exactly food for gentry, but Jamie will be back by then and Aunt Maggie and Uncle Joe will probably be glad to eat with us to save them cooking after their journey.'

'I have never pretended to be gentry and the food sounds heavenly. You don't know how much I look forward to your company, Marie, and your uncle's and Jamie's too of course. It's a relief to be treated like a normal person. People round here treat me as though I've come from a different planet because I own their land, yet I can't pretend I like the company my parents cultivate.'

'It's because you're the local laird now, even if the estate is run down and a lot smaller than it used to be since Lord Tannahill bought five of the hill farms for shooting.'

'I've no interest in shooting but I shall look forward to Rupert and his uncle coming to stay at Stavondale Tower. Rupert and I have been friends since boarding school, then we were at Oxford together.'

'That is another hurdle. You are so well educated compared to us lesser mortals.'

'Don't say that, Marie. I never met a girl as intelligent and knowledgeable as you. I find it refreshing. The girls I know are too busy batting their eyelashes to hold a decent conversation.' His tone was almost savage. Marie raised her eyebrows in surprise.

Uncle Jim and Doug Lamont were bringing in the cows for milking when they returned. Marie slid lightly from Duke's back.

'I'll need to change but I will be out to help with the milking in a minute, Uncle Jim. Don't forget to save me the quietest cows.'

'Aye, we'll do that lassie, if ye're sure you want to help us? We can use an extra pair of hands with Jamie away, can't we Doug?'

'We can that. Alice had meant to come up to help but her mother couldn't come to look after the wee fellow and he would only get into mischief if he was running loose in the byre.'

'I read about a man trying to invent a machine for milking cows,' Mark said. 'He was using a vacuum to draw the milk out but I believe it injured some of the cows. It would save a lot of time though if the machine had been a success, don't you think?'

'I read something about that,' Jim said. 'I believe it was mentioned in the *Scottish Farmer*. I reckon it will be a long time before anybody can invent a machine to milk cows though. It's not natural. I'd want to be sure it didn't do my cows any harm,' Jim said firmly.

'I'll take the ponies and unsaddle them,' Mark said with a smile. 'We shall never need a machine for that. Shall I attend to the other horses too, Mr Sinclair? I'd like to help.'

'Ernest always looks after the horses,' Jim said. 'He takes a pride in them. He's not so good with cows though. There's calves to feed and water and the sheep to feed in their troughs in the field. If you wait while Doug and I tie up the cows in their stalls I'll show you where to find everything and tell you how many scoops of feed to give them. How did you get on with Robin by the way?'

'Oh, you were right. He seized the chance to rent Glenside and he's taking over my animals right away. His son Billy is really happy about it.'

'That's a good day's work then? You'll be writing to Lord Hanley now?'

'Yes, I shall write as soon as I get home tonight and post it at the village. If he does want me I shall probably go at the end of next week. I hope you don't think I'm taking advantage of Marie, leaving her to attend to my correspondence.'

'I doubt if anyone will take advantage of my niece, Master Mark,' Jim said wryly. 'She would not have offered unless she wanted to help. If you ask me she's more interested in estates and how they're managed than she realises.'

'She certainly has a better understanding of what needs to be done than I do.'

'She was considering training to be a nurse before she came up here. I suspect Emma and Maggie arranged this visit between them. I think they knew Rina's condition was serious. I'm thankful Marie is so capable, although she's so young. We don't want to prevent her making new friends, or stop her helping anyone else though.'

* * *

The men were just cleaning up the byre for the night and Marie was cooking the dinner she had prepared earlier when Joe drove into the yard. Marguerite had been sleeping and Jamie lifted her out of the car and carried her into the house, while Maggie climbed out stiffly and stretched her arms above her head, stifling a yawn. In the kitchen the little girl ran to Marie holding up her arms. 'Mama . . . ? Ree-ree?' Jamie smiled wanly at his younger sister.

'She didn't seem to recognise Rina when we first arrived at the hospital,' he said. 'It really upset Rina when she clung to Aunt Maggie. She was in tears and that upset this wee rascal. I thought Aunt Maggie was going to do the same but she hugged Rina, then Marguerite seemed to accept it was all right for her to hug her too.'

'She's very young,' Marie said sympathetically. 'She's bound to be a bit bewildered with her mama in hospital and me here all the time. Did she travel well in the car?'

'Oh yes, she slept most of the way there and again on the way home. She will not be ready for bed tonight.'

'She'll be fine once she's had a little play and eaten her supper and had a bath. Mother always says a warm bath helps to settle toddlers so I hope she's right.'

‘Well she should know. She’s had plenty of experience with all of us.’

‘Yes, it has made a tremendous difference since Lord Hanley installed the bathroom with hot water from the taps.’

‘It made a difference here, too,’ Jamie agreed, ‘thanks to Uncle Joe’s influence.’

‘Mother is really proud of Uncle Joe making such a success of his life,’ Marie said, ‘but you haven’t said how Rina really is, Jamie. You don’t look as cheerful as I expected now you have seen her.’ Marie gave him an anxious look, meeting and holding his troubled gaze.

‘We’ll talk about it after we’ve eaten. When we’re on our own,’ he added in an undertone and Mari’s heart sank. She guessed the news was not as good as they had all hoped now that Rina was having rest and medical care.

CHAPTER FIVE

Maggie was tired after her journey to Glasgow. She knew it was partly due to tension and the headache which had developed. Seeing Rina still looking so ill had distressed her.

'Ye're a good lassie, Marie, making a meal for Joe and me, as well as helping Jim with the milking. I didn't feel like cooking. In fact I didn't think I could eat anything but I enjoyed it. You're a grand wee cook. Emma has made a good job of you all.'

'You should go home and put your feet up, Aunt Maggie. You do look tired and I expect Uncle Joe will be glad to relax after concentrating on driving to Glasgow. I will soon clear away and wash the dishes.'

'No, no. I'll dry if you wash. You still have Marguerite to bathe and get to bed.'

'Jamie and Mark are entertaining her at the moment,' Marie said with a smile. 'I'm not sure who is enjoying it most, the pair of them building up bricks or her knocking them down, but she sounds happy and they will tire her out.'

'He's a nice laddie, Mark. It's easy to forget his family are gentry.' She looked anxiously at Marie. 'I wouldn't like to see you getting hurt while you're here, lassie.'

'Hurt? Mark wouldn't hurt a fly, let alone a woman.'

'I didn't mean physically,' Maggie said hastily. 'I meant — well if you fall in love with him and then he goes off and marries one of his own class.'

'Oh, Aunt Maggie,' Marie chuckled, lifting her soapy hands from the wash bowl as though she was going to give her a hug, but Maggie stepped back hastily. 'Mark and I are friends because we're both strangers in this area. He admits he doesn't find it easy being regarded as the local laird. I think he's grateful for someone to talk to and as a riding companion. We went to see Uncle Robin this afternoon. Mark offered him the tenancy of Glenside. He seized the opportunity for Billy and his bride to be. It was Uncle Jim's idea.'

'I'm sure it's a good idea,' Maggie said drily, 'but I know you're changing the subject. It has happened before and it could happen again when a man fancies a girl from a different background, but when it comes to marriage it's a different story. No doubt Mark's parents will have one of their own circle lined up as a wife when he's ready.' Marie was silent, as she tried to remember what she had heard about her own family's history. Hadn't something like that happened to their Granny Sinclair? Jamie had said she was a bitter old woman. She must ask him about it. She had a vague recollection of hearing Aunt Maggie's real father had turned out to be the old laird but nobody spoke about it.

'I'm not looking for a husband, Aunt Maggie, so don't worry about me. I can't make up my mind what I would like to do, except I like to be busy and needed, but I want to use my brain as well. I think Lord Hanley understood that better than I did myself.'

'You may feel that way, Marie, but I see Mark looks at you with great affection.'

'He regards his friend Rupert with affection. He misses his company.'

'Mmm, well be careful.'

'Dear Aunt Maggie, I will, so don't worry about me. Anyway, I think Mark may be going down to Yorkshire now he's solved the problem of Glenside.'

'It will be good for you to have a break from his company for a bit.'

'I thought you and Uncle Joe liked him?'

'We do. He's a nice laddie, pleasant and well mannered, and not a bit arrogant. In fact, he's a bit lacking in self-confidence. That's strange considering his background.'

'I have a feeling Mark's family are not close like ours. We all help each other, even if we do squabble sometimes. I really missed Meg when she got married. I think Mum did too.'

When everyone had gone home and Marguerite had settled down to sleep, Marie was impatient to hear news of Rina. After a last inspection of the few ewes which were still waiting to lamb Jamie came into the kitchen and flopped down into the wooden armchair beside the range. Marie perched on the leather-topped fender stool beside him.

'Tell me how Rina is getting on, Jamie,' she said quietly.

'She wept when we left.' Jamie said the first thing which came into his head. It had been on his mind all the way home. Marie heard the gruffness in his voice and knew Rina's distress was upsetting him. 'She wanted to come home with us.'

'I can't blame her. There's no place like home, especially when the two most precious people in her world are here. Did you see Mr Chambers?'

'Yes. He asked to see me on my own when we arrived. Mel's husband must have told him we were there. He seems very stern. He said Rina was fortunate to have Melissa and her husband to care about her because most women only see a midwife. Even those who see their local doctor are usually only advised to rest. He admits specialists like him still have a lot to learn about pregnancy and childbirth, even though it's supposed to be part of nature. Rina says he is gentle and cheerful whenever she sees him.

'I'm glad about that or she would be even more desperate to get home.'

'I know b-but he–he says he fears for Rina's life unless they can operate to take away the baby within the next two weeks. That is by the end of May, a month before it is due if Rina's dates are correct. I told him Rina matters more to me than any baby and if it will help her to recover the sooner he operates the better.'

'Did he agree?'

'He said the first Caesarean operation, that's what he called it, had been performed about thirty-odd years ago, by a German doctor in 1881. He says they have learned a lot about operations since then,' Jamie shuddered and covered his eyes for a moment. 'He gave me another of his stern looks, then admitted all operations carried a risk. Performing a Caesarean operation is a last resort as far as he's concerned.'

'Oh Jamie . . .' Marie's voice shook.

'He says it is unlikely Rina will be able to have any more children judging by her present condition. He has discussed it with her. She pleaded with him to give her baby the best chance of survival.'

'Poor Rina,' Marie sighed. 'Does she realise delaying could cost her own life?'

'Mr Chambers said he had tried to explain that. I told him he must save Rina at all costs. We already have Marguerite and Rina is the most important person in the world to me. He seemed surprised I was so insistent, but he looked relieved. He promised to talk to us together, before I left.'

'And did he?'

'Ye-es. Aunt Maggie and Uncle Joe understood. They took Marguerite for a walk and then waited at the car for me. Rina is dreadfully upset at the prospect of losing the baby, but I think I convinced her, as well as Mr Chambers, that her own life is the most important thing to Marguerite, and to me. I believe Marguerite's need made Rina see things in perspective. The danger is that her kidneys may already be damaged.'

'Oh I pray not, Jamie.' Marie turned to him then and hugged him tightly. 'We all loved Rina as soon as we met her when you brought her to Moorend. She was so full of life and energy and so very happy — you both were.'

‘We didn’t know then what the future might hold.’

‘No wonder Aunt Maggie and Uncle Joe were so subdued. I expect you had to tell them how things are.’

‘Yes, briefly. I didn’t tell them everything so it would be better if you don’t mention it to Aunt Maggie, or in your letters to Mother. You know how they discuss everything.’

‘Very well, but I’m glad you have confided in me, Jamie.’

‘Yes,’ he summoned a wan smile. ‘Who would have thought my little sister could be such a comfort. I’m glad you’re here, Marie. In fact, I don’t know how we would have managed without you. Rina would never have agreed to stay in hospital if you weren’t here to look after Marguerite, and it’s all too much for Aunt Maggie.’

* * *

Monday afternoon brought another surprise. Marie was clearing away the midday meal at Bonnybrae when Mark rode Bali into the yard in a great hurry.

‘I’ve had a telegram from your friend, Lord Hanley, Marie. He wants me to go to Yorkshire immediately. He says he will meet the train at Wakefield this evening.’ Mark sounded both excited and apprehensive.

‘So you have brought Bali to stay here?’ Marie asked, looking anxiously at Uncle Jim.

‘It’s all right, lassie. Mark already asked me about that before he said he could go to Yorkshire,’ Jim assured her, ‘but how do you mean to get to the station, Mark?’

‘We-ell, er, I wondered if Marie could ride there with me and bring Bali back.’ Marie looked helplessly at Jamie. He had Marguerite on his knee but she was needing a nap.

‘Marie can’t leave the house while Marguerite is asleep. Uncle Jim and I are going to sort out the sheep this afternoon. How about you leave your horse here now? You can borrow my bicycle to ride to the station. Ask the stationmaster to keep an eye on it. I’ll collect it in the morning when I’ve delivered the milk to the station.’

'You'd do that, for me?' Mark asked gratefully. 'I knew Marie would be busy with Marguerite but I couldn't think what else . . .'

'That's okay, Mark. You can return the favour someday,' Jamie said with a smile.

'You haven't much time if you're to collect your clothes and get to the station,' Marie said, taking her sleepy niece in her arms. She was surprised at the frisson of homesickness she felt at the thought of Mark travelling to Yorkshire when she was staying here indefinitely.

'Give my love to Mam and Dad,' she said huskily, reverting to her childhood names for her parents. 'I-I'll just take this wee angel up now. Goodbye Mark.' He quickly crossed the floor and kissed her cheek.

'I shall miss you, Marie. You will write, won't you? Tell me what's happening with Rina and — and everything?'

'Of course,' Marie nodded.

'Thanks for arranging this for me.'

Marie felt a lump in her throat.

'I hope you get on all right with Lord Hanley. Bye Mark.' She lowered her head to Marguerite's soft cheek and hurried away with her.

'I think Marie's a bit homesick because you're going to Yorkshire without her,' Jim said. 'Tell her mother and father she misses them and we all send our regards.'

'I will. I'd better get going. It will not make a good impression if I miss the train.'

Marie missed Mark's company more than she had expected but Aunt Maggie came up to Bonnybrac most afternoons to listen for Marguerite wakening from her afternoon sleep while she exercised Bali or Duke on alternate afternoons. Sometimes she met some of the Stavondale tenants and they enquired about Mark's absence, letting her know they had not seen him around for a while. Most of them were pleasant, even if one or two dropped hints about their barn, house or stable waiting for roof repairs. The tenants who were owing rents tended to keep a low profile if they saw her riding by. They knew she had typed the letters asking for their outstanding rents to be paid and they guessed she would be keeping an eye on things and reporting back to their new laird. They all knew Robin Sinclair and his son had taken over the lease of Glenside but only one man complained of favouritism. Once a week Marie took the key which Mark had left with her and called at Stavondale Manor to check if there were any letters needing attention and to make sure everything was in order. Sometimes she ran into Mrs MacCrindle who called each day and kept things clean and tidy. She was not a young woman, but she kept herself fit and busy and she was reliable. Marie guessed she was lonely with no one to care for after years spent looking after Rina's grandfather. She always offered Marie a cup of tea and a scone but she rarely had time to stay.

'I must get back before Marguerite wakens,' she explained. 'I know Aunt Maggie would never neglect her but she is getting heavy for her to carry downstairs.'

'I understand lassie. It's a good job you could come to help with Miss Rina being so ill.' She shook her grey head. 'I pray for her every night and hope she'll come through. I don't suppose her lady mother has been in touch has she?'

'Not as far as I know,' Marie said gently, 'but she may have written to Rina.'

'I'll bet ma life she doesna want tae ken. She never looked after her bairns herself.'

When Marie got back to Bonnybrae she asked Jamie if Rina's mother knew she was ill, and in hospital.

'I don't think so. She has never been in contact since she went to France. I don't think Rina has an address for her.'

'But, Jamie, that's terrible.' She wanted to say 'what if Rina were to die' but she couldn't even contemplate such a thing, even less say it to Jamie. 'Surely any normal mother would want to know how her only child is getting on. Our parents always want to know if we are well and happy, even though there are so many of us.'

'Yes, I suppose they do,' Jamie said thoughtfully, 'but I didn't believe they loved me when I first came up here, or at least I thought father didn't.'

'Oh, he did! I was only four when you ran away but even I can remember how worried they both were. I'd never seen Mam cry before. Even now you're grown up they both look forward to getting your letters and hearing your news.'

'Do they? I wonder if they know illegitimate children can be legitimatised now, when the parents marry, even though the marriage is after the birth.'

'Even if that's true I don't suppose they think about it. Dear Jamie, none of us think about it, and neither should you. You're the eldest of our family. You're the same as us. How do you know about such things anyway?'

'They passed a law in parliament last year. Wives can divorce their husbands as well now, if they can prove they have been unfaithful. Before that it was only men who wanted to divorce their wives for being unfaithful. Some even fabricated evidence.'

'Goodness I didn't know that. That's unfair. I'll bet men are more likely to be unfaithful than women anyway. It's a good job they changed that law. No wonder those two women were determined to be accepted as British lawyers last year.'

'Women lawyers?' Jamie laughed. 'I didn't think there were any!'

'There are now. One of them was called Ivy something. Anyway why shouldn't women be lawyers? How else can we get a fair deal if everything depends on men to make the judgements? No wonder Aunt Maggie is so much in support of women having the vote.'

'I had no idea you had such radical views, Marie, or that you were such a wee firebrand. I'll bet Lord Hanley would never have had you in his house if he'd known.'

'He does know,' Marie said indignantly. 'We talked about all sorts of things. He encouraged me discuss such things, even if we disagreed sometimes. He always gave me the newspapers to read, and books from his library. He said if he'd had a daughter he would have made sure she had the same opportunities of education as he gave his sons.'

'Did he? Maybe losing his sons in the war has mellowed him.'

'I don't think it's that,' Marie said indignantly. 'I believe he realises many women are as capable and intelligent as men. You said yourself that Meg was one of the cleverest pupils at Silverbeck School when you were both there.'

'Yes, she was.' Jamie agreed.

'Not all parents are like Rina's mother and have nannies and tutors for their children. Lord Hanley and his wife truly grieved for their sons. They have no nephews or close relatives to carry on the estate either.'

'There can't be many people as selfish as Rina's mother,' Jamie muttered. 'I'd work down a coal mine before I would ask her to help with the hospital fees. I pray to God Mr MacQuade is right about the value of the things he has sent to auction. Mr Dixon, the bank manager, has been understanding so far, but Mr Chambers speaks as though Rina is going to be in hospital for weeks yet. I expect the operation alone will cost a lot.'

'I'm sure Mr Dixon knows you will repay the money one way or another,' Marie said. 'I overheard Uncle Joe and Aunt Maggie discussing it. They're willing to help with the cost.'

'It's my responsibility. Rina is my wife,' Jamie said desperately.

'Of course she is but they love her too. We must be thankful Melissa and her husband are friends or she — she . . . well she would never have gone to hospital. Who knows what might have happened?' She couldn't tell Jamie how worried their mother was about Rina's condition, or that she had known mothers die if they did not get attention, and even sometimes when they did. She shivered inwardly and changed the subject.

'I think Mark's mother must be a bit like Rina's. I feel sorry for him sometimes.'

'Do you, Marie?' Jamie frowned. 'Don't confuse sympathy with love. Maybe it's a good thing he has gone away for a while.'

'Don't talk rubbish, big brother!' She would not admit she was missing Mark's company more than she had expected.

'It's not rubbish. I saw the way he looked at you before he left. He's certainly very fond of you.'

'He only wants my help with the correspondence for the estate. He never expected to become a landowner. All the repairs are a bit depressing.'

'Uncle Jim says there have been no repairs done for years. Rina blames her father.'

'Yes, she told me that when she knew I was helping Mark,' Marie said. 'She said it grieved her grandfather dreadfully. Our parents are afraid something like that will happen to Lord Hanley's estate because he has no relatives to take over. They are saving every farthing in case they need to buy Moorend someday. I think they have only thought about it since you and Uncle Jim bought Bonnybrae. I feel sorry for Allan though. He and Lynn would be happy with a cottage or small farm to rent if it meant they could get married.'

* * *

Jamie couldn't wait for Saturday when Joe would take them to visit Rina again.

'I'm really grateful to you, Uncle Joe, but I must pay for the petrol at least.'

'Eh laddie, you hold on to your money,' Joe said, noting how tired and anxious Jamie looked these days. 'Ever since we married Maggie and I have considered you and Rina as the children we never had. We want to visit her too. She'll be longing to see Marguerite.'

'Yes, she asks loads of questions in her letters and she draws lovely little pictures for me to show Marguerite.'

Mark wrote regularly to Marie, but in his last letter he had asked if she could find time ride over to Stavondale Manor to search for a certain letter in his desk.

'If you could post it to me, Lord Hanley would like to see it. He thinks he may be able to advise me about handling matters concerning the cottages in East Lowrie village. We have not considered them yet, have we? We have not seen them either. Maybe we can arrange that as soon as I get back.' Marie felt a little troubled at the way Mark used "we", as though he expected she would be here indefinitely. He was staying at Silverbeck Hall with Lord Hanley but he had been to Moorend with Bob Rowbottom and enjoyed meeting her parents. She was pleased he did not consider their modest lifestyle beneath him. Mark was not like that, he judged people rather than their surroundings. In fact, he admitted he felt more at home here, at Bonnybrae, than he did in his own spacious Stavondale Manor.

Marie decided she would ride over there on Saturday when Aunt Maggie and Jamie took Marguerite to the hospital. She would be back to help Uncle Jim and Doug Lamont with the milking in place of Jamie. Sometimes Ernest exercised Duke for her in the evenings after he finished work if she hadn't time to exercise both horses. Ernest loved all the horses but he had been used to Duke when he worked for Rina's grandfather.

As soon as she had waved Jamie and Marguerite off in the car with Uncle Joe she scurried around tidying the kitchen and putting away her niece's toys then she saddled Bali and set off for Stavondale Manor. She tied Bali to the hitching post beside the gate and waved to Mrs MacCrindle who was in her garden. The elderly woman waved back eagerly and began to walk up the track to meet Marie. Marie's heart sank. She really needed to get on and search for the letter. Mark was not the most methodical person when it came to correspondence. However, she had been brought up to consider her elders and she guessed Mrs Mac was lonely with Mark away. She walked to meet her. She always asked after Rina so Marie gave her the latest news.

Eventually, she declined the offer of a cup of tea and her oat biscuits and let herself into the large echoing house. There were several letters on the floor behind the door and two which had arrived earlier in the week and which Mrs MacCrindle had placed on the polished hall table. Marie flicked through them and guessed they were bills, except one in a thick cream envelope with black handwriting. She gathered them into a pile, wondering whether Mark would want her to open them and deal with them, or would he expect her to post them to him. He was casual about such things and often left the letters for her to open and sort through even when he was here. She had a fair idea what she was looking for in Mark's desk but she searched each drawer methodically and failed to find the letter. Only one deep bottom drawer remained and it was always locked because Mark kept the leases for the farms in there. Marie sighed. Time was passing. She went through to the small sitting room where Mark kept his keys in the small drawer of a cabinet beside the fireplace. She was searching for them when she was startled by a haughty voice.

'What are you doing, girl? What business have you prying in those drawers? You should not have those keys. Give them to me at once.'

'Who — who are you?' Marie asked, her fair skin flushing beneath the icy glare. Marie knew about the quality of materials from her mother so she knew the woman was well dressed in a straight green woollen coat with a brown fur collar and a matching hat. Although the fashion now was for shorter lengths the coat was only about four inches above her highly polished leather shoes. Marie bit her lip, aware of her own dishevelled appearance. Usually she borrowed Rina's breeches for riding but today she had kept on her black working skirt. She had shortened it to mid-calf, not to be in fashion, but because it was more convenient for working, especially collecting eggs or trudging across a muddy field, and even for carrying Marguerite up and down stairs. Her hair was always a mass of wild curls when she had enjoyed a good gallop. She could see the woman's disapproval in her flint-like eyes.

'Inform my son we are here. Then tidy yourself and bring us tea.'

'I'm sorry? I don't think you are expected, at least not here, at Stavondale Manor. This house belongs to Mr Mark Blackford.'

'Of course we're expected! I wrote to Mark. I informed him we intended paying him a visit.' So this was Mark's mother. Was she plain Mrs or did she have a title?

'Your letter may be amongst the unopened ones on the hall table. Mark is in Yorkshire.'

'Yorkshire?' Marie thought the woman was going to have an apoplectic fit the way her colour rose with her voice. 'He has gone to Yorkshire without informing us? When is he due home, girl?'

'He will be staying with Lord Hanley for a few weeks. Now if you will excuse me I need to search for a letter regarding the estate. He has asked me to post it to him without delay.' She went to pass Mrs Blackford but the woman barred her way.

'How dare you be so insolent?' she hissed. 'We have journeyed a long distance. Serve us with some refreshments at once.' Marie's colour, and her temper, began to rise.

'I am not a hireling,' she said coldly. 'I help Mark with his correspondence for the estate. Apparently he had not expected to spend his life managing an estate especially one as run down as Stavondale. Now I must find the letter and be on my way.'

'You must what? Who do you expect to look after us?'

'I really don't know, madam. Mark does not employ any staff. He says he cannot afford such luxuries.'

'Can't afford staff? He is my son!'

'Maybe but he does not have money to spare. Mrs MacCrindle cooks a meal for him in the evenings but she is elderly and he does not employ her. She needs warning of extra cooking so it would be kinder if you were to find accommodation elsewhere.'

'You insolent chit . . .'

'Now, now, my dear. This young lady is quite right. I have been speaking to Mr McGill, the farm manager for Lord Tannahill. Apparently Mark is away from home. I think I saw your letter unopened on the hall table as I came by.' His wife stared blankly.

Marie liked the look of Mark's father. His mouth was meant for laughter, quite the opposite to his wife's thin pursed lips and scowling brows.

'I am sorry,' she said, 'I would make a cup of tea but I don't think there is milk or anything else in the larder, and I really do need to get back to Bonnybrae. My sister-in-law is very ill. I am keeping house and caring for my brother's wee girl. Please excuse me.'

'Of course my dear,' Mr Blackford said. 'Mr McGill told me you have been helping Mark with the estate business. Apparently Stavondale is more run down and neglected than I realised. I understand Mark has left his horse in your care too.'

'Yes, I rode here on Bali to give him exercise. Now I must go.' His wife sniffed angrily. She was obviously used to having everyone do her bidding. Marie didn't like her at all. Poor Mark. He had her sympathy.

She found the letter she needed amidst a pile of leases so she took it out and locked the drawer again. She went through to the room to replace the keys where she had found them. Mrs Blackford was sitting upright in a chair beside the empty fireplace looking furious. Her husband came back from the direction of the kitchen.'

'I'm afraid Miss er . . . Miss?' He looked questioningly at Marie.

'Sinclair. Marie Sinclair,' she said, closing the drawer and edging towards the door.

'I'm afraid you are right, Miss Sinclair. There are no provisions even for a cup of tea.'

'There must be a servant somewhere,' his wife insisted. 'Can't you tell someone we require their services, girl?'

'I'm sorry. As I said Mark does not employ any servants. Mrs MacCrindle keeps the house tidy out of the goodness of her heart. She likes having someone to mother.'

'Mother! I am Mark's mother. He doesn't need . . .'

'But you're not here to care for him, my dear,' her husband reminded her. 'Do you know of anyone who would come in to work while we are here Miss Sinclair?'

'I'm afraid I don't know the people around here very well. My home is in Yorkshire. As I said, I came to help out while my sister-in-law is ill. I really do need to go,' she said urgently and made her escape.

Uncle Jim and Doug had started the milking by the time she got back to Bonnybrae but Bali had enjoyed a gallop on the way home. Ernest was crossing the yard and he offered to take care of the horse and rub him down. Marie thanked him and hurried indoors to get the coarse apron she wore for working outdoors. Both Jim and Doug were pleased to see her and have her help and Marie thought how good it was to feel appreciated. She doubted if Mark's family ever made him feel like that.

When the milking was finished, the byre cleaned for the night and all the pails sparkling clean and upended again, Marie went indoors to set out the casserole she had put into the oven earlier. The rest of the family had still not returned.

'They were back earlier than this last week,' Jim said. 'I hope they have not had a breakdown with the car.'

'Oh surely not. Jamie says Uncle Joe is a careful driver.'

'Well I'm hungry,' Jim said. 'We had lunch early today so they could get away.'

'That's true. Shall we have ours, Uncle Jim? I can stand the dish in water and put it back in the oven so it will be ready when they do return. It will not spoil. That's what Mother does if Dad is late home from the market. The pudding is cold anyway. I used the first of the rhubarb to make a large pie and I thought we could have it with cream for once.'

'That sounds good to me lassie. You'll make some man a fine wife one day. Your mother has made a grand job of teaching you how to keep house. No wonder that Lord of yours wanted to keep you.' Marie smiled and dished up their meal. As they ate she told him what had delayed her at Stavondale Manor. She described Mark's parents.

'They expected him to be there and someone to wait on them. There were no provisions to make them anything, even if I'd had more time. Mrs MacCrindle will stock up for Mark when he's due back. Mrs Blackford's haughty manner would have had the poor woman in a panic.'

'So you didn't like Mark's parents then?' Jim remarked.

'Mr Blackford seemed all right, but his mother . . .' She shuddered. 'I hope I never have to meet her again. If she had been a sweet old lady, or someone like Aunt Maggie who appreciates everything, then I might have brought them here for a cup of tea and rhubarb pie.'

'I'm glad you didn't. It tastes delicious,' Jim said with a laugh.

'Mrs Blackford wouldn't have expected to sit at our kitchen table like Mark does. She would have demanded to be served in the dining room with the best china. I know how to set a dining table to suit gentry since I stayed with Lord Hanley and his wife, but it takes time. You need some warning, or a troop of servants. Anyway they had a car so they can easily drive into Strathlinn and look for somewhere to stay. They should have given Mark more warning instead of expecting him to be hanging about waiting for them to visit. I think it was only a spur of the moment decision because they had been staying in the Lake District.'

'Dinna upset yourself over folks like that lassie. It's not your fault they found an empty house,' Jim soothed.

'No, it's not. You're right Uncle Jim. We'll have a cup of tea.' She grinned. 'That's Mam's cure for everything.'

She made the tea and then cleared and washed their dishes. Still Jamie and Marguerite had not returned so she settled down to write to Mark, enclosing the letter he required and telling him his parents had visited and found an empty house.

'Your mother was very annoyed. No doubt you will be hearing from her when you return.' She had just finished writing the letter and was putting everything in a larger envelope when she heard the car. She pushed everything aside and ran outside. Aunt Maggie looked pale and tired and Marguerite was fretful. Marie opened the door and lifted the little girl into her arms, stroking her flushed little face.

'Want a drink, Mama . . . Ree-ree. Pwease?' she added.

'Of course my little angel, you can have a drink and some lovely dinner. How are you Aunt Maggie? You look tired and weary. I've made dinner so you must come and eat.' Her aunt nodded silently and glanced towards Jamie. Marie raised her eyes to her brother and drew in her breath. His young face looked pale and strained. She felt he might burst into tears if she said the wrong thing. Instead she turned back into the house.

'You will all feel better when you have eaten. I have a mutton casserole all ready with lots of vegetables and some savoury dumplings like mother makes,' she said with a cheerfulness she did not feel. She knew instinctively something was wrong. Even Uncle Joe had lost his cheery smile.

CHAPTER SIX

Jamie was glad Marie did not ask any questions. He didn't think he could force any food into his churning stomach.

'Wash your hands and face, Jamie,' Marie said quietly, as their mother might have done. He obeyed automatically. All the way home his thoughts had been with his beloved Rina and her sweet, tear-drenched face. He could still feel the dampness on his chest from holding her close against his heart. It had been a wrench to leave, although he had stayed longer than allowed.

Surprisingly they all ate Marie's delicious stew. Marguerite had already drunk a cup of milk but she enjoyed the mashed carrots and potatoes, onions, mushrooms and tiny pieces of tender meat, as well as a sizeable portion of dumpling.

'Ye're a fine cook, lassie,' Maggie said gratefully. 'I feel a bit better now.' She glanced at Jamie with sympathy but she said no more.

'Wait until you taste the rhubarb pie,' Jim said, doing his best to add a note of cheer to the sombre atmosphere. 'I swear it is as good as you make yourself, Maggie, and you made the best pies in the district.' There was a small piece left when they had eaten their fill, so Jim said he would finish it off with another cup of tea to clear the plate. Jamie didn't wait for a cup of tea. He pushed back his chair.

'I need a breath of fresh air. I'll take a walk up the hill round the sheep.'

'Eh laddie, don't go too far up the hill,' Jim said anxiously, though he sensed his nephew needed to be alone. 'I know we're at the end of May but it's already eight o'clock. The darkness and the mist can come down fast.' Jamie nodded but made no reply. Maggie bit her lip as she watched him go, then she offered to help Marie clear away and wash the dishes.

'No thanks, Aunt Maggie. You look tired to death. I will change Marguerite first and get her ready for bed. She will not be long before she's asleep tonight. I'll wash up later. You're much later back than you were last week.'

'Aye, ye are that. The news is not so good by the looks of Jamie,' Jim said anxiously.

'No, I expect he will tell you everything when he's got his feelings under control,' Joe said. 'He didn't want to leave Rina and she clung to him and sobbed as though her heart would break.'

'Is Rina worse then?' Marie asked nervously, feeling a tremor of fear for her young sister-in-law. Rina had been so full of life and love, with her generous heart and warm smile. Could it be only three years since they married? Surely she could not die so young and leave her darling toddler without her mother. Life could not be so cruel — could it?

It was the following morning when Jamie joined Marie in the scullery after breakfast. Marguerite was playing happily with a stuffed toy cat on the hearth rug.

'I'm sorry we were so late back yesterday, Marie. Mr Chambers, the surgeon, made a point of coming into the hospital to speak to me, before we left. That's what kept us late. I think the traffic was busier because it was Saturday with people shopping then trying to get home,' he said dully.

'The time doesn't matter Jamie. The main thing is you all got back safely. We were beginning to worry.'

'Mr Chambers doesn't often come in on Saturdays unless there is an emergency or a special patient he needs to see, but Mel says he calls in to see Rina every day, even on a Sunday. He told me he is deeply concerned about her. He asked me again if her life was more important than the baby's survival. I told him I would never change my mind about that.'

'I'm glad. I agree, however sad it is to lose a baby. Rina is far more important.'

'Apparently not all men think that if they are hoping for a son. Mr Chambers seems to doubt Rina's dates. She has always thought the baby was not due until the end of June, but she was not sure about exact dates when Marguerite was born and everything was fine then. Mr Chambers says her condition is deteriorating. It's much worse than it was last week. Oh Marie, he's going to operate, on Monday.'

'Jamie!' Marie turned and hugged him. 'He'll take away the baby?'

'Yes. She is terribly upset. She says the baby needs longer if it is to have a chance of surviving. She doesn't realise her own survival is the most important thing in the world to me. She has been reading all about incubators for premature babies. I remember when she was nursing she always read everything she could to do with her work and treatments and any new discoveries. She says it was a Frenchman who first thought of incubators for babies after he saw an incubator for chickens at a zoo. It was not a great success then but that was forty years ago, in 1880. Then she read about closed in incubators but they didn't allow enough ventilation and babies had difficulty breathing. She has been pestering Mel's husband to get her the latest information.'

'She will be desperate to give the baby a chance,' Marie said with compassion.

'I know, but honestly, her face and hands are so swollen and she can't get her feet into her slippers, even though Aunt Maggie bought her some two sizes larger. I-I can't bear to lose her. What does the baby matter compared to Rina? We have Marguerite.'

'Oh Jamie,' Marie repeated softly. She barely knew what words of comfort she could offer. 'I know it must be a big operation to remove a baby, but surely Mr Chambers will be able to save Rina once he takes away the baby?'

'I think it depends whether her kidneys are affected, or any other side-effects. They have done all sorts of tests to her blood and for protein and sugar in her urine, but she still wants him to wait. If only I could be with her.'

'She will be asleep won't she? They use anaesthetic for operations since the Great War. Lord Hanley said before that the shock and pain killed a lot of soldiers when they cut off their limbs without anaesthetic.'

'B-but . . . I'd be there to comfort her until she went to-to s-sleep,' he stammered desperately, 'and when she wakens up and there is no baby for her to cuddle I could try to comfort her. She was so happy when she first held Marguerite. We both were.'

'Yes, I can understand it would comfort Rina if you can be there.'

'Och, there's no use talking about it. I can't be up in Glasgow and leave Uncle Jim and Doug with all the work. I know that really. Apart from the milking we were going to start shearing the sheep if the weather stays dry.'

'I'm sure the sheep could wait another few days. I don't mind helping with the milking but I'm afraid to leave Marguerite in bed. Even if Aunt Maggie came up here early in the mornings, she is getting heavy and a real wriggler. They might fall coming downstairs.'

'That would never do,' Jamie agreed.

'I'm sure if they know how bad things are for Rina, Alice will ask her mother to come and stay overnight to watch their children to let Alice help with the milking. They all think the world of Rina and Alice enjoys being at the byre. She says it's not as tiring as running after the children.'

'I suppose I could ask them, but it still leaves a lot for Uncle Jim, apart from the sheep.'

'Did I hear my name?' Jim called from the kitchen. It was Marie who explained Jamie's predicament.

'Don't worry about me, Jamie. You need to be with Rina at a time like this. I understand how worried ye are laddie. We all are. I went down to talk to Maggie and Joe last night while you were up the hill. They explained how serious things are. I know the doctors should know better than me but I was convinced Rina must be carrying two babes when she got so big so early on.' He sighed heavily.

'Yes, Mr Chambers thinks it is twins but he says that would worry Rina even more so he has not mentioned it's a possibility. He says there's something called an X-ray now but he doesn't want to take any more risks with Rina's health.

'You need to be with her at a time like this, Jamie. Maggie says Melissa must think so too because she offered you a bed so you can stay on Monday night. She thinks it would keep Rina calmer. Anyway,' he grinned, 'Maggie has offered to come and help with the milking.'

'Aunt Maggie?' Jamie and Marie echoed in unison.

'Once you learn to milk you never forget and Maggie was better than any of us. She enjoyed it.'

'But Aunt Maggie milking? At her age?' Jamie repeated.

'She says it would be safer than her looking after a lively toddler like Marguerite. Remember she's never had children of her own. Anyway, she's only fifty-seven and she's been milking since she was eight years old. When she's not worried sick about Rina she's still fit. She's only a year older than I am. Lots of women are still milking at her age. I'll bet your mother will be.'

'You're right there. Mother enjoys milking.'

'So does Maggie but she hasn't needed to do it often since she married Joe. He's proud and independent and he insisted he would provide for his wife. Anyway, in this case Maggie offered to help and Joe agrees. They both think the world of Rina and they think you ought to be with her at a time like this, Jamie. I'll ask Ernest to come to the byre and carry the pails of milk to the dairy and empty them over the cooler so Maggie will not be lifting any heavy buckets.'

'Oh, Uncle Jim, that's splendid,' Marie said with relief.

'Joe and Maggie had everything planned when I went down to Braeside. Remember Jamie, you're not on your own. We all care about both of you, and wee Marguerite. God knows she needs her mother.' Jamie gulped and his eyes were over bright. He nodded.

'Joe is taking Maggie for a Sunday afternoon drive today. They're going to call on Mr and Mrs Courton to explain what's going on and let them know Joe will not be at the factory for a few days. He's says they will understand. He'll be coming up to tell you he'll drive you into Glasgow early tomorrow morning so that you can be with Rina as soon as you're allowed in the hospital. Joe intends to call on the MacQuades this afternoon on the way home and tell them what is happening. They will telephone Mel so she'll be prepared for you staying overnight and Dr Meadows will tell Rina you will be with her. It will give her something to look forward to.'

'That's wonderful.' Marie turned and hugged Uncle Jim. 'You're all wonderful — you and Uncle Joe and Aunt Maggie. We're so lucky with our relations, especially when you think of poor Rina. She has no family except her mother and she may as well not have a mother for all she seems to care.' Out of the corner of her eye, Marie saw Jamie surreptitiously brush away a couple of tears with the heel of his hand.

'Marie's right, Uncle Jim,' he said throatily. 'We are lucky to have you all. I'll never be able to repay you for everything.'

'Eh laddie, you owe me nothing. Imagine what a crusty old bachelor I would have been if I hadna had you to help me here at Bonnybrae — not to mention sharing a home with Rina and the wee one. My life has turned out better than I ever dreamed.'

* * *

As Joe had expected, Bob Courton understood how anxious he and Maggie felt about Rina. He and his wife had no family since they lost their wee girl, and they had followed Rina's progress with kindly interest since they learned she was having problems with her second pregnancy. Mrs Courton had insisted on making tea for him and Maggie on Sunday afternoon. Later, Bob couldn't resist a wide grin as he waved them off saying, 'I knew you'd find buying a car was good advice!' Joe smiled back at him and admitted he was very glad he had the car now, and so were his family.

When Joe and Jamie set out for the hospital at the crack of dawn on Monday morning Jamie couldn't eat his breakfast. His stomach felt knotted with tension. Marie made up a small basket of buttered scones and cheese, slices of Aunt Maggie's fruit cake and two bottles of cold tea so they could eat after the drive to Glasgow and before Jamie went into the hospital. She added a bacon sandwich for Jamie.

'You have to keep up your strength and you might feel hungry by the time you get to Glasgow. Besides it would never do if you fainted, Jamie. The doctors and nurses will be busy enough without you becoming another patient.'

'Anyone would think you were my mother instead of my young sister,' Jamie said.

'Maybe, but you know I'm right. Anyway, Uncle Joe will need a break before he sets off home again.' Jamie nodded and gave her a wan smile as he took the basket of food. Impulsively Marie turned and hugged him tightly.

'Good luck, Jamie.' She whispered huskily. 'Give Rina our love and all our good wishes.' She turned away to hide her tears and hurried upstairs to Marguerite who was rattling the bars of her cot and calling in her baby prattle. She was at the stage where she tried to climb over the bars and she could almost manage the stairs herself.

* * *

Rina was relieved when Frank Meadows told her Jamie would be with her first thing on Monday morning and he would be staying overnight with him and Mel.

He had explained to Rina that she would feel very groggy and probably disorientated after the operation and she would need to stay in hospital for a few weeks to recover.

'I shall not mind that so much if my baby survives, Frank. You will make sure Mr Chambers gets an incubator ready? I have read the book and the pamphlets you and Mel got for me.' She frowned. 'I also read about the man named Couney who took the babies in their incubators to an amusement park in America, I wouldn't like my baby to be exhibited like a freak show.'

'I read about that myself,' Dr Meadows said gently 'but I don't think Couney regarded the babies as freaks. He charged the public to see them in their incubators to raise funds to get more incubators and to improve them after Julius Hess and DeLee had perfected the thermostat which keeps them at an even temperature. They are much safer than depending on changing hot water bottles every few hours. It would have been easy for a busy nurse to forget or to delay. The thermostats have been a big benefit, and now Hess is trying to improve them even more by incorporating oxygen for the babies who have difficulty breathing.' He smiled at her. 'It is just like we were as students at the fever hospital, Rina, always trying to find a new and better way to save our young patients.'

'Yes,' Rina said softly. 'I remember.'

'Even so you must remember we could not save them all, however hard we tried?'

'I know. Whatever happens with my baby I shall try hard to accept it if I know you and Mr Chambers have done all you can to save it.'

'We shall certainly do that, I promise. Now here is Jamie, come to keep you company until Mr Chambers is ready for you.'

'Before you go, Frank . . . I read about gavage feeding if babies are too weak to suckle from their mothers.'

'What is that?' Jamie asked with a frown.

'I only read about it,' Rina said, 'but the babies are fed milk through a tube up their noses and into their stomachs until they grow stronger.'

'That sounds horrible,' Jamie muttered. 'I hope . . .'

'Oh Jamie,' Rina was almost in tears, 'I only want to be sure Frank and Mr Chambers will do everything — everything possible to give our baby a chance to live.'

'I know, I know Rina,' Jamie looked up at Dr Frank Meadows apologetically, 'but you know yourself they will do everything in their power, just as you did when you were a nurse. You would not have expected the parents to question your work, would you?'

'Of course not. I always did my best to help them,' Rina said indignantly.

'I know you did, and so you must have faith in all the people here.'

'I-I do.' Rina's voice trembled and Jamie knew the tears were not far away. She was strung as tight as a violin. He looked at Frank.

'Please tell Melissa I appreciate her giving me a bed for tonight so I can come in to see Rina in the morning before Joe comes to drive me home. Now Rina you'll never guess what Aunt Maggie is going to do . . .' He glanced at Frank and gave an imperceptible nod. He had already had instructions from Mr Chambers to keep Rina as calm as possible and try to divert her attention from the forthcoming operation and any consequences, but Jamie knew that was easier said than done, for himself as well as Rina. She had no thought for her own life, only for their unborn babe, but Rina was his wife and the most precious person in his world. Mr Chambers had been honest with him. Her life was at risk too. It was the reason for performing this operation and that in itself was a hazard.

Jamie felt it was the longest day he had ever lived through. When they had come to wheel Rina away he had kissed her tenderly but she was already drowsy. Mel's husband had advised him to go to the shop a few hundred yards away where the widow woman who owned it made good soup for the nearby workers.

'She bakes fresh bread and rolls every day and she will make you a cheese roll if you ask her, and a cup of strong tea. You must eat and keep your strength up for Rina's sake. She is going to need you after the operation but you will not be able to see her for some hours. Even then she may not be aware you are here. If she is very upset Mr Chambers might ask matron if you can stay with her instead of going home with me. They may put her in a small room on her own for tonight, but it all depends on Mr Chambers and matron. It is not good to upset the other patients in the ward if Rina is very distressed. Mr Chambers always does his best for all the patients but he has taken a great liking to Rina from the beginning. He says she reminds him of his own daughter. She lost her first baby so he understands.'

* * *

Late that afternoon Maggie's heart sank and the blood drained from her face when she saw the red bicycle and recognised the son of the post-mistress from East Lowrie. She knew immediately he was delivering a telegram, and telegrams always seemed to bring bad news. Fortunately Joe was in the garden and he had seen the telegraph boy stopping at their gate. He reached Maggie's side in time to catch her before she fainted.

CHAPTER SEVEN

Joe held Maggie in his arms, and beckoned the boy to place the telegram in his hand. The boy obeyed, jumped on his bike and pedalled off down the road. Joe helped Maggie into the kitchen at Braeside and sat her down at the table.

'I've never swooned in my life before,' she muttered. 'How — how b-bad is it? R-Rina?' She tried to swallow the lump which had gathered in her throat like a stone.

'Before I open it you need a drink of brandy,' Joe said gruffly and made for the corner cupboard near the fireplace. He poured two small tots and insisted Maggie drink hers, but she was already tearing at the flimsy paper with fingers which trembled so much they would scarcely do her bidding. Gently Joe held the glass to her lips.

'Drink this first,' he commanded. He waited until the fiery liquid had slipped down her throat, then he tossed back his own, and pulled out a chair as close to his wife as he could get. They opened the telegram together, barely aware they were holding their breath.

Rina not waken from operation yet. Twin boys. Very frail but alive. Mel phoning parents at 7.00 pm.

'Thank God Rina is still with us,' Maggie breathed.

'The news is not exactly good,' Joe said cautiously, 'but it's not bad either. At least the poor lassie has survived this far. I don't know how long it takes to regain consciousness. I don't know anybody who has had a serious operation.'

'Neither do I,' Maggie murmured. 'Please God let her be all right.' She sat up straighter and looked at Joe. 'Two babies! Jim's instinct was right!

'Listen Maggie,' Joe said. 'We'll go up to Bonnybrae and tell Jim and Marie the news. We'll ask Jim to start the milking early so you can get away. I'll make us a bite to eat, then we can drive to Strathlinn. We could be at the MacQuades by seven o'clock when Mel phones her parents. We would hear if Rina is . . . if she has come round.'

'Oh yes, Joe. That's a good idea, if you're not too tired? You were up very early to drive Jamie to Glasgow this morning.'

'I'm fine, and I'd sleep better if I knew Rina was conscious and if she's going to be all right.'

'All right. Jim and Marie will be as anxious for news as we are. Ernest will help Doug and Jim to finish off outside so I can get away as soon as the milking is finished.'

'Aye, I believe everybody here is waiting for news and wishing Rina well.'

Maggie and Joe arrived at Strathlinn shortly before seven o'clock. Mary MacQuade welcomed them eagerly.

'Mel phoned this afternoon. She said Jamie had sent you a telegram but she would phone this evening with an update. We know how anxious you must be so Neil said we would come to bring you the latest news. It is even better now you are here. Telephones are so wonderful at a time like this.' She ushered them into the room where Neil MacQuade was seated, smoking a pipe and reading a newspaper. They were no sooner seated than the telephone rang in the hall.

'I think you should come too Mrs Greig in case you want to ask Mel any questions, although she only knows whatever Frank can pass on to her.'

'Oh no, I couldn't,' Maggie was flustered. 'You go, Joe. You're used to telephones. I wouldn't know what to do.'

'Both of you go with Mary,' Neil MacQuade said with a smile. 'Then you can hear what's happening, even if you don't speak to Mel yourself, Mrs Greig.'

'Oh please call me Maggie,' she said hurrying into the hall after Joe.

Mel told them Rina had come round briefly from the anaesthetic.

'Mr Chambers is satisfied with her condition so far but he has given her medication to ease the pain so she is very drowsy. He thinks she understands there are two babies, though they are very small and weak.'

'Thank God Rina has survived so far,' Joe said huskily into the phone.

'Frank is on late shift,' Mel said. 'He will bring Jamie home with him when he finishes and take him back to see Rina in the morning.'

'I will collect him about midday at the hospital entrance,' Joe said.

'I'll tell Frank. Rina may be less drowsy when he sees her in the morning. Jamie looked through the nursery window to see the babies in their incubators. Frank says it upset him to see them so tiny and attached to tubes but Mr Chambers says their breathing is fairly good. One twin is slightly stronger. I'm praying one of them survives for Rina's sake,' Mel said tearfully.

When Joe had replaced the receiver, and reported everything Mel had said, Mary MacQuade insisted on making a tray of tea and biscuits and bringing it through to the room.

Maggie slept better that night than she had for weeks. Rina had survived the operation and there were two tiny babies with a chance of life. That had to be an added blessing. She decided to accompany Joe to fetch Jamie home.

'I reckon you need a good sleep by the looks of you,' Joe said when he collected Jamie at the hospital.

'We didn't get back to Mel's until late last night. Even then I couldn't sleep. Frank was on early shift so we left early this morning.' Jamie said. 'I believe these doctors work as many hours in a day as farmers.'

'But how is Rina?' Maggie persisted anxiously. Jamie half turned towards her.

'I honestly don't know, Aunt Maggie.' His voice shook with nerves and exhaustion. 'Mr Chambers says he's satisfied so far. Frank said after a major operation she is bound to take time to recover but — but she has barely spoken. She recognised me the first time she regained consciousness but today she slept all the time I was there. One of the nurses said it was due to the pain relief because it is a big wound. I wish we were not so far away.' Maggie patted his shoulder comfortingly.

'I'm sure she is in good hands with Mr Chambers. Are both the babies surviving?'

'Yes, so far. I only saw them briefly through the window. They seem no bigger than a puppy. It's hard to believe they can survive when they need all those tubes.' He shuddered. 'Rina has not asked about them again. It's . . . it's as though she's not really aware of where she is or what's happening.' His voice shook. 'I'm not even sure she knew it was me when I kissed her goodbye.'

'Oh laddie, I expect it's because they're giving her a lot of medication,' Maggie said in troubled tones. They all fell silent, each occupied by their own thoughts.

Uncle Jim was crossing the yard when Joe drew up at Bonnybrae. He came across to the car to greet them.

'Eh, Jamie, ye look all in, laddie! Is Rina getting on all right?' Jamie nodded silently. 'I think you'd better get to bed for an hour or two,' Jim said. 'I'll call ye in time to start the milking. Maggie is a grand help with the milking but we've missed ye.' Jamie nodded again. It was hard to talk over the lump in his throat. He walked towards the house.

'I think he's exhausted,' Joe said, 'and he's worried about Rina, although the doctors are satisfied.'

'It must be a big operation,' Jim said. 'I've never heard of anybody having it. Rina has gone through a lot already. It's bound to take time to recover.'

'Aye, I hope Jamie's worries are unfounded,' Maggie muttered doubtfully.

'He has a good instinct when it's sheep, or his dogs,' Jim said, 'but what do any of us understand about human beings and new ways of treating things that are supposed to be natural.' He strode away to work, but he was frowning anxiously.

After a couple of hours sleep Jamie felt brighter. He was glad to get back to the routine of the milking and taking his dogs round the sheep in the evening. The following morning they were finishing milking and Doug crossed the yard to the dairy. He saw the lad from East Lowrie post office knocking on the farmhouse door and holding a flimsy yellow envelope. Doug's heart beat a rapid tattoo and he hurried back to the byre to tell Jamie. Marie had just accepted the telegram as Jamie reached her. Joe had seen the red bicycle passing Braeside and he waited for the laddie to cycle back again.

'Do you know what was in that telegram?' he asked when the lad slowed. He shook his head. 'Who was it for?'

'Mr Jamie Sinclair,' he called, peddling on his way home for breakfast. Joe's heart thumped. He hoped Maggie had not seen the red bicycle going by. He hurried up to the farm, knowing he would probably be late for work, but Bob Courton would understand.

Marie, Jamie and Jim were all standing at the open door of Bonnybrae as Joe hurried towards them. Jamie was holding the flimsy yellow paper and his face was white.

'What does it say?' Joe gasped. 'Wh-what's wrong?'

'It's from Dr Frank Meadows,' Marie whispered hoarsely. Jamie handed him the telegram in silence.

Rina delirious. I think you should be here. Frank.

'Oh dear God,' Joe said, and wiped his forehead. He had often had to make snap decisions at work. 'Get washed and changed Jamie. Marie make him some food. He can eat in the car. We'll go to Glasgow right away.'

'But your work, Joe? You were going back today, weren't you?' Jim said.

'This is more important. I'll go and tell Maggie then I'll come back for you with the car Jamie. Get yourself ready.'

'B-but I can't . . .' he opened his arms wide, 'I can't leave Uncle Jim and Doug with — with everything to do.'

'Ye might regret it for the rest of your life if ye dinna go now, Jamie,' Uncle Jim said quietly. 'We'll do what we can and the rest will wait. Do as Joe says.'

Jamie went inside, his young face whiter than the milk in the jug he was holding. Marie packed some food for Jamie, then she folded the nightdresses she had washed and ironed and added two of her own. Her brother John had been gassed during his time in the trenches and when he returned home her mother had managed to save him twice. The third attack had proved fatal but Marie remembered how often her mother had sponged him down and changed his nightshirt when it was damp with sweat. She had said it was essential to cool someone down if they had a temperature. Instinct told her that Rina must have some sort of fever to make her so ill.

Maggie arrived in the car with Joe and she obviously thought the same thing when she saw Marie packing the clean nightdresses for Jamie to take to the hospital.

'I've come up to see if I can help with anything. Jamie you must remember how ill Rina was when she had that fever while she was working at the hospital. She nearly died then if it had not been for the care of Home Sister and Matron Gilroy, but she recovered. She will again. If there are no nurses available to do it, then you keep sponging her and changing her nightgown. She's your wife after all. Do anything you can to keep her cool if a high temperature is the problem. Of course you must listen to Mr Chambers first. He has done this operation before, hasn't he?'

'Yes, but he said a Caesarean operation is a last resort. He said he had not lost a patient yet . . .' Jamie's voice tailed away and Marie guessed he was close to breaking down. He loved Rina so much.

'Here's the things to take with you,' she said briskly, 'Eat something on the way.'

'Thanks.' Jamie's voice was gruff. He hurried to the car. Joe had the engine running.

Joe had intended to drive to work after he had dropped Jamie at the hospital, but when they arrived he knew he could not leave without hearing the latest news of Rina. Eventually one of the nurses told him the doctors were afraid she had developed an infection. Her temperature was very high. Joe asked if Jamie would be able to stay with her.

'It is unusual but I believe Mrs Sinclair is a close friend of Dr Meadows and his wife. We understand she was a nurse herself. She is in a small side ward on her own and both Dr Meadows and Mr Chambers agree it could be beneficial if her husband can be with her. She will need constant observation until the temperature breaks or . . .'

'I understand,' Joe said quietly. 'Thank you for being frank.'

For the first time in his life Joe had no inclination to go to his work. He felt sick at heart for Rina, the happy, smiling girl who had found a place in his and Maggie's hearts when she was ten years old. He knew Mr Courton would understand something unforeseen had developed. Even so Joe knew he should let him know he might be absent for several days. He wondered if there was a public telephone box in Glasgow and where he would find it. Maybe it would be quicker to set off home right away and call at the MacQuades. He could tell them the latest news and ask if he could telephone Bob Courton from there.

As soon as he knocked on the MacQuades' door Mary MacQuade opened it and drew him inside.

'I am so glad you have called Mr Greig. I will make a tray of tea if you will come through to the sitting room.' Joe wiped his brow.

'I would prefer the kitchen. I can't stay long and I haven't come to put you to any trouble. I have taken Jamie to the hospital to be with Rina.'

'It is no trouble but come through here then. Dear Rina, she always liked the kitchen best.' Mary MacQuade sighed heavily as she led the way. 'Mel phoned early this morning. She is dreadfully upset because Rina is so ill. Frank will not let her visit. He says Rina would not know her. You know Mel is expecting a child, though not for some months yet, but Frank is afraid it may upset her to see Rina. Poor Jamie . . .'

'It is better for him to be with Rina, whatever happens,' Joe said, his voice trailing to a husky whisper.

'Yes, I agree,' Mary MacQuade nodded, her face troubled. She busied herself making tea and brought scones and cheese for Joe.

'I-I'm not really hungry,' he said wearily, 'but a cup of hot tea will be very welcome. I wondered if you would allow me to telephone Mr Courton to explain what has happened and let him know I may not be in to work for a few days until we see . . . until we know how things are. I will pay for the call of course.'

'My dear Mr Greig, you don't need to pay. You're welcome to use the telephone. We're very lucky to have the lines as far as Strathlinn. It is such a boon when you need to contact someone urgently.'

'Thank you. Please call me Joe.'

'Very well, Joe it is,' Mary MacQuade smiled. 'The telephone is in the hall.'

Joe returned to the kitchen after making his call.

'If — if we have not heard anything from Jamie by tonight, would you mind if I called on you tomorrow morning to hear if Mel has any news?'

'Of course, you must do that. Neil and I are both dreadfully worried about Rina so we know it must be ten times worse for you and your wife.'

Half an hour later Joe turned up the road for Bonnybrae, passing his own house at Braeside. He was sure Maggie would have stayed up at the farm and he knew it was better for her to be occupied and to have company, rather than being on her own with time to brood.

Marie was churning butter and he could hear her singing nursery rhymes to Marguerite while she played with her rag doll and the small wooden cradle he had made for her. He knew the women never liked to stop in the middle of churning — something to do with turning the butter, though he never understood what. He put his head round the door.

'I'm back but there's no news. I expect I'll find Maggie in the kitchen?' Marie nodded, smiled and kept on singing in her sweet, clear voice. Marguerite was beginning to pick up the words of some of the rhymes herself and Marie was pleased about that. She knew she was going to miss her young niece terribly when she returned home to Yorkshire. She had written short letters to her parents and to Mark as soon as Rina's operation was over and to let them know about the birth of the two frail babies. Mark must have written back immediately because she had received a letter that morning asking if she would be home soon and telling her he was looking forward to seeing her. He had not mentioned the estate correspondence she had forwarded to him several days ago. She couldn't think of anything but Rina lying so ill and unconscious in a hospital bed. Perhaps she shouldn't have written so soon about the twins. Aunt Maggie had promised to write today and tell her mother that Rina's recovery was not progressing as they had hoped. Even if she recovered from this latest setback Marie knew it would be some time before Rina was well enough to come home and be able to look after Marguerite, let alone care for premature twins, if they survived. She would not go home to Yorkshire and leave Jamie and his family when they needed her so badly. She would not allow herself to think what would happen if Rina didn't recover.

Maggie had helped prepare the meal for all of them and she and Joe stayed to eat at Bonnybrae. When they had finished Joe eyed Marie keenly as she carried Marguerite up to her cot.

'I reckon she's getting too heavy for you to carry upstairs so often, lassie,' he remarked with a frown.

'I don't think she'll need an afternoon sleep much longer, but she gets up so early and she would be tired and cross before bed time. Anyway, it's no problem carrying her up because she's usually drowsy. It's worse coming down. She wriggles all over the place when she's fresh from her sleep, don't you rascal?' she laughed, gently poking Marguerite's soft ribs. 'That's why I don't want Aunt Maggie to carry her and have a fall herself.'

'Aye, I can understand that,' Joe said thoughtfully.

Maggie insisted on helping Marie to clear and wash the dishes.

'You should have a rest yourself now, Aunt Maggie, while Marguerite is asleep. I'm going round the hen houses in the field to collect the eggs. I'll collect the two near the farmyard later then she can come with me.'

'I'm going down to Locheagle,' Joe announced. 'Is there anything either of you need from the grocer's or the butcher?

'I want to write to Emma,' Maggie said. 'I'll keep it short if you will wait and post it please, Joe? We ought to let her know Rina has had a relapse after I was so optimistic.'

'Aye, I suppose it would be better to prepare them,' Joe said slowly.

'Were you going to call in at David's and Richard's?'

'No, I hadn't intended to call. We'll wait and hope Rina turns the corner soon.'

'Why are you going to Locheagle then?' Maggie asked curiously.

'Oh, just a bit of an idea I've had. I want to see the joiner. I'll tell you later if anything comes of it. How long will that letter be?'

'Aunt Maggie, will you add a note to Mother from me, please? If she, or Dad, see Mark ask them to tell him I shall not be home for several more weeks.'

'Oh? Was Mark expecting to see you down there soon?'

'He seems to think because Rina has had the operation everything will be back to normal in no time.'

'Aye, that's a typical man I suppose,' Aunt Maggie said.

'Even without this latest problem I think Rina will need a lot of help until the wound heals properly. I mean, she'll not be able to lift Marguerite, or buckets of milk, or do lots of the other work she did before, will she?'

'No, I don't suppose she will,' Maggie said slowly. 'I hadn't considered that far ahead. None of us have, but ye're right, Marie. It will take time.'

'Then if the twins do survive, they will take a lot of time feeding.'

'Aye, and a lot of washing with two lots of nappies,' Maggie nodded. 'Are ye happy to stay a while longer lassie? It would be the best thing for all of us if you can.'

'Well even if I do decide to train as a nurse they wouldn't accept me until after my birthday, in January. I can't make up my mind about it. Lord Hanley spoiled me a bit, taking me under his wing and giving me so many opportunities. Mark says he has a job waiting for me in the Estate Office when I go back, if I want it. I can't decide what to do.'

'Well there's no doubt Jamie and Rina need you, lassie. We all do, but you're not earning any money while you're here.'

'I have a warm bed and plenty to eat,' Marie said with a smile. 'Not everybody is so lucky. I'm not complaining.'

'I know, but most young folk seem to want money in their pockets these days, though we never had money of our own when I think about it,' Maggie added.

'Lord Hanley paid me generously during the eighteen months I was there and he opened a bank account for me so I saved almost all of it. I haven't needed to buy anything much. Mother sent me a new dress and it isn't even my birthday.'

'She was expecting you would be going to the local dances with your cousins. She wanted you to have something new and enjoy life a bit too. We all think you've been brilliant the way you've got through so much work.'

'Mother was married when she was my age, and from what Polly says they all had to work terribly hard. She said there was not a clean room to sleep in, or to eat, and Jamie was a baby when they went to Moorend.'

'None of us knew all that at the time but William still praises the way your mother faced all the difficulties, as you're doing now lassie. You'll get your reward someday.'

* * *

There was no news the next morning when Joe called on the MacQuades.

'Mel phoned last night,' Mary MacQuade told him. 'They are having difficulty getting her temperature down. She doesn't recognise Jamie, or anyone else. She doesn't seem to know where she is, or that she has had an operation.'

'How are the twins doing?' Joe asked quietly. He dare not think how they would look after two frail babies without their mother even if they did survive.

'They are holding their own. Jamie stayed overnight at the hospital. Frank said he couldn't bear to leave Rina, but he is worrying about all the work he has left behind at Bonnybrae. He told Frank they had planned to shear the sheep this week.'

'The sheep will have to wait. He can't be in two places at once,' Joe said. 'He needs to be with his wife at a time like this. We're all agreed on that. Do you mind if I call tomorrow? It's at times like this I really wish the telephones would come to country areas.'

'I don't mind at all, Joe. You're very welcome to come for news. Neil and I are as worried as you are about Rina. She is the best friend Mel has ever had.'

Joe passed on the little information he had when he returned.

'Jim has had a bit of good news as far as the work's concerned,' Maggie said, 'but you may need to go to Locheagle to buy extra groceries. He saw Robin at the station when he dropped off the milk this morning. He and Billy and young Robert are coming to help with the shearing. They have finished clipping their own sheep so they've offered to come today and tomorrow to help Jim. Robin says one good turn deserves another and he's sure it was Jim's influence which got them the tenancy of Glenside.'

'Aye, it probably was, once Mark decided he needed a tenant. It will be a big relief to Jim, and to Jamie, if they can get all the sheep clipped before the weather breaks. I expect there'll be extra food needed though. Is that why you want me to go to Locheagle?'

'Yes. Marie is making a list of things.'

'Well that suits me. I think my stuff will be ready to collect at the joiner's yard.'

'You're being very secretive, Joe. What are you going to make?'

'You'll have to wait and see in case it doesn't work out as well as I'm hoping. It's for Marguerite, but I hope it will help both you and Marie to look after her.'

'I see. If it's like the other joinery work you've done I'm sure it will work, Joe.'

'Here's the shopping list, Uncle Joe,' Marie said. 'I hope you don't mind putting a bag of flour in your lovely car? We must have plenty for bread and scones with three extra men to feed. Aunt Maggie has offered to help. Do you mind?'

'Of course I don't mind lassie, so long as you feed me as well. I expect they'll find a job for me, even if it's only chasing sheep back to their pasture after they're shorn or pushing them up to the shearing pen to save time for the shearers.'

'You sound like an old hand, Uncle Joe,' Marie remarked.

'It might not be my line of work but I've seen sheep being sheared lots of times and helped often too. It will be grand if they can get them finished, then you can write and tell Jamie. It will be one thing less for him to worry about.'

When he knew his brother and nephews were coming Jim had rounded up the first batch of sheep and brought them into the yard before he had his breakfast. They needed time to empty their stomachs before they were turned this way and that during shearing. He had told Doug about his brother's offer of help.

'They don't have as many cows to milk as we do so his wife, Evelyn, his daughter and his daughter-in-law to be, have volunteered to do the milking to let Robin and the boys stay until dark if it stays dry. They have an old man who helps as well. He's been with them since they married.' When Doug told Alice the plans for the day she asked Jim if Ernest could ride Duke up the glen to her parents' house and ask her mother to come down to look after the baby and three-year-old Freddie so that she could help with the afternoon milking and give the men longer at the shearing.

'Aye we'd be pleased to have another milker, Alice, if you're sure,' Jim said gratefully. 'The more we can get done today the better, while the weather is so good. I'll send Ernest to you. It will exercise Duke at the same time and that will help Marie. The lassie hasna enough time for everything she wants to do.'

Alice's father, Ed Vickers, had been a shepherd all his life so when he heard his wife was going to Bonnybrae to help he seized the chance to go too.

'There's always a job for a spare man at shearing time,' he said. 'I can still work my collie if there's more sheep to bring down for clipping, or shorn ewes to get back to their lambs.'

Before Mark Blackford's father had bought the Stavondale Estate for him, Lord Tannahill had already purchased the six hill farms. He had joined two of the smaller farms together, originally tenanted by the Lamonts and the Vickers. It had been an amicable settlement because Alice's brother, Tom Vickers, was already married to Doug Lamont's sister, Sue. Doug and Alice's own wedding had followed as soon as they got a job with a cottage at Bonnybrae. Alice's father had been unable to part with his elderly Clydesdale mare or his two faithful collies. The dogs he kept at home and the mare grazed away her retirement at Tom's place in return for pulling an odd cart of hay or straw, or a few sacks of feed. Now Ed decided it would save their time and energy if he and his wife collected the mare and rode her down to Bonnybrae.

'But Ed,' his wife protested, 'I haven't ridden on the back of a cart horse since I was a lassie.'

'Aye I remember,' her husband grinned. 'I held ye tight pretending to keep ye safe. I can do the same again. Come on Millie, ye'll be fine.'

'B-but I could never get up on one now . . .'

'There's always a way. I'll stand ye on the garden wall, then pull ye up in front o' me. Come on, lassie, we're not that old yet, and I always enjoyed the shearing. We'll go over to Tom's and tell him and Sue where we're going. Bess will run along beside us. The exercise will be good for her. She's not such an old dog yet.' So together they walked the short distance along the track to their son and daughter-in-law's farm. Ed explained what was happening at Bonnybrae.

'Oh dear, does that mean Miss Catherine is still in hospital,' Sue asked. She remembered Rina coming round on her pony with her grandfather when they were both young girls.

'Aye, I think the news canna be good.' Millie said soberly. 'It was Ernest who came to ask me to go down to Bonnybrae. He said Master Jamie was staying at the hospital. The doctor had sent for him early yesterday morning so it doesn't sound good. Ernest is a grand horseman and he's a grown man now, but I thought he was going to burst into tears at the mention o' his young mistress. He thought the world o' Sir Reginald and Miss Catherine.'

'We all did,' Sue said. 'I pray to God they'll make her well.'

'So what are you going to do, Father?' Tom asked, 'if Mother is going to look after the bairns?'

'I always enjoyed the shearing. There's always room for another pair o' hands. Jim Sinclair's brother and his sons are coming to make up a team. The Sinclairs help each other when there's trouble, and they're having plenty o' that with Mistress Catherine's illness.'

'Right, I might come and lend a hand myself then when I've finished my work here. We only have three cows milking just now. Could you manage them on your own Sue?'

'Don't I always milk our few cows myself my braw man?' Sue asked grinning saucily up at him. He smiled back fondly and patted her cheek.

'Aye ye're a good wife and I'm not complaining. Aye, I liked Miss Catherine and Jamie Sinclair is a grand man with his dogs.'

Jim was surprised and pleased when he found he had Ed and Tom Vickers as extra helpers and Joe had already volunteered to help keep the sheep coming forward to save time for each of the shearers. Ernest would be hard pushed to keep up with rolling the fleeces.

In the kitchen at Bonnybrae, Marie had just given her two uncles and her cousins a cup of coffee and shortbread before they started.

'I thought I had asked Uncle Joe to bring enough beef for two days,' Marie said anxiously, 'but we must feed them all. Do you think I should cook it all today, Aunt Maggie?

'We don't want a big feed while we are bending and wrestling with the ewes,' Uncle Robin said overhearing her. 'We'll be glad of a good feed when we're finished though. All we need through the day is plenty o' drinks and maybe some scone and cheese at dinner time. If you can keep sending it outside for us it will save us taking time to come into the house.'

'All right we'll do that,' Marie said, glad she had ordered extra flour and put off the churning for another day. She would bake fresh bread and some girdle scones.

'Joe brought a huge piece of cheese,' Maggie said, 'but maybe the men would be glad o' a drink of soup at dinner time if it's tasty and not too thick.'

'I boiled a piece of ham yesterday so I can use the stock for pea and ham soup. I put dried peas to soak last night before we knew about all this,' Marie said. 'We can mash in some of the vegetables to keep it tasty but make it thin enough for them to drink from the enamel mugs. We'll send that and a can of tea out at dinner time. I'll make a basket up with ham sandwiches, as well as scones and cheese, then they can please themselves what they eat. Mother always feeds the men well. She says strength goes in at the mouth and if men are to work hard they need fed. One of the men, who has been at Moorend since before any of us were born, has a huge appetite but he's very strong and he works hard.'

'Yes, I remember him from when Joe and I stayed with you,' Maggie said with a smile. 'His name is Cliff something or other, isn't it?'

'Yes, that's right. I'd better get the bread made first to give it time to rise. I shall need to use the biggest pan to make a huge pot of beef stew with plenty of vegetables and some dumplings for dinner tonight. It will take up all of the oven. There will be no room for a big rice pudding. Maybe I should make plenty of pastry and put it in the pantry where it's cool. We have lots of rhubarb in the garden now and Uncle Jim loves rhubarb pie. I could bake three pies while the oven is hot when the bread comes out. If I make plenty of custard that will help fill them up when they haven't had a substantial meal all day. I hope Marguerite will continue to be good and play happily with her toys while I'm working with floury hands.' Marie smiled. 'That's always when she decides she needs a pee or something urgent.'

'I'll look out for Marguerite, lassie, until you finish baking. Emma and William should be really proud of you the way you're coping with everything.'

'Thanks, Aunt Maggie. I enjoy the bustle really, and it will be a huge relief to Uncle Jim if they can get most of the sheep sheared by tomorrow.'

'Aye, it was good of Ed and Tom Vickers to come to lend a hand. They are both good at working their dogs so they will probably bring the rest of the sheep down from the hill to let them get emptied out. Jim would have had to stop shearing to get them himself and he says he can't work the dogs as well as Jamie. He reckons Jamie and the two dogs are worth three men when it comes to herding sheep.'

'Mother says he always liked the collie dogs and he longed for Dad to get sheep at Moorend, even when he was very young,' Marie said softly. 'I pray with all my heart that Rina will improve soon. How long can she go on like she is, Aunt Maggie?'

'Not much longer, I fear,' Maggie said soberly. 'A high temperature is dangerous if they don't get it down.'

Marie carried a large basket of food and a gallon can of soup out to the pens where the men were clipping.

'I have brought enough for everybody. I'll be back with a can of tea in a minute. Doug, I'll call and tell Alice you'll not be in to eat. Does anyone want fresh water?

'Nah, nah, lassie,' Ed Vickers chuckled. 'We can all drink that frae the spicket if we need it.'

When Marie returned to the house for the can of hot tea she looked puzzled.

'What's a spicket, Aunt Maggie? Is it another name for a burn?'

'Och no lassie, it's a water tap. I expect they'll drink water if they're very thirsty.' Marie delivered the can of tea and a set of clean mugs. She called at Alice's cottage on the way back to say the men were all eating together up at the sheep pens.

'Will you come in, Marie? How are they getting on?' Alice asked.

'I'll not come in just now. We're going to have our dinner. There still seemed a lot of sheep to clip but Uncle Jim says they're getting on faster than he ever expected. Your father and my cousin Robert are going up the hill to bring down the rest of the sheep when they've eaten. Apparently Robert is almost as good as Jamie at handling the dogs. Uncle Robin says they take it from Grandfather Sinclair and he would have been proud of his grandsons. I never knew him.'

'Och, he was a fine looking man and a good farmer. Everybody in the glen thought so,' Alice's mother said, coming to the door to see Marie. 'If ye'd care to bring wee Marguerite here at milking time I'm sure she would play fine with Freddie. I could easily watch them both if ye'd like to help with the milking? I know Maggie is helping while the young mistress is in hospital and Jamie away. It's a hard time ye're all having.'

'Are you sure you don't mind? Will it be all right to leave all three of the children?'

'Och, wee Anne will probably be asleep in the pram. Such a good wee bairn she is. It will be no bother and an extra pair of hands at the milking will save time. I wouldn't be surprised if the men work on until dark if they're getting on well. The weather is perfect.'

'All right. I'll tell Uncle Jim I'll be at the milking as well. He will be pleased about that. Thank you.'

Robert Sinclair had never met Ed Vickers before but they were both proud of their dogs and the way they worked the sheep on the hill.

'Gyp and I will take the left side if you like Mr Vickers?' Robert offered, seeing the sheep high above them and knowing the other man was old enough to be his grandfather.

'Aye. That suits me grand, laddie. Your young legs will get to the top a lot faster than mine. I'll take this side with Bess. We'll round up the stragglers and meet together lower down.'

Robert had climbed some way up the hill when Gyp stopped and looked back at him, awaiting his command. He shielded his eyes and stared ahead to see what was amiss. He was amazed to see the sheep were already gathering and beginning to head down towards him. Then he saw they were being kept together in a neat flock by a man with and two collies working either flank. He whistled Gyp, turning her towards a gully where he could see forty or fifty sheep grazing peacefully, but he guessed they were hidden from the view of the man above. He and Gyp could bring them down the gully and with luck they would join the main flock now descending in a steady stream between himself on one side and Ed Vickers on the other. Whoever the man was he was proving a good neighbour and saving them a great deal of time. Robert knew he had been despatched to gather the sheep because he was the slowest of the shearers present, but he was also one of the best at working the dogs. Even so he was not so slow at clipping that he wouldn't be missed and every animal shorn made the task less for tomorrow. Moreover, he was enjoying the camaraderie of working with a team.

As expected the three men came almost together mid-way down the Bonnybrae hill.

'What's this then Ed, I didn't expect to see you here. Is this your laddie? I note he's a grand hand with his collie for all he's so young.'

'No, this isna my laddie but I'd be proud o' him if he was. With that hair and the way he can handle a dog ye should have guessed he's a Sinclair. Robin is his father and they're at Bonnybrae to help Jim with the shearing.'

'I see.' The man strode closer to Robert and held out his hand. 'I'm Walter Harvey frae North Braehead. Pleased to meet ye, son.'

'Pleased to meet you too, Mr Harvey. I'm Robert Sinclair. You have saved us a lot of time and energy bringing the sheep down from the top.' He gave his boyish smile. 'Uncle Jim will think we sprouted wings when we're back with them so soon.'

'We neighbour Bonnybrae land just over the hill' Walter said, returning the smile. 'Jim has done me many a good turn and we're repairing the boundary wall up there today so I saw Jim gathering the sheep frae lower down early this morning. I guessed he was going to be shearing the day. When I saw you two and your dogs coming for the rest o' the sheep I thought it would help a bit if I began bringing them down to ye.'

'It has that,' Ed Vickers said. 'I know I'm getting past ma prime when I see this young fellow striding up yon hill.' He shook his grey head in disgust.

'But you have been a great help, Mr Vickers,' Robert protested. 'I know Uncle Jim is really pleased to have so many pairs of willing hands to make the job quicker.'

'The least I can do. Jim gave my lassie and Doug a job and a house when they wanted to get married. It pleased me and my wife because they didna have to leave the glen to find work and we like being able to see our grandbairns now they've come along. Alice says Jim's a good boss and he always pays her if she helps out at the milking. Some bosses take a man's wife for granted.'

'My wife was down at East Lowrie post office. She heard Mistress Catherine was in hospital in Glasgow,' Walter Harvey said, looking questioningly at Robert.

'Yes, she is,' he replied, his tone subdued because he knew how concerned his parents were at the news Jamie had been sent for. 'Jamie is with her. That's why Dad suggested we should come and help Uncle Jim get the shearing done.'

'It's grand when families stick together and help each other in time of trouble. Tell Jim I'm real sorry to hear about Mistress Catherine and I hope she'll soon be well again.'

'I will, but we'd better keep the sheep moving now or they'll scatter. 'Thanks for your help Mr Harvey.'

'Aye, thank 'ee,' Ed, repeated.

Jim was amazed when the rest of the sheep were coming into the gathering pen almost before they had started clipping again after their brief rest to digest their own food.

Later that afternoon Maggie, Alice and Marie brought in the cows for milking and tied them up in their respective stalls. Jim joined them but they told him if he milked the few difficult ones, including a young blue roan heifer who was inclined to kick for no reason, they would manage the rest and take them back to the field.

'Are you sure? Where is wee Marguerite?'

'Alice's mother volunteered to look after her as well as Freddie and Anne,' Marie told him. 'I do hope it will not be too much for her.'

'Och Ma loves bairns. Besides we're all pleased to help at a time like this.'

'Well, I appreciate it. All of you,' Jim said. 'Be sure to tell your mother Alice.'

'Marie, the men enjoyed the tea and scones, and the fruit cake you brought before you started the milking so now they all want to keep on going until it's getting dark. It will be late before we get in for our dinner.'

'That's all right, Uncle Jim. I'll get Marguerite fed and bathed so she will be asleep before I need to attend to you all. Will you send Ernest to tell me about half an hour before you finish so I can get the potatoes on to boil and cook the vegetables. The meat is simmering in the oven but I can't cook the vegetables too early.'

'Don't worry, lassie. I'll send Ernest to warn you. Will there be enough for everybody?' he asked.

'I'm sure there will,' Maggie chuckled, 'if ye could see the big pan of beef stew our lassie has cooked and she's added carrots and onions and fresh mushrooms, just as you like it. The dumplings have still to go in but I expect Marie will put them in when we finish here. You have no idea what a grand wee worker she is.'

'Aah but I have,' Jim smiled. 'I keep telling her we couldna have managed without her. I reckon Master Mark knows she's a treasure because he writes to her nearly every day.'

'Alice, your mother ought to join us for the meal too,' Marie said to change the subject from Mark. 'She will have earned it looking after all three rascals.'

'She'll not mind. She'll look after my two though if I'm invited?'

'Of course you are,' Marie said warmly. 'You must come in with Doug and your father, and your brother. Be sure to bring Ernest in too. I know he is a bit shy. It sounds as though it will be after nine o'clock before they stop.'

'We're making the most of the good weather,' Jim said.

When the milking was finished, Marie fed the young calves while Maggie and Alice guided the cows back to their field for the night, then Marie collected a sleepy Marguerite.

'They have played well together,' Mrs Vickers assured Marie. 'It made it a lot easier to entertain Freddie having a little friend. He even played with Marguerite's rag doll when he got a chance. She does love it, doesn't she?'

'She has cuddled it more since Rina has been away,' Marie said sadly. 'I think it must give her some kind of comfort.'

The men continued shearing until darkness began to fall but they didn't want to risk nicking the skin of the ewes due to the fading light. Jim was delighted with the day's work.

'There's only fifty-five left to shear,' he told them. 'I can scarcely believe it. Doug and I will soon finish them tomorrow with Ernest to roll and Joe to keep the ewes coming forward. I can't thank you all enough. Now let's get into the house and enjoy a good dinner.'

So the ten of them made their way into the house amidst some laughter and teasing as they did their best to wash their hands and sweaty faces. When they were gathered around, Jim stood at the head of the table, his face tense. Maggie notice the twitch of his eye. He had had that as a boy whenever he was nervous. He cleared his throat a couple of times.

'You all know I attend the kirk the same as the rest of you because we were brought up that way, but you'll know I'm not known as a religious man. Today, I have such a lot to be thankful for so I'd like to offer a prayer before we eat.' As one, the men and Alice, rose to their feet.

'Dear God, accept my humble thanks for this day's work, for the good friends and neighbours who have made it possible, and for my niece and sister for bringing us sustenance all day long. And please God,' he cleared his throat again and his voice when it came was gruff with emotion. 'Dear God we ask that Rina will be spared and restored to health again.' There was a spontaneous Amen to that, and a few murmurs of heartfelt agreement before they all sat down again.

Maggie and Marie had already eaten with Marguerite. Now Marie stood beside the pile of hot plates and ladled out generous portions of the beef stew, while Maggie brought the dishes of vegetables, broad beans from the garden and buttered cabbage, in addition to the vegetables in the stew and dishes of creamed potatoes.

'My, but this smells good,' Robin said and there were murmurs of agreement. Cousin Robert looked up at Marie and grinned appreciatively. He was young and he was famished and he saw she had given him an extra-large helping. He loved dumplings and Uncle Jim had told him she made the best he'd tasted. The gravy was rich and brown and Robert knew his uncle had been telling the truth.

'There's rhubarb pie and custard to follow,' Marie said, 'but if anyone doesn't like pie there's custard with bottled pears.' There was a chorus they all liked pie and Marie was thankful she had made three large ones. She knew if there was any left Uncle Jim would enjoy it tomorrow. Afterwards they lingered over tea and shortbread and chatted about events in the district and the day's work, teasing Ernest a little because he was so quiet. It was dark outside by the time they all rose to go with grateful thanks for their meal.

Marie carried the dirty plates to the sink to begin washing them. Maggie got wearily to her feet to help.

'No, Aunt Maggie, you must go home with Uncle Joe,' Marie said firmly. 'You've been on your feet all day and you look tired to death.'

'I can't leave you with so much to do. I'll dry the dishes and put them away,' Maggie insisted, trying to stifle a huge yawn.

'Marie's right, Mrs Greig,' Alice said. 'You do look tired. I'll wash the dishes if Marie dries them. She knows where they go. Please let me? That was the most delicious meal I've ever tasted.'

'I don't suppose it was,' Marie laughed, 'but it's very late and hunger makes even the plainest food taste good.'

'Well it really was good, honestly.' Alice raised her voice to call her husband. 'Doug will you tell Mr Greig his wife is ready to go home before she falls asleep on her feet, and tell Mum and Dad they can go home now if they want, or stay the night if they prefer. I'll be back at the cottage in ten minutes.'

'Thank you, Alice,' Marie said quietly. 'Aunt Maggie really is tired and the worry over Rina doesn't help. If there had been any news Uncle Joe thinks the MacQuades would have come to tell us. They have a motorcar so it doesn't take long from Strathlinn and they care for Rina too. Uncle Joe is going first thing in the morning to see whether they have had a telephone call from their daughter.'

'I pray to God she'll be spared,' Alice said. 'Doug was just saying he doesn't know how Jamie will cope if she doesn't get better. They were so much in love long before they got married. I don't believe either of them have ever looked at anyone else.'

'I think you're right,' Marie said slowly. 'We all loved Rina from the first time we met her. It doesn't seem possible that such a happy person can die so young. She was so full of life before all this trouble, and she loves Marguerite.'

Robin and his sons had come in their pony and trap but it was very dark for driving home so Joe offered to drive them in the car.

'I could stay,' Robert volunteered eagerly, 'if you can find me a bed for the night, Uncle Jim? I could help you finish the rest of the sheep and drive them back up the hill then I'll drive the pony and cart home when we're finished.'

'I'm sure we can find you a bed, laddie, and it's good of you to offer, but what do you think Robin? Can you spare him?' His brother chuckled.

'I reckon young Marie has fed him too well and he wants to stay for more.' Then he added seriously, 'I never expected we would get through so many in one day but it saved a lot of time having so many pairs of hands. We had expected to come again tomorrow, so if you can put up with Robert you're welcome to keep him until you've finished. He enjoys working with sheep more than the cows anyway. I'll have to have a word with Mark Blackford and tell him if any of his hill farms come to let, Robert would be interested.'

'Yes, it's better if he knows. He's not familiar with his tenants yet,' Jim agreed, 'now we'd better let Joe get Maggie home before she falls asleep on her feet.'

'I'm not that bad,' Maggie protested.

'No, lass, but I'll drop you off at Braeside as we go down the road.'

'I wondered if the MacQuades might have had any news of Rina,' Maggie said in a subdued voice. 'Maybe they'll have left a note for us if they found an empty house.'

'I doubt if they'd leave a note, Maggie. They would have come up to Bonnybrae to tell somebody if they'd heard from Mel. It's no good getting your hopes up, lass. I promise I'll drive over to Strathlinn first thing tomorrow.'

Joe was right. There was no note waiting. The fire was out. There was no hot water. Maggie felt her spirits plummet, but she knew she felt worse because she was so tired, even though it had been such a satisfying day. She splashed her face and hands and got into her nightgown. The best place to wait for Joe was under the bed covers so she snuggled down in their big feather bed. She hadn't expected to fall asleep.

Joe did not waste any time chatting when he dropped Robin and Billy off at home, but even so Maggie was sound asleep when he returned. He looked down at her with a tender smile. How lucky they were to have found each other, even though they had had to wait so long before they could live together as man and wife. He had already removed his jacket and boots downstairs and he was just about to strip off his shirt and trousers when he saw a light flash across the bedroom window. He peered out wondering what it could be. Before the lights went out he glimpsed the shape of a car and he guessed the lights had flashed across the bedroom as it turned. He ran downstairs, his heart racing. He knew of only one man likely to call who had a car.

CHAPTER EIGHT

Joe pulled open the door as Neil MacQuade was about to give a tentative knock.

'We saw the house was in darkness,' he said. 'I was wondering whether to knock.'

'Do you have news of Rina?' Joe asked breathlessly. 'Come in. Please come in.'

'I can see you're getting ready for bed and Mary is in the car, so I'll not stay. We thought it might be too late to come but Frank didn't get home until . . .'

'Rina . . . ?' Joe asked and sank onto the stool they kept beside the back door for removing their boots or clogs.

'Her temperature has broken. Mel says that's the best news we could have, even though she is still very ill.'

'Thank God for that,' Joe breathed. 'It — it does mean she has a ch chance n-now?'

'Yes. Frank says the first face she saw was Jamie's. She recognised him and she gave him a lovely smile and whispered his name. He said they knew then she has a chance to pull through. She is very weak. She went to sleep almost immediately but the main thing is her mind has cleared. It is the first sign they have had that she might recover. Mel said we should warn you it is going to take a long time.'

'It doesn't matter how long, or what it costs, so long as Rina is going to live,' Joe said fervently.

'Mary and I are relieved and happy too. We felt we must come and let you know there is light and hope now.'

'I can't tell you how thankful I am, or how grateful we are to both of you. It is terrible keeping you on the doorstep after all your hospitality to me. Won't you both come inside?'

'No, I can see you're getting ready for bed.'

'I'm afraid Maggie is already asleep,' Joe said apologetically. 'It's been a hectic day.'

'Busier than usual?' Neil asked politely.

'Yes. Oh yes! If you are speaking to Dr Meadows tomorrow ask him to tell Jamie nearly all the sheep are sheared. We have had a truly satisfying day. He'll never believe it could be done without him but it will be one thing less to worry him. Tell him he must stay with Rina as long as she needs him now.'

'I will. Frank says he's been torn in two between staying with her and worrying about leaving his uncle with so much work. How did this miracle happen?' Neil asked curiously.

Joe explained about Jim's brother and nephews coming to help with the shearing and how other willing hands had turned out to help and get so many done.

'Some of them came because they know and love Rina. Maggie is exhausted. I shall waken her to tell her the good news though because Rina's health has been on her mind all day. Jim is a quiet man but he said a heartfelt prayer for her before everybody sat down to eat and they all echoed his sentiments. Tell Jamie there are only fifty-five ewes left to clip and they will be finished by midday tomorrow. His cousin is staying overnight. He'll help to finish before he goes home in the afternoon.

'That's splendid,' Neil MacQuade said, 'and such cooperation and neighbourliness is a sure sign of respect and liking for the Sinclair family I believe.'

'And especially for Rina. They all know and love her. Today brought out the best. I shall go to bed with a truly thankful heart for this day's blessings,' Joe said sincerely. 'I'll come with you to the car and thank your wife too, if you don't mind.'

'We are as pleased and happy for Rina as you are, I think,' Mary MacQuade said with a smile. 'Even though it will take a long time for a complete recovery.'

'Did Mel mention the twins?' Joe asked. 'I almost forgot about them in our anxiety about Rina.'

'She says they are fairly sure the bigger twin will survive. The smaller boy is struggling. She is going to suggest to Jamie that he should have them baptised as soon as Rina is strong enough to discuss it. That will not be for some days though.'

'Rina would want that, I'm sure. My sister, Jamie's mother, lost a baby and it distresses her still because he didn't live long enough to be baptised.'

'Mmm. We'll tell Mel what you said. I believe they have a priest and a minister who visit the hospital regularly.'

'Will you tell Jamie we'll drive up on Saturday or Sunday please? He can tell us then how long he wants to stay. He should take the chance to spend time with Rina now she's aware he's there. I can imagine the relief he must feel. I can't thank you enough for coming to tell us the good news tonight.'

Joe could have done with a cup of tea but he knew the fire had been out for most of the day and he was too tired to kindle it to boil the kettle. He poured himself a glass of milk instead and took one up to Maggie in case she fancied a drink. Tired though he was he felt like dancing a jig at the news that Rina was going to recover. The dread which had hung over them all had been like a heavy weight.

* * *

The following morning Maggie couldn't wait to tell Marie and Jim the news about Rina when she arrived at Bonnybrae to start the milking.

'Oh Aunt Maggie!' Marie threw her arms around her aunt, almost sobbing with relief. 'That's the most wonderful news I've ever heard.'

‘She’s still seriously ill, and very weak,’ Maggie warned cautiously.

‘But she will recover? Wee Marguerite will have her mammy back?’

‘Aye, they believe so. I hope you will stay for a good many weeks yet, though lassie? Getting over a big operation, and then days with a fever and no food, I darena think what effect it will have had.’

‘Yes, but she’s young,’ Jim said on a positive note. ‘Rina loves life. Remember how well she recovered from the fever when she was nursing, once she got some fresh air and your good cooking, Maggie. We must be thankful that she’s turned the corner. Are the twins still surviving?

‘Yes, but Joe says the smaller one is struggling. Speaking of Joe, I hope you don’t mind Jim but he felt he ought to get back to work today, now we’ve had better news. He said you would have Robert to help to finish the clipping.’

‘Yes, of course. Joe has been a big help in a lot of ways, besides the clipping. And he hasn’t objected to you helping with the milking, Maggie. That’s made a big difference with both Jamie and Rina away. Tell him I’m grateful.’

‘A sign of respect for the Sinclair family, Mr MacQuade says it is, when people volunteer to help, as they did yesterday.’

‘I don’t know about that,’ Jim smiled ‘but it was a great day and good to have such camaraderie. I’ll tell Doug the good news about Rina.’

‘And I’ll write mother a letter the first chance I get,’ Marie said. ‘I know how worried she has been that Jamie might end up without a wife and wee Marguerite without her mother. Maybe the postman will take it if he brings us any letters.’

‘Aye, he’ll take it, lassie. Leave it on the wee table by the back door. Put a weight on it so it doesna get lost.’ Jim advised. He grinned at Marie. ‘He’s sure to have something to deliver. I never knew a young man write as many letters as Master Mark writes to you.’ Marie blushed. Uncle Jim didn’t miss anything.

'I owe him at least two replies but I'll write tonight.' He seemed to see her parents regularly so he would know how anxious they all were. Her mother appeared bemused that such an educated young man should want to visit them, but Marie knew a warm welcome and friendship meant a great deal to Mark. Her father accepted people as he found them and welcomed any decent young person away from his friends and family. William Sinclair neither bowed down to people who thought themselves above him, nor did he look down on those less fortunate than himself, like Cliff Barnes who had suffered a raw deal in life. In fact he was kind and considerate to people like Cliff and he had never shunned the gypsies for having a different way of life to his own. On the other hand he refused to show deference to those who considered themselves high and mighty, when they were no better than himself — people like Gerry and Thora Wilkins who lived at Mountcliff. They might rent the largest farm on Lord Hanley's estate, but they were still tenants, as he was.

Marie had been surprised to find Lord Hanley's views were much the same as her father's, even though he owned all the farms and most of the cottages in and around Silverbeck. He believed people should earn respect. He valued Bob Rowbottom as his agent because he was reliable, conscientious and trustworthy. It didn't matter that he and his wife lived in a tied house on the estate, any more than it had signified that she was a daughter of one of his tenants. He valued people who were genuine and sincere and he had appreciated even the smallest thing she did for his wife. In return they had both treated her with a kindness and friendship far more important than money, or the gift of Lady Hanley's jewellery. That still embarrassed Marie. Sometimes she looked at the various pieces but she had never worn any of them. She knew, as Lord Hanley himself had pointed out, that some of them were simply pretty, but she was sure some were quite valuable.

Mark was enjoying working with Mr Rowbottom. He said he had learned a tremendous amount already and got his own ideas into perspective. It was clear from his letters Mrs Rowbottom had taken him under her motherly wing.

The postman called before Marie had time to write a letter for her parents. Sure enough there was another letter from Mark. She tucked it in the pocket of her pinafore to read later. She needed to churn the butter which she had not been able to do yesterday. Meanwhile Maggie peeled vegetables for a pot of leek and potato soup, knowing her nephew Robert had a healthy appetite. They both knew he would not want to leave until the shearing was finished and that was hard work, not to mention driving the sheep back to the hill, even with his skill at handling his own dog and Jamie's. Marie knew Jamie would have appreciated seeing his cousin work the collies. Between them the menfolk had finished off the huge pot of stew and dumplings yesterday so Marie made a pork casserole and added the fresh mushrooms Uncle Joe had picked at dawn this morning. She set it in the oven to cook while she got on with making the butter. Marguerite toddled between Maggie in the kitchen and herself in the dairy. Fortunately it was attached to the house along a passage beyond the pantry.

When Uncle Jim and Robert came in for their meal at midday they wore smiles of satisfaction and announced the shearing was finished and the sheep were back on the hill.

'I've enjoyed being here,' Robert said. 'It makes a change working with different people. Doug Lamont seems to be a good man. He tells me you're a grand boss, Uncle Jim.'

'Och I don't know about that, but Doug works hard and his wife is always willing to lend a hand with the milking when she can organize her bairns. It was Rina who suggested they should come to Bonnybrae and we have been glad to have them.'

'Speaking of Rina, now the news is a little better, how about letting me take Marie to the village dance next Saturday?' He grinned and winked at Marie. 'Things will get even busier here when Rina gets home if both babies survive, and I hope they do after all the heartache she's had.

You would like to go to a dance, wouldn't you, Marie? I mean you're too young and pretty to slave away here all the time.' Maggie looked at her nephew and her niece, then at her brother.

'I suppose he's right, Jim. We ought to let Marie have some fun and you do like dancing, don't you lassie?'

'I've only been to a few dances with my brother. Dad told Allan to keep an eye on me and see me home as though I was six years old. It was a shame because he wanted to see a girlfriend home. They're courting seriously but Dad doesn't want to think about Allan needing a farm of his own.'

'Is she a nice girl?' Maggie asked.

'Oh yes. Her aunt and uncle rent the neighbouring farm to Moorend. Mum and Dad get on well with them when they meet, or when Lord Hanley holds a tenants' dinner. Her name is Lynn. Lynn Tindall.'

'So shall we meet you at the bottom of the track, Marie, just below Braeside? Can you ride Jamie's bicycle?'

'Of course I can ride a bicycle, but I'm not sure about leaving Marguerite,' Marie said. She had missed Rina's company. It would be nice to spend time with young people.

'Och, the bairn hardly ever wakens once she's in bed for the night,' Jim said, 'and Robert is right. It will be a busy household when Rina comes home.'

'I think you should go lassie,' Aunt Maggie said. 'Joe and I will come up to Bonnybrae and listen for Marguerite so Jim can get to his bed.'

'All right I will meet you at the road end, Robert.'

'We'll hide the bike in the hedge. Billy and Fran will be going so we can take the pony and trap. Laura will want to come when she hears, but Dad think she's too young yet.'

It was later that evening before Marie found time to write a long letter to her mother telling her Rina was conscious, though she was very weak. She told them about the shearing of the sheep and how Uncle Robin had volunteered to help and others had come to lend a hand, and how the evening had ended with everybody enjoying a huge meal, with a lot of laughter and cheerful conversation after a hard day's work. She reported that Marguerite could almost climb up and down the stairs now. She didn't realise how much her love for her young niece shone through her words. She sealed the envelope, ready to sleep now, but she wrote a short letter to Mark, enclosing two estimates she had received for repairs to roofs on three farms most needing attention.

> *You will see that one estimate is slightly more expensive than the other but Mr Thomas is willing to start the repairs straight away and wait for payment until the rents are paid at the end of November, so long as you guarantee he will get his money then. Perhaps it would be better to get the repairs started as soon as possible or they might cost a lot more if they have to survive autumn gales. He understands it must be your decision, Mark. It is not my business. I asked Uncle Jim about both tradesmen. He says they both do a decent job.*

She was too tired to describe the sheep shearing again, but she did say Cousin Robert was taking her to a dance in East Lowrie village hall on Saturday night.

The postman took both letters the following morning, but she knew Mark had replied straight away because she received an even longer letter than usual from him the very next day. She was surprised when he began by saying how much he wished he was back in Scotland so he could take her to the dance. She had told him it was only a village dance with local musicians. She was sure it was not the sort of entertainment he and his friends would be used to, but he mentioned it again at the end of the letter. He said her brothers, Allan and Peter, had suggested he could go to a local dance with them but he had refused because it wouldn't be the same without her as his partner. Marie chewed her lower lip as she read. She wondered whether Mark was feeling homesick. She was too innocent and far too modest to consider Mark was falling in love with her and missing her company. He was enthusiastic about everything regarding estate management but she guessed he was enjoying driving Lord Hanley's car and chauffeuring Bob Rowbottom round the farms. Apparently the land agent's broken leg was healing normally but his shoulder had been broken in two places and it was still tightly strapped up and very painful. The doctor at the hospital in Wakefield had told him he would have to be patient as it could take several months before he could ride his horse again. Meanwhile Mark told her he exercised both Bob's horse and Lady Hanley's, sometimes accompanying Lord Hanley for a gallop over the Common, or round the Home Farm, in the evenings now the days were longer.

He mentioned several visits to Moorend and said her parents always made him welcome. He was glad Rina's health was improving at last, but he was sorry she would not be returning to Yorkshire herself for many weeks yet. Her mother had explained there would be a lot of extra work with a tiny baby — and maybe two, since the smaller twin was putting up a fight for life. Eventually he mentioned the roof repairs. He asked her to write to Mr Thomas, confirming the costs in writing and promising he would be paid at the end of November if he would start the work straight away.

He went on to say that Lord Hanley had told him he held a rent dinner from time to time, inviting his tenants to a dinner but making it clear they were expected to pay their rents to him in the farm office before leaving at the end of the evening. Mark went on.

> *He says he has not held one since Lady Hanley died because he needs a hostess, and you were there to help organize the last one so you know what should be done and how to arrange everything. He is sure you would make an excellent hostess and you are more than capable if I am willing to hire a cook and staff to serve. It seems you will still be up there when I return and I would prefer the idea of persuading our tenants to pay their rents with a carrot, rather than reminding them they are in debt and could face the stick of eviction. I couldn't do it without you though, Marie. Please,*

please promise you will help me? I thought we should hold it the night before the November term day, so long as Rina's health is improving by then.

There was a little more, repeating that he would like to be going with her and her cousins to the dance. As usual he signed off "with love from Mark". She had never paid much attention before, assuming it was his usual way of finishing, just as she always finished her letters to Meg or her parents sending her love. She ended her letters to Mark more formally.

She bit back a smile when she thought of the dance in the village hall at home and she supposed the dances would be the same at East Lowrie or Locheagle, or any other country village. She could only imagine the kind of balls Mark and his friends usually attended. Lady Hanley had reminisced about the customs when she was young, before the Great War. She described the etiquette and the gentlemen's manners, and the fine dresses of the young ladies when they attended balls in the large houses. She said many things had changed since the war. Men and women no longer wanted to be subservient and most big houses could only employ enough staff for their daily needs. Marie knew Mark's mother still had servants and she would disapprove of her son attending dances in a village hall with ordinary folk like her and her brothers.

* * *

On Saturday evening Marie bathed Marguerite and put her to bed, thankful when the toddler settled down to sleep without a murmur of protest.

'Are ye not wearing the new dress your mother made for you, lassie?' Aunt Maggie asked, looking over her steel spectacles from the newspaper Joe had brought earlier.

'No. It's really lovely but I'd like to keep it for something special. I like my yellow cotton and if I get wet cycling home it will wash and iron as good as new.'

Marie was fond of the yellow dress with its full skirt and narrow waist, the pin tucks on the bodice and short puffed sleeves. She had a pretty cotton petticoat trimmed with lace to wear beneath and she knew they went well together for the country dances when strong young men delighted in whirling girls off their feet.

'That makes sense,' Uncle Jim said, looking at her with approval. 'It looks as though we'll have rain before morning.'

'Ye're pretty as a picture, lassie,' Uncle Joe said. 'Enjoy yourself.'

'I'm sure I shall. I hope Marguerite doesn't cause you any trouble. Robert said we would be back before midnight. The dances finish at half-past eleven so that everyone can be home before the Sabbath.'

'Aye, that's the way it was in my day,' Uncle Jim said with a sigh, 'but I don't know whether young folk observe the Sabbath as much we did. Times are changing.'

* * *

Marie heard the sound of the pony's hooves on the road as she was reaching the end of the Bonnybrae track.

'That was well timed,' Cousin Billy said with a grin, drawing the pony to a halt while Robert jumped down and helped her stow the bicycle in the hedge bottom, then handed her up into the trap with a beaming smile. He was a handsome lad this cousin of hers, Marie thought. Aunt Maggie had told her he was the image of her father when he was a young man. Fran welcomed her with a shy smile and made room for her on the bench seat along one side of the trap.

'You and Robert are so much alike, Marie, you could almost be twins,' she said. 'I wish I had hair that colour.'

'Do you really?' Marie asked incredulously. 'I'm sure you would soon be longing for your own lovely dark curls.' She had suffered a lot of teasing at school due to the reddish glints in her hair, and Fran was lovely with her long dark hair and big brown eyes. 'The sun bleaches my hair in the summer and people call me a ginger knob in the winter.'

'Anyone would envy those streaks of gold and silvery blond. It's lovely, isn't it Billy?'

'Our cousin is a pretty lassie,' Billy agreed. 'We shall have to watch her with some of the lads from East Lowrie. Do you have a temper like Robert's to match the red in your hair, Marie?' he asked with a teasing grin. He had inherited his mother's dark hair and blue eyes. Marie glanced questioningly at Robert but he simply smiled and shook his head.

'My temper is no worse than yours, big brother.'

'I don't think I have a bad temper either,' Marie said slowly, 'but I don't like people who try to take an unfair advantage. I tell them what I think if they try.'

'That's the spirit,' Robert cheered. 'A real Sinclair. Dad says your father used to get into a temper when he was young and lived at Bonnybrae with Grandmother Sinclair.'

'I don't know about that,' Marie said. 'I know he believes our grandmother treated him unfairly. Jamie didn't like her.'

'I love dancing, do you, Marie?' Fran asked, changing the subject. Billy smiled fondly at her. He knew Fran hated quarrels and did her best to avoid them. In this case neither he nor Robert could remember much about their Grandmother Sinclair so they were not likely to argue anyway. They knew their father considered his youngest brother had been treated harshly and he was genuinely sorry Uncle William had settled in Yorkshire.

'I haven't been to many public dances,' Marie said responding to Fran's question, 'but Dad often gets out his fiddle and we have a bit of a dance round the kitchen at home. I love the music. Polly, our maid, knows all the steps, and she taught me and my brothers, Allan and Peter. I'm looking forward to tonight.'

Long before they reached the village hall they could hear the music of the accordion band with at least one fiddle and the drums.

'It's a good band tonight,' Robert said and jumped out of the trap almost before they had stopped. He turned and seized Marie round the waist and lifted her out too.

'Gosh,' she gasped in surprise.

'You're light as a feather,' Robert chuckled. 'Come on we'll leave those two to deal with the pony and steal a kiss and cuddle in the dark.' Billy flicked his shoulder lightly with the whip.

'Behave yourself Kiddo or we shall leave you to walk home, and remember, no promising lifts to girls you barely know tonight.' Robert grinned up at his elder brother.

'There'll be no need. I shall have the best looking girl for my partner already.' His blue eyes twinkled at Marie and he clasped her hand and danced with her to the door of the village hall.

'I've only been to this village once,' Marie said. 'We mostly go down to Locheagle to the shop and post office.'

'I suppose it's about the same distance to either village from Bonnybrae but East Lowrie is part of the Stavondale Estate. Most of the sons and daughters and workers of Stavondale tenants come here to the dances, although the ones who are really keen walk or cycle for miles to the other villages, wherever there is a dance.'

Robert lost no time in leading her onto the dance floor and from then on the evening seemed to fly. Marie was never without a partner and both the girls and men smiled warmly and made her welcome. Some of the names were familiar because she had seen their parents' names as Mark's tenants, but some of them lived in or near the village and she was pleased to meet them too. She knew almost everyone in Silverbeck, the village at home in Yorkshire, and it would be good to recognise familiar faces here too.

Only one partner proved obnoxious. He was large and sweaty with greasy dark hair and small grey eyes which seemed to peel the clothes off her as his stare moved slowly from her shoulders down to her waist and on down to her legs, as he pulled her hard against him, barely giving her space to breathe, even less to dance. His loud voice was embarrassing, rising above the dance music and she wished it had been one of the country dances where she could keep moving out of his grasp. He told her his name was Fred Lorrimer and his father was a tenant on the Stavondale Estate. He sounded proud of the fact as though his family were of great importance, but Marie recognised the name. His father was one of the few people Mark openly despised, although he was usually the least judgemental of people. She soon understood why he felt such antipathy. Instead of feeling ashamed both father and son were apparently proud of the fact they had not paid their rent in full for several years, and none at all for the last two years. Fred Lorrimer bragged about it and declared they had no intention of paying anything until a long list of repairs had been carried out. Marie grimaced.

'Don't give me your sour face. I hear the new laird has strutted off south to enjoy himself.' His eyes narrowed to mean slits. 'Aah, that's it! You must have written the nasty letter threatening my pa with ejection for not paying his rent! Well you can tell the new bloody upstart we don't owe anything to him.' Marie fumed inwardly on Mark's behalf. He was the last person anyone could accuse of being an upstart.

'Your father will find the debts are part of the estate. He must pay the rent owing, whether or not any repairs are carried out.' One of the neighbouring tenants had warned Mark that the Lorrimers did nothing to maintain their farm, or the house. The list of complaints would keep on growing as an excuse to put off paying any rent. Uncle Jim had agreed the Lorrimers had a reputation for being sly and dishonest when Rina said they thought it was a clever strategy to go on inventing repairs as an excuse for not paying. Her grandfather, Sir Reginald Capel, had come close to evicting the grandfather Lorrimer more than once for similar tricks. Unfortunately, since Sir Roger had dismissed the land agent, the family had ignored all demands for rent.

'Mr Blackford will not allow the situation to continue. He needs the rents to pay for the repairs. If your father is making such a poor job of farming he cannot make enough money to pay his rent it is not the landlord's fault.' Marie knew her words were offensive but she couldn't stand Fred Lorrimer's arrogant manner and Mark deserved better tenants than him. 'Tenants who do not pay their rent arrears will face eviction.'

'Why you . . . you! My father was never short of bloody money.' Fred Lorrimer blustered loudly, jerking her so hard he almost squeezed the breath out of her. Marie guessed he would like to strangle her. A few couples nearby raised their eyebrows and one of the young men winked at Marie while his partner offered her a sympathetic smile and shook her head as much as to say "ignore him". That was easier said than done. She had angered him and he was not about to let her get away with it but he lowered his voice and hissed angrily.

'I know it was you who wrote that bloody letter!' he sneered. 'My father should have known the laird wouldn't pay a solicitor for such a piffling thing as owing rent.'

'Owing rent is no paltry matter,' Marie said indignantly. 'If you expect your landlord to pay for repairs he needs an income from the rents to pay for them.'

'You would take his side when you work for him, wouldn't you, you snooty bugger!'

'I don't work for Mr Blackford. I help him as a friend.'

'Friend? Oh aye, and how does he pay you then, like this . . . ?' he sneered and pulled her sharply against him, lowering his face to hers. She kicked his ankle and jerked her head to the side.

'You've no need to be haughty with me. We all know your brother married the laird's granddaughter for her money.'

Marie gasped. 'My brother married Rina because he loves her . . .'

'Go tell that to the bloody bluebirds!' he scoffed. His small eyes narrowed to slits and he gave a scornful laugh. 'Now I get it! You're helping the new laird to trap him the way your brother caught Miss Catherine. You Sinclairs!

You're all bloody fortune hunters and. . . .' Marie jerked herself out of his arms, wanting to slap his face but he twisted her wrist cruelly. Across the room Robert had seen the crimson patches staining Marie's fair skin and her furious expression. He knew he showed the same signs of temper when he was angry. He ought to have warned Marie to avoid Lorrimer.

'I must rescue my cousin from Lorrimer before he causes a scene,' he whispered to his partner, but he had no sooner released her than the dance finished.

Marie breathed a sigh of relief and hurried away from Lorrimer without a backward glance. She vowed she would not go near him again, not if she saw him first. She hoped Mark would be asking Lord Hanley's advice on dealing with people like him. They were not the only tenants owing rent but none of the others owed as much, and they didn't boast about it as though it was an achievement. She resolved to help Mark make them pay what they owed whatever it took.

Billy came to claim her for a Scottish waltz and she smiled at him with relief.

'The dance will be ending soon,' he said, 'Have you enjoyed the evening, Marie?'

'I have, we-ell except for the last dance.'

'I saw you dancing with Lorrimer. None of the girls like him. We should have warned you to avoid him, but he can be persistent.'

'Thank you for bringing me all the same, and for introducing me to so many people. Everyone else has been friendly and Fran is a lovely girl. I'm sure you will both be happy.'

'I'm sure we shall. Her parents were a bit anxious because she is only nineteen and I'm twenty-six, but now that we're going to set up home on our own at Glenside they're a lot happier. I know we have your friendship with Mr Blackford, and Uncle Jim's prompting to thank for that. How is our young laird getting on in Yorkshire?'

'Mark's not that young. He will be twenty-five at Christmas. He never expected to be a landlord. He is more interested in engines and machines. He knows all about Uncle

Joe's motorcar and he went with him to see the machines at the factory. Uncle Joe said he was quite knowledgeable about the way they worked and what they did. He is enjoying working for Lord Hanley in Yorkshire though. He says he has learned a lot about estate management.'

'So why did he come to Stavondale then?'

'His parents didn't ask him if he wanted to be a landowner. He had come up here with his friend. Then he had the accident when he shot Sir Roger.'

'Everyone believed the estate would have had to be sold anyway to pay off the laird's gambling debts,' Billy said drily.

'Yes, Rina thinks Lord Tannahill advised Mark's father that the Stavondale Estate would be good value for the money and within Mr Blackford's limit. He had already purchased six of the farms and Stavondale Tower and Home Farm for himself. I can't believe either of them realised what a bad state of repair the farms are in. Mark has no other capital so it will be a burden for years with only the income from the rents to pay for repairs but he is determined to improve everything. He lives very frugally you know. He doesn't have servants or anything. That's why I was so furious with Lorrimer. Lord Hanley is paying him for being a chauffeur while he is in Yorkshire. It may not amount to much but as Dad would say, every little helps.'

'You're right about the estate repairs being a burden!' Billy agreed. 'There have been none done by the estate since Sir Roger took over. My father says it's a wonder the old laird hasn't risen from his grave.'

'Rina adored her grandfather,' Marie said, 'but she says Jamie would never have married her if the estate had been as wealthy as it used to be, so she is not sorry things have turned out as they have.'

'Money is not everyone's God, even though we all need enough to get by.'

'Rina never hears from her mother. She hasn't even got her address in France. We were terribly worried when we thought she might die.'

'The tenants blamed Lady Capel more than Sir Roger for the lack of money. No one respected her. The maids and the cook disliked her so maybe Rina is better without her.'

'I suppose so.' Marie shivered. 'I'd hate to think my parents were so uncaring.'

'We're coming up to the last dance so I'll go and claim Fran.' He grinned down at her. 'I see Robert and two other swains hurrying towards you, Marie. I'll have the pony and trap waiting outside so we can get away when it ends. We usually have "Auld Lang Syne" and "God Save the King" to finish.' Marie just had time to nod and smile her thanks before Robert was at her side, along with two other young men she had danced with earlier. She took Robert's arm but she smiled warmly at the other young men.

'I think they were both hoping to walk you home,' Robert said with a grin.

'I have really enjoyed myself tonight,' Marie announced happily.

A little while later they were all settled in the trap again and on their way home.

'I'm glad you could come,' Robert said with a grin. 'There were a lot of fellows pestering me for your name and wondering if they dare ask you to go to the next dance.'

'I hope you told them I'm only up here temporarily to help until Rina is well again. Several people asked how she is. They all seemed genuinely sorry she has been so ill.'

'Aye. I've heard my parents say the old laird took her round all the farms with him as soon as she was big enough to sit on a pony,' Billy said. 'All the tenants liked to see her and her grandfather. Things changed with Sir Roger.'

* * *

The following morning there was a letter for Aunt Maggie and Uncle Joe from Jamie confirming he intended coming home on Sunday. He said Rina was well enough for a short visit so he hoped Aunt Maggie would come and bring Marguerite if Uncle Joe was coming.

> *The problem is, he wrote, the twins are still in their incubators. They are holding their own and have regained a little of the weight they had lost. They are still being fed through a tube and Mr Chambers says they will need to stay for a few weeks yet and he is advising Rina to stay for a week or two longer until she has built up her strength. She is fretting to get home because of the cost of her stay in hospital, and she is missing Marguerite. Mr MacQuade has sent the vases and things to a saleroom in London but we have had no word of them being sold. I am doing my best to persuade her to follow Mr Chamber's advice because she is so unsteady and frail.*
>
> *Will you please tell Marie that we hope and pray she will be able to stay for a few more months? We desperately need her help, especially when the twins are able to come home. The nurses seem to expect they will both survive now so that is helping Rina's spirits.*

There was a little more saying how much he was longing to get back home although he hated the thought of leaving Rina.

As usual Marie wrote to her parents with the latest news. She also told them about her cousins, Billy and Robert, taking her to the dance and how much she had enjoyed it. She knew her father would be pleased his nephews were making her welcome. She did not mention the dance at all when she wrote to Mark, but it was the first thing he asked about when he wrote, again telling her he wished he could have been with her. When she replied she said everyone had been friendly and welcoming and she had met several of his tenants from the cottages in the village of East Lowrie and none of them had grumbled. Then she told him about Fred Lorrimer and how angry he had made her, promising to do everything she could to make sure they paid all the rent owed or she would help him get them evicted.

CHAPTER NINE

Marie and Aunt Maggie had been puzzled by the wood which Uncle Joe had purchased from the joiner. While he was at work Maggie examined the rods he was making with such care on the machine which helped him make ridges and curly bits.

'I think he must be trying to make another cot,' she said. 'Marguerite will soon move into the small bed we stored in the attic, but they will need two cots for the twins.'

'Better wait until they are all safely home,' Jim said cautiously. He couldn't quite believe there could be two more wee Sinclairs running around Bonnybrae next year.

'I've never been up in the attic,' Marie said. 'If there is a bed up there shouldn't we bring it down and get it washed and polished and the mattress aired?'

'I suppose we should,' Maggie said. 'I don't think Rina will want to spend money on a new one. She's worried enough about the hospital fees. The one in the attic is not wood though. It is made of iron but it has a spring base. It will probably need a new mattress after all this time.'

'I'm sure it will,' Jim said, 'if it's the one we all used, until the next sibling came along or we grew too big for it. Your father would be the last to sleep in it, Marie. I'll help you get it down. If the old mattress is still there I'll take it over to the saddler in East Lowrie and ask him if he can make a new one, the same size and shape. It had rounded ends instead of square didn't it, Maggie?'

'Aye, I believe it did, now you mention it.'

Marie unearthed the bed from under a pile of rugs which were stored in the attic. She looked at it doubtfully. It had once been black but the paint was scuffed and shabby. She couldn't imagine Marguerite wanting to sleep in that instead of her cot.

'Do you think I could paint the top and bottom, Uncle Jim? We could carry it out to one of the sheds until I get it done if you bring me some paint and a brush from the village.' She ran her hands along. 'I'll need some sandpaper to smooth away the chipped paint.'

'All right, lassie, if you're sure you haven't got too much work to do already.'

'The evenings are light so long now. I'll paint it when Marguerite has gone to bed.'

As it happened Uncle Joe was not making a cot. Triumphantly he produced a square pen with a moveable wooden bottom. Three of the sides had hinges so that it could be folded flat and the fourth side was made to fasten with three secure latches to make a sizeable rectangle. The wooden bottom had tiny blocks for feet to keep it a couple of inches off the floor so that Marguerite would not feel the cold or damp while she played.

'I made it so Rina wouldn't need to worry about her wandering off when she is busy bathing or feeding the new baby,' Joe said. 'She can play in here with her rag doll and other toys. I thought you might sew her a big cushion Maggie. If she's tired she can lie down and sleep there instead of upstairs.'

'What a splendid idea, Uncle Joe,' Marie said in delight. 'And I love these bells you've attached, and those big wooden beads on the opposite end. You're a genius.' Joe flushed with pleasure at his niece's praise and Maggie smiled proudly.

'Perhaps we could put one of the sheepskin rugs in the bottom until you get her cushion made, Aunt Maggie?'

'That would be a good idea, lassie. You washed three of the rugs from the bedrooms didn't you?'

'Yes, I've still two more to do when I get time and a good blowy day to dry them. I'd no idea they came up so lovely, or so creamy and soft.'

'Of course they do,' Uncle Jim chuckled. 'They're my best sheep you're talking about, lassie. The rugs were their best jackets, made to stand wind and rain, aye and snow.'

'I suppose they are,' Marie said with a smile. 'I must tell Dad, then maybe he'll get some sheep and cure one for Mum's bedside.'

* * *

Mark sounded jubilant when he replied to Marie's letter in which she had told him of her anger with the arrogant Lorrimer and her resolve to help him recover the debts.

> *I am relieved you agree I should make Lorrimer pay up, he wrote. He is the worst offender. Lord Hanley says, if we teach him a lesson it will let the others see we mean business. Now that I know you will still be up there I would like to take his advice and hold a tenants' dinner if you will help me. I will write to Lord Tannahill and ask if I can hire his staff from Stavondale Tower, especially the cook and the maids she needs to help. If you can find time, dearest Marie, could you call on Mrs Mac? I wouldn't like to hurt her so it would be better if she hears of our plans from you. Maybe she would recommend a person to clean, someone she can supervise. She might have some useful suggestions herself.*

Mark was learning everything he could from Mr Rowbottom and Lord Hanley and Marie was relieved he was finding his stay beneficial, but it troubled her the way he frequently mentioned "we" in his letters, as though they would always work together. It was true she loved being at Bonnybrae and she could understand why Jamie had settled so happily. It would be a wrench when she had to leave, especially, Marguerite. All her cousins had made her welcome and Aunt Maggie, Uncle Joe and Uncle Jim treated her with real affection. More importantly they regarded her as an adult. Her parents, and even Polly, their maid tended to think she was still a child. She would be eighteen in January and she would have to decide whether she wanted to train as a nurse or whether she should accept Lord Hanley's offer of employment in the Estate Office and as his chauffeur when he had taught her to drive.

It was a long time until November and the proposed tenants' dinner but Marie knew how quickly news spread in a country area and if Lord Tannahill mentioned anything to the cook at Stavondale their plans would be all over the glen. Consequently, as soon as Uncle Joe and Aunt Maggie set out for the hospital with Marguerite at the weekend she saddled Duke and took him for a good gallop to Stavondale Manor. She took the key to check everything was in order and to collect any correspondence for Mark. She recognised his mother's handwriting on one of the envelopes. She was surprised he had never sent her his address in Yorkshire, even though it was temporary. Then she led Duke down to Mrs MacCrindle's cottage and gave him a long rein so that he could graze the grass verge. She saw Mr McGill walking across the field behind the cottage and acknowledged his cheery wave, smiling at how friendly everyone was when she still considered herself a stranger here.

'Hey, but I'm pleased to see ye lassie,' Mrs Mac said welcoming her inside. 'I'll make us a cup of tea and a freshly made scone.' They chatted easily as they waited for the kettle to boil. 'Now draw up a chair and help yourself to the butter and raspberry jam.'

'Oh please, Mrs Mac, you mustn't bring out any more food,' Marie called when the elderly woman disappeared into her small pantry to bring gingerbread and shortbread.

'Och lassie, I'm pleased to have somebody to feed. When is Master Mark coming back? Is there any word?'

'No, not yet. I came to tell you of his plans though and to ask whether you have any suggestions which might help. You spent so many years with Sir Reginald Capel.'

'What sort of suggestions?' Mrs Mac asked with a worried frown.

'Mark is planning to give a dinner for the tenants and their wives on Thursday, the twenty-seventh of November, the night before rent day. It is Lord Hanley's idea. That's the landowner he is staying with and who is instructing Mark on managing the estate. He is my parents' landlord. He is fair and wise . . .' She broke off when they heard a knock at the door.

'That will be Mr McGill. He will be wondering if there is news of Master Mark's return. We all miss him.' She hurried to the door and invited Mr McGill inside. Almost before he was seated at the table, Mrs Mac had brought him a cup and saucer and was pouring tea for him.

'Would you pass him one o' the plates from the rack on the dresser behind ye, please lassie? And a knife out o' the left-hand drawer?' Marie did as she asked and placed them in front of the farm manager with a smile and a twinkle in her blue eyes.

'I really called to see if you had brought any news, Miss Sinclair, 'he said with a grin, 'but I guessed there'd be a cup of tea going.' Mrs Mac told him about the proposed dinner.

'Mmm, I've heard of some landlords holding a rent dinner when the tenants pay their rent,' he said. 'It would take a mean and cold-blooded man to gorge himself, then leave without paying his dues, especially when the other tenants were paying theirs,' McGill said thoughtfully. 'It makes sense that landlords need the rents before they can pay for repairs. Some folks have no shame though. We all know there's a couple of tenants who boast about being behind with their rents. It's not due to hardship either. They need to be taught a lesson.'

'Yes,' Marie's soft mouth tightened. 'It is not my business of course but I've heard one of them bragging. Now that he has talked to Lord Hanley, Mark agrees, but he is afraid he might not be able to get new tenants when the farms need so many repairs. Uncle Jim says farming is not as profitable as it was during the war. The government are importing cheap food from abroad again because they don't want wages to increase for factory workers who are producing goods for export.'

'That's true,' McGill said. 'The politicians only think about keeping costs down to export goods. They've forgotten already that the people nearly starved during the war.'

'My father and Lord Hanley would agree with you,' Marie said, 'but Uncle Joe studies the newspapers and he talks to workers in his factory. He says there are a lot of families who can barely afford enough food for their families.'

'Aye, he probably understands more about these things than we do. Most folk get enough to eat in the country areas.'

'Uncle Jim thinks some younger sons of Stavondale tenants would seize the chance to rent a farm of their own, and they would be willing to work hard and pay their rents. I hope Mark will deal with the bad tenants if they don't pay up after the rent dinner.'

'I wouldn't have the cheek to attend the dinner if I'd no intention of paying my debts,' Mr McGill said.

'That's because you're a decent and honest man,' Mrs Mac told him.

'Thanks for that compliment, Mrs Mac,' McGill said with a wide smile as he helped himself to a generous slice of gingerbread.

'Anyway,' Marie said, 'Mark is still making plans but he wanted you to be the first to hear about them, Mrs MacCrindle. He knows you spoil him when he's here,' Marie said, smiling, 'so he doesn't want you to do any work yourself, but he wondered if you know of a maid who would come in to clean nearer November, and if you would supervise?'

'Aye, I have a niece who would be glad to help. She's well trained and a good worker.'

'Lord Hanley is paying Mark for working with him and his land agent, and for acting as chauffeur. Mark says it's a pleasure and he doesn't consider it work at all, but the money will be useful to pay towards the dinner and staff.'

'Yes,' Mrs Mac said, looking worried. 'There will be a lot of cooking though.'

'Mark is going to ask Lord Tannahill if he can hire his cook, with whatever maids she will needs from Stavondale Tower, but he wants to hold it here, at Stavondale Manor, so she would need to use the kitchens.'

'Oh that's all right then,' Mrs Mac smiled with relief. 'There is a rent table somewhere in the house. Sir Reginald used it when he was collecting the rents. It has drawers all round it with different letters of the alphabet for the names of the tenants, or was it the names of the farms? I forget now. I know Miss Catherine left it at Stavondale Manor because she said she had no use for it. It was part of the furnishings when Master Mark bought the manor. How is Miss Catherine?' she asked anxiously.

'I was just wondering that myself,' Mr McGill said.

'Jamie is coming home from the hospital today with Uncle Joe and Aunt Maggie, but in his letter he said Rina is fretting to come home too. She is still very weak and the twins will need to stay at the hospital until they are feeding normally. They are still being fed through a tube.'

'It's been a worrying time for them all,' McGill said sympathetically.

'But Miss Catherine is going to be all right?' Mrs Mac persisted. 'Do the doctors think her babies will survive?'

'Yes, they say they need time and patience, and Rina needs plenty of good food and rest. I don't know how long I shall be here but I shall stay for as long as Rina needs me.'

'That's grand,' Mrs Mac said with a beaming smile. 'Sir Reginald would have been so pleased to see the lassie with a couple of wee boys, and her young daughter too of course. I've knitted one baby jacket but my heart wasna in it. Now I know they're going to be all right, I shall get on with knitting some more.'

'Aye, my wife was feeling the same,' McGill said. 'Tell Miss Catherine she's knitting two pairs of cot blankets. One pair in pale yellow and the other in pale blue wool. She will get on with them when I tell her the good news.'

'How kind you all are,' Marie said warmly. 'Catherine will be so pleased when I write to tell her. We're all looking forward to her getting home again, but I hope she will agree to wait until she's stronger. She must feel torn in two when the twins have to stay up there and she wants to be with Jamie and Marguerite at Bonnybrae.'

'That's true,' Mrs Mac said, 'but tell her there will be years to enjoy all her family together so long as she gets herself well again. You tell her I said so. I've known her all her life and she's as dear to me as if she was my own bairn.'

'Thank you, Mrs Mac. I shall tell her that in my next letter. I try to write often so that she will not be so homesick.'

'She's lucky to have you, lassie,' McGill said. 'I knew your Grandfather Sinclair and he was a good man — one of the best, a hard worker and kind too. I can see he's passed his good qualities on to his grandchildren, or at least to you and Jamie. Robin Sinclair's three are grand young folk too.'

'Don't forget Jack Sinclair,' Mrs Mac reminded him. 'They tell me his son is a hard worker, and his lassie too.'

'I don't know them very well,' Marie admitted. 'I've only met them once at Aunt Maggie's. Uncle Jim and Aunt Maggie are kind and generous to Jamie, and to me too while I've been here.'

'Well, I'll do all I can to help you and Master Mark make this rental dinner a real success,' Mrs Mac said.

'Aye, and if there is anything me or my wife can do you only have to say, even though we're not part of the estate. I like Master Mark and it will be grand if he can make Stavondale Estate a place to be proud of again.'

'Thank you both. I shall tell him when I reply to his letter. Mr Thomas has already started on the roof repairs to one of the farms and he hopes to complete three of them by the end of November. That should let the other tenants see he is doing his best to improve each farm when he can afford it.'

'He doesn't live extravagantly, that's for sure,' Mr McGill said, 'and Lord Tannahill seems to have known him a good many years. He has a great word of the laddie.'

'I must be getting back,' Marie said with a smile for both of them. 'Thank you for my tea, Mrs MacCrindle, the scones are delicious. I'm supposed to be helping with the milking while Aunt Maggie is away at the hospital. She has taken Marguerite with her.'

'Ye'll make some farmer a grand wife one day,' McGill said with a twinkle in his eye.

* * *

Jamie seemed subdued when he returned from his stay at the hospital but Marie sensed Uncle Jim was more relaxed now he was back. She realised her brother shared a lot of the responsibility for Bonnybrae. He was young, strong and hard working. She wondered if her father would miss her brother Allan as much if he moved away from Moorend. He was seven years older than she was but she understood his frustration at always taking orders from their father. Uncle Jim had shared decisions and responsibility with Jamie gradually. They didn't always agree but they discussed things amicably. Allan was in love with Lynn Tindall and they wanted to marry but there were no cottages at Moorend Farm and neither of her parents seemed to understand his increasing dejection.

Mr Rowbottom had told her he remembered Allan going to war as an innocent lad of seventeen but he had returned eighteen months later a mature man, grieving for the loss of their brother John. Since she had worked away from home herself she could understand and sympathise with Allan's feelings.

Marguerite had been hot and grumpy when she returned from the hospital so it was a relief when she was bathed and settled down to sleep.

'Rina will have her hands full with two babies to care for,' Aunt Maggie reflected. 'Our wee angel will have to learn to share her mama. Rina has been away so long Marguerite barely seems to realise she is her mother. That upset Rina, especially when we had to leave. She burst into tears. Of course that upset both Jamie and Marguerite.'

'Oh dear.' Marie looked anxiously at her aunt. 'I hope Rina doesn't think I'm usurping her place. I love Marguerite dearly but I shall have to return home soon.'

'I know dear, but Rina is pleased you're here. She knows her wee lassie is safe.

'That must be why Jamie seems so subdued,' Marie said.

'Yes, he hates to see Rina distressed but Dr Meadows says it is a sign she is still very weak. He hopes another week will make a difference so long as we can persuade her to take things easy when she comes home. We couldn't manage without you, Marie.'

'I shall stay until Rina feels she's ready to manage on her own.'

'Ye're a good lassie. Maybe it will not be such a bad thing for Rina to come home on her own for a week, or even two, if the twins have to stay in hospital for a bit. It would give her time to get back to normal, and for Marguerite to have her mother to herself.'

'That would be a good idea for Marguerite,' Marie agreed. 'The boys don't know who their mother is yet so they will not miss her as Marguerite does.'

'They are being well cared for. Mr Chambers is pleased with their progress, but he would like them to gain a bit more weight and make sure their wee lungs are developing before he allows them to come home.'

As promised Marie wrote to Rina passing on the news from Mrs Mac and the McGills and telling her they were all longing for her to come home. 'But I shall only stay on condition you promise to rest as much as possible, otherwise I might as well go back to Yorkshire.'

Rina replied immediately saying she would promise anything if only she could be home again but she insisted they must pay Marie a proper wage for as long as she was able to stay. Apparently the jade collection she had inherited from her grandfather, and which Mr MacQuade had despatched to the London saleroom, had made almost twice as much money as the local valuation they had been given. Marie understood what a great relief that must be to Rina and Jamie because they could repay the bank loan.

'It is true,' Jamie said, his usual smile returning briefly. 'Rina had a letter from Mr MacQuade yesterday and he couldn't believe the vases were so valuable, or that the jade pieces had made so much. They are going to a collector in America. At least Rina can stop worrying about money now, but she still wants to get home. We really do need your help Marie. We discussed things and we agree it would be easier if we pay you from now on. We could never have managed without you. Uncle Jim agrees. We shall not feel quite so bad at keeping you here if we pay you. It could be ages before the twins get into a routine. Mr Chambers says it may be a year before they catch up and it is vital Rina should not get exhausted and ruin her own health.'

'I enjoy being here at Bonnybrae so long as I'm needed.'

'Aye, but Jamie is right lassie,' Uncle James said. 'Now that they can afford to pay you a wage you should accept it. They have their pride. There must be things you need.'

Marie wrote to Mark, telling him Rina hoped to get home in another week and they expected the twins would get home in two to three weeks' time. She went on to say Mrs MacCrindle had promised to hire a cleaning maid before the rent dinner in November, but she reminded him that she would probably be back in Yorkshire herself by then so she would be unable to help him organize the dinner or collect the rents.'

Marie smiled when she received two letters from Yorkshire by return of post. Mark insisted that he couldn't manage the rent dinner without her, both as his hostess and to help him keep a record of the tenants and what they were paying. Marie had told him she couldn't do both, even if she was still here and she didn't feel it was her place to act as hostess, but he insisted he was depending on her. Would she please promise not let him down?

I have never met a girl like you, my dearest Marie. I miss you more than I thought I would ever miss anyone. You are my friend and companion. I feel so at ease in your company and I know I can depend on you.

Marie couldn't help feeling a little flattered and warmed. It was true she and Mark had felt at ease with each together from the beginning. He told her he was getting to know Lord Hanley's tenants better than his own and he vowed to remedy that as soon as he returned. He told her Mr Rowbottom's condition was improving slowly but it didn't look as though he would be able to ride his horse for a few months yet. Mark felt the land agent was down in spirits and considering giving up his work so that Lord Hanley could employ a new agent. Marie gasped at that. The Bob Rowbottom she knew had always been so cheerful and optimistic, with a wry sense of humour. Moreover her father got on well with him and respected his opinion, both as a friend and as the agent for the estate. He would not be happy if there was a change.

In the letter from her mother Marie learned that she was sending two small cribs for the twins.

'Emma didn't say anything about cribs in her letter to me,' Aunt Maggie said.

'Jamie was always good friends with Garridan, one of the gypsies. We call him Dan for short. When he heard Jamie and Rina had got twin sons he refused to believe they wouldn't survive with Jamie for their father.'

'He's been proved right about that,' Aunt Maggie said, 'even though none of us believed they would live.'

'Dan and his wife set about making two woven cribs for them, with willow or hazel I suppose. Mother is sewing a padded lining for each of them. She says they're oval and beautifully made with little handles on either side for carrying. She thinks they would fit side by side in a big cot at night and keep the draughts away, but she says Rina could carry them downstairs and let them sleep in the cribs during the day where she can hear them. She thinks they will be big enough to last the first six months, or maybe longer, when the twins are so small. She was fretting about parcelling them up but Allan said he would send them by train when he takes the milk to the station.'

'Well isn't that lovely. I'll be writing to Rina tonight so I'll tell her. It will be a lovely gift and so thoughtful.'

CHAPTER TEN

In one of his letters Mark mentioned attending one of the dances in Silverbeck Village Hall with her brothers Peter and Allan and Lynn Tindal, but it was Peter, in one of his rare letter writing phases, who had mentioned that Mark had danced nearly every dance with Irene Wilkins. He went on to ask if she remembered the Wilkins and that made her smile. Everyone in Silverbeck knew the Wilkins. Neither Mrs Wilkins nor Irene allowed anyone to forget they were the largest tenant farmers on Lord Hanley's estate. In her heart Marie was dismayed to realise how dejected she felt to hear Mark was as attracted to someone else, especially a girl as shallow as Irene Wilkins, yet she herself had insisted they were only friends.

> *Of course,* Peter went on, *Mark didn't know anyone else and Irene Wilkins was quick to introduce herself now she knows Mark owns land of his own. He had a couple of dances with Meg. In fact he seemed keen to talk to her, even though she is married. He danced with Lynn a couple of times but our Allan is a bit possessive in that quarter.*

Marie could almost hear Peter chuckling as he wrote. He didn't pay much attention to girls yet.

Later that night when Marie lay in bed her thoughts returned to Peter's letter. Mark was a free agent so why should it bother her if he brought back a wife. She had no claim on him, they were only friends, even when he did insist he couldn't manage without her. He was a thoroughly nice person though and she hoped he would get someone better than the snooty Irene Wilkins. Are you sure you're not a bit jealous? A little voice whispered in her head.

* * *

Maggie decided they wouldn't take Marguerite to get Rina home from hospital.

'She gets fidgety and sleepy by the time we're coming home and she can be tiring. It will make more room for Rina and me in the back of the car too. I have made her a new dress though. Here it is Marie. I thought you might dress her in it after she's had an afternoon nap then she will look fresh and pretty to welcome her mama.'

'Oh Aunt Maggie, that's lovely,' Marie exclaimed holding up the small dress.

'Och, that's nothing. It's only a wee muslin dress.'

'You're so clever and so modest,' Marie chuckled and hugged her aunt. 'Rina will be thrilled when she sees her.'

'Aye she'll get a surprise when she sees what a fine job you have made to that old bed too. It's like new since you rubbed it all down and painted it.'

'It's the new mattress Uncle Jim got the saddler to make. It fits perfectly. It must be comfortable because Marguerite has slept in it for three nights now and so long as she has Raggy doll and Teddy she goes to bed and settles without a murmur.'

'What have you done with the cot then?'

'I folded it up and put it in the box room. I thought it would be better if she forgets about it then she'll not mind when the twins need it.'

'You have a wise head on your young shoulders lassie. You'll make a good mother yourself one day.' Marie blushed.

She would need to find a husband and get married first and she was not sure that's what she wanted yet. Her thoughts flew unbidden to Mark. She wondered if he really liked Irene Wilkins. She shrugged. It was not her business. She was only a friend acting as his unpaid secretary. He was the local laird — far beyond her league.

* * *

Uncle Jim had just come in for his afternoon tea before starting the milking when they heard Uncle Joe's car drawing into the yard. A few minutes later Jamie came in holding Rina'a arm to steady her after sitting so long in the car. Dr Frank Meadows, had warned him it would be a while before she got her muscles back after being confined to bed for so long. As they entered the kitchen Jim rose and moved quickly round the table.

'Eh lassie, welcome home. It's good to see ye back where ye belong,' he said gruffly, giving her a warm hug. To his surprise, and her own, Rina threw her arms around his neck and burst into tears. Maggie, watching from the door, shook her head in silence. Bachelor he might be but she knew her brother had grown to love Rina as much as she and Joe had. She was the nearest he would ever have to a daughter of his own. Even so he had never been a demonstrative man and she was surprised how gently he stroked Rina's dark hair and spoke soothingly until she regained her composure and blinked away her tears. Marie had tried to prepare Marguerite for her mama coming home but she stared wide eyed, a little uncertain whether this really was her mama. She looked up at Marie and held up her arms, her soft mouth trembling, ready to burst into tears herself. Marie swept her up in her arms and lifted Raggy doll with her.

'Mama is crying happy tears because she is so pleased to be home again.' she said softly. 'Look Raggy doll wants to give her a hug. Will you help her?' Marguerite looked uncertainly from Marie to her mother then she seized Raggy doll and held out her arms. Rina couldn't quite stem her tears as she hugged the small warm body to her and Marguerite laid her cheek against hers.

'We need some fresh tea I think,' Marie said briskly. 'Come on Aunt Maggie sit in at the table. Try one of my cherry scones. Marguerite helped chop the cherries but I believe she ate more than she put in the mix. Come on Uncle Joe you must be ready for a drink after all that driving.' As they all took their seats Rina regained control of her emotions.

'Keep Marguerite on your knee for now,' Marie said quietly. 'She needs you close. Shall I spread a scone for you?' Rina swallowed hard and nodded, looking up at Marie and summoning a watery smile.

'Thank you for everything, Marie,' she whispered, but Marie squeezed her shoulder and nodded her understanding, feeling a lump in her own throat at the sight of Marguerite nestling into her mother's breast. Jamie pulled out a chair close beside his wife and daughter.

'Here's your cup of milk, Marguerite. I'll put your bib on to protect your pretty new dress then you can show your mama what a clever girl you are now Daddy has taught you how to drink from your own special cup.'

As soon as tea was over Jamie and Uncle Jim had to get on with the milking. Rina pushed back her chair and set Marguerite on her feet then began collecting the crockery for washing up.

'I've lit the fire in the sitting room, Rina' Marie said. 'I think Marguerite needs you more than the cups and saucers do. Anyway, you must see the playpen Uncle Joe has made. Take them into the room and show off your skills, Uncle Joe.' She grinned at him.

'Yes you do that,' Aunt Maggie said. 'I'm glad to stretch my legs after sitting in that car so I'll wash the dishes and Marie can dry them.'

As they worked together companionably Aunt Maggie told Marie it must be weakness that was making Rina so tearful. Marie nodded. She had heard her mother say women were often tearful after their babies were born due to changes in their bodies and it was worse if they were tired or weak.

'I expect Rina will soon regain her good spirits as she gets stronger,' she said. 'I don't suppose it was easy for her to leave the twins behind.'

Two weeks later Uncle Joe drove Jamie and Rina back to the hospital in Glasgow to collect their baby sons. Rina had been delighted with the two small basket cribs which Jamie's gypsy friend, had made, and which Emma had padded and lined so beautifully. William James and Reginald Joseph Sinclair slept the whole way home.

'I expect they will probably make up for such good behaviour tonight,' Marie predicted wryly. Twins were a novelty and they were no sooner home to Bonnybrae than Alice Lamont brought her own two children and her mother up to see them, and bring little gifts of tiny knitted bootees, jackets and leggings to keep them warm when the colder weather arrived. Doug's mother also sent a gift of two nightgowns which she had made and embroidered herself and a message to say she looked forward to seeing the boys before they were much older. Rina was overwhelmed with the kindness of the many people who sent gifts when they heard she was safely back home and her twin sons were thriving at last, even if they were still very small. The wedding of Cousin Billy and Fran drew nearer as the harvest progressed. They were all invited and Maggie had made a new dress for herself. She offered to make one for Marie too, but she still had the dress her mother had made. It was very pretty and this was the sort of special occasion she had been saving it for, but she got a big surprise.

When they met a couple of weeks before the Harvest Home dance Fran shyly asked if she would be her bridesmaid along with Billy's sister, Cousin Laura. Fran was very diffident about making this request but Marie felt honoured to be asked. She gave Fran a spontaneous hug and told her she would love to be her bridesmaid.

'My mother wants to make the dresses for you both,' Fran said anxiously, 'but she does make a lovely job. She made this dress for me.' Fran held out her skirt but it was the beautiful embroidery on the bodice which caught Marie's attention.

'Goodness me she must be very clever with her needle. My own mother and Aunt Maggie are really good. I've often envied them both, but your mother could sew for Queen Mary.' Fran laughed and looked relieved.

'You're about the same height as Laura but you are a lot slimmer, so Mother wondered if you could ride over to our house next Sunday afternoon so she could take your measurements. I've seen some lovely material. It is a sort of turquoise and mother has lots of patterns, so she thought you and Laura might like to choose a style. What do you think, Marie? I thought turquoise would suit your lovely fair skin and red-gold hair, but it also suits Laura's dark curls.'

'I'm sure it will suit both of us. It is thoughtful of you to consider us, Fran. After all, you're the bride. I was looking forward to your wedding anyway and now I'm so excited.'

'Laura will be pleased when I tell her. She was nervous about being on her own.'

Emma and William had received an invitation to the wedding but they could not be persuaded to attend. Marie was more disappointed than she had expected and she knew Jamie had thought they might come to see his twin sons. Rina still tired easily and she pleaded with Marie to stay at Bonnybrae, at least until Christmas. There was certainly plenty of work to do with the extra washing of nappies and baby clothes, as well feeding and the usual cooking, cleaning and churning, not to mention looking after two infants and a toddler.

'I shall have to return home eventually,' Marie said to Jamie as they watched the last load of oats being carted home. 'I think you ought to get a young maid to help Rina with the children, or if you don't want anyone living in the house maybe there would be an older woman who would come two or three times a week to wash and clean.'

'Do you think so?' Jamie asked anxiously.

'Yes, I do. There's more work to babies than men realise. Mother always said that. The twins are very small so they take longer to feed than normal and there are two of them. They take up a large chunk of Rina's time, and Marguerite needs some attention too, although Alice has been very good at taking her to play with her own children and they seem to get on well.'

'I must look for somebody at the term then. That's the end of November up here, but we're hoping you will stay with us until after Christmas, Marie?'

'I will so long as Mother and Father agree,' Marie promised. 'Mark is hoping I shall still be up here to help him when he holds his dinner for the tenants at the end of November but I said I couldn't promise. Now that I've been to more of the local dances with Robert and Billy and Fran I'm beginning to feel I know more people in this area than I do at home but I'm glad I've never met that horrible Lorrimer fellow again.'

'No, I hear he's unpopular with everybody, especially the girls. I wonder if his father will attend Mark's rent dinner?'

'I don't know but Mark sounds more assertive since he has been with Lord Hanley and Mr Rowbottom. He says he will definitely give the Lorrimers notice to quit unless they pay most of what they owe by rent day. He has agreed I should ask Mr Thomas to repair the slates on their house roof and the byre. It was my suggestion but he said Lord Hanley agreed because it left the Lorrimers without any excuses and, more importantly, a new tenant would expect a dry home and a decent byre to milk his cows.'

'That's true for a new tenant but the Lorrimers only have a house cow. They don't keep many sheep either. They're bone idle. It's Mrs Lorrimer who keeps them fed with her hens and a pig for the house.'

'I think Mark is hoping they will leave. In his last letter he told me he had been teasing Allan about coming up here to farm. He said he would probably be looking for tenants after the rent dinner. He was surprised when Allan said he would take up any offer of a tenancy if it meant he and Lynn could get married and have a house of their own.'

'I don't know what our parents would say to that!'

Marie knew Fran and Billy had sent Mark an invitation to the wedding to show their appreciation because he had granted them the tenancy for Glenside, but she knew it was unlikely he would be able to attend. The last she had heard was that Bob Rowbottom was still unable to mount his horse and Mark was still chauffeuring him on his farm visits. In England these were especially important at this time of year because the end of September, Michaelmas Day, was one of the two dates when tenants paid their rent or gave six months' notice to their landlords of their intention to move out on the next rent day of March twenty-fifth. The same applied to landlords when they wanted to give notice to their tenants. Marie knew Lord Hanley was a good landlord and well respected, so she doubted if there would be many, if any, farms changing hands. Even so she knew, from her short time spent in the Estate Office, that Mr Rowbottom would make a point of paying them all a visit to hear of any complaints or any other change in circumstances.

Normally in Scotland the moving days were the end of November and the end of May, but in Billy's case it had suited Mark for him to take over the tenancy of Glenside immediately. Both Billy and Fran preferred to spend their savings on their new home rather than a honeymoon, so Fran and her mother had spent all their spare time scrubbing and cleaning and distempering the rooms so that it would be fresh and clean. Billy had bought a dressing chest for Fran which matched the oak of the new bed the joiner had made for them. He had also bought a carpet square for the sitting room, and Fran had been busy making a rag rug for the kitchen. Various friends and relatives had contributed kitchen utensils and the previous tenants had left a large iron kettle and a cauldron to hang over the fire for cooking, as well as a wash tub, a posher and a rubbing board in the wash house. Fran already had a mangle with large wooden rollers inherited from her grandmother, along with a dresser and an assortment of crockery. Aunt Evelyn and Cousin Laura had been sewing curtains and bedding which Laura was embroidering. Uncle Joe had promised them two pairs of woollen blankets from his factory for a wedding present, in addition to the pretty quilted patchwork cover which Aunt Maggie was making. They would have the main essentials to begin their life together, especially once the wedding gifts, large and small, had been moved from Fran's home into the house at Glenside. There would be a show of presents two nights before the wedding. Marie learned this was a Scottish custom, quite different to the way things had been for her sister Meg's wedding in Yorkshire. As bridesmaid she had promised to bake and help Fran and her mother, then stay overnight and help to move everything to Glenside so that the couple's new home would be as welcoming as possible.

'They're so much in love I dinnae think it will matter whether they have everything they need or not,' Fran's mother said happily.

Life seemed to have been particularly hectic for Marie between wedding preparations, finishing the harvest and the busy pace of life at Bonnybrae, so she was worried about leaving Rina on her own for a couple of days, although Aunt Maggie said it was her duty as a bridesmaid to help Fran before the wedding. She went down to Braeside to discuss her concern about leaving Rina and the twins.

'Rina has gone to bed herself this evening although it's so early, but the twins waken about midnight.'

'You deserve a bit of time to yourself, lassie,' Uncle Joe said, giving a satisfying pull on his pipe. 'It will help Jamie understand Rina needs help when you go home again.'

'He does understand,' Marie defended her eldest brother. 'He feeds one of the boys while Rina feeds the other during the night.' She grinned suddenly. 'He hasn't learned to change a nappy yet though. Rina said he tried, but wee Reggie was soaked through by the next morning.'

'I don't blame Jamie over that,' Joe said with a smile. 'I doubt if I'd make much of a job of changing nappies either.'

'He has promised to look for a maid at the November term,' Marie told them.

'Joe's right, Marie,' Aunt Maggie reassured her. 'You should be free to help Fran and her mother. I hope you enjoy being bridesmaid. I know you've got everything organized as far as you can at Bonnybrae. Rina said you churned the butter and made enough bread for an army, as well as baking two cakes to take to Fran's for the show of presents. Folks always enjoy a cup of tea and a bite to eat after they've had a good look at everything, some out of interest but most because they are curious to see what their neighbour has given.'

'Oh Aunt Maggie, it's not like you to be cynical,' Marie said with a laugh.

'I'm not cynical. It's the truth but the women enjoy a show of presents. Have a word with Alice. I'm sure she'll lend a hand with Marguerite if she can.'

'I'll run you over to Fran's house in the car in time for the show of presents,' Uncle Joe offered. 'After all, you'll need things for the night and a change of clothes if you're going to be shifting things to Glenside the next day.'

'Oh thanks Uncle Joe!' Marie gave him a kiss on his weathered cheek. She had intended riding over on Duke but she had pondered how she would manage her clothes and if there would be anywhere to stable and feed a pony. Now she could pack her suitcase. 'I'm really looking forward to Meg and Ranald coming. It seems ages since I saw my big sister.' She grinned. Big sister had been a family joke for a few years now. Marie was not very tall herself but she had grown taller than Meg and their mother by the time she was fourteen.

'Joe is meeting them at Strathlinn,' Aunt Maggie said, 'but you'll not see them until the wedding.'

'I know. That's the worst thing about doing my bit as a bridesmaid. Ranald's relations are all from Scotland too so they are going on to visit some of them.'

'But they'll be back here for a night before they travel home,' Aunt Maggie reminded her. 'You'll be able to catch up with all Meg's news then. I'm sure you'll enjoy being bridesmaid, Marie. You have worked hard for months now. You deserve a change.'

* * *

Marie was amazed at the number of people who came to the show of wedding presents on two evenings before the big day. A few came in a pony and trap, some on horseback, but most of them walked, some for several miles. They made the most of the event, only leaving as darkness was falling and after drinking several cups of tea and eating numerous sandwiches, biscuits and cake. Marie was glad Aunt Maggie had warned her about the custom so she had baked two batches of biscuits as well as the cakes. Aunt Maggie had sent one of her famous fruit loaves and Aunt Evelyn and Laura had brought baking. Fran and her mother had been busy too. Fran was an only daughter and her family were well known, so friends and neighbours made the most of the open invitation. Marie stayed overnight and Fran's mother expressed her heartfelt thanks several times during the evening as they washed and dried the unending flow of cups, saucers and plates. The following day cousin Laura returned to help move the wedding gifts over to Glenside in readiness for Fran and Billy. Fran insisted on being there in person when it came to making up the bed with the new sheets and blankets.

'I daren't trust you two on your own in case you make us an apple pie bed, or something worse,' she said. They all surveyed the bedroom with satisfaction once the furnishings were in place.

'I know the carpet is very shabby but it was here already and there's plenty of wear in it yet. Dad helped me lift it and we gave it a thorough beating out in the orchard.'

'It looks fine to me,' Marie assured her. You can't see much of it for the lovely new bed and the massive oak wardrobe. The sheepskin rugs on either side look so cosy.'

'Yes, they're lovely. Billy's uncle Jim sent them. I must remember to thank him.'

'Shall I lay a fire in the grate in case it's cold by the time you arrive here after the wedding?' Marie asked.

'I've already set the fire in the kitchen but Billy says we shall not need it until the next morning.' She blushed a bright pink. 'He says we shall soon keep ourselves warm in bed,' she mumbled shyly. Marie nodded but her own cheeks were pinker than usual. She knew she had a lot learn about love and marriage. She might be capable of managing a household and looking after children, or even writing a good business letter and doing accounts, but when it came to relationships between men and women she was as innocent as a babe in arms.

Everything had been set into place by late afternoon.

'What a difference all your lovely new things have made, Fran,' Marie said in admiration. 'It really looks like home now and so welcoming.'

'Yes, it does, doesn't it,' Fran beamed. 'We've been so lucky to get so many useful gifts and the new oil lamp to hang from the ceiling is beautiful. The light will reflect in the new mirror on the far wall too. That was a gift from Aunt Betty. But it's all thanks to Mr Blackford and your Uncle Jim that we can set up in a home of our own. I do hope he will be able to come tomorrow.'

'Mark? Are you expecting him?' Marie asked in surprise. Her pulse quickened. He hadn't mentioned coming in his last letter.

'I don't know. He said he would love to attend but he was not sure he would be able to get away. Father wrote back and assured him he would be welcome even if it was a last-minute decision. The reception is very informal anyway. It's in the village hall so that we can fit everyone in and the tables can be cleared away for a dance afterwards.'

'I didn't know there would be a dance,' Marie said, thinking her Scottish relations were far more sociable than she had expected. 'We didn't have many relations at my sister's wedding. Both families are from Scotland so most of our relations are up here.' She felt a pang of regret that her mother and father would not be here to share this family celebration.

They were all feeling grubby by the end of the day and Laura opted to go back home to wash her hair. Fran's mother had guessed how they would be feeling.

'I lit the copper boiler in the wash house so there's plenty of hot water if you want to bathe. It is cosy in there too with the fire and the water steaming so I set out the tin bath and clean towels for both of you.'

'Oh Mum, thank you.' Fran said, giving her mother a hug. 'That's just what Marie and I need, but everything looks lovely at the house now. Billy will be pleased.'

'Your turn first, Fran,' Marie said. 'You're the bride and the most important person.'

'Thank you so much for all your help, Marie,' Fran's mother said warmly. 'I didn't expect so many people at the show of presents last night. I don't know how I would have managed without you to help me. Are you going to wear your hair up tomorrow?'

'I don't know what to do with it.' Marie sighed. 'I haven't had it cut since I came to Scotland. It's never been as long since I left school. I've been tying it back for working.'

'You would suit it dressed on top of your head,' Fran's mother said. She moved behind Marie and held up her thick tresses. 'You have such an elegant neck and pretty oval face. I will pin it up for you tomorrow if you like. It's a beautiful colour but you must have caught the sun as it is darker auburn underneath and a mixture of gold and silver on top. Fran was right you will suit the turquoise dress and the headdress.'

'Thank you,' Marie said, smiling. 'I would like to try it up if there's time to do it.'

'Mum's good at that sort of thing. It will not take her long,' Fran said with a grin, coming through from the wash house swathed in a large towel with another around her head. 'She's very creative, aren't you Mum? She can make almost anything with her hands.'

'Oh, I don't know about that,' Mrs Burnie said, her cheeks pink.

'You have certainly made two very pretty headdresses for Laura and me,' Marie said. 'Did you make the silk roses too? I do wish my mother could have seen them.'

'Yes, Mum made the roses so you can take the head-dresses home if you want them.'

Fran herself was to wear the tiara and veil her mother had worn for the something old with her beautiful new white brocade wedding dress. She had a pair of blue satin garters and Marie had offered to lend her a pretty bracelet made up of silver flowers, each with a small blue sapphire in the centre for something borrowed. It was one of the many pieces of jewellery she had been given by Lord Hanley. She was sure he hadn't really been aware of how much he had given her in his wife's casket, but he had insisted he had neither daughters nor daughters-in-law to whom he could pass them on and he wanted her to enjoy wearing them. She had chosen to wear a necklace of gold facetted links and a matching bracelet herself. She would like to have worn the necklace with three emerald teardrops which was her favourite but she knew the green would clash with the turquoise of her dress. Laura was borrowing a silver necklace and bracelet from her mother.

As Marie relaxed in the warm bath in the wash house she realised how fortunate they were at Moorend since Lord Hanley had installed a hot water system with an upstairs bath and a water closet. He had done the same at Mountcliff to keep Mrs Wilkins satisfied. He planned to do the same for two of his farmhouses each year if finances allowed. Bonnybrae had the same facilities so she had become used to them now but Marie knew that was due to Uncle Joe's influence because he had installed a bathroom at Braeside for Aunt Maggie. None of the Stavondale farms had bathrooms. It would be several years before Mark would have spare cash to spend on anything but essential repairs.

The morning of the wedding dawned bright and clear with a hint of autumn crispness in the air. At fourteen Laura had not been a bridesmaid before. She was excited and nervous when she arrived at Fran's.

'Laura, you're making me nervous,' Marie teased. 'It's Fran who is the bride. We're supposed to be supporting her.'

'I'm glad I'm not on my own,' Laura said. 'You've been a bridesmaid once. Please will you take Fran's bouquet? I'd be sure to drop it or forget to give it back.'

'All right,' Marie said easily, 'but keep calm or you'll make Fran and me edgy too.'

'Dad says you're the most capable and composed young woman he's ever known. He hopes I shall grow up like you.'

'Everybody gets nervous sometimes, Laura. Anyway, we have to be an example. Remember Marguerite is going to join us when we walk back down the aisle behind the bride and groom. Aunt Maggie has made her a lovely white silk dress with an organza overskirt and she has embroidered it down the front with dainty sprigs of rosebuds and tiny green leaves. Uncle Joe has decorated a wooden spoon with silver ribbons and a smiling face for her to present to Fran. They love Marguerite as if she was their own grandchild.'

True to her promise Fran's mother came into the bedroom to dress Marie's hair high on the crown of her head then she pinned the circlet of silk roses firmly into place.

'You both look perfect,' she said with satisfaction, pinning the other circlet of roses firmly on top of Laura's dark curls, before drawing two plump ringlets over one shoulder to the front while the rest cascaded in glossy waves down her back.

Marie did feel a little panicky when she saw so many people gathered outside the church to await the bride. She knew Fran's family had lived in the same area for several generations and although her father owned and worked the smallholding where the family lived he was better known in the district as their local builder, as his father and grandfather had been before him, and his only son was already following in his footsteps. Inside the little village church was already full with invited guests. Marie thought how lovely it looked decorated with flowers for the Harvest Festival Service to be held the following day, but she only saw a blur of faces as she and Laura followed Fran and her father down the aisle.

Both Billy and Fran repeated their vows clearly and with conviction. How happy they look Marie thought. She gave a little smile to herself when she saw Robert wink at her behind their back after he had handed over the ring. She guessed he had been on edge too. Then the whole atmosphere seemed to relax and they were following the bride and groom back down the aisle. Marguerite was at the end of the second pew beside Rina and Jamie but she was already hopping excitedly from one foot to the other waiting to grasp Marie's hand. The congregation gave a happy sigh and many smiles as she stepped from the pew and gave a wide smile, so like Rina's own. Marie bent to take her tiny hand in hers. She couldn't help smiling into the upturned, happy little face. When she raised her head again her eyes widened. There in the next pew, sitting beside Aunt Maggie, Uncle Joe and Uncle Jim sat Mark Blackford. Marie had never seen him look so smart or so much a gentleman but there he was in his dark suit with his hair neatly parted and brushed back from his face in a wave. He seemed broader and taller somehow and his healthy tan and sun-bleached hair showed he had spent the summer outdoors. He was smiling at her and the admiration in his eyes made her feel warm all over. She caught her breath. Her pulse raced. She had never felt like this before.

CHAPTER ELEVEN

Fran's father had insisted they must have proper photographs to remember the wedding of his only daughter so they assembled in front of the church. Marie had no opportunity to speak to her sister, Meg, or to Mark, but she saw them both smiling at her from the crowd. When that was over, they walked the short distance to the Church Hall for the reception but Mark appeared at Marie's side and took her arm, drawing her round the corner of the church away from the crowd.

'I got photographs of the wedding group but now I would like one of you on your own.' He placed his hands on her shoulders and bent his head. Marie thought he intended to kiss her cheek but instead his hands moved to cup her face before he pressed his mouth to hers in a lingering kiss. They had never exchanged anything more than a friendly hug before but Marie found she hadn't the willpower to resist even if she had wanted to. The blood tingled in her veins. Emotions she had never experienced before seemed to take over her whole body. Her knees felt weak. Mark raised his head and smiled at her. 'You'll never know how much I've longed to do that, Marie,' he whispered gruffly. 'I have missed you terribly.' Before she could reply he bent his head and kissed her again and this time he was rewarded by the tentative parting of Marie's innocent lips. When he released her, he said, 'I only accepted the wedding invitation so that I would have an excuse to see you again. I knew you were to be a bridesmaid.'

'How — I — er . . . It's a long way to c-come Mark.'

'It is worth it. I didn't realise I was going to miss you so much when I agreed to go to Yorkshire. Now,' he straightened and reluctantly stepped back from her. 'I promised to take a photograph. I'd better get on with it before people wonder where we've got to.' His grey eyes sparkled as he removed the leather strap from his shoulder and held up a camera, grinning at her surprise. 'This was a birthday gift a few years ago, from Rupert's uncle, Lord Tannahill. He has always understood better than my own parents how much I appreciate gadgets. Lord Hanley requested a photo of you when he knew I had a camera and I'm sure your parents would like one too since they can't be here to see how beautiful you are. If you stand over here beside this tree I can make a real picture of you. You look so much taller, and so very elegant, with your hair like that, Marie.'

'Fran's mother pinned it up for me,' she said with a smile. Mark clicked the camera.

'Stay there. I want a few more. You're the most beautiful girl in the world to me.'

'If I didn't know you better, Mark, I'd swear you've been drinking brandy, or some other tongue-loosening liquor,' Marie chuckled, refusing to take him seriously.

'I don't need brandy. It's the truth, Marie,' he declared. 'And I don't mean only physical beauty. It takes more than that for true beauty. I hadn't realised how much I would miss your company when I was seeing you almost every day. Seeing you in church, looking so regal, well it was like seeing you, I mean really seeing you, for the first time.'

'Mm,' Marie mumbled thoughtfully, but she was too shy to tell him she had felt something like that herself when she caught sight of him in his dark suit and pristine white shirt. 'You seem different yourself Mark, since you've been away — more assured somehow, and I don't think it is only your very smart suit. Or your haircut, handsome though they make you.' He took her hand and grinned.

'I'm glad you noticed the haircut. Bob Rowbottom said you would. He said you always notice the details. We'd better join the others though, before they send out a search party.' He led her back towards the parade of people heading for the Church Hall. 'I know you have to dance with the best man, and other duty dances as bridesmaid, but please promise you'll save as many dances as you can for me, my sweet Marie.'

'We have never danced together before but Allan tells me you're a very good dancer. Apparently Irene Wilkins thinks so too.'

'Irene who? Oh you mean the Wilkins' daughter from Mountcliff? I have only been to one village dance. It's true I danced with her more often than I wanted. If she had been a nicer, kinder person, I might have felt sorry for her after hearing the village rumours.'

'When do you go back to Yorkshire?'

'I promised Lord Hanley I shall be back by Monday afternoon so I need to leave around five o'clock on Monday morning. You will spend some time with me tomorrow, Marie? Just the two of us?'

'I-I will try, but I must spend time with Meg too. She is my sister after all.'

'I know. You have a lovely family, so close and more loving than mine have ever been. Mrs Greig has invited me for Sunday lunch. She said Meg and Ranald would be there too, so I'm hoping you will be there.'

'It will depend how Rina is but I hope we shall be able to get organized in the morning before I go down to Aunt Maggie's.

'That will be splendid. Maybe we can go for a run on our own later.'

'A-a run?'

'Lord Hanley loaned me his car so I could drive up. That's why I need to leave very early Monday morning. I don't want to let him down when he has been so generous.'

'Gosh, he must trust you, Mark. That's a long journey.'

'Yes, but he said I'd earned it. I'll tell you about that later,' he added as they entered the hall.

'Jamie and Uncle Jim are leaving the wedding festivities after the meal. They need to go home to do the milking. Rina says she will leave then too and take the twins and Marguerite home to bed. Uncle Joe is taking them but he's coming back for the dancing and to chauffeur Aunt Maggie and me home later.'

'Maybe I shall be able to drive you home if I'm lucky,' Mark said with a twinkle in his eye. His expression sobered. 'I noticed Rina is still pale and very thin.'

'We're lucky she has come through everything. She has had a tough time. The twins still need fed during the night. That takes a while and disturbs her night's sleep.'

'I see your aunt beckoning to me, Marie. I believe she has found my place name.'

'Yes. I think you're going to meet two more of my relations who are also your tenants. I barely know them myself so I hope they are pleasant.'

'I'm sure they will be if they are your relations. That's more than I could say for any of mine,' he added with a grimace, 'but at least we can choose our own friends. Remember to keep some dances for me, and that I'm taking you home.' He bent his head and kissed her lightly on her cheek but she blushed when she caught the glance and the smile Aunt Maggie and Uncle Joe exchanged. They were old romantics she decided, and they didn't miss a thing. She went to take her own place with Laura beside the bride and groom and the rest of the main wedding party. Everyone was in high spirits and the hall had been decorated with greenery and coloured balloons and strategically placed vases of tall bronze chrysanthemums and white dahlias.

'It all looks so warm and festive,' she whispered to Fran, 'and I don't think I've ever seen so much delicious food.'

'I hope you will tell Mother and Father that, Marie. They have been so worried in case things didn't turn out right, but they should have known the Wright sisters wouldn't let us down. Emily Wright has a bakery shop in the next village and when she caters for weddings and parties her sister, Evelyn, helps her. They're both wonderful cooks.'

'If that large roast ham is anything to go by it makes my mouth water looking at it, not to mention the chicken and the large pork pies. Every table has several bowls of fruits and nuts and salads.'

'Yes, they try to cater to suit everybody but they're coming round with bowls of hot soup to start us off. Do you want chicken or broth? They can only do one course hot. They bring it hot in huge pots in the back of their pony and trap and they have two spirit stoves to keep it piping hot.'

'Mm, I hadn't realised I was so hungry until the delicious smells wafted this way. I think I'll have the broth.' Someone was passing round baskets of freshly baked hot rolls and there were already curls of golden butter on little dishes up and down the table.'

'Be sure to save room for the trifle,' Cousin Billy said, leaning forward to grin at her. 'They make the most delicious trifle I ever tasted. I'm glad Mark Blackford managed to get here,' he added. 'It's thanks to him we're able to get married today. I haven't spoken to him yet but please tell him how much we appreciate his help, Marie.'

'I will. I see Aunt Maggie is making sure he is well looked after,' she said with a grin.

During the meal Mark seized the opportunity to tell Joe and Maggie he would like to take Marie home after the dance.

'Can you do that?' Joe asked. 'How did you get here? Do you have a pony and trap?

'I came by car.' Mark said calmly. 'Lord Hanley suggested I borrow his and drive up if I promised to be back by Monday afternoon. I must leave very early Monday morning.'

'His lordship must have a high opinion of you to trust you to drive all this way.'

'He knew how much I wanted to come to the wedding, but I'd already decided it was impossible to get away so near the September rent day when Mr Rowbottom visits each of the farms to see whether there are likely to be any changes of tenancies. The car had broken down the previous week and there are no local garages or even a mechanic. Lord Hanley bought the car from a garage in Leeds so he expected he would need to get a mechanic to come out to fix it. I asked if I could look at it first. It was easy to see a small part that should drive the fan was broken. I showed him what was wrong, then I got it off and went to Leeds on the train for a replacement part so that I could fix it myself. I took the chance to clean the plugs and change the oil and generally give it a going over as I'd been longing to do.' Mark grinned boyishly and Joe had to smile.

'You're a better man than I am,' he said. 'Next time you come up I'll get you to check mine. No wonder Lord Hanley thought you deserved to borrow his car.'

'He did more than that. I left my dress clothes at my parents'. I left in a hurry and I couldn't pack everything,' he added ruefully, remembering his mother's anger. 'Lord Hanley introduced me to his tailor, a Jewish man living in Leeds. He insisted on him measuring me up and making me "a dark suit suitable for a well-dressed country wedding". That was his description.' Mark's fair skin flushed slightly. 'He explained that it wouldn't do if I was more formally dressed than the groom. Anyway the tailor measured every inch of me and this is the result.' Mark held out his arm for Joe to inspect the material. 'I expect you'll disagree of course but he reckons the best woollen cloth in the world is made in Yorkshire.'

'It's certainly excellent quality material,' Joe said, feeling the sleeve.

'No wonder you're looking so smart, Mark,' Maggie remarked.

'It's the best fitting suit I've ever had,' Mark agreed. 'Perfectly comfortable everywhere. The tailor says he will keep my measurements and I can let him know whenever I need a suit. He will send some patterns. Lord Hanley wouldn't even let me pay. He said he would have needed to pay more for a mechanic to come.'

'Aye, he could be right about that, Mark, but it's good to know he appreciates you. Marie told us he had been very generous to her.'

'He's not a greedy man. In fact he's a sincere man I believe, but he's no fool and he wouldn't let anyone take advantage of him. One or two of his tenants have tried that. It has helped me to know such things happen everywhere. When I return to Stavondale I intend to deal with my own tenants as he handles his. I'm hoping Marie will still be here to help me with the rent dinner at the end of November. I don't think I could manage it without her as my hostess. Doesn't she look beautiful today, and her hair is dressed so elegantly?'

'Aye she's a pretty lassie,' Joe said and winked at Mark. He and Maggie were convinced he had attended the wedding to see Marie more than to oblige his new tenants.

'Rina is hoping Marie will stay at Bonnybrae until Christmas so she should be here to help you with the dinner,' Maggie said. 'I expect she'll return home for her eighteenth birthday or Emma will think she has lost her daughter completely.'

'When is her birthday?' Mark asked.

'She will be eighteen at the end of January.'

* * *

As soon as the speeches were over some of the local farmers had to return home to milk their cows, including Jamie and Uncle Jim, Aunt Bessie's husband, Albert, and Uncle Jack, but most of them would return for the dancing. They enjoyed a good celebration and it was a local band who were well known for good music. Maggie introduced Mark to her sister Bessie and her brother Jack as he had not met them before, although they were his tenants. They were surprised to see their new landlord was so young and that he seemed to be so friendly with their niece from Yorkshire, and other relatives.

When Marie had danced with Robert, as best man, and Fran's father, then Uncle Robin, Meg's husband, Ranald, and the groom himself, she made her way to join the group where relations young and old had gathered around a long narrow table facing the dance floor. Mark had been watching for her. He stood up at once and took her hand before she could sit down, making sure no one else could claim her. He drew her close. Never before had he wanted to hold a girl in his arms as much as he wanted Marie.

'I have waited ages for this,' he whispered, smiling down at her. 'I don't think I shall let you go. Too many others will claim you.'

'I doubt if I'd be that popular, Mark, even if I am a bridesmaid,' she laughed.

'I'm not taking any chances. It's you I've come to see. Lord Hanley guessed that. I've fixed it with Mr and Mrs Greig that I'll take you home.'

'What did they say?'

'They were surprised Lord Hanley had offered me his car.'

'You're a wonderful dancer, Mark,' Marie said with a sigh, relaxing into his arms. 'You will be in great demand.'

'I have already danced with Mrs Greig, and your sister, Meg, and your Aunt Bessie. Now all I want is to dance with you. Let's stay on the floor for now,' he added in a low voice, still holding her hand as the dance drew to an end. 'I think I have met all your family now, Marie. They are all pleasant people.'

'I barely know some of them myself,' Marie admitted as he drew her into his arms for the next dance. He drew her closer and sighed softly.

'I think I'm in love with you Miss Marie Sinclair. I've missed your company so much, and now,' his voice was husky, 'now I want to hold you and go on dancing with you forever.' Marie caught her breath. They had shared an easy, uncomplicated friendship from the beginning but she was enjoying the feel of his strong arms around her as they danced together to the music. She felt safe and happy.

'I-I've never been in love,' she said in a small voice. In fact she had never had a boyfriend or wanted one, but now . . . ? Mark smiled tenderly down into her upturned face.

'Neither have I. In fact I've always scorned the word when my brothers went on about being in love,' Mark admitted, 'but I hadn't met you then, Marie. I have always known instinctively I wanted a girl who could be my friend and companion, my soul mate. You're all of that, but tonight,' his voice deepened, 'you stir my senses in a way I have never known before.' The light in the hall was dimmer now the sun was sinking. The autumn day was drawing to a close but the oil lamps had not yet been lit. Mark lowered his head and brushed his lips gently against her temple, his arms tightened a little. 'My brothers, and especially my mother, think marriage is finding a woman with wealth and producing the next generation of Blackfords. I knew they were missing something. Do you feel it too, Marie — a bond of real friendship drawing us together, and now,' he said softly, holding her close, 'now I know we could have so much more. Holding you in my arms makes my heart sing and the blood tingle in my veins.' His lips were very close to her ear, his cheek resting on the soft coil of her hair. 'I wish this waltz could go on forever,' he said with a sigh as the music ended.

A singer came on to give the band a short break. Mark smiled at Marie and drew her down to two empty seats well away from her family. Marie looked across at Aunt Maggie and saw Uncle Joe wink at them. He grinned and gave a little nod. Obviously he was not offended that they were not re-joining the family yet. When the band began to play again Fran and Billy joined them. Fran's eyes were sparkling with happiness.

'We have come to seek your help. We know Robert and his friends intend to play tricks on us but we'd like to give them the slip.' They discussed a plan in whispers then Billy led Marie onto the floor for the next dance, leaving Mark to partner Fran.

* * *

It was during the Sunday lunch at Braeside that Uncle Joe looked across at Marie and Mark and chuckled.

'That was a fine escape Fran and Billy made last night. I noticed you had changed partners. When they lit the lamps I knew it must be getting time for the bride and groom to leave, but you all looked content circling the floor. I assumed you two girls had gone to change when you went out. Then Mark went to the toilet, or so I thought seeing Billy sitting there waiting for you all to return.'

'That's what you were meant to think,' Mark grinned. 'Billy hoped no one would notice us. I went first to make sure the car would start at the first swing of the handle in case Robert guessed and came after them. It started perfectly and Fran and Billy reached their new home without showers of confetti or the pranks Robert and his friends had planned.'

'He couldn't believe it when he realised all four of you had disappeared,' Joe grinned. 'Perhaps it's just as well you two didn't return either Marie, or he might have played his tricks on you instead.' He eyed the colour rising on Marie's fair skin. Mark reached for her hand beneath the table and gently squeezed her fingers. He wondered if Joe knew, or guessed, it had taken them a long time to reach Bonnybrae after they parted from the newlyweds.

'It was a lovely wedding,' he said calmly, 'but it was nearly time for the dance to end and you knew I would see Marie safely home.'

'Aye that's true. You must have driven a long way round about though,' he mused, hiding a smile. 'Jamie said he was feeding one of the twins when he heard you return, lassie.'

'Oh Uncle Joe,' Meg admonished, seeing Marie's colour rising. 'Stop teasing them. Don't tell me you never dallied in the moonlight with a pretty girl.'

'Aye well I agree it was a beautiful evening with a full harvest moon.' Joe sighed and glanced at Maggie. They exchanged their own smiles. They might have been deprived of moonlight sorties when they were as young as Marie but they had found their happiness together eventually and they were content. Joe liked to tease though.

Marie was lost in a dream of her own as she half listened to the conversation around the table. It had been a long time before she slept last night. The romance of the wedding, the atmosphere of joy and happiness, and the time alone with Mark driving home in the moonlight. Everything had conspired to fill her with a rapture she had never known before. Billy and Fran had expressed their gratitude to Mark for helping them escape from Robert, but he had laughed and brushed their thanks aside.

'One day,' he said, 'if I am lucky enough to persuade Marie to marry me I shall expect you two to come to our rescue if we need it.'

'So Uncle Joe is right! That really is the way the wind blows!' Billy crowed with delight. 'I thought he was being an old romantic but he has seen a lot more of the pair of you than we have. Thanks anyway and good luck.' He had closed the car door and Mark drove on in silence for a while.

'It's early enough yet so maybe we can park somewhere and talk for a bit?'

'All right. It's been such a lovely day, hasn't it? I'm sorry it has to end.'

'So am I, and I'm even more sorry I must return so soon, but Mr Rowbottom thinks he will be able to ride his horse again in two or three weeks so I hope to be back for good by the end of October.' He sighed. I suppose we should go through some of the estate's affairs at Stavondale Manor tomorrow, before I leave?'

'That would be a good idea, especially the repairs Mr Thomas has done.'

'Fine. At least it will be a good excuse for keeping you to myself for the afternoon,' Mark said with a grin, 'but we'll forget about work for now.' Marie had not really believed what he had said to Billy about marrying her but when Mark stopped the car and took her in his arms there was no doubting his passion, and for the first time in her life Marie experienced a desire and exultation she had never imagined. She knew Mark was sincere when he said he had never felt so close, or so at ease, with a girl before. She remembered his diffidence when they had first met on the train to Strathlinn, and his boyish gratitude when Uncle Joe had offered him a lift on his motorbike. There was nothing arrogant or conceited about Mark, in spite of his background and education, but there was a new strength — both physical and mental — which she had not noticed before. She felt safe in his arms but as his passion increased and she felt the hardness of him she drew back a little. She knew so little about men, or about life beyond her family circle, but she knew there were men who would take advantage especially with someone as naive as herself. Mark sensed her nervousness.

'I cannot deny my desire, Marie. I yearn for you, and after today, I long to make you mine, but please believe I would never hurt you, or cause you shame and distress. I will wait for ever if I have to because I know I love you and you are the one I want to share my life with.' He had taken the pins from her hair then and watched it cascade around her shoulders before he buried his face in it, revelling in the silken strands.

'You smell of lavender and roses and lemons, Marie, and you're the kindest as well as the most beautiful girl I know.' He lowered his head and made a trail of little kisses from her ear and down her neck before his mouth found hers in a gentle kiss. Instinctively her lips parted. The kiss deepened arousing a passion neither of them had expected or experienced before. Slowly, reluctantly, Mark lifted his head. 'Dear God, Marie, you don't know what you're doing to me. I love you with every part of me,' he whispered gruffly.

'Oh Mark,' Marie murmured when he released her, 'I had no idea I-I could feel like this.' For the first time she understood what temptation really meant.

'I know, but please believe me Marie, however much I want and desire you, I promise I will never take advantage. You can trust me, I swear. You have my word.'

'Oh Mark, I do trust you. I-I'm not so sure how much I trust myself now . . . now you have awakened such feelings in me. I have never felt like this before.' Even to herself she knew she sounded young and innocent.

'I am glad. I hope I shall be the one to show you what real love can mean between a man and a woman. I know it is much too soon to ask you to promise yourself to me, Marie. Your Aunt Maggie reminded me that you are not yet eighteen. Since I met your parents I know how much they love all their children, including Jamie, so I understand they will be disappointed if you move away to live in Scotland, but all the opposition in the world will not prevent me hoping that one day you will marry me.'

'Marry you?' Marie drew in her breath. 'Can you be so sure it is what you want, Mark? Your parents would never approve of you marrying someone like me.' She shuddered at the memory of his mother's haughty manner and supercilious sniff of disapproval.

'I am sure. I will face opposition from the devil himself if I have to, if you can learn to love me, and if you want me as much as I want you. This will be our secret for now, but perhaps when you have your eighteenth birthday? Perhaps then you would allow me to buy you an engagement ring to tell the world you will be mine when your parents give their consent. I shall understand if they insist we must wait another year but . . .'

'Marie, dear, that is the third time I have asked you,' Aunt Maggie said, bringing Marie's attention back to the present and the dinner table.

'I-I'm sorry, Aunt Maggie,' she stammered. 'What did you ask me to d-do?'

'I asked whether you want apple pie or raspberry sponge and cream.'

'Oh, raspberry sponge please.'

'Marie was away in a world of her own,' Meg said, smiling. 'It must have been a nice dream judging by your expression little sis. Have you remembered Ranald and I must leave soon after lunch to catch the train to visit Ranald's relations? The Kerrs of Lochdaroth. We shall be staying with his cousin until Thursday but we shall be back here for our last night with Aunt Maggie and Uncle Joe. We get the train home on Friday.'

'Yes, I know. Perhaps we shall have a chance to catch up then,' Marie said. 'Jamie and Rina are hoping you will all come up to Bonnybrae if you're back in time for lunch.'

'Oh we will certainly try. Marguerite is adorable. I know Mother and Father called me after you, Aunt Maggie, but Marguerite has almost the same name as us.'

'She does indeed. We're all Margarets in one form or another.'

* * *

As soon as Marie and Meg had helped clear the dishes and wash up it was time to leave. Mark had promised to give them a lift to the station to save Joe going out, then he and Marie planned to call at Stavondale Manor to see Mrs MacCrindle and discuss estate affairs.

'What were the Silverbeck rumours you mentioned?' Marie asked idly after they had dropped Meg and Ranald at the station.

'I'd forgotten about that. Do you remember the Wilkins'?'

'Of course,' she smiled wryly. 'The biggest tenants in the area, what else.'

'Mm, the higher you climb the further you have to fall,' Mark remarked with unusual cynicism. 'I would feel sorry for them if they were not so haughty and arrogant but Mrs Wilkins reminds me a bit of my mother.'

'What has happened?' Marie asked.

'Rumour has it Mr Wilkins is considering giving notice this Michaelmas and he will give up the tenancy of Mountcliff in March. Rumours say he plans to move in with his lady-love, at least that's what Mrs Rowbottom calls her, but she says Miss Cody is a very nice person. She also reckons Mrs Wilkins only has herself to blame. I don't know why. She said Lynn's grandmother, Mrs Tindall, could tell me why but of course I wouldn't ask.'

'B-but Miss Cody's father was a vicar. I can't believe it. In Silverbeck!'

'It may only be village gossip. But if Mr Wilkins does give notice Mr Rowbottom thinks Lord Hanley would favour your parents as the next tenants. Whatever happens Irene Wilkins seemed upset the night of the dance, even if they are only rumours.'

'Gosh!' Marie was silent for a moment, forgetting her momentary distrust of Irene as she considered the effects the news might have on her family. 'I suppose my parents would have jumped at the opportunity a few years ago but I can't imagine my mother wanting to move now, or Dad either really. He has made so many improvements to Moorend and he already milks more cows than Mr Wilkins, even though he does have fewer acres.'

'It is because your father has proved himself such a good farmer and the best tenant that Bob Rowbottom thinks he and his sons deserve the chance to rent Mountcliff, in addition to Moorend. Remember none of this is official, Marie, so best not mention it in your letters. It would be a splendid opportunity for Allan and Peter though if it comes off.'

'It would mean Allan and Lynn can get married and they're certainly getting impatient. I'm not so sure about Peter though. I doubt if he would want to live with Allan and Lynn when they're newly married. Anyway it would be a big outlay buying more stock and equipment,' Marie said thoughtfully. 'I remember Lord Hanley saying there was at least fifty acres of hill land on Mountcliff. Maybe Dad could run sheep there.'

'We should forget about it for now, unless your parents tell you themselves. I thought your mother might have mentioned the rumours in her letters.'

'No.' Marie gave a wry grimace. 'My parents still think I'm a child. It would never occur to them I might be interested, even less have an opinion.'

'I know you are not a child, Miss Marie Sinclair, not the way you make me feel.'

'Oh Mark,' Marie blushed, then sighed. 'I'm really going to miss you when you leave this time.'

'Not as much as I shall miss you, my sweet Marie. But you do understand I can't let Lord Hanley — or Mr Rowbottom — down. They have been very good to me, and I have learned a lot in a short time.'

'Then we had better pay attention to your own estate now,' Marie said. 'We could drive past the farms where Mr Thomas has been working. We don't need to go in because you can see most of the roofs from the road. When I have ridden past on Bali I thought the improvements looked good.'

'All right we'll do that before we call on Mrs MacCrindle. I know she will have tea and scones waiting for us. I don't want to offend her. In fact I don't know what I would have done without her.'

'She has a kind heart. Rina still regards her almost as part of her family.'

* * *

Marie missed Mark badly when he returned to Yorkshire again. Her mother made a vague mention of the rumours circulating in Silverbeck Village in her next letter so Marie told her she had heard them too. If they were true, and if Mountcliff tenancy became available, she hoped her father would seize the opportunity to rent it for Allan's sake, unless they wanted to see him do something rash and follow Jamie to Scotland to farm. She added her suggestion that her father might enjoy keeping sheep again, and maybe teach her youngest brother, David, to handle the dogs as Jamie had done. She knew he already had his own young collie.

She smiled when she received her mother's prompt reply.

> *You sound so grown up and mature, Marie. I can't believe my own daughter can consider farm tenancies and make such sensible suggestions. Your father is amazed. He has only seen the hill land at Mountcliff from a distance. Your idea of keeping sheep and working his dogs again has stirred his interest, even though Mountcliff is equipped as a dairy farm. It would cost a great deal of capital to stock it with milk cows but we could keep all our own dairy heifers and increase the numbers gradually. Meanwhile William admits grazing sheep and growing more corn could bridge the gap. Between ourselves, Marie dear. These last few words were underlined and Marie was pleased her mother remembered she was good at keeping secrets. She went on, Ever since Jim and Jamie managed to buy Bonnybrae your father has been saving every spare penny in the bank so we can buy Moorend if it comes to sell because Lord Hanley has no heirs. Your letter made him consider Allan's future more seriously. It is only fair Allan should be able to get married and live his own life but I wouldn't like him to move away, as Jamie has done. You are right, Marie, Mountcliff would be convenient and they could work the land together. Allan is a young healthy man and we're not exactly old folks yet. I'm only forty-three. Your father is forty-nine but he's as fit as he has ever been. Peter is a hard worker too. Perhaps distance has made you see things more clearly, or maybe you have inherited my own mother's wisdom.*

There were the usual questions about Marguerite and the twins and lots of good wishes to everyone else before the letter ended but Marie felt much closer to her mother now. She wondered how her parents would feel if she did marry Mark and live in Scotland. Her sister Janet was nearly fifteen and had left school at the summer term. Then there was

Fiona, the baby of the family. Maybe they would not miss her as much as she would miss them. She knew without doubt that Mark's family would never accept her as a suitable wife for their youngest son but Mark didn't seem to care about their opinion. At least they were far enough away not to cause trouble if she and Mark did marry. She had not reckoned on the distance being less of a problem for those who owned a motorcar, or worse, Mrs Blackford's penchant for interfering.

CHAPTER TWELVE

The twins were thriving and sleeping most of the night now. Marguerite adored her tiny brothers and watched intently when they were being fed or changed. She spent ages tending Raggy doll as her mother did the twins, then putting her into the tiny crib and Joe's playpen was a boon. Reluctantly Rina acknowledged she had not yet regained her former vitality and she admitted she would need help when Marie went home if she was to continue churning the butter and keeping her poultry, as well as running the busy household.

'I was so determined to be a good farmer's wife,' she sighed. 'I am truly grateful to you, Marie, for helping me, and caring for Marguerite for so many months.'

Marie exercised the two horses more regularly, and kept the estate affairs up to date, now Rina was at home. Mr Thomas had almost finished the repairs. There were more needing to be done but until Mark saw how many tenants paid their rent in full he could not commit himself to more expense. Marie doubted if the small estate would be enough to occupy Mark's mind after spending time on an estate more than twice the size of Stavondale but she was looking forward to his return at the beginning of November. Uncle Joe had offered to drive her to the station to meet him and Aunt Maggie had invited them both to Braeside for a meal.

Mark stepped off the train carrying a large, brown-paper parcel as well as his case. He kissed her cheek and grinned at Joe as he thrust the parcel into her arms.

'This is from your mother, Marie. She says you can count it as an early Christmas present since you will not be home for Christmas. I told her you were going to be my hostess at the rent dinner so she has made you a new dress.'

'Another new dress? I've never had so many dresses in my life. She made me one for the dances. I was saving it for a special occasion, but I got a lovely bridesmaid's dress.'

'I believe Emma and Maggie have been consulting about this one,' Joe said with a chuckle. 'I hear it's shorter than you usually wear to show off your pretty ankles. Maggie can't wait to see it. She has promised to do any alterations if it's not a perfect fit now you are thinner. Maggie and I are going to buy you an early Christmas present too — a pair of leather shoes, but you will have to choose them and try them on.'

'I can't believe this! Does everyone expect the tenants' dinner to be a posh affair, Mark? I'm not sure I am up to it.'

'Dearest Marie, you can manage anything as far as I'm concerned,' Mark said earnestly. 'Your mother says everyone dresses in their best clothes. I know you'll be lovely whatever you wear. All I ask is that you will be my hostess, then help me afterwards to collect the rents. I wonder if Mrs MacCrindle and the cook from Stavondale Tower have organized the waitresses and a wine waiter yet.'

'They had a meeting. Cook came to Stavondale Manor to inspect the kitchen. She was very impressed. Rina remembers the young man who acts as wine waiter. She says he was the gardener's youngest son so he will know the tenants. I'm sure everything will be fine but we must have a final check to be sure how much each tenant is owing.'

* * *

A few mornings later Jamie was measuring the milk in the churns and securing the lids with the lead seal for the train journey to the creamery. Marie was filling the smaller cans which each household received for their own use, a perk which Ernest and Doug appreciated. Uncle Joe walked up to Bonnybrae each morning to collect the milk for Braeside. He was on his way back home when he met a youth panting up to the farm.

'What ails ye, laddie?' he asked. He was fighting for breath and brushing the sweat from his brow. He looked about twelve or thirteen.

'Mither sent me to bring Mistress Lamont,' the lad gasped. ''tis her father, Mr Forbes.' Joe caught his arm.

'What's wrong with him?'

'He d-died in the night. Mrs Forbes is in an awfy state. Mither says it's the shock an' I must hurry but 'tis a long way frae Craig's Hill.'

'It is a long way to run,' Joe agreed with a frown. 'Take this can of milk to the house you have just passed. I'll break the news to Alice myself. Tell my wife what has happened. Mrs Greig will give you a drink and a bite of breakfast. Tell her I'm going to take Alice and you back to East Lowrie in my car to save time. Alice has two young bairns.'

'Thank ye, oh, thank ye mister,' the lad breathed gratefully. He had not had any breakfast because his mother had despatched him in haste.

Joe retraced his steps and told Jamie and Marie what had happened.

'But Mr Forbes seemed so fit!' Marie said incredulously. 'He helped us with the sheep shearing while you were at the hospital with Rina, Jamie.'

'None of us know what's afore us,' Joe said. 'I'll have to break the news to Alice. Her mother needs her.'

'I'll come with you, Uncle Joe. It will be no place for two young children. I'll have to bring them here and look after them for today at least.'

'But you'll never have time to . . .' Jamie started to object but he saw the stubborn set of his sister's chin.

'I must,' Marie insisted. 'Alice helped us when Rina was in hospital remember. She'll be dreadfully upset.' She lifted the can of milk for the Lamonts and went with Joe to their cottage. Alice bust into hysterical tears at their news. Marie comforted her until she was calm.

'It's the shock, Alice. I'm so sorry, but your mother needs you. Uncle Joe is going to drive you there in his car to save time. Have you had any breakfast?'

'Aye but the bairns are not out o'bed yet. I can't . . .'

'Yes you can,' Marie said firmly. 'I'll look after the children. Once they're dressed and fed I'll take them with me to play with Marguerite. Now you change your pinafore and get what you need while . . .' Doug came running in.

'Jamie told me what's happened. I can't believe it!' He gathered Alice in his arms.

'That young laddie was fair exhausted,' Maggie remarked to Joe that evening when he returned from work. 'He'd had nothing to eat and he ran all the way from East Lowrie village.'

'Aye, Forbes' death is a terrible shock to them all, as well as his wife. He was only forty-eight. He thought he had indigestion. Alice's brother, Eddy, was at his mother's when we arrived. He said his father never left the farm until they were finished for the day, but he had left early the previous afternoon.'

'Yes, Alice came back about ten minutes ago. She stopped on her way past. She's terribly upset but she's grateful to Marie for looking after the children. Eddy is going to sleep at his mother's until after the funeral. He understands Alice can't leave two young children for long and it's not far between his mother's house and the farm.'

'I was glad Marie came with me to tell Alice,' Joe said. 'She took over so calmly and comforted Alice, poor lass, then she organized the two bairns. She's as capable as a woman twice her age. She reminded me of her Granny Greig. My mother helped many a body in trouble and she was always calm in a crisis.'

'Aye, Doug was full of praise for Marie. He said she is always ready to help. Jamie brought him in for his dinner at Bonnybrae and that helped reassure the bairns.'

'Aye Marie is a good lassie. Emma will miss her if she marries Mark and settles up here, but I think Rina would be pleased. They've become good friends.'

'Aye,' Maggie sighed, 'life is full of ups and downs. Mark is a nice laddie and I'm sure he cares deeply about Marie whatever his own background.'

* * *

Alice's mother was still staying with Alice and Doug at Bonnybrae three weeks after her husband's death.

'She's nervous about staying on her own but it makes a big difference having her with us,' Alice told Rina. 'I've always enjoyed milking and now I can go to the byre with Doug without worrying about the bairns. I know mother is dreading going back,' she said, her expression troubled. 'I think she's worried how she'll pay the rent to Lord Tannahill too. It was different when Dad was working with Eddy. I think he paid the rent for them. Do you think I'm being selfish if I ask her to live with us?'

'What does Doug say?' Rina asked. 'Would he mind?'

'Oh no. He always says she's his second mother. We were always close, the four of us you know, Doug and Eddy, me and Daisy. We're all family now we're married.'

'So long as you all agree I can't see why it wouldn't work.'

Two days later a very diffident Mrs Forbes came to the house to see Rina. She had seen Marie taking Marguerite out to gather eggs with her own tiny basket so she knew she would find Rina alone.

Rina drew her into the kitchen and asked how she was keeping.

'I'm all right, Miss Catherina. Oh, I'm s-sorry, I mean Mrs Sinclair.'

'Mrs Forbes you're trembling. Please have a seat and I'll make you a cup of tea.'

'Oh no, please don't go to any trouble. I came to ask a favour o' ye.'

'I will help if I can,' Rina said gently, seeing the older woman's nervousness.

'Alice and Doug have asked me to live with them. Don't get me wrong. There's nothing I'd like better. They're a lovely pair and I love my grandbairns.'

'So what's the problem?' Rina watched Mrs Forbes ringing her hands in agitation.

'I-I'd like to be a wee bit independent still. I'm only forty-five. I'm not old, am I?'

'Of course you're not, Mrs Forbes. Would you rather stay in your own home?'

'No! Oh no.' Mrs Forbes shuddered. 'It willna be like home without Forbes. I-I heard Miss Marie is going home after Christmas and Master Jamie is going to the hiring fair next week to hire a wee maid for ye?'

'Yes, I'm afraid so.' Rina sighed. She was not looking forward to having a stranger living with them. 'I need some help with the washing and cleaning while the boys are so small. I want to get back to doing the churning and my poultry, and helping when we have lambs again.'

'I-I would ye consider me, Miss Catherina?' Mrs Forbes asked in a small voice. 'I'm used to washing and all the work there is about a farm. I-I've worked hard, all ma life.'

'I know you have Mrs Forbes. I remember when I used to come round with grandfather, before Lord Tannahill bought the hill farms and made yours and the Lamonts into one. Grandfather always said you were a good, hardworking wife.'

'Aye, I tried to be.' She wiped a tear with the corner of her apron and sniffed hard.

'Then if you're sure you want to work here at Bonnybrae I'd be pleased to have you,' Rina said, her own spirits rising. 'I would need to discuss it with Jamie and his uncle first of course, but if you could work for me . . . say four mornings a week?'

'Oh Miss Cath . . . Mrs Sinclair, I would like that beyond all.'

'Well let me discuss it with my husband tonight and I'll let you know for sure tomorrow. Does Alice know?'

'Not yet, but I'm sure both o' them would be happy to know I want to keep my independence and help them as well.'

Jim and Jamie were as delighted as Rina to hear they would have a familiar face helping in the house when Marie went home. They knew Elsie Forbes was a hard worker, honest and reliable, and fond of children, all qualities it was difficult to judge when choosing from a line of strangers. It was agreed that Elsie would start work straight away for one morning a week to get used to the Bonnybrae routine before Marie left after Christmas.

'Rina, as soon as the rent dinner is over,' Marie suggested, 'How about you let Mrs Forbes and me give the whole house the annual spring clean while there are two of us. It would still leave the blanket washing when winter is over but it would get things off to a good start so you don't get overtired. It would let her see the way you like things done too.'

'You're so good to me, Marie,' Rina said gratefully. 'It is a splendid idea if you're willing. We're going to miss you dreadfully when you return to Yorkshire.'

'If I'm honest I shall miss your friendship too, Rina, and the children, especially Marguerite.' She sighed. 'I feel very unsettled. I can't make up my mind whether I want to train to be a nurse now or not. Mother doesn't really need me at home when she has Polly and now Janet has left school. She loves being at home and helping with the milking. I know

Dad still wants me to work for Lord Hanley. I would probably become a sort of personal assistant and chauffeur, from what he suggested before. I don't know whether that would be enough.'

'When you get back to Yorkshire maybe everything will become clear,' Rina suggested. 'I loved nursing, but I loved Jamie more. I've no regrets about giving up.'

Mrs Forbes working one morning a week gave Marie time to help Mark with the rent dinner only two days away. He had delivered an invitation to each of his tenants and they all assured him they were looking forward to attending, even the Lorrimers. He had also invited the Masons. Mr Mason was the blacksmith at East Lowrie but he rented the small farm behind the forge, on the approach to East Lowrie village. The Hendersons, who ran the grocery store, and also the local bakery, with their son and daughter-in-law, also rented forty acres and some buildings so the four of them were included.

'Mr Henderson expects the young couple to take over both businesses and his bit of land eventually,' Mark said. 'It's a pity the Masons have no son to follow on. He thinks he will have to give up the smiddy in another year.'

'That would an awful miss,' Marie said. 'Mr Wright, the blacksmith back home, is always in demand.'

'Maybe he'll find a young apprentice. Can you manage so many people, Marie?'

'Yes. I'll tell Mrs Bell, the cook, and Mrs MacCrindle. The table is all set beautifully in the dining room. Come and see. I have written out the place names so you can help me seat everybody where you want them. There will be six Sinclairs,' she grinned, 'so we should spread them out so no one can say we're favouring my family. Mr Lorrimer is the only one I'm dreading but Rina says Mrs Lorrimer is a pleasant woman and quiet as a mouse.'

'Speaking of Rina,' Mark said, 'Do you think she and Jamie would join us after the meal and bring the twins? All the tenants' wives ask after her. They would love to see her again. They could talk while you and I are in the office dealing with the rents.'

'I'll certainly ask her. Now come and help me set out the place names where you think they should be seated? I'd rather like Mr and Mrs Massie and the Hardies at my end. I know them and they are friendly.'

'All right. We'll seat the Lorrimers in the middle but away from the grocer and the blacksmith. They're owing both of them money.' Mark took some of the place names. 'My word these are beautiful! Who did you get to write them, Marie?'

'I did them myself,' Marie said.

'You did? They look professional. I could never attempt anything so beautiful.' Marie blushed when he wrapped his arms around her and kissed her longingly. 'You do know I can never let you go my clever girl?'

'I'm not clever. We learned to do calligraphy at school,' Marie said, although she knew few in her class had mastered the technique properly. She glanced down at the cards with a glow of pride. Rina had admired them too.

* * *

In spite of all their careful planning, plus the diligence of Mrs Bell and Mrs MacCrindle and their helpers, a dark cloud was descending over the proceedings in the shape of an uninvited, and most unwelcome, guest.

It had never occurred to Mark to mention the rent dinner in the rare communications he had with his parents, but he had consulted Lord Tannahill about hiring his cook. His friend Rupert had written to wish him every success with the rent dinner and to say he would be visiting Stavondale Tower around the end of November with his uncle and his young cousin, Sylvia. It transpired that Rupert had run into Mr Blackford in Bath around this time and innocently commented on Mark's splendid idea of holding a dinner to persuade his tenants to pay their rents on time. He passed on the snippet of news to his wife, never dreaming she would insist they must go to Scotland at once. She was confident it was her place to be there, to act as hostess and to prevent Mark making a muddle of things.

* * *

Marie had finished checking everything on the day of the dinner. Mrs Bell was in control in the kitchens. She and Mark had agreed on a suitable menu with Mrs Bell early on and Mark had explained he wanted the food to be of the best quality with a reasonable selection and adequate quantities, but he did not want a lavish banquet. Everything had been delivered to Mrs Bell's satisfaction and she was looking forward to the evening. Mrs MacCrindle and her niece had enjoyed bringing the house to life. Everything was spotless. Marie had arranged fresh flowers in the hall, the dining room and the drawing room. On Rina's suggestion Marie had had two of the young men carry the rent table into the office which she and Mark would be using. It was the one Sir Reginald Capel had used when the tenants came to pay their rents. The drawers around the perimeter were labelled alphabetically. She had made sure an updated record for each tenant was in the appropriate drawers. One or two were woefully behind. It was while she was doing a last check in the office that Mrs Blackford entered the house leaving her husband chatting to Lord Tannahill.

Earlier that morning Marie had ridden to Stavondale on Duke and he had grazed in one of the paddocks all day. Mr McGill had promised to bring him up for her and tether him to the hitching post at an agreed time. Glancing out of the window she saw that her mount was waiting patiently and now she was ready to ride back to Bonnybrae and change into the lovely dress her mother had sent for her. At Mark's request she had agreed to dress her hair on top of her head as she had worn it for Fran and Billy's wedding. Aunt Maggie had offered to help her and Uncle Joe had promised to drive her back to Stavondale Manor in his car in good time to help Mark welcome their guests. She felt the excitement mounting inside her. Surely the evening would be a success after all their careful preparations.

She was crossing the hall towards the front door on her way out when she was accosted by Mrs Blackford with twin flags of angry colour on her high cheekbones. Her thin lips were tight and her pale eyes were cold with anger.

'You girl! Are you Sinclair?'

'I am Marie Sinclair, yes.' Marie's heart beat faster. She remembered Mark's mother from the earlier unpleasant meeting. This was almost like a replay, especially when she ordered, 'Give the servants instructions to prepare rooms for myself and my husband. They are refusing to take instructions from me. As for the cook, the menu she is proposing is frugal. It is barely fit for peasants. There is no fish course. Now she is threatening to leave . . .'

'What! Surely you have not upset Mrs Bell?' Marie hurried towards the kitchen. Her heart pounding. Mark's mother followed protesting angrily about needing her room. Marie ignored her and went through to the kitchen. She saw Mrs Bell was upset and near to tears.

'That woman says she's Mr Blackford's mother and she is in charge from now on. She says the food I'm preparing is only fit for peasants.' Marie put an arm around the plump little woman's shoulders, reassuring her that the menu had Mark's complete approval. She turned back to face Mrs Blackford struggling to control her temper.

'Mark insisted the menu must not be formal or excessively elaborate. He makes no secret of the fact that he is relying on the tenants paying their rents tonight before he can pay for this meal. He doesn't want to give the impression he can afford to live off the fat of the land when the estate is badly in need of repairs. He cannot afford such luxury himself. The food will be good quality, well cooked and more than adequate. Mrs Bell's reputation is renowned. She cooks for Lord Tannahill's guests at Stavondale Tower but no doubt they pay him well to attend the shooting and eat the best dishes available. I must ask you to leave the kitchen and not interfere.'

'Leave the kitchen? Do you know who I am girl?'

'Oh yes! We met on your last visit. Mark would have warned me if he had expected you. Please take a seat in the drawing room. I will try to find him.' She turned to Mrs Bell. 'Please go ahead as we planned,' she said firmly. 'I must get home to change now if I'm to be back in time to help Mark greet his guests and act as his hostess.'

'Hostess? My son cannot have a mere maid acting as hostess!' Mrs Blackford glared indignantly. 'I shall be his hostess this evening.'

'I see. Then you must consult Mark about that.' Marie said abruptly. Her stomach was churning with nerves and anger. She went outside, untied Duke and jumped on his back.

She met Mark on his way back to the house. He was talking to Rupert Shearman and it was clear something was wrong. She drew Duke to a halt but she didn't dismount. Mark saw the colour in her cheeks and the fire in her blue eyes and guessed she had met his mother.

'Honestly Mark, I'm truly sorry,' Rupert was saying. 'It never occurred to me your father would give our conversation a thought, even less that your mother would come all the way to Scotland. I thought she said she had washed her hands of you?'

'She did, but if she can criticise anything I do, she does, as you should know.' He turned to Marie. 'I can see from your expression that she is already meddling. God knows where my father is but he will have to get her away.'

'You had better go and tell her that before she stirs up any more trouble,' Marie said. 'She told Mrs Bell the menu is only fit for peasants. She was ready to leave.'

'Oh no!' Rupert gasped, then groaned aloud.

'I think I have smoothed things over for now.' Marie said, 'but your mother is demanding rooms to be prepared.'

'She can't stay! Especially not tonight . . .'

'Then you will have to tell her, Mark. I shall not be returning. She has decided a mere maid is not suitable so she will be your hostess . . .' Before she had finished speaking Mark seized her in his arms and lifted her from Duke.

'You must be here! I want you here. We have planned the tenants' dinner together and I can't hold it without you to help me, Marie. Rupert, this is the girl I intend to marry as soon as I can persuade her to say yes, and let me ask her parents' permission.' There was both anger and pleading in his grey eyes. What lovely thick sooty eyelashes he has, Marie though irrelevantly.

'I can't act as hostess with your mother in the company, Mark. If you insist I will return after the dinner to help you to deal with the tenants in the office.' Mark pulled her closer. She could feel his heart beating and she knew he was as upset as she was.

'There will be no dinner if you're not here as my hostess,' Mark said stubbornly. He turned to Rupert. 'Marie is more important to me than all my family put together. Do you understand that?'

'I'm beginning to,' Rupert said. 'I've never seen you so dynamic in all the years we've known each other.'

'Then you must get my mother out of the house. She must stay somewhere else.'

'There's plenty of rooms in the shooting lodge but I can't do anything until my uncle and your father return. They have gone for a walk over the hills.'

'They may be away ages then.'

'I know, but I promise you, my friend, I will get your mother away from the manor before your guests appear.' He turned to Marie, still held firmly within the circle of Mark's strong young arm. 'You must return. You have to be Mark's hostess or he will never forgive me. You will end a beautiful friendship.' Although she knew he was serious Marie wanted to laugh at the way his black eyebrows seemed to dance up and down in a comical fashion. She turned to Mark uncertainly.

'Maybe your mother would add a more dignified presence and impress the tenants.'

'She would probably call them all peasants,' Mark said darkly. 'You don't know how condescending and insulting my mother can be, even to me, and I'm supposed to be her own flesh and blood,' he added bitterly. 'I want the tenants to be at ease and see that I'm human too. I have a living to make. I need their cooperation.'

Marie chewed her lip. 'You're sure?'

'I am certain. Rupert must get her out of the house before any of the tenants arrive.'

'Then I must hurry or I shall never be ready in time.' Mark smiled his relief. He kissed her firmly on her mouth before he lifted her onto Duke's back. Over his shoulder she saw Rupert's surprise.

'You really do love her don't you, Mark?' she heard him say before she urged Duke to a canter.

'I do,' Mark said, 'but my mother can be poisonous. You must get her out of my house, even if I never see her again.'

Rupert nodded realising Mark was deadly serious. Mrs Blackford had never struck him as motherly or loving towards Mark. It would be wonderful if his old friend found a wife who really loved him as he deserved and Miss Marie Sinclair certainly seemed a sincere young woman. He already knew how intelligent and capable she was because Mark's letters had been full of praise for her. He should have guessed how things were, but there would be difficulties with Mark's family. His brothers were already climbing the social ladder and they were as arrogant as their mother. They would never acknowledge the daughter of a farm tenant as their sister-in-law, however lovely, intelligent and kind she might be, no matter how much Mark loved her.

It did not occur to him that Marie's family might have objections of their own, especially her father. William Sinclair remembered the Stavondale Estate as it had been in his youth, twice the size it was now, and prosperous. However greatly reduced, Mark was still a landowner and from a different class of people to his with his fine education. It was clear from their letters that Maggie and Joe believed the young laird of Stavondale was in love with Marie. William had liked Mark Blackford when he first came to Moorend with Bob Rowbottom. If Lord Hanley did offer him and his sons the chance to farm Mountcliff, it would be partly due to Mark Blackford's influence. All the more reason why he could not imagine a daughter of his being the wife of a local laird, acting as lady of the manor and sitting in the laird's pew in the village church. How long would it last before Mark and his family felt ashamed of Marie? He could not visualise a lifetime of happiness ahead with such a marriage. He didn't want Marie to marry the first man who asked her, and then regret it. Marie was like him, she thrived on challenge. All his children had been brought up to work hard. Had he known William's views Rupert Shearman would have regarded them as inverted snobbery, and as negative as Sybil Blackford's pretensions and self-importance.

Before she knew Joe and Maggie suspected Mark Blackford was in love with her daughter, Emma had taken a liking to him. He was well mannered and polite but he never pretended to be a gentleman or better than other men. He drank tea and ate scones at their kitchen table with the same enjoyment as her own sons. Bob Rowbottom and his wife had also been pleasantly surprised by Mark's attitude to life, to his ability to work hard, and to his acceptance of people for themselves and not for their influence or wealth. They considered him a thoroughly pleasant, down to earth, genuine young man.

Consequently Emma disagreed with her husband regarding Marie's ability to make her own choice when it came to friendships, and even to marriage.

'Marie may not be eighteen yet but she is already older than I was when we were married,' Emma told William sharply. 'She is not a silly, flighty child. She loves children and most women find enough challenge, and satisfaction, in rearing a happy, healthy family and helping their husbands make a success. In our case we have worked hard to bring prosperity to Moorend. According to Maggie's letters, Stavondale Estate is greatly reduced, run down and neglected, and Mark has no capital to improve it. He has his own problems to overcome, even if they are different to ours. He told us he was depending on Marie to look after the estate's affairs while he was down here learning from Lord Hanley. I am telling you now, William, I shall not oppose their marriage so long as I am sure it is what Marie wants, and that Mark can make her happy.'

'It hasna come to that yet,' William reminded her. 'The laddie hasna mentioned marriage so put it out of your mind. Don't encourage Marie to have foolish dreams beyond her station. And remember he owns a fine big Manor House so he's far from destitute.' Emma pursed her lips and didn't reply but William knew his Emma well enough to realise she would make up her own mind and neither of them wanted Marie to live as far away as Scotland.

* * *

Marie's encounter with Mrs Blackford had severely shaken her confidence about the tenants' dinner and the evening ahead. Had she been wrong to agree to be Mark's hostess? She did her best to calm her nerves. Rina and Aunt Maggie tried to reassure her. One thing was certain she would do her best to make sure Mark had no reason to be ashamed of her. The dress her mother had made was in one of the newer styles with the hemline around mid-calf. The green velvet suited her pale auburn hair and fair complexion and there was a short fitted jacket to match with a nipped in waist. Aunt Maggie had helped her pin her mass of freshly washed curls on top of her head except for one on each side of her face which Rina thought softened the effect. It made her look and feel elegant. She had new shiny black shoes with a small heel, something she had never worn before. She truly appreciated Lord Hanley's generosity in giving her his wife's jewellery when Rina helped her choose the necklace of green emeralds, like a string of small gold flowers with sparling green emeralds in the centre. There were earrings and a bracelet to match.

'I hadn't realised they were real emeralds, Marie,' Rina said in admiration. 'You look beautiful, and you can hold your head high, even if the king and queen are in attendance.'

'I hope Mark agrees,' she said uncertainly.

'Of course he will. His mother sounds a — a bitch.' She stifled a giggle. 'Some of the girls at school used that word when we had a nasty teacher. I'm really looking forward to joining you all later and showing off my little family. It was kind of Mark to include Jamie and me.' Jamie was not so sure. He felt he had no right to be there but, as Uncle Jim said, they had been tenants until not so long ago and his two uncles and Cousin Billy would be there.

The November day had been surprisingly mild for the time of year but the custom of changing the clocks by one hour, which had begun in Germany in April 1916, had been adopted in Britain. It seemed to make the days of November and December incredibly short. As darkness fell there was an added chill, so Marie slipped her winter coat around her shoulders as she climbed into Uncle Joe's car. They arrived in good time but Mark was already dressed in a dark suit with a white shirt and a tie. He was waiting for her in the hall. He took her coat as she slipped it from her shoulders. He looked stunned as he gazed at her.

'You're so beautiful, Marie,' he breathed. He couldn't resist lowering his head to kiss her soft lips, before he whispered, 'Mother is still here but Lord Tannahill and father are back from their walk and Rupert called in to say they are arranging rooms in the East Tower and will collect her shortly. He had no sooner finished whispering than Mrs Blackford appeared at the door to the drawing room. Her annoyance was obvious. Her mouth was tight. She saw no reason why she couldn't stay here and dine with her son's guests.

'I heard voices. Is Lord Tannahill here yet . . . ?' She stopped short. As she took in Marie's appearance her eyes widened. Angry colour suffused her cheeks. 'So this is your hostess for the evening, dressed in the latest fashion too. I have no doubt she persuaded you to buy it for her.' Marie gasped at her effrontery, but Sybil Blackford stepped closer, her eyes narrowing as they fixed on the emerald necklace, then her ear rings. 'Are those emeralds, Mark? You must be out of your mind to spend so much money on this — this chit of a maid. Then you claim you have no money to provide a decent meal! The girl has wrapped you around her little finger. She'll bleed you dry. Can't you see she is taking advantage?'

Mark stared at his mother. For a moment he was speechless. He saw Marie's eyes mist with tears at the mention of her necklace and her hand now lay at her throat.

'How dare you suggest . . .' Fury drained the colour from his face and Marie laid a hand on his arm and shook her head. She blinked rapidly and met Mrs Blackford's cold stare, her blue eyes honest and proud.

'The lady who owned these jewels was a *real* lady, in every sense of the word. It grieves me that she is no longer here to wear them herself.' Her voice was low but it held a thread of steel. Her words were enunciated with such clarity no one could fail to hear the scorn, or grasp her meaning that Mrs Blackford was no lady. She was a spiteful, embittered woman with twin flags of angry colour in her withering cheeks.

Mark placed a protective arm around Marie's shoulders and confronted his mother. The rage in his eyes made her step back a pace. 'Your insults are contemptible. You come to my home uninvited, you criticise our arrangements, and you stir up trouble with the cook. I will tell you now, Marie and her family, have too much pride to allow me to buy her clothes or anything else. You are insulting the girl I intend to marry.

'The girl you . . . You want to marry a — a dairy maid?' Mrs Blackford repeated incredulously. Mark squeezed Marie's shoulder and looked down at her tenderly.

'Marie Sinclair is the only girl I shall ever want for my wife. I intend to marry her if, and when, I can persuade her to agree.' None of them had heard the approach of Lord Tannahill and Mr Blackford. They had listened in astonished silence. Neither of the men could believe the malicious invective Sybil Blackford had uttered, neither had they ever heard Mark speak with so much authority and pride. He had addressed the woman he believed to be his mother with ruthless candour, but both knew she deserved his contempt for her interference and her demeaning innuendoes. The girl had a dignity and pride all her own, but it was clear she also had character, and possibly a temper she was striving to control. It was time to make their presence known and get Sybil away before the guests arrived.

'We have heard enough, Sybil,' Mr Blackford said sternly. 'It is time we left.'

'I'm sure the evening will be a success,' Lord Tannahill said calmly. 'You both deserve it from what I hear in the district. Now forget this confrontation and enjoy yourselves then your guests will too.'

'You can't possibly condone Mark dressing up one of his maids to act as hostess!'

'Miss Sinclair is not a maid and she will make the perfect hostess for Mark and put the tenants at ease. This is a new idea to them.' Lord Tannahill's face was grim, his tone sharp. He clenched his jaw, then made up his mind. 'Mark, before your parents leave tomorrow, there are things you need to know. I'm beginning to suspect even you are a little in the dark, Douglas, at least over some aspects.' He looked keenly at his old friend. 'It is time you and Mark learned the truth Sybil has been at pains to hide.'

'No!' Sybil Blackford literally screeched. She rushed at Lord Tannahill and jerked his sleeve. 'Our family has nothing to do with you.'

'I rather think it has, and when I hear the way you speak to Mark I realise he should have been told the truth long ago, but I only learned of it recently myself.'

‘Your grandfather! I thanked God when I heard he was dead. He was a senile old man. You can’t believe anything he told you!’

‘I can, and I do, Sybil. It is true he was ninety-eight, but he was far from senile. I hear a pony and trap. Your guests are arriving Mark. Enjoy the evening both of you.’

‘Well!’ Mark exclaimed. ‘What was all that about, I wonder?’

CHAPTER THIRTEEN

We had better be prepared to welcome people in,' Marie said. 'I will call Victor with his tray of drinks. Rina says he knows most of the tenants. His father was the gardener at Stavondale Tower, still is I think, but for Lord Tannahill now. Victor used to fill in as a footman when her mother was trying to impress people.'

She made time to have a reassuring word with Mrs Bell in the kitchen and inform her that Mrs Blackford had left and would not be returning tonight.'

'Thank the Lord for that! How can a nice young man like Mr Mark have such a nasty woman for a mother? Everything is ready now though, Miss Sinclair.'

'Thank you.' Marie smiled warmly. 'It looks and smells wonderful.' Mrs Bell relaxed.

* * *

The evening went remarkably well and neither Mark nor Marie had time to mull over the earlier encounter. Everyone seemed to enjoy the good food and the conversation. When Rina and Jamie arrived with their little family the women were delighted, as were the older men who remembered Rina as a child. They crowded into the drawing room, all wanting to greet Marguerite, who clung shyly to her daddy, or to hold one of the twins.

'What are their names?' Mrs Massie asked, rocking one of the babies on her lap.

'He is Reginald, after my grandfather, but we call him Reggie. Mrs Hardie is holding William but I fear he is going to end up as Liam, at least that is what Marguerite calls him and we are beginning to use that name too.'

Marie accompanied Mark into the farm office and one by one the tenants came in to settle up their rents. Some thanked Mark for doing their roof repairs and he asked all the tenants what each one considered the most outstanding repairs for them. Marie made a note of each farm and the tenant's requests. Two of them, whose rents were overdue for the past year, were sincerely apologetic but they had brought what they could spare. In both cases they paid a six-monthly term in full plus two and three months into the present term.

There was only one sour note of the evening. Mr Lorrimer had not brought his wife but he had brought his son in her place, without asking anyone's approval. Both were loud at the table, demanding additional helpings of meat or the delicious desserts. Marie had overheard Mrs Fletcher telling Aunt Evelyn that Jenny Lorrimer had been looking forward to spending an evening out with the other tenants' wives. Apparently she had known most of them when she was a girl. Lorrimer had made the excuse that she was unwell but Mrs Fletcher said he had beaten her so badly she had lost two teeth and had a black eye.

The Lorrimers were on their way towards the front door, avoiding the farm office, but Victor had a sharp eye on them. He had already refused both of them more drinks.

'It's this way gentlemen,' he said politely, but firmly. He shepherded them through the door into the farm office. When Marie saw both of the Lorrimers coming in, she tensed, remembering how belligerent and boorish Fred Lorrimer had been at the dance. She went into the hall to get an extra chair but she took the precaution of asking Victor to hover near this end of the long hallway. If he heard raised voices or sounds of trouble, he should enter immediately, using any excuse if it proved a false alarm.

'They've both had quite a lot to drink,' Victor said anxiously. 'They meant to get away without seeing Mr Blackford.'

'Call my brother Jamie if you think we need help,' Marie advised quietly and disappeared back into the office to take her place beside Mark again.

'Now Miss Sinclair, do you have the records for Mr Bert Lorrimer please?'

'Yes, here they are.' Marie selected a white card from the appropriate drawer. It was neatly laid out with the Lorrimers' name and address at the top but there were no entries of rent paid. 'Rent has not been paid for seven terms, or three and a half years, including the term finishing now.' She gave the total of rent in arrears.

'What the hell does she know about it? I don't owe that. Ye've only been the laird for five minutes,' Mr Lorrimer snarled. His son sniggered mockingly at Marie, but she and Mark had discussed how they would proceed formally with the Lorrimers.

'Mr Lorrimer the estate was purchased as it stood, including debtors and creditors. The creditors were few, mainly tradesmen who had not been paid for repairs. You are by far the largest debtor. As your new landlord I insist you pay the arrears for rent due to the estate, plus the rent for the term which is finishing now — the twenty-eighth of November.'

'Like hell I will,' Bert Lorrimer growled.

'Repairs?' Fred sneered. 'What're they? You've not done any, and neither did the bugger who owned Stavondale before ye.'

'Fred's right! We've had no repairs at Southhill. So, m'lord, ye get no rent,' Bert mocked and got to his feet to leave, a triumphant grin on his broad face.

'No rent, no land to farm,' Mark stated coldly. He stood up too, looking down on Bert Lorrimer. His lean jaw was clenched with determination. Marie felt a glow of pride to see his resolve. She knew how much they had both dreaded the prospect of dealing with the Lorrimers. Fred stood up too, sending his chair crashing to the floor.

'Ye canna take our land!' he bawled. 'Ye canna put us off our farm! We'd hae no hoose and no place tae keep oor stock.'

'You should have considered that when you whined about repairs yet did nothing to help yourselves. The solution is simple,' Mark leaned down to pick up his fountain pen and leisurely screwed on the end with an air of finality. 'You pay the rent you owe, all of it, or you move out of Southhill by the end of the year.'

'End of the bloody year!' Bert Laurimer yelled. 'That's only a month away. We canna do that!'

'The solution is in your hands. The notice to quit will be delivered to you by the first day of December unless you have paid what you owe. You must be out of Southhill by the end of that month. You are a bad influence on the rest of the tenants, bragging about not paying any rent. They will see where your cunning has landed you.'

'You canna dae this, not to us Lorrimers!' Fred shouted furiously. Pushing his father out of the way he seized Mark by his lapels. The door opened to admit Victor with both Billy and Jamie Sinclair behind him. They were in time to see Mark deliver a robust right hook to Fred Lorrimer's chest, swiftly followed by a left punch to his jaw. Marie stared in surprise. She had no idea Mark had practised fencing and boxing, amongst other sports while he and Rupert were at boarding school, and later at Oxford. Fred reeled like a deflated balloon. He would have fallen to the floor had his father not caught him.

'We heard angry shouts,' Victor said, 'but it seems you don't need any help, Mr Blackford.'

'Thank you, Victor,' Mark said calmly. 'Show these 'gentlemen' out, will you?'

When the door closed behind them Mark flopped back into his chair and gave Marie a sheepish grin. 'I didn't expect to come to blows with any of my tenants,' he apologised.

'I'm proud of you, Mark. Proud and astonished. You don't look like a boxer though.'

'I'm not really. My greatest asset was always being nimble on my feet so I avoided many of the blows, but Fred Lorrimer took me unawares. I couldn't let him get away with it.'

'I'm glad you didn't. Fred Lorrimer is a bully. They both are, but I feel sorry for Mrs Lorrimer. I heard a rumour tonight that she is going to stay with her brother up north. Mrs Massie says she's had enough. I think East Lowrie and the whole district will be better without the Lorrimers.'

'We shall have to do some repairs to Southhill but I hope we shall be able to get another tenant to take it on.'

'I don't think there'll be any difficulty if Uncle Jim is right.'

* * *

It was only when she lay in bed later that evening that Marie remembered about the confrontation between Lord Tannahill and Mrs Blackford. She didn't know either of them well but she had never seen his lordship look so grim and resolute. She wondered what he had to tell Mark. Her thoughts wandered back to the evening, especially the end. Jamie and Billy had been full of praise at the way Mark had dealt with Fred Lorrimer. He had earned the respect of all the young men in the area by the end of the week.

Mark had not forgotten Lord Tannahill had something to tell him but he was puzzled and his mind was more taken up with the way the evening had gone. He was impressed with the efficient way Marie had kept a record of everything, even tallying up the rents as they came in. Only the five larger tenants had paid by cheque. The rest had paid in cash. At the end of the evening they were able to set aside enough cash to pay Mr Thomas for the roof repairs. Marie had put it in a thick brown envelope and written his name on it. The remaining cash, which was not a great amount, she had put into his strong box, and handed him the key for safe keeping. They were both satisfied with the way the proceedings had gone. He had tried to pay her for all her help during his absence in Yorkshire and since his return, but she shook her head.

'I haven't done all that much, and to be honest I have enjoyed having something to occupy my brain as well as keeping house for Jamie and Uncle Jim and looking after Marguerite. I can't decide what I want to do when I go home after Christmas. I don't think I want to train as a nurse.'

'Oh, Marie, I know what I want you to do, even if it is selfish of me to ask you to be my wife when there's so little money to call our own, at least until I can get the estate back into good order. We get on so well together and I love you more than anything in the world.'

'Your mother would never accept me as your wife, Mark and I really don't want to cause a rift between you and your family.'

'There is no contest, Marie. I want to spend the rest of my life with you. I have already grown away from my family. I never was that close. I spent most of my holidays with Rupert and his family you know, either at his own home or very often with his uncle, especially after his wife died and Sylvie was a baby. Rupert's mother spent a lot of time there, making sure Sylvia was properly cared for. Now the rascal spends her time riding her pony and accompanying her father, or so Rupert says. Mother never once invited him to stay with us, even if he had wanted to. He thinks my brothers are arrogant. Father isn't like that.'

Mark wandered downstairs and glanced in the rooms which had looked so good yesterday evening with candles and flowers and all the people eating and talking and enjoying themselves. Now the house echoed with emptiness and he made his way to the kitchen to make himself a pot of tea and a slice of toast. Even here it didn't feel like a home, warm and welcoming and lived in. No wonder Rina had preferred to stay with Mr and Mrs Greig. When he had finished he went into the office and slipped the envelope for Mr Thomas into his pocket. On the spur of the moment he decided he would ride on to Strathlinn and take the cheques to the bank. He might be able to buy himself some breakfast there too. He brought Bali in from the paddock which Lord Tannahill had given him permission to use. He was riding past the turning into the Stavondale Tower when he saw Rupert already mounted and ready for a morning ride.

'Where are you off to, Mark?' he called cheerily. 'I thought Uncle Fordyce said he was having a meeting with you and your parents this morning?'

'We are but Mother will not be up for hours yet.' He grimaced. 'Have you any idea what it's about?'

'No. He didn't say but he looked very grim last night. So where are you going? Shall I ride along with you?'

'You can come if you like. I'm going to pay off my debt to Mr Thomas, the roofer, then I'm riding into Strathlinn to get the rest of my money in the bank. It will be good to be solvent again.' He grinned. 'Not that it will last for long with more repairs needing done.'

'Things do seem to be in a poor state.' Rupert agreed. 'I'm a bit surprised at Uncle Fordyce encouraging your father to buy the remaining Stavondale farms. He must have known how dilapidated things are.'

'I expect that's why my father could afford it. I suppose I'm lucky to get any kind of settlement — being the youngest of three sons, especially when I displeased Mother by refusing to consider either of the two wealthy simpering misses she had selected for me.'

'We haven't seen so much of each other since you moved to Scotland and I've been busy learning all the things I'm supposed to know before I take over the family estate.' They cantered along chatting pleasantly. Mr Thomas was surprised, but pleased to see them.

'I heard ye were holding a dinner for your tenants yesterday evening,' he said. 'Didn't expect ye'd be parting wi' the money so soon though, did I?'

'You have been patient to wait so long, Mr Thomas and you made a good job.'

'A few more roofs there are needing done, but Miss Sinclair said I was not to go near the Lorrimers at Southhill. Telling you the truth now, it's glad I was about that. Difficult man he is. That lad o' his will be worse in a few years' time. Nasty with it they are. I wouldn't work there on my own. Another man I'd be taking with me. Couldn't trust him not to do me an injury see.'

'I understand, Mr Thomas.' Mark said. He sighed. 'I expect the village grapevine will be singing loud enough before long so you will hear the Lorrimers are moving on to plague some other landlord, if they can get anyone to take them.'

'Is that so?' Mr Thomas whistled. 'Well, I can't say as I'd be sorry, except for Jenny. Too good for him she was. 'Tis said he caught her one night on her own. The next thing they were getting married and a bairn on the way.'

'We'd better get on,' Mark said. 'I will let you know when I can give you more work but I need a builder and a joiner first.'

'Aye well you be telling your little Miss Sinclair to write me a list when you're ready. Efficient she is, and clear about what's needing done. She promised you would pay me as soon as you could, and here you are!'

'Seems your Miss Sinclair is popular with everybody,' Rupert remarked, as they rode away. 'My father said she looked really beautiful last night and every inch a lady.' Mark's fair skin coloured but he was pleased Lord Tannahill approved of Marie.

They finished their business at the bank and then persuaded the landlord of the Crown and Feathers to serve them with a substantial breakfast of bacon, eggs, sausages and potato scones and a good pot of strong tea. Hunger satisfied, and with their horses rested a little, the two friends cantered back to Stavondale in high spirits, never dreaming of the news they were about to hear.

As Rupert and Mark approached Stavondale Tower they saw Lord Tannahill talking to Sylvia who was sitting astride her pony in neat little breeches and a smart jacket.

'Ah Rupert, just the man I need. Can you take Sylvia for a canter around the grounds? I need to have a talk with Mrs Blackford before she leaves. Are you ready Mark?'

'Can't I come too?' Rupert asked. 'If it's anything bad Mark might need my support.'

'No, this is between Mark and his family. He will tell you later if he wants you to know.' Both young men caught the stern inflection in his voice.

Mark was surprised to see his mother looking less haughty and assured than usual. Her face seemed pale in spite of the amount of rouge she had used, but Mark knew his father loved her whatever her faults. Sometimes he had felt disloyal and considered his father weak for not standing up to her, but now that he loved Marie he knew he would defend her with his life if needed, but he couldn't imagine her being mean or perverse like his mother. He couldn't remember her ever being gentle and loving, at least not with him, not the way Marie was with Marguerite and the twins.

'Good morning, Sybil.' Lord Tannahill's tone was cool. 'We shall go into the room I use as an office when I have shooting parties here, then we shall not be disturbed.' They followed him into a pleasant room with comfortable leather chairs and a whole wall lined with books. Mark shuddered. He was glad there were no guns or pistols decorating the walls. As long as he lived he would never forget the day he had pulled a trigger and seen a man dying in front of his eyes. That had really shaken his self-confidence.

'Would you like to tell Mark the truth about his family, or shall I?'

'I reared him as a son, ungrateful wretch that he is.'

'Very well.' Lord Tannahill looked at Mark. 'This news came as a shock to me so I understand it may be a greater shock to you, but it pleases me more than ever to know you and Rupert have always been good friends. I have always enjoyed, and encouraged, your visits to my home, Mark, because I admired your firm character and integrity. Believe me, I had no idea then you were connected to my own family.' Mark stared in bewilderment. 'I didn't know until my grandfather sent for me and told me your story before he died.'

'He was a senile old man,' Sybil Blackford hissed. 'You can't believe a word.'

'I didn't at first. He often visited me when Rupert and Mark were home from Oxford. He enjoyed their company. So I thought he had become confused. However he insisted I must consult the legal firm who had acted for him. Reluctantly they supplied proof of every transaction from the day Mark was born.'

'I don't understand what you're talking about,' Mark said as the remaining colour drained from Sybil Blackford's face.'

'Is this really necessary?' Douglas asked, taking his wife's hand in his.

'Yes, it is,' Lord Tannahill declared, 'because Sybil has not been honest with you either, Douglas. A large portion of the money which my grandfather settled on Mark has been used by Sybil for the benefit of herself and her own two sons.'

'Surely not!' Douglas Blackford said, looking at his wife. She did not meet his eyes.

'It is true.' Lord Tannahill's voice was grim. 'At Sir Roger's funeral I realised from our conversation that you were unaware of the full settlement on Mark. I had examined the figures and I found there was barely half of the original settlement left. I knew estate management was not Mark's first choice of occupation, especially one as run down as Stavondale, but I realised the money needed to be invested without delay, and in something your wife could not touch. You attended the funeral without her, so I took the opportunity to urge you to buy land — that is the remaining Stavondale Estate plus the Manor House, in Mark's name using the money that was left from my grandfather's settlement.' He turned to look at Mark. 'I know the farms have been badly neglected but land holds its value over time. It will be a challenge but if you can improve things, you may be able to sell at a decent profit and do as you wish with your life. I fear you would have been left without anything unless you married a wealthy wife, as Sybil hoped.'

'It was his duty to do as I asked, but he was always stubborn. He was barely polite to either of the girls I chose for him,' Sybil snapped. She looked sullen.

'I don't understand.' Mark was confused and impatient. Lord Tannahill nodded.

'Your natural mother was Sybil's cousin. Your father was my uncle, my grandfather's youngest son by some years, which meant he was only a few years older than myself,' Lord Tannahill said. 'Grandfather admitted he had been spoiled and was rather wild. He and your mother planned to marry, but a month before the wedding he was thrown from his horse and broke his neck. It became clear the girl, Doreen Whiteley, was expecting his child. Grandfather set her up in a pretty cottage in a village a few miles away. He made sure it was legally hers, in her own name.' He glanced at Sybil Blackford's set expression and tight lips. 'He promised he would settle some money on her and the child when it was born. As the birth drew nearer Doreen yearned for someone of her own for company. She was grieving and frightened. She and Sybil had been close as children so Sybil went to stay with her to make sure Doreen got a fair settlement. Apparently you were expecting your third child Sybil, and pleased to leave two boisterous boys in the care of their nanny.' He met Sybil's cold eyes, but he went on. 'Doreen had a long and difficult labour, according to the midwife, whom I have traced and spoken with . . .' Sybil Blackford gasped.

'She was an interfering busybody,' she muttered.

'Doreen had lost a lot of blood. She was very weak and she knew she was dying. She begged Sybil to take care of her baby. Sybil didn't believe the midwife's opinion that Doreen was dying so she promised to care for her baby as her own.'

Sybil Blackford snorted in a most unladylike fashion but Mark was listening incredulously.

'Two weeks later her own baby was born, a month early, a little girl. The midwife seemed genuinely sorry that you lost her.'

'So she should be sorry. She was no help!' Sybil snapped.

'Anyway Mark, when my grandfather learned what had happened he visited the cottage and made an agreement. Sybil would bring you up as her own child and he would pay for your keep and for your education — which is probably the reason you were sent to boarding school while you were so young,' he added drily. 'He also paid your fees when you went to Oxford.'

'I didn't know that,' Douglas Blackford mused. 'I thought we paid.' He frowned wondering where his money had gone if not for Mark's education. He sensed his wife's anger and remained silent, at least until they were alone.

'I wish I had known someone else was paying,' Mark said. He looked at Sybil. 'You were always telling me I was a burden, although I was never as extravagant as my brothers. Now I know why you were always so happy for me to stay with Rupert's family . . .'

'You're causing trouble in my family!' Sybil Blackford glared balefully.

'I'm not finished yet. Mark and Douglas need to hear the rest. My grandfather settled a considerable sum of money on Mark to be given to him when he reached twenty-one to set him up in whatever life he decided to pursue, whether that be in a legal profession, a career in the army, as a landowner or whatever other interests he developed. I was unaware of any of this until last year. Grandfather had had his suspicions for some time and he decided it was time someone else should be made aware of the provisions he had made.'

'He would have squandered every penny trying to manufacture motorcars. That's all he thought about. His hands and clothes were always black with grease,' Sybil snapped.

'It was only when Douglas came up here on his own for Sir Roger Capel's funeral that I realised how little he knew about Mark's background and finances. Grandfather expected you would be as trustworthy as himself. He had made his solicitor and you, Sybil, as the trustees. You did exactly as you wished with the lawyer.' There was no doubting his anger. He turned to Mark. 'There is nothing we can do about it now, but that is the reason you have ended up with a dilapidated estate. I hope you agree it is better than nothing, which is what would have happened before long. I believe you will grasp the challenge to improve Stavondale, especially as you seem to have chosen a very capable young woman to help you.' Sybil sniffed angrily. Lord Tannahill ignored her. 'I hope you will be able to embark on whatever business holds your interest one day, Mark. I suspect that may have something to do with engines and motorcars. You have always been interested in that sort of thing. I'm only sorry I didn't know the truth earlier. Now I think we must take our leave and find Rupert. I believe you plan to leave soon, Douglas?'

'Yes, yes we do.' Douglas Blackford seemed stunned. His wife looked mutinous.

Mark followed Lord Tannahill to the door but then he turned and shook hands with the man he had believed to be his father.

'I know you always treated me as a son. I thank you for that,' he said quietly. He held out his hand to Sybil Blackford but she stood erect, fists clenched at her side.

'Get out of my sight,' she snarled. 'You've got more than you deserve.' Mark raised his eyebrows, nodded and headed for the door.

'I hope you are not too upset by all these revelations, Mark,' Lord Tannahill said sadly. 'I wish I had known the truth a long time ago. Apart from appropriating your birth right Sybil appears to have treated you badly if last night is an example. She was always affable in my company.'

'She can be charming,' Mark said drily. 'Thank you for all your kindness.'

'I'm sorry you've ended up with such a poor deal.'

'It is not so very bad,' Mark said with a smile. 'I like a challenge, as you know. Stavondale Estate is certainly that, but I'm learning how things should be done, and how to handle the tenants, since I spent time with Lord Hanley in Yorkshire. More importantly I would never have met Marie Sinclair if I had not had reason to come back up here. I have a feeling it will prove to be the most important occurrence in my life.'

'She is certainly lovely and I gather the local people like and respect her. Do you really love her, Mark?'

'I do. The problem will be persuading her father I can take care of her and make her happy. He will not be pleased if another of his family comes back to Scotland to live.'

'I see. I'm sure if Marie Sinclair loves you in return you will find a way.'

'I hope we can,' Mark said fervently. 'We had a really good evening with the tenants and most of them paid up. This morning the manor feels empty and forlorn.'

'I know what you mean, Mark.' Lord Tannahill nodded. 'That is the reason I have kept the east wing of Stavondale Tower as my home when I'm up here. Sir Reginald Capel found it a more homely place to live than the large west wing where Sir Roger lived. The shooting parties seem to enjoy staying there.'

'Would you think me ungrateful if I sold Stavondale Manor in the future?'

'Not at all, my boy. Douglas paid a good price for it but I wanted him to invest everything that remained of your inheritance. It was the only way to prevent Sybil getting her hands on any more. He is a good man but easily manipulated. Sybil knew that. I'm afraid I took advantage of him, but it was on your behalf. Will you come in and see Rupert now?'

'If you don't mind I would like some time to consider everything. I'm feeling a little bemused by today's discoveries. You can tell Rupert everything. It will save me explaining.'

Even before he reached the house Mark knew he wouldn't be able to settle. He felt dazed by the revelations.

He couldn't believe the man he had regarded as a kindly father was not even related to him. In a way he thought he understood a little of his proxy mother's bitter resentment. He had been no substitute for the girl child she had craved. She had given him a home and a name but she had done it for money, not for love, or with tenderness. He led Bali to the stable, unsaddled him, gave him a brisk brushing and left him with a scoop of oats. He patted his neck and murmured, 'You're having a busy day today old boy. We'll take a good gallop after lunch.' He longed to call on Marie and tell her of his astonishing discovery but she had given him most of her time the past few days and she was here to help Rina after all.

Mrs MacCrindle followed him into the house. She had seen him going to the stables from her kitchen window.

'I came to tell you there is plenty of food to satisfy a hungry man for two days at least. Mrs Bell put it in the pantry but I thought you might not think to look in there, Master Mark.' She beamed at him. 'I might as well heat the soup for you now I'm here. There's cock-a-leekie or cream of celery. Which would you like today? And there's plenty of meat left — venison, sirloin of beef or roast guinea fowl.'

'I think I will save the meat until tonight, thank you Mrs Mac. Is there any cheese?'

'Oh yes, and I've brought ye a newly baked loaf. There's fresh butter.'

'Then that is what I shall eat for now with the celery soup please. Was there any of Mrs Bell's delicious lemon pie left?' he asked with a boyish smile.

'There is, and some trifle. I told her you had a sweet tooth.'

'Then I shall have the trifle with my meal tonight.'

'All right. I'll warm the soup now then and set it in the wee room.'

'That's all right. I'll come through to the kitchen to eat. It's warmer and cosier there — more like I've always imagined a home ought to be. Help yourself to anything you fancy.'

'Ye're an easy man to please, Mr Mark. I'll come this evening and cook some fresh vegetables to go with the beef. Beautiful and tender it was. Everybody seemed to enjoy their meal. The whole evening went well. It was lovely to see Miss Catherina and her babies.'

'I suspect there was one pair who did not enjoy themselves.'

'Aah, ye mean the Lorrimers? Well they ate plenty, and drank more than was good for them.' Her face split into a big smile. 'Ye'll not have heard the latest gossip about them?'

'I don't think so.'

'Mr McGill heard it at the station when he was putting the milk on the train. Mrs Lorrimer has left Southhill. She had packed her things and waited until they were at the dinner, then she went to the station and caught a train. Rumour has it she has gone to live with her brother. He's a shepherd in Aberdeenshire. He lost his wife a year ago so maybe he'll be glad of her company.'

'It's a long way from Southhill to Strathlinn to catch the train, especially with a case.'

'McGill thinks she planned it after the latest beating. The porter told him she arrived in a pony and trap, with a big suitcase, a cardboard box tied with string and a pillowcase full o' stuff, as well as a basket. We have an idea who would drive her to the station, but Lorrimer would use his fists if he knew. It seems the village folk have warned Constable Wallams in case there's trouble. He hasna been at East Lowrie long so he doesna ken how vicious Lorrimer can be. Mr McGill was fair pleased to hear ye'd sent Fred Lorrimer home with a thick lip last night. He said all the farmers at the station this morning would have awarded ye a medal if they'd had one. They're delighted somebody has had the courage to stick up to that bully.'

'Is that so?' Mark grimaced. 'Maybe the rumours have not got around yet that I expect the Lorrimers to quit Southhill by the end of December?'

'Really? I don't think anybody's heard that, Mr Mark? Is it true?'

'I have told them to be out by then unless they pay all their rent arrears. I doubt if they will. It will let the other tenants see that Lorrimers bragging has not gained him anything.'

'Now that Jenny Lorrimer will be in a safe place, I'm glad Bert and his son are getting what they deserve. After last night, McGill says all the tenants are regarding ye with new respect. When they hear the latest they'll think ye've grown ten feet tall overnight.' Mark grinned. Mrs Mac smiled back at him with motherly pride.

When Mark had eaten, he moved restlessly into the office. He glanced through the cards where Marie had made notes of the repairs needed for each of his tenants. Three of the farms needed urgent building work before the joiner could begin his repairs, and with winter coming they must be done without delay. He decided to call on Mr Caldew, the builder who had premises on the outskirts of East Lowrie village. He would ask him to carry out the repairs as soon as possible now the estate could pay him for his work. Then he would have a word with Mr Gordon, the joiner and see whether they could come to a similar agreement to the one he had had with Mr Thomas. Lord Hanley had assured him most tradesmen were willing to come and go a little if it meant getting work over the longer term.

* * *

Later, after the satisfaction of a good gallop, he had reached an agreement with the builder. He had had an enlightening conversation with the joiner, and an understanding he would do repairs in stages. The day had been worthwhile so why did he feel as though a dark cloud was hanging over him.

He slowed his horse to a walk as he turned onto the track up to Bonnybrae. In his heart he knew he had occupied himself deliberately so that he need not dwell on Lord Tannahill's revelations. No one wants to feel as unloved and unwanted as his surrogate mother made him feel. Maybe part of her felt bound by her promise to a dying woman but he knew she had only cared about the money. He had to tell Marie the truth. What would she think when she knew he was an illegitimate orphan? He knew he should be grateful that Sybil and Douglas Blackford had given him a home and a name, whatever the reason. Would Marie see it that way or would she only see his real mother's shame? If she truly loved him would it make a difference? And what of her parents? They would have to be told the truth. Would they refuse to consider him as a son-in-law?

It was a solemn, distracted Mark who rode past Braeside and failed to see Maggie collecting her eggs, or notice Joe's car parked in the drive when it would normally be at his place of work. When he arrived at Bonnybrae Jamie and Jim were with the rest of the family in the kitchen having tea before starting the milking. They all welcomed him warmly and Jamie pulled out a chair for him while Rina brought another cup, saucer and plate.

'I heard you had a good evening, Mark,' Jim said with a grin, 'and dealt very efficiently with the Lorrimer bully boys.'

'I didn't have much option,' Mark said. 'He would have hit me again if I hadn't defended myself.'

'Even so I heard you were impressive,' Jim said. 'It was high time someone put them in their place. You have gone up in the estimation of the other tenants from what I heard at the station this morning — and not just for dealing with the Lorrimers. They all said they had enjoyed a splendid meal and good company.'

'Speaking of the station,' Marie said, 'I expect you would see Uncle Joe's car still at Braeside, Mark. He had to go to work on the train this morning. There is something wrong with the car.'

'I could take a look at it if you think he wouldn't mind,' Mark offered, biting into his scone and jam with relish in spite of his apprehension.

'I'm sure Joe would be grateful,' Jim said. 'None of us know anything about engines. That is if you have time. You seem . . . preoccupied. Are you worried, laddie?'

'No, no I-I'm fine,' Mark stammered. Gathering his wits he told Marie he had been to see the builder and the joiner. They had asked if she would make them a list of the jobs with their prices, as she had for Mr Thomas.

When Jim and Jamie went out to the milking Jim remarked, 'Did you notice the way Mark keeps Marie informed about his arrangements with Caldew and Mr Gordon? He discusses things as though it's her business as much as his. He'll miss her when she goes back to Yorkshire.'

'I know,' Jamie said slowly. 'Most of the tenants last night seemed to regard them as a couple. I still think of Marie as a young sister, but she looked stylish and competent with her hair up and in her smart new dress. They all say she is very efficient. It's a pity Mrs Blackford upset both the cook, and Marie. Rina says she sounds arrogant and haughty, like her own mother.'

'They could have trouble from both sets of parents then if they're serious about each other. I think they make a good couple but I don't suppose William and Emma will want another of their offspring settling in Scotland, any more than the Blackfords will consider a farmer's daughter a suitable match for their son.'

* * *

Mark held Bali's reins in one hand and reached for Marie's as they walked down to Braeside to look at Joe's car.

'I have things to tell you but I'll wait until we shall not be interrupted. You might not want to know me when I tell you what I've learned about my family today.'

'Oh Mark,' Marie squeezed his fingers. 'Is that why you look so anxious? Even Uncle Jim noticed. Things can't be that bad.'

'I'll tell you later,' he added as Maggie came to her gate.

'Mark's going to take a look at Uncle Joe's car,' Marie told her. 'If he can get it going we will go to meet him to try it out and save him the walk home. We'll leave in good time in case the car stops on the way.'

'You have that much faith in me? I may not get it going.' Mark knew Marie was trying to arrange time for them to talk, but he found himself wanting to put it off now he was with her. He didn't want to tell her he had been born out of wedlock, or that the woman he had believed to be his mother had been paid to take care of him. It made him feel as worthless as he had felt as a child when she had continually compared him with the boys he had believed were his brothers.

Marie talked to Aunt Maggie at the garden gate while he checked the oil filter and the plugs and various things which might be at fault. Eventually he swung the handle several times but the car didn't start. He adjusted something under the bonnet and swung the handle again. The engine fired and died. Marie pulled a face.

'Fingers crossed he'll be third time lucky, Aunt Maggie.'

'I pray so. Joe would miss his car badly now he's got used to the convenience of it.'

'We all would,' Marie said. 'He's so generous at giving us lifts and he will never take money for the petrol.'

'He's a kind man, Joe. I've been a lucky woman to have him for a husband. I hope you will be as blessed as I am, whatever your future holds. We had to wait a long time to be together, but it was worth it. Don't be too disappointed if your parents want you to wait a while before you marry, Marie. If you truly love each other everything will work out right.'

'You think my father will object to Mark?'

'I expect he'll think you're too young to commit yourself to the responsibility of a husband and family, even though it's what your parents did themselves.'

'Hey! We're going at last and she's ticking over sweetly,' Mark called triumphantly. It always gave him the greatest satisfaction to repair things, especially engines. He so rarely got the opportunity. 'I'll leave her going while I wash the oil off my hands then we'll see if she will go all the way to the station.'

'Is it safe to leave it?' Maggie asked anxiously. 'Will it drive itself into the fence?'

'No, it'll be fine. I've made sure the brake is on. If it stops I shall know it's still not right.' A few minutes later he was back, drying his hands on Maggie's kitchen towel and grinning when he heard the engine still running. 'Jump in Marie, and we'll see if she will keep going all the way to the station.'

'You'll be far too early. Joe will not be at the station until six o'clock,' Maggie said.

'It will give me time to adjust things again if she stops on the way there,' Mark said.

'We don't mind waiting if we're too early,' Marie grinned mischievously. Maggie smiled back, wagged her head and gave them a wave.

'I'll have a meal ready for when you get back,' she called.

'Thank you.' She turned to Mark. 'I promised to be back for Marguerite's bath time, but we should still have time to talk. Now tell me what Lord Tannahill said. I suppose it was bad news to make you look so uneasy, but if it means you have to sell the estate you can always become a mechanic. You said yourself the number of motorcars will grow, as well as engines to drive other things. Look how many trains there are all over the country now and nobody believed they would ever become popular.' She saw his wistful look.

'Tell me what's troubling you, Mark?' she said and laid a hand on his sleeve.

'I would like to ask you to promise that what I have to say will never come between us, but that would be unfair of me, unreasonable in fact . . .'

'I can't imagine anything Lord Tannahill could say would come between us. I don't care if you end up without any money. We'll work for our living as my parents have done all their lives.'

'My mother was a fallen woman,' he blurted.

'I don't understand.' Marie stared at him, tempted to laugh at the idea of Mrs Blackford doing anything which was socially unacceptable.

'The Blackfords are not my real parents,' he muttered. 'I'm an orphan. My mother died giving birth. She was not married.'

'I see.' Marie said, trying to take this in. 'So Mrs Blackford is not your real mother? If you ask me that's good news. At least it is to me. It means her spite and jealousy doesn't flow in your veins, so it wouldn't be in our children either . . .' she blushed bright pink. 'I –I mean if-if we do marry, and if we have children . . .'

'Oh Marie!' Mark placed one hand on her thigh for a moment, then he gave something between a sob and a chuckle. 'Trust you to see a completely different angle, and a brighter side to this lousy tangle. My real mother was Sybil Blackford's cousin. She knew she was dying and asked Sybil to promise she would look after me.'

'She kept her promise,' Marie said quietly, 'so she must have some good in her.'

'You think so?' Mark muttered bitterly. 'You would have looked after Marguerite, and loved her, and never asked anything in return, because you're that kind of sweet girl. *She* was paid to look after me. Apparently my father was an uncle of Lord Tannahill, the youngest in the family by several years. He and my mother intended to marry but he was killed before the wedding took place.'

'Lord Tannahill's uncle?' Marie frowned. 'That means you and he shared the same grandfather? How strange.'

'Yes, isn't it?' Mark still sounded bitter. 'Apparently he died last year, aged almost ninety-eight. I had met him several times when I spent holidays with Rupert. He always seemed to ask me a lot of questions, but in a kindly way.'

'I expect that's because he knew you were his grandson. You and Rupert have always been close friends, haven't you? Even without knowing there was a family connection.'

'Yes, we have, since we were eight years old. Lord Tannahill only learned the truth himself shortly before the old man died. He was only a few years younger than his uncle — my real father. He says my grandfather paid the Blackfords well to look after me and he paid for my education. It seems he had settled a sum of money on me to set me up in in life, whatever I decided to do. My — my mother had been using it for her own sons. That's what made Lord Tannahill tell me the truth. She thought I wouldn't need it if I married a wealthy wife, as she intended. She didn't think anyone else would know.'

'How awful!' Marie gasped and squeezed his arm in a gesture of comfort. For a moment his fingers clasped hers. She saw the hurt in his eyes.

'Grandfather must have guessed she was taking advantage of the solicitor so he confided in Lord Tannahill. He looked into things and realised what she had been doing. My father came to Scotland alone to support me at the funeral of Rina's father. I was still in shock and upset. He was always kind towards me. While he was up here Lord Tannahill took the opportunity to persuade him to invest what was left of my inheritance in land — that is Stavondale Estate and Stavondale Manor in my name. I can guess how furious Mother would be. She had not told my father that she had been using the money bit by bit.'

They were almost at Strathlinn so Mark drew to a halt on a quiet stretch of road.

'I can't believe anyone would want to be so unkind. You're such a fine man, Mark.'

'Even if I am someone else's bastard?' He muttered bitterly. 'I'm not the person I thought I was so I shall understand if . . .'

'Hush Mark! I'm not interested in your pedigree. You are kind and sincere. You're never greedy or jealous.'

'To tell the truth I'm not worried about who I am either. I was made to feel worthless and inferior to my so-called brothers. I can't regard them as my family now I know the truth.'

'I can understand that.'

'But the fact is my mother died unmarried and in shame. Other people might care about that.'

'It will not make any difference to the people who know you Mark. They will still be your friends.'

'Maybe you feel like that with your generous spirit, Marie, but what about your parents? What will they say if

I ask them for permission to marry their daughter, be the father of their grandchildren? I can't blame them if they put me out of their home and tell me never to come back.'

'I'm sure they would never do that! They will probably ask us to wait a while but that's because they think I am too young. Aunt Maggie thinks that, even though she approves of you. I know from Mother's letters that father has been worried history might repeat itself. Our grandmother wanted to marry the laird — Sir Reginald Capel. He was Aunt Maggie's father but he married someone else. I think he's afraid that might happen to me.'

'Never! I would never allow that to happen to you. I love you, Marie.'

'It troubled father terribly when Jamie and Rina wanted to marry because their families and backgrounds were so different. Now he sees how much they love each other so he has accepted it. Maybe he will feel the same about us if we give him time.'

'Things are different now. Lord Tannahill admits Stavondale Estate is not the best inheritance I might have had but he says land is a valuable asset because we can't manufacture more of it, and everybody needs it. I believe he's right about that and I'm sure we can improve things as time goes on if only we can be together. He says I may want to sell it when it is in a better state, then decide what I really want to do, but at least I shall have some capital of my own, even though it is not as much as his grandfather had intended. Since you and I have worked together, the estate has begun to hold more interest for me and I enjoy a challenge.

'I'm afraid my help, and my love, are all I can give you,' Marie said simply. 'My family are not wealthy. The boys always come first with Father and he has brought them up to want to be farmers.'

'Oh Marie,' Mark turned towards her and drew her into his arms. 'If I have your love, and if you will still be my wife, that is all I ask of life.' He kissed her then, a long lingering kiss, until he remembered they were supposed to be meeting the train.

* * *

Joe looked weary and dejected as he walked out of the station, but his face lit up when he saw them waiting for him with his car.

'I think she's going all right since I've cleaned the filter, Mr Greig. Do you want to drive?'

'No, no laddie. I am pleased to get a ride home. I don't know how to thank you.'

'There's no need to thank me. You know I enjoy messing about with engines.'

'You looked terribly tired and exhausted when you came out of the station, Uncle Joe,' Marie said with concern. 'Have you had a bad day?'

'You could say it's been a wearying day, lassie, and the thought of the three-mile walk at the end of it seemed too much. It never used to bother me. I must be getting to be an old man.'

'Of course you're not. I expect you've been working too hard.'

'Well we've had some trouble with one of the machines. It was not the weaving part. I'm usually able to put that right. This seemed to be the mechanics of it. To make matters worse, Mr Courton's car is giving him trouble too. It was stuttering the same as this one did, then it wouldn't start no matter how I swung the handle. He was going to drive into Glasgow to get a new set of cogs but in the end he had to phone the firm who makes the machines. They can't send anyone out for two days. That made both of us a bit short tempered. So you could say it's been a lousy day.'

'Can I ask where you buy your petrol?' Mark asked.

'I get it at the petrol pump about a mile from the factory. The only other pump is in Strathlinn so it wouldn't do to run out.'

'Does Mr Courton get his at the same place?'

'Yes, it's the nearest for both of us.'

'That may be the problem,' Mark suggested tentatively. 'I cleaned the plugs first, but this little lady has gone well since I cleaned the carburettor and the filter. It could be that the petrol from the pump is not as clean as it should be.'

'But they've only just got the pump filled up. A tanker came with it a couple of days ago. I was waiting to fill my car before I set off home, so I saw the tanker leaving.'

'Maybe it stirred up sediment from the bottom of the tank. It's an idea since you're both having the same problem. It's probably time to change the oil again too. It's better with the thicker oil in the summer but we could use thinner oil for the winter.'

'My but you're a clever laddie, Mark. I don't suppose you'd like to come with me tomorrow and have a look at Mr Courton's car, would you? I know he would be very grateful. He'll pay you well.'

'I would be glad to come, and I don't need paying. Perhaps you could show me the machine that's giving you trouble too in case I can see the fault — not that I know anything about weaving machines or looms and such like. I'd be glad of something to take my mind off things,' he muttered, more to himself than to Joe.

'Eh laddie, you're too young to have a weight on your mind,' Joe teased but he saw Mark's pained expression. 'Sometimes it helps to share your problems,' he added quietly. 'You know Maggie and I would be happy to help if there's anything we can do?' Mark was silent for a while. He hadn't meant to tell anyone locally of his discovery about his family but he knew Joe and Maggie Greig were not gossips. He found himself confiding in Joe as they drove along while Marie listened in silence in the back of the car. She couldn't see why it should make any difference who Mark's parents were. She was pleased Sybil Blackford was not Mark's real mother, and at least his grandfather must have cared what happened to him.

'Come in and share a meal with us,' Joe said. 'Maggie will understand all this better than anyone. She knows how it feels to find out your parents are not who you believed.'

'You go in with Uncle Joe, Mark. I promised Rina I would be back in time to give Marguerite her bath and help with the twins,' Marie said.

'We'll drive to the farm and drop you off then, if that's all right?' He looked at Joe.

'Drop me at my gate and I'll tell Maggie you're joining us for supper.'

* * *

It eased Mark's mind when he had confided in Mr and Mrs Greig. They understood so well how unsettled he was feeling, how he felt cut adrift in some way, but at least James Sinclair had treated Maggie in every way as though she was his own daughter. It was harder for Mark.

'Mark, has it occurred to you that Mrs Sybil Blackford might have been jealous because your grandfather was so generous in providing for you, and for your future? That is probably why she appropriated some of the funds for her own sons. Also, it seems clear to me that you benefitted greatly from your education and you are highly intelligent — possibly more so than her own two sons. She wouldn't like that. She probably tried to make you feel worthless as a result.' Mark considered her reasoning and decided she might be right about the jealousy at least, and without conceit he knew he had a far quicker brain than either of his brothers. Even Lord Tannahill had said that, when he bought the parts to put together to make a car engine. He nodded silently and ate his meal, but when he had cleared his plate he looked up at Maggie, his blue eyes grave.

'I do appreciate you being so understanding. I'm sure Rina will understand too, but — but I love Marie and I want to marry her. Her father may think she is too young and I would wait if I have to, but now — now I shall have to tell him I'm not who I thought I was. Even if my mother had lived I would have been a — a bastard. Can you blame him if he doesn't want me to marry his daughter?'

'I know Sybil Blackford may not be the kindest of women and she may not have loved you as she loved her own sons,' Maggie said gently, 'but she gave you a name and a home. Oh, I know she was paid generously for doing so, but it was better than being left in an orphanage, Mark. Can you find it in your heart to forgive her?'

'I suppose so, once I've recovered from the shock, but my main concern is how it will affect Marie's parents and their opinion of me as a suitable husband.'

'I can understand how you feel,' Joe said. 'Emma is my sister and we had a wise and kindly mother. I know she'll understand that none of this is your fault, laddie, and they liked you when you were down there. William may be the boss of his household but when it comes to family matters I believe Emma has a great influence. So long as you and Marie love each other that is what will matter to Emma. Why don't you let Maggie write to them and tell them what you have discovered? It will give them time to get used to the idea without you or Marie being there. In the end I suspect their lassie living so far away from them, will bother them more than who your mother is.'

'I have already promised Marie that I will take her to visit them at least once a year, and if we have children I shall save every penny to buy a car to make the journey possible. Maybe they will come to stay with us.'

'We should all like that,' Joe nodded.

So Mark agreed that Maggie could write to Emma and William and explain how he had discovered his real identity, and in the morning Joe would collect him and take him to his work to see whether he could repair Mr Courton's car, and take a look at the factory machine.

As Mark had suspected the fault with the car was the same as Joe's, the gritty petrol. He knew nothing about the workings of the weaving machines but when he saw the others in operation it seemed clear to him that the machine had not been cleaned or oiled and one of the cogs had become badly worn. He offered to collect a replacement from the Glasgow manufacturer if Joe would allow him to borrow his car.

'You can borrow mine,' Mr Courton said immediately.

'I will try to get the machine going when I return but I can't guarantee anything,' Mark said. 'These machines are new to me.'

'Maybe they are laddie, but you seem to understand more about them than I do.'

Mark managed to get a demonstration and few hints on the common faults from the engineers where the machines were made. He succeeded in fixing the machine and even giving it a trial run before the shift ended. Mr Courton was highly satisfied with his day's work and insisted on paying him, as he would any other engineer.

'I couldn't possibly take all that!' Mark protested.

'You repaired my car as well as the weaving machine, laddie. Have you any idea how much that has saved us? We should have lost another two day's work, maybe three while we waited for the engineer from Glasgow, and then his time doing the repair.'

So Mark reluctantly accepted what he considered an exorbitant sum. On the way home he confided in Joe.

'I have been saving up. I would have liked to buy Marie a diamond engagement ring for Christmas but I daren't until I can get her father's permission to marry her. Do you think she would like a gold wristwatch? I know she doesn't have one and with such generous payment I could buy her a really good one now.'

'A good watch is very useful, but shouldn't you keep your money until you buy her the ring? She will have her eighteenth birthday a month after Christmas. Maybe William will agree to an engagement even if he insists you should wait a while to marry.'

'I shall miss her dreadfully when she goes back to Yorkshire,' Mark said. 'It's not only all the help she gives me with the accounts for the tenants and the tradesmen, but we are so easy together, if you understand what I mean? We're good friends and companions, as well as all the other feelings I have for Marie.' He blushed and Joe glanced sideways at him then grinned.

'I understand exactly how you feel, laddie. Maggie and I must seem old to you, but we have not forgotten how impatient we were to be married once we discovered how we felt about each other. We're on your side remember — only please keep the other feelings under control for a while yet, for all our sakes. I know it's not easy to resist temptation when you're in love, but Marie is so young.'

'You're good to me, you and Mrs Greig. I value your opinion and your support.'

'The family usually gather at Bonnybrae for Christmas. Will you join us? I know Rina intends to ask you anyway, but I hope for Marie's sake you will come.'

'I would love to join you if you're sure? Rupert and his mother always go to his uncle's at Christmas. It is company for Sylvia. He has invited me to go but he will understand, especially when it is a long way to travel for a few days.'

Marie knew Mark had given Aunt Maggie permission to tell her parents about his family and she trusted them to plead his case, as Uncle Joe had promised. Even so she was not surprised when she received her mother's letter telling her how much they were looking forward to her coming home as soon as Christmas was over, especially now that Rina would have Elsie Forbes to help in the house for five mornings a week. She went on to say that she and William had both enjoyed meeting Mark when he was with Lord Hanley. They had found him pleasant and not in the least arrogant. Marie could tell her mother was choosing her words with care, She imagined her biting the end of her pen as she considered. She went on, *His discoveries about his family do not worry us. We felt he was a kind and genuine young man whatever his parentage*. The letter went on to say they both believed she was too young to make up her mind about such a serious step as marriage, especially when Mark's background was so different to her own. Whatever skeletons he might have in his past he had been educated at Oxford and mixed with a different class of people. He was the local laird, even if Stavondale Estate was much smaller than it had been when they had known it.

Marie felt dispirited by her mother's reply and she showed Mark the letter.

'The nearer the time comes to me going home to Yorkshire and us being apart the more I dread it,' she said. 'I know now I love you very much, Mark.' At her words he seized her in his arms and kissed her with passion.

'Your words are music to my ears,' he murmured gruffly and kissed her again. He tasted the dampness of tears on her cheek. 'Please don't cry, Marie,' he pleaded. 'I shall save up and buy an old car that I can repair myself then I can come down to see you more often.'

'Will you, Mark? Will you do that?'

'I will now. I'm very relieved your parents don't hold my family's transgressions against me. It is only your age they consider a problem and that is changing every day.'

'But I do know what I want. I know what sort of life we should have together. It's not as though you will be one of the landed gentry who never does a day's work and attends dinners and balls and the House of Lords.'

'Heaven forbid,' Mark said. 'I could never live like that. I enjoy messing about with cars and machines too much. My main fear is that I may get bored with being a small landowner, if we can ever get all the repairs done and keep them up to date. You could probably run the estate yourself my clever little love. Anyway, cheer up, Marie. Your Aunt Maggie has a romantic soul and has invited me to stay at Braeside for Christmas and to join you all for Christmas dinner at Bonnybrae. Apparently she and Rina have discussed it and are in agreement. What's more your Uncle Joe has offered to loan me his car if we want to go to the Christmas Eve dance. Will you go with me?'

'Oh yes, I'd love that. We have not been to any of the local dances together yet.'

CHAPTER FOURTEEN

The Christmas Eve dance was a great success with everyone in high spirits. Marie was relieved to see Fred Lorrimer did not appear. There was one new face neither of them had seen before but they did not know everyone from the village, or those who might be home for Christmas. It was Mr Fletcher, who played the fiddle with the band, who told them the young man was a nephew of Mrs Mason, the blacksmith's wife. The boy's mother, Mrs Mason's sister, had died a year ago. His father had remarried a week ago, so Angus was staying with his aunt and uncle for Christmas.

'I dinna suppose newlyweds want a teenage laddie hanging around even if they are getting on a bit. The Masons have no bairns o' their own so they'll be kind to him. His twin died. Maybe that's why he's small for his age. He'll be fourteen soon, ready to work.'

'Will he live with his father then?' Marie asked, feeling sympathy for the boy.

'I dinnae ken. His father works at the flour mill. Young Angus is good with horses. He would like to be a blacksmith, like his grandfather. Mrs Mason's family were all blacksmiths. She and her sister were born at the smiddy. Mason came as a young apprentice. That's how they met. I hear he's giving up next year?' Mr Fletcher looked at Mark.

'Yes, he gave a year's notice at the rent dinner. His wife doesn't want to leave but he says the work is getting too much for him with both the forge and his forty acres.'

'He'll be badly missed. There isn't another blacksmith for miles. We all depend on him for shoeing our horses, and a wee bit of welding o' the ploughs and such like.'

'Mr Sinclair was dismayed when he heard. He says it's a three-mile trek to Locheagle and three back. It will be further for you, and the Massies, being two miles up the glen.'

'Aye, and it's as far to take them the other way and the road is steep.

'I asked if he couldn't take on a man to help with the work,' Mark said. 'He says there's no one locally. We shall have to advertise the premises.'

'It will upset Emily,' Mr Fletcher said, 'but we really need a blacksmith.' He wiped crumbs from his mouth. 'They're tuning up. I'm needed to play again. Enjoy the rest of the dance.'

On the way home Marie was quieter than usual.

'Are you all right, Marie? Did you enjoy the dance?'

'Oh yes, I loved it. The band was good too. I didn't know Mr Fletcher played the fiddle. He was telling me I must stay for the New Year's Eve dance. He says it's the best time to be in Scotland with all the first footing.'

'Is that why you've been so quiet? You will be in Yorkshire then unless . . .'

'No. It's . . . I was thinking about the forge and the blacksmith. Uncle Jim was quite depressed about having no blacksmith in the district. I was wondering . . . Do you think Mr Mason would take on his nephew as apprentice? I mean it's not the same as having a stranger in your home. Surely he could pump the bellows, even if he's not strong enough to shoe the horses yet? An apprentice wouldn't need as much money as a man, would he?'

'I suppose Mrs Mason must have considered that, don't you think?'

'I don't know. I-I had another idea. Please don't be angry. It's only a suggestion.'

'Oh Marie, of course I wouldn't be angry with you.' Mark drew the car to a halt and pulled her into his arms, taking the opportunity for a lingering kiss. He tucked Marie's rug more firmly around her knees and kept her close in his arms, keeping each other warm.

'Tell me what's in that curly head of yours?'

'I-I know how angry your parents — well Mrs Blackford — would be if you did this, but how would *you* feel about selling Stavondale Manor and building a smaller house? One a bit like Aunt Maggie and Uncle Joe's at Braeside?' She trembled and his arms tightened.

'I don't feel any attachment to Stavondale Manor,' he said slowly, 'or anywhere else for that matter. If I had a home, filled with love, as Braeside is, I wouldn't care how small it was. Why do you ask, Marie?'

'However much we love each other I-I'm not sure I could make Stavondale Manor into a proper home. I do want children — your children, Mark, but it's so large we would need servants just to keep it clean.'

'I know exactly what you mean. I felt the warmth and welcome of your parents' home the first time I went. I believe Lord Hanley and Mr Rowbottom feel the same. I suppose we could always shut off part of Stavondale Manor?' he mused. 'But it seems a waste after Rina's grandfather went to so much trouble to make it bigger.'

'Shutting off a part of it would not be the same. Surely it would be better used and lived in by people who appreciate that sort of style? I don't see me ever feeling that way. Neither did Rina. She told me that herself.'

'I'm not sure I know what a real home is like. That's why I was happy to spend so much time with Rupert and his family.'

'So would it be a crazy idea to sell Stavondale Manor and use some of the money to build a house for ourselves? If the

Masons want to give up their land we could build a house there, on the outskirts of East Lowrie? Maybe you would like a yard near the blacksmith's for mending cars. You did say you think you will get bored with only the estate . . .'

'That's true . . .' Mark agreed, 'if we ever get everything into good repair.'

'Maybe you could install a petrol pump when it is near the village so that people did not need to travel to Strathlinn. I know there are not many cars yet, but you keep telling me there will soon be more and — and you reckon there will be more machines on farms too. You could build a shed where people could come if they want your help to repair things.'

'When did you think of all this, Marie? Is that why you were so quiet when Mr Fletcher was going on about the smiddy?'

'It sort of popped into my head that it might suit you to have something more than the estate. Being near the blacksmith's could prove convenient, especially if you can persuade him to take on his nephew as an apprentice and keep going for a few more years. It would be easier for him without the land and Mrs Mason wouldn't need to leave her family home.'

'I would like to have the land around us if we did build a home together. Our home together sounds wonderful, Marie. I pray your parents don't make us wait too long.'

'So do I,' Marie agreed fervently. 'I can't wait for us to be together. I would enjoy it if we could keep a couple of cows for milk, and to make butter. Some of the villagers might like to buy it when we have some to spare. I'd like some chickens like Aunt Maggie, and a pig. You would have grazing for Bali, and maybe I could have a pony of my own to ride with you.' She chewed her lower lip anxiously. 'I know that is not the sort of life your parents expect you to have, but I could never pretend to be a lady.'

'I love you the way you are, Marie, and I want you to be happy,' Mark declared firmly. 'I don't care what my so-called mother thinks anymore. You've given me a lot to think about my darling girl. I suppose the first thing would be to see Mr MacQuade to find out if there would be any demand for a house like Stavondale Manor.'

'Wouldn't you need to consult your parents first?'

'No.' His voice hardened. 'Lord Tannahill made sure it is in my name. Now I know they have been paid to look after me all these years I shall not feel the least bit guilty if I do something to please myself — so long as I have your approval, and your love, Marie. That is all that matters to me.'

'You will always have that, Mark.' He smiled and put a gentle finger under her chin, tilting her face for his kiss.

Reluctantly they drew apart.

'It will be Christmas day in half an hour. It is time we returned to Braeside. I really wanted to buy you an engagement ring for Christmas, Marie. I can't wait to let everyone know you're going to be my wife, but I know I must wait until I obtain your parents' permission.' He sighed. Marie reached up and drew his face to hers to kiss his lips.

'We know I belong to you,' she said softly. 'Nothing can change that.'

The following evening with the twins and a very tired Marguerite tucked up in bed Mark looked around the cosy room at Bonnybrae and sighed happily.

'This is the happiest Christmas I can ever remember,' he said. 'I can't thank you all enough for including me in your family circle.'

'As far as I can see you'll soon be a permanent part of it,' Jamie chuckled, 'and very welcome you will be. Rina and I will be pleased, but I can't imagine what our parents will think of another of their children retuning to our Scottish roots. I expect they'll blame me.'

'I'm sure they will accept it once they're convinced you two really love each other,' Aunt Maggie said. 'Their loss will be our gain.'

'It's kind of you to say so Mrs Greig,' Mark said sincerely.

* * *

Mark lost no time in calling on the Masons to see whether he could persuade Mr Mason to take on his wife's nephew as an apprentice and carry on as the blacksmith.

'I've tried to persuade him,' Mrs Mason said. 'Angus is a grand laddie and he's strong even if he is small. I'm sure he'll grow and it's in his blood to be a blacksmith.'

'It's not only the work at the forge,' her husband protested. 'We have forty acres of land and where there's animals there's always work needed, even though Emily milks our two cows and looks after the hens.'

'Why not keep on the forge with your nephew and give up the land?' Mark suggested.

'But they're all part of the same tenancy. I would keep going a while longer with young Angus here to help me, if the house and forge were on a separate lease? But then I suppose whoever took the land would need the house . . .' he finished glumly.

'Not necessarily,' Mark said. 'We could find a way around that. This district really does need a blacksmith for the sake of all the farms on the estate.'

'Oh Mr Blackford, if only you could find such a solution,' Mrs Mason said, ringing her hands. 'You'd be the answer to all my prayers. It would be a pleasure for us to keep Angus. Mason would teach him to be a blacksmith like his grandfather.'

'Consider what I've suggested and let me know,' Mark said getting up to leave.

'I dinnae need to consider, if I can keep the house and the forge without the land. I — er, would I need to keep paying as much rent?' Mason asked diffidently.

'Of course not. You would only pay for the cottage and the forge. You have a decent-sized garden so you could still keep your hens, Mrs Mason, and a pig if you wish, but that would be up to you.'

'Oh I thank ye Mr Blackford.' Mrs Mason said gratefully. 'Sir Roger would never have agreed to such a plan. It's the answer to my prayers.' Her husband smiled at her with affection and put a brawny arm around her shoulders.

'You've brought us the best Christmas present we could wish for. Emily was born here,' Mr Mason explained to Mark. 'We'll be forever in your debt if ye can arrange everything. Angus will be happy too,'

'The rest of the tenants will be relieved to know they still have their blacksmith so we'll fix things without delay,' Mark said confidently, unaware he might have problems with his own plans.

Marie felt the few days after Christmas had flown on wings and she could not hold back tears as Mark kissed her tenderly on the last evening they would spend together for some time.

'I shall see you in the morning, dearest Marie. Joe asked if I wanted to accompany him when he drives you to the station. I will ride Bali over in good time. I didn't think your uncle looked very well tonight. That cough seems to have exhausted him.'

'I know. Uncle Joe is so rarely ill we tend to forget he is getting older.'

* * *

The following morning Maggie came up to Bonnybrae looking anxious.

'Joe is in bed with a pounding headache and a temperature. Mark will drive you to the station, Marie. We had all intended seeing you off but I don't like to leave Joe.'

'Of course, you mustn't leave him, Aunt Maggie.' Marie hugged her warmly. 'Give him my love. You've both been wonderful to me. Mark didn't think Uncle Joe looked well last night. Do you think we should make a detour and ask the doctor to call?'

'I think the lassie is right,' Jim said before Maggie could reply. 'Joe is never ill so he must be feeling bad if he has taken to his bed.'

'It's his chest and that racking cough.' Maggie said.

'It sounds like influenza to me,' Rina said quietly. 'In her letter Mel said there was an epidemic going around in the city. They have admitted a lot of extra patients. I think it would be wise to have the doctor, dear Aunt Maggie.'

'All right, will you call and ask him to come, Marie?' Maggie agreed hesitantly. They so rarely needed a doctor, but she had been dreadfully worried about Joe during the night. He had thrashed about the bed and talked without making sense. She knew he still had a temperature. 'I must get back to him now but I'll ask Mark to collect you here with your suitcase. I see you have accumulated extra baggage. I hope you'll manage the journey all right on your own?' Maggie looked fondly at her niece.

'I'm sure I shall,' Marie summoned a smile. 'You will write and tell me how Uncle Joe is? And what the doctor says? I wish I wasn't going away. I could have helped you.'

'Don't you worry, lassie. We'll be fine,' Maggie said and gave her one more hug.

Mark felt dejected as he watched the train draw away, taking the love of his life with it. They had clung to each other and Marie could not hold back her tears. As he strode out of the station Mark decided he would call at the offices of Mr MacQuade and tell him of his plans to sell Stavondale Manor and build a house on the smiddy land near East Lowrie. He would have something to tell Marie when he wrote and if things moved quickly and her parents knew he was building a house especially for her they might give their consent to her marriage more readily.

Mark was greeted cordially when he was shown into Mr MacQuade's office. He explained his plans and that he and Marie hoped to marry if her parents gave their consent.

'It is a wise decision to build a house nearer the community and I'm sure you will soon build up a demand for your services with your knowledge of cars and machines. I shall probably be one of your first customers. As we get more motorcars on the road a village petrol pump will be a great asset too.' His smile faded though when Mark outlined his plan to sell Stavondale Manor to finance his plans for a new house and a workshop. The solicitor formed his fingers into a steeple and frowned at them.

‘I’m afraid I can’t see much demand for a house the size of Stavondale Manor when there is no land attached. There’s nothing in the area to attract a buyer. If I am honest, it was a relief when Lord Tannahill told me your father wanted to buy it as a residence to go with the Stavondale Estate.’

‘We hadn’t considered that aspect,’ Mark said feeling disheartened.

‘I will do my best of course. I can advertise it in the various property sales, but I can’t promise you will get anything like the price your father paid for it.’

As a small boy Mark had learned to hide his emotions and he hid them now but as he drove back to Braeside he felt sick at heart without Marie. His hopes and dreams for their future seemed hopeless.

He forgot about his own disappointment when he delivered the car back to Braeside. The doctor was just leaving.

‘Oh Mark, I’m so glad you’re back. I was giving Doctor MacClean a cup of coffee in the hope you would be home soon. He is having trouble with his car and I thought you might know what to do.’ The doctor described the stopping and starting and jerky driving he was having and Mark said he would take a look.

‘How is Mr Greig?’ he asked as Maggie hurried back indoors.

‘He is a sick man,’ the doctor said gravely. ‘I believe he was in contact with a man at his workplace who had the same racking cough and difficulty breathing. He has a bad dose of influenza but I fear he is on the verge of pneumonia by the sound of his chest. It is vital to get his temperature down. I have instructed Mrs Greig to keep sponging him and changing his clothes. You are her nephew I presume?’ he asked suddenly, wondering if he should be discussing his patient so freely. He was new to the area and fairly young.

‘I am not her nephew yet but I am hoping to marry her niece. If there is anything I can do to help I will. The Greigs have been kind and made me very welcome.’

'If you could stay with Mr Greig and make sure his wife gets some sleep it is the best I can suggest. She looks exhausted already and it is unlikely she will get much sleep tonight. The condition is likely to get worse before the temperature breaks. The best we can hope for is it will break before it proves fatal. I have promised to call again in the morning. If there was anything more I could do I would return today but diligent nursing is all I can suggest.'

'Then I will do whatever I can to help. When did you last change the oil, doctor?'

'Change the oil? Oh, in the car? I have never changed it. I don't know how.'

'Well I've sorted a loose connection and cleaned the plugs so that may help but if you're coming back tomorrow bring a can of oil with you and I will change it while you attend to your patient. Now you get in and I'll turn the starting handle.' The engine started on the second swing and the young doctor gave a sigh of relief and thanked Mark profusely.

Mark knew the doctor was more concerned than he had allowed Maggie to see and he went straight up to Bonnybrae to tell them things were not good with Joe.

'We're just going in for our dinner,' Jamie said. 'Come and have some with us.' Rina was upset when she heard how ill Joe was.

'I ought to go down and help,' she said. 'They have both done so much for me.'

'No, no,' Mark said hastily. 'Mrs Greig doesn't want to come near in case she carries an infection, especially to the twins. She says they will not have much resistance yet. Anyway she knows you will be missing Marie's help until you get into your own routine.'

'Oh, I am. I'm missing her already and Marguerite is too. She asks for Marie continually.' She looked across at Jamie and he smiled at her. The previous night Rina had wept in his arms because she felt so disorganized. 'I so wanted to be a good farmer's wife for you, Jamie.' He had comforted her in the best way he could by making love to her — not with the wild passion of their first love but with gentle teasing and touching until she had forgotten her troubles and responded to him with all her love.

'We could do that after dinner, couldn't we? Jamie!' Uncle Jim's voice brought Jamie's attention back to those around him. Rina's cheeks were pink. She knew exactly where his thoughts had been.

'I'm sorry. What did you say?' he asked blankly.

'Mark is suggesting we should bring a bed down to the sitting room for Joe. It would save Maggie carrying coals upstairs for the bedroom fire and Mark is offering to stay overnight with Joe to let Maggie get a proper rest as the doctor has advised.'

'He is coming back in the morning,' Mark explained 'but he says it is vital we get the temperature down. I think he is more concerned than he admitted to Mrs Greig. I am stronger than she is for lifting Joe to help him drink and to change his nightshirt. She had changed him twice last night he was sweating so much and his temperature is still too high.'

'Of course we'll bring a bed downstairs,' Jamie said, 'but I expect Aunt Maggie will protest at us for going near.'

'If you could send Doug Lamont down with me we could manage,' Mark suggested, 'then Mrs Greig need not be concerned about Rina and her little ones.'

So it was arranged, but Joe barely seemed aware of the two young men carrying him down the stairs or Maggie tucking him up in clean cool sheets.

'I am going to ride home now to collect a few things and call on the joiner who is doing some repairs at one of the farms,' Mark said. 'I will return early in the evening if you will promise to go to bed and sleep.' Maggie began to protest. 'I know all about sponging people down to reduce their temperature,' he assured her. 'That is what matron used to do to us when we had an epidemic of measles and once when there was a serious influenza outbreak.'

Maggie agreed, but only on condition Mark called her if there was any change in Joe's condition. Mark nodded, but her haggard face and the strain in her eyes made her look much older than her sixty-two years.

Mark told Mrs MacCrindle where he was going. All country folk liked to hear what was happening but Mrs Mac deserved to know. She made him a cooked meal every evening and if he was at home during the day she always provided soup and freshly baked bread, as well as fruit and cream or a pie and custard for dessert.

He collected his leather writing case and the Waterman fountain pen with its gold nib, making sure he had filled it with ink. It had been a gift from Lord Tannahill for his twenty-first birthday. He found it hard to believe they were cousins. He was glad he had been regarded as a worthy friend to Rupert long before they were aware of their relationship. Tonight he would write to Marie, but he would not tell her how seriously ill her Uncle Joe was, neither did he want to tell her his hopes for selling Stavondale Manor had been dashed, but the more he thought about it the more convinced he was that Marie had found an ideal solution to keep both of them occupied and happy together. He understood the reasons for Mr MacQuade's misgivings but he knew Marie would be as disappointed as he was.

Maggie's anxiety for her beloved Joe increased. He did not recognise her. Beads of perspiration stood on his brow no matter how often she sponged him. She was exhausted. Joe's raving frightened her even though she knew it was due to the fever. It was a relief when Mark returned straight after his evening meal. He persuaded Maggie to go to bed then he settled down to write to Marie, full of everyday trivia and telling her how much he was missing her already, and how much he loved her. Several times he stopped to sponge Joe's damp skin, using the basin of warm water and cloth Maggie had left ready. He held Joe up to drink sips of water but he seemed glad to flop back against the pillows. Around four o'clock in the morning Mark's anxiety increased. He knew he must call Maggie. She would never forgive him if Joe died and she was not there. He had no medical knowledge but his instincts told him Joe had reached a crisis.

CHAPTER FIFTEEN

Maggie pulled on her shawl, thrust her feet into slippers and followed Mark downstairs. She knew he would not have wakened her without reason. Her heart thumped painfully. How could she survive without Joe?

'I have changed his nightshirt twice,' Mark said, 'but even the sheets are damp. If I sponge him down from head to toe and lift him into that easy chair could you change the bed? It is the best I can think of.'

'Aye laddie, I think ye're right,' Maggie agreed. 'I have sheets on the clotheshorse in front of the kitchen fire. I'll bring a clean shirt. Are you sure you can lift him yourself?'

'I will pull the chair nearer the bed but I'll wash him down first if you don't mind.' Maggie nodded. She knew it was touch and go for Joe. She prayed fervently that the fever would break. Mark carried out his task methodically then, with Maggie's help, got him into a clean shirt before lifting him into the chair with a blanket around him. Maggie quickly changed the sheets. Together they lifted Joe back onto the bed. His eyes rolled. He mumbled incomprehensibly but he showed no sign of recognition. 'I will hold him up if you can persuade him to drink a little water.' Maggie obeyed without questioning the young man. He treated Joe as gently as a mother. Together they watched and waited in silence.

'It seems such an effort for him to take each breath,' Maggie whispered tearfully. 'I want to breathe for him.' Mark didn't answer but he understood. She got up and restlessly added coal to the fire and swept the hearth, moving around the room, unable to keep still.

Mark stood up abruptly. He put his hand on Joe's brow.

'He's not sweating now. His brow is cool. Listen! Surely he is breathing more steadily?' Maggie hurried back to the bedside.

'I-I think the fever has broken.'

'Shall I add the extra blanket?' Mark asked. 'Isn't this when he must not get chilled?' Joe was quiet now, his breathing less laboured too. Mark felt a surge of relief. It was as though he had seen a miracle. Maggie nodded. She put her face in her hands and began to weep softly. Mark carried away the basin of water and the towels. When he returned Maggie had wiped her face and was praying silently, kneeling beside Joe's bed. Mark crept away again. He pushed the kettle over the fire to make a cup of tea for both of them.

It was barely light when Dr Maclean arrived. The lines of weariness changed to relief when he saw Joe was still alive and sleeping naturally at last.

'You have made an excellent job of nursing him, Mrs Greig. I confess now I didn't hold much hope for him yesterday. We lost two more patients during the night. One young man only in his twenties.'

'I couldn't have managed without Mark. He's been wonderful,' Maggie said candidly. The doctor turned to look at Mark.

'So you're a genius with sick men as well as sick motors?' he said with a brief smile. 'I remembered the oil in spite of the turmoil. We need the motor to get round everyone.'

'I will change it now then. Do you have more patients waiting for you?'

'Yes, too many, I'm afraid,' the young doctor said gravely. He turned back to Maggie. 'It will take several weeks before Mr Greig returns to his former health. He will be very weak for the first ten days or so but keep him warm and feed him small nourishing meals whenever he can eat them. I'm sure you know all that of course but I advise him not to return to work for at least four weeks. Yesterday I feared it had turned to pneumonia.'

'I will write to Mr Courton and let him know,' Maggie said. 'He is Joe's partner.'

She was a bit surprised, and hurt, when Mr Courton did not acknowledge her letter and she wondered if he was well himself. When two weeks passed she asked Mark if he would take the car and drive to the factory to explain why Joe had not returned to work yet. Mr Courton was relieved to see him. Mark thought he seemed to have aged ten years in the few weeks since they last met. He soon learned that Mrs Courton had also had the influenza and almost died.

'I got two nurses in to care for her night and day. She is recovering but she is very weak,' he told Mark. 'I understand how bad Joe must have been. I'm sorry I didn't reply to Mrs Greig's letter. Things are in a muddle without Joe. A number of people are off sick. One woman has died. Another man has lost both his wife and his mother.' He sighed heavily. 'Will you tell Joe I will visit him at home as soon as I can? I think the time has come to sell this place. The two of us should retire and enjoy whatever years we have left.'

'Oh dear,' Mark said. 'I am sorry to hear things are so bad. Is there anything I can do while I am here?'

'Do you mean that, laddie? We have two machines down. I have no idea what's wrong. Have you time to take a look? Joe is such a good all-rounder. We've missed him badly. There's orders not sent, and wrong orders despatched. Nobody else understands the machines. Joe was training one of the younger men but he has been off sick almost as long as Joe. He has a wife and a young family so I know he'll be back to work as soon as he's able. He'll need the money. Meanwhile . . .' Mr Courton gave a defeated shrug.

'Show me the machines,' Mark said. 'I'll do my best if it's not too complicated.'

* * *

Back in Yorkshire, Marie missed Mark even more than she had expected. It was only when he was sure Joe was definitely recovering that he told Marie how ill he had been. They understood then why Maggie had not written her usual weekly letters. Mark also mentioned his meeting with Mr MacQuade and reluctantly passed on the solicitor's fears that there would be little demand for a house as big as Stavondale Manor, certainly not to sell at its true value. Marie sensed he was feeling as disappointed as she did at the news, but she wrote a cheerful reply, encouraging Mark to continue following his own dreams.

She was glad when Lord Hanley called at Moorend in person to ask if she would help out in the Estate Office again with Mr Rowbottom. She had been there less than a week when he gave her a lesson in driving his motorcar.

'He has missed you while you have been in Scotland, lass,' Bob Rowbottom said. 'He's lonely since his wife died. He has taken to you like the daughter they never had.'

'Maybe he needs a new project to take up his time and his interest,' Marie suggested, thinking of Mark.

'You may be right about taking on another interest,' Bob Rowbottom agreed, 'but I think he's hoping you're back home for good. I reckon your dad's hoping so as well. I ran into him at the blacksmith's.'

'I know.' Marie pulled a wry face. 'He says he didn't rear a family to send us all back to Scotland and I'm too young to get married, but Mark and I know what we want. Anyway, my parents were young when they came to Moorend.'

'What's his name, this young man you think you love?'

'You've already met him. He came down here to learn about estate management.'

'Ah, so it is young Mark Blackford then? He's a real nice lad. He has a lot to learn about tenants and estates but he knows a lot about motors.'

'That's right. He would like to start up a garage of his own if we get married. He is coming down for my birthday next week. He was going to drive my aunt and uncle down too but Uncle Joe is still recovering from influenza so he's not well enough to come. He and Aunt Maggie like Mark, and they approve of us getting married before too long.'

The day before her birthday Lord Hanley suggested he and Marie should meet Mark at the railway station and she could drive. He said coping with more traffic would be good for her. Mark was astonished when he saw her and Lord Hanley waiting for him outside the station but it did not stop him taking Marie in his arms and kissing her thoroughly, before he turned to greet Lord Hanley.

He had bought Marie a dainty silver wristwatch for her birthday. It was set on a very pretty bracelet of intertwined silver leaves. He presented it to her at the breakfast table on the morning of her birthday. He looked up and met William's gaze.

'I would have liked to buy Marie an engagement ring, but I could not do that without your approval. We would dearly like your permission to marry, even if we have to wait a year, or even two.'

'We have only just got her home again,' Emma said gently. 'We have missed her very much, although we are very glad she was able to help Rina.'

'We love each other,' Mark said simply. 'You have my word I will bring her to see you at least once a year.'

'That is more than you and father managed to do,' Marie said reproachfully. 'I never knew Granny Greig. Jamie says she was lovely and so was Granddad Greig.'

'It is getting easier to travel now,' William said, 'and your mother and I were too busy earning a living. Besides the circumstances were different,' he added, his mouth tightening as he remembered the way he and Emma had had to marry and move to Yorkshire, even though he had no regrets now.

'If you wait another year,' Emma said, 'and if your plans work out and you're both still in love, then — then perhaps your father will give his consent?' She looked at William.

'We'll see. Meanwhile you might as well enjoy the time you have together. Lord Hanley has invited all of us for a meal tonight at The Hall. Mr and Mrs Rowbottom will be there as well. It's a pity Joe and Maggie couldn't come.'

'It would have been lovely to see Jamie and Rina again too, and the children,' Emma sighed, 'but it is such a cold time of year for travelling with two young babies.'

'There is a solution, Mrs Sinclair,' Mark said with a twinkle in his eye. 'You could visit them. Jamie and Rina would love to see you and show off their family.'

'Mark's right. They would love to see you both,' Marie agreed. 'I'm surprised you haven't been to see Uncle Joe after him being so ill.'

'He has not regained his health or his decisive manner yet,' Mark reflected gravely. 'It's as though he can't be bothered anymore. Mrs Greig couldn't believe it when Mr Courton visited them and suggested they should sell the factory and retire. He just nodded listlessly.'

'It sounds as though Joe is too tired to make such a big decision,' William said.

'They have had one mill-owner looking over the mill and another making enquiries about the sales side of things, but Mr Courton is afraid their record for efficiency will go down without Mr Greig,' Mark said. 'At least they have had some interest. That's more than we've had for Stavondale Manor.'

Later, when they were alone together, Marie did her best to comfort Mark.

'We shall get by so long as we're together,' she said. 'I will do my best to make the manor into a real home, warm and welcoming, where there is love and a place for those who want to visit us. Wherever we live I'm sure your friend Rupert will come, and Jamie and Rina, Aunt Maggie and Uncle Joe will come too when he is well again.'

'I know you will bring love and happiness wherever we make our home, my love,' Mark said and drew her into his arms for a long and passionate kiss. 'Sometimes I wonder how much longer I can wait before you are my wife. I never believed I would feel like this.'

'Neither did I,' Marie agreed snuggling closer. 'I know it is your heart's desire to be a motor expert. Perhaps we could still build a garage on your land near the village.'

'Our land, Marie. It will always be ours my love, because without you it wouldn't matter where I lived, or what I did.'

'All right. I am suggesting near East Lowrie because Uncle Joe says when the telephones and electricity spread out from the towns the poles and wires will come to the villages first.

'Already a few houses in Silverbeck have a telephone and there is electricity too. Lord Hanley says it will be reaching here, at Moorend in the next few years.'

'Yes, there are more people in this area, but you're right, Marie.' Mark hugged her to him and grinned. 'I knew you would cheer me up and find a bright side to things. I'm not looking forward to leaving tomorrow though.'

Mark travelled down to Yorkshire whenever he got an opportunity. Eventually he persuaded Joe and Maggie to come with him for a weekend. Joe agreed so long as they took the car and Mark did the driving. Although he had returned to work at the factory, he had not regained his usual zest for life. Both he and Bob Courton seemed relieved when they thought they had a prospective buyer willing to pay the price they wanted, and who agreed to keep on the workers and the sales side of the business. There was only one snag. The man was moving from Yorkshire. He had a family of three with another on the way and his wife wanted a large house away from the factory. Joe suggested he look at Stavondale Manor.

'He thought it was too far away from the factory,' Joe told William and Emma, 'until he realised I travel three miles further than that every day. He said he would bring his wife and children to Scotland to see it. That's why we must get back on Monday. Even if they like the house I think there will still be a problem. He would like his children to have ponies so he wants a bit of land. Mark has written to Lord Tannahill to see whether he would be willing to sell or rent a field from the Home Farm.'

'I don't know whether to hope Mark is lucky and gets a sale or not,' Emma said with a sigh. 'It's hard to think of losing Marie again. Sometimes I wonder why we ever moved so far away. That will be two of our children settled back in Scotland and we shall hardly see out grandchildren.'

'Don't fret, Emma,' Maggie soothed. 'You know you can always come and stay with us and visit them. You said Meg is expecting a child too?'

'She is. It will be due in September.'

'Eh, lassie,' Joe chuckled and put his arm around Emma as though she was still the little sister he and his brothers had loved and protected all those years ago when she had first worked as a maid at Bonnybrae. 'I'd have thought you would have seen enough of babies when you've had so many of your own.' Emma smiled up at him.

'I love all my bairns. I'm reluctant to see them going so far away, but I suppose Mother and Father must have felt the same about me.'

'Aye, they did. You've done well together though, you and William.'

Marie wept a little as she waved Mark and her aunt and uncle goodbye. She knew she was lucky to have such a generous boss as Lord Hanley, and Bob Rowbottom was always good-natured and tolerant if she seemed subdued. Ever since his accident he avoided riding long distances so Marie now drove him out to the half dozen farms which were located some miles away towards the moors. The tenants' wives always made them welcome and plied them with afternoon tea or a hearty lunch if they appeared in the mornings. Marie enjoyed meeting people and listening to their problems and their successes, perhaps winning prizes for their sheep or their children's achievements at school.

So when Marie appeared at Silverbeck Hall one morning with red-rimmed eyes and the look of an unhappy young woman who has spent a sleepless night both Lord Hanley and Bob Rowbottom were dismayed. Marie got on with her work typing up the letters and doing the estate's accounts but her distress was evident and her silence prohibited questions. The next two days were the same and it was clear to the two men that their favourite young woman was deeply unhappy and upset. Shortly after lunchtime on the third day Mr Rowbottom rode over to Moorend hoping to see William and perhaps learn how they might help Marie overcome her unhappy state. William was ploughing in one of the fields some distance away but Emma invited him into the house for a cup of tea.

'I'm not here about the farm or the tenancy,' he replied in answer to Emma's query, 'but we're worried about Marie. She is so pale and tired, she looks ill. Usually she can raise a smile on the busiest of days.'

'Is her work suffering?' Emma asked anxiously.

'No, she is working harder than ever, as though she wants to fill every second of her day so she has no time to think. We eat our lunch with Lord Hanley but she's barely eating enough for a sparrow.'

'She is the same at home. Four mornings ago the postman brought her a letter. It was not from Mark. He writes at least three letters a week and we all recognise his writing by now.' Emma gave a wan smile. 'William wonders what he finds to say.'

'We wondered if it was a lovers' quarrel. If there is anything we can do please let us know. It is so unusual for Marie not to have a smile.'

'I don't know who sent the letter, but I'm sure that is the cause of Marie's misery. The colour drained from her face as she began to read it. She was in the middle of eating her breakfast but jumped up from the table and ran to her bedroom. I know she wrote to Mark later that day because she went to the village herself to post it instead of leaving it for the postman to take, as we usually do.'

'I see. I'm sorry to see the lass so unhappy. We both are, but if we don't know the cause we can't help.'

'William says the same.'

'Something has really upset her. Lord Hanley has grown very fond of her, and of young Mark.'

A couple of weeks passed. Marie remained an unhappy shadow of her former self. She had lost weight and looked permanently tired. Several times she wondered if she had made the right decision in telling Mark she had changed her mind about marrying him. She had asked him not to contact her. Contrarily she knew in her heart she had hoped he would try to reason with her, even though she had made her wishes plain. Twice her young sister Fiona had climbed into bed beside her to offer comfort when she had heard her weeping. But nothing could heal the sorrow in her heart. She would always love Mark.

* * *

Emma was startled, then flustered, the afternoon two well-dressed gentlemen drove into the farmyard at Moorend. William was not at home. The two men stepped out of their shiny black car. The younger man was the driver and at first glimpse she thought it was Mark. Her heart hammered against her ribs, but then she saw he was not as tall as Mark and he had fair hair.

'I am Lord Tannahill,' the older man introduced himself with a smile, 'and this is my nephew Rupert, a close friend of Mark Blackford.' He asked if he could speak with Marie. Emma had been collecting eggs and she was carrying a basket full on her arm, as well as four in a ladle. They had been cracked in the nest and she didn't want them to make a mess of the rest. 'May I carry your basket?' Rupert asked. 'It looks heavy.' He smiled at her and took the basket from Emma.

'I-I'm sorry but Marie is not here.'

'Not here?' Rupert echoed in dismay. 'Has she — has she run away?' It had been his idea to make this detour and call on Marie.

'She is at Silverbeck Hall. She works there for Lord Hanley in the Estate Office.'

'I'm afraid we have taken you by surprise, Mrs Sinclair. May we come in?'

'Well y-yes, of-of course.' Everyone used the back door at Moorend and the front door was always locked as it was near the road, even though it was a quiet road. Emma flushed as she led the two gentlemen through the kitchen into the sitting room. At least it was neat and clean but the fire was not lit. She began to apologise and, ever hospitable, she asked if they would like a drink of tea. They both declined politely explaining they still had a long journey ahead but they wanted to see Marie because they were anxious about Mark. In spite of his uncle's warnings Rupert could not resist asking Emma if she and her husband had forbidden the marriage and caused Marie to break things off with his friend.

'Oh no,' Emma said. 'We could not forbid it when they both seemed so much in love, but we did ask them to wait at least six months, and preferably a year. Marie is still so young. My husband thought they should wait until Mark had carried out his plans to sell his house and build a home and a garage near the village.'

'Then why has Marie written to say she cannot see him again, and that he must not contact her?' Rupert demanded.

'Marie would not write such a thing!' Emma exclaimed. 'She loves Mark. She has told us so often enough.'

'I'm afraid she did write. Mark is devastated. He is talking of selling the whole estate and travelling abroad. He doesn't care where,' Rupert declared angrily. His uncle laid a restraining hand on his arm. 'I-I'm sorry, but Mark is my best friend, my oldest friend. I have never seen him so unhappy. Why would she . . . ?'

'I can't believe it,' Emma interrupted. 'We are all worried about Marie too. She neither eats nor sleeps as she should. She will not tell us the reason for her unhappiness. It all began the day she received a letter. She will not tell us who sent it, or what it said.'

'A letter?' Lord Tannahill repeated, frowning. Rupert stiffened.

'Whatever was in it upset her badly. She has been distressed ever since.'

'I see, then we must call on Marie herself and see if she can tell us the reason for such unhappiness,' Lord Tannahill said and stood up. Rupert had no option but to do the same. Emma was about to plead with them not to make Marie anymore upset, but she bit back the words. Marie could not be any worse.

Rupert was quiet on the way to Silverbeck Hall. As it happened Lord Hanley was in the Estate Office with Bob Rowbottom and Marie when the young maid announced he had visitors. Lord Tannahill lost no time in introducing himself and saying it was Marie they had come to see. Bob Rowbottom was already on his feet and he put an arm around Marie's shoulders fearing she was going to faint at the sight of the two men. He felt her trembling. Rupert saw how protective the two older men were and swiftly made a shot in the dark before they put him out.

'What did Sybil Blackford say in her letter to you, Marie? How did she succeed in parting you and Mark so — so cruelly?'

'Y-you know?' Marie whispered, her eyes widening in alarm. 'D-did she write to Mark too?' Rupert shot his uncle a look of triumph.

'We should have guessed that spiteful women was at the root of the trouble!' Rupert declared. 'She's poisonous. She has never cared about Mark's happiness. All she wanted was for him to repay them by making a good marriage.'

'That's enough, Rupert,' Lord Tannahill said sternly.

'No, Uncle Fordyce. It's not enough! I'll bet her letter was pure venom.' He strode across the room to Marie and hugged her. She sagged against him as though her remaining strength had drained away. 'Mark is heart sick without you. He has had a good offer for Stavondale Manor, if Uncle Fordyce will sell or rent the new buyer a field for grazing ponies. But now — now he doesn't care about anything. He says without you the estate can go to the devil. He is talking of going to Africa.'

'Oh no . . . Oh no,' Marie said and for the first time in public she put her head in her hands and wept. Lord Hanley and Mr Rowbottom looked at each other and nodded. Marie's tears were like the lancing of a wound.

'We will leave you to talk to Marie on your own,' Lord Hanley said. 'When you are ready, cook will have a meal waiting for you — all three of you. Bring them into the small parlour, Marie, my dear. And Marie, if they can help you and Mark to heal the rift, let them try. Life is too short for so much unhappiness. You have suffered enough these past few weeks.' Lord Tannahill thanked him then turned to Marie.

'May I see the letter you received, Marie?'

'It — it is not a nice letter,' Marie said. She shuddered. 'Honestly, I never cared whether Mark had money. B-but I-I could never let her shame Mark so — so publicly, or — or with such m-malice . . .'

'I would like to read it myself,' Lord Tannahill said very firmly. Marie crossed to her bag and drew out the letter. She handed it over reluctantly, biting hard on her lower lip as he began to read. Rupert smiled at her encouragingly and led her to a seat near the fire. She gave him a pleading look.

'I am not a money grabber,' she whispered. 'I would love Mark even if he had no money. In — in fact it would be better if he had never had an estate. He didn't ask for it. I would never . . .'

'Don't distress yourself, my dear.' Lord Tannahill said quietly. 'This is pure evil.' He strode to the fireplace and placed it in the flames.'

'Uncle!' Rupert exclaimed indignantly. 'I wanted to see . . .'

'The letter is venomous beyond belief. It is not fit for anyone to read. I knew Sybil resented Mark receiving what remained of his inheritance. She was unscrupulous about stealing the money for herself and her sons, but she must be deranged to write with such malice. It is better that Mark should never know how evil she can be.'

'She has always been bitter. However well he did at school she always belittled him and made disparaging comments. He achieved so much more than his brothers at university, but she still criticised him. I had never known him so happy and — and sort of complete, as he has been since he met Marie.'

'The love of a good woman can make a man, as I hope you will find out for yourself one day, Rupert. Right now, the best thing you can do for Mark is drive to the village post office and send him a telegram. Tell him to go ahead with the sale of the manor. Everything will be all right.'

'Shall I do that, Marie?' Rupert asked uncertainly.

'Certainly, you must,' Lord Tannahill insisted. 'Even if Sybil did spread malicious rumours they cannot hurt Mark so long as he has Marie at his side. As for you my dear, Marie, you must do your best to put that poisonous letter out of your mind. Forget Sybil Blackford ever existed. Any hatred she spreads will reflect more badly on herself than on Mark. Will you do that?'

'I-I will try.' Marie shivered. It would be easier said than done.

'I shall tell her I insisted on reading the letter myself. I rather think she will be sufficiently ashamed never to want to speak of it again — to you or to me. I doubt if she will be able to face either you or Mark again, but you will both be happier that way. If she had been left to her own devices she would have appropriated all of Mark's inheritance. I am glad my grandfather confided in me before it was too late. Apart from the money I was pleased to learn he is a young relative of mine. I can assure you Mark's friends will stay his friends.'

'Th-thank you,' Marie whispered hoarsely. 'Shall I take you through to see Lord Hanley now? It is time for me to go home.' She felt bewildered and emotionally wrung out, yet a tiny well of hope was beginning to spring inside her. Would Mark come to see her after she had told him so emphatically she didn't want to see him again? She shuddered. How could she forget the horrid things his mother had written?

As she showed Lord Tannahill along the hall towards the small sitting room he paused, his attention caught by two of the framed photographs.

'Who can this be?' he pondered aloud, frowning at one of the pictures.

'These are Lord Hanley's sons when they were younger,' Marie said quietly. 'They were both killed during the war. Their deaths caused Lady Hanley great sorrow. I'm sure Lord Hanley grieves deeply for them too.'

'Yes, I'm sure he must. Has he no other children?' he asked, still gazing intently at the elder of the two boys.

'No, he only had two sons. It is tragic that they both died fighting for their country.'

Lord Hanley smiled in welcome when they entered the small sitting room. It was only small in comparison to the other rooms, but it was large enough for a decent-sized dining table as well as several comfortable chairs around the huge fireplace.

'I prefer to dine in here when I am alone, or with just a few friends,' he explained to Lord Tannahill. 'It is nearer the kitchens and handier for cook and her helpers.'

'I will go home now,' Marie said, 'unless you would like me to finish typing the letters first?'

'No, no, my dear Marie. You have done enough work for today but you must stay and eat with us. I asked Rupert to call in at Moorend and tell your parents you would be dining here tonight. Lord Tannahill, it is getting late, and I understand you have a long way to go? It would give me great pleasure if you would stay here overnight and continue your journey in the morning?'

'That is very kind of you. I would be happy to accept. When Rupert suggested making this detour into Yorkshire, I had not anticipated we should be so long. It has been worth every minute.' He smiled at Marie. 'Rupert was right for once. I had no idea how badly things had gone wrong. I'm sure things will work out well now we have got to the root of the trouble.'

'Indeed I do hope so,' Lord Hanley agreed, 'even though I fear it means Marie will return to Scotland and we shall miss her badly. Isn't that so Bob?' He turned to smile at his land agent and Bob Rowbottom agreed.

'If you will excuse me I'll ring for Jenny and ask her to make up the beds.'

'I'll help her,' Marie said, rising to her feet at once.

'No, my dear. You stay by the fire and relax.' He looked seriously at Lord Tannahill. 'Now you see why I shall miss Marie so much. She is always willing to help however mundane the tasks, and there are few things she cannot accomplish. I think our young friend, Mark, will be surprised when he sees how well she drives my car now.'

'Mmm, I see what you mean,' Lord Tannahill said thoughtfully with a speculative glance at Marie. 'Your willingness may prove a solution to one of Mark's immediate problems. We shall see.'

Eventually Rupert came bounding in, smiling widely.

'I'm sorry to have taken so long,' he gasped. 'You'll never guess what's happened!' he grinned. 'Uncle Fordyce, can we book in somewhere near to stay tonight?'

'Lord Hanley has kindly offered to put us up here, Rupert. So what brings that big smile to your face?'

'I called to speak to Marie's parents, as Lord Hanley suggested, after I had sent the telegram. I took a wrong turning on the way back. I came to a junction and I saw the telegraph boy coming in this direction. I stopped to ask if I was on the right road. He said I was and he was bringing a telegram to Silverbeck Hall for a Rupert Shearman. I said that was me so he handed it over. Here it is.' He waved the flimsy paper triumphantly. 'It's from Mark. He says: *Arriving on last train into Wakefield tonight. Thanks a million. Mark.* So you see Marie, he can't wait to see you.'

Marie's face went white, and then pink. She didn't know what to say but her shining eyes and sweet smile told the onlookers all they needed to know. 'I can't believe it,' she whispered tremulously.

'Whatever you said in that telegram seems to have done the trick,' Lord Tannahill said drily. 'I hope Mark doesn't miss the opportunity to close the sale on Stavondale Manor when his mind is preoccupied.'

'Maybe he'll call on MacQuade on his way to the station,' Rupert said.

'I-I think I ought to go home now and — and . . .'

'There's no need, sweet Marie,' Rupert grinned. When I read the telegram I turned the car and went back to tell your parents Mark would be arriving late tonight and I would be taking you to the station to meet him.'

'Oh . . .' Marie gasped, 'B-but . . .'

'Your mother said she would have a bed ready for him but she thought you might want to change your clothes so she sent a dress and coat and shoes so you can change here before we set out for the station. It will be nearly midnight before the train gets in I think.'

'That's all right,' Lord Hanley said. 'It will give us all time to enjoy a good dinner. After that, Marie, you can use the room you had when you stayed here with my wife. There's plenty of hot water if you care to bathe or wash your hair, or whatever young ladies do before meeting their sweethearts,' he said with a teasing smile. 'Bob has a daughter so he will know about such things better than I do. We only had sons.'

'Oh yes, hair washing always seemed to be essential. Taking a bath at short notice was not so easy then though as none of us had bathrooms as we have now.' Bob Rowbottom winked at Marie. 'Young Mark will be pleased to see you lass, whatever you look like, and you're always as pretty as a picture anyway, especially now you've got the colour back in your cheeks.'

Rupert was sitting next to a small table on which there were several photographs in silver frames. His attention was caught by one of them. He possessed none of his uncle's caution, or his careful reflection. He picked up the photo of a young boy on a pony.

'How strange that you should know the Winkworths of Feltham Grange, Lord Hanley. They're almost neighbours of Uncle Fordyce.' Lord Tannahill's head jerked up. He tried to catch his nephew's eye in warning, even though he himself had noticed the likeness when he saw the photograph in the hall. Rupert was looking expectantly at Lord Hanley. Fordyce quickly intervened.

'I believe the photographs are of Lord Hanley's sons,' he said quietly. 'They were both killed during the war.' Rupert heard the warning in his tone and flushed.

'I-I am so s-sorry, Lord Hanley,' he stammered. 'I didn't know. It's just . . . this photograph is the image of young Dickie Whitelea. I have seen him following the hunt with his Grandfather Winkworth. He's only about eight years old but he's a fine horseman already.' Too late he glimpsed the flash of irritation in his uncle's eyes. He saw Lord Hanley frowning and rushed on in confusion. 'Th-that's why I thought you must know the Winkworths, Sir. I'm so sorry.' Lord Tannahill bowed his head. Rupert didn't notice Bob Rowbottom and Marie waiting tensely.

Lady Hanley had talked a lot about her sons to Marie in the latter months they had spent together. She knew Richard was the eldest but his friends called him Ricky. She also knew he had had a girlfriend called Thea Winkworth whom he had met at the house party of one of his old school friends. Thea had come to stay at Silverbeck Hall several times. They had seemed to be very much in love and had planned to marry as soon as the war was over. She also knew Lord and Lady Hanley had been dreadfully hurt when Thea failed to attend Ricky's memorial service, and even more so when she married less than two months after Ricky's death, even though she had known the man all her life.

As for Bob Rowbottom he had known Ricky and his brother, Douglas, since they were born. He and his wife had met Thea, and liked her. They had felt disappointed too.

CHAPTER SIXTEEN

Bob Rowbottom had long since gone home to his wife when Rupert and Marie set off to meet the train at Wakefield. Rupert had regained his lively spirits and he told Marie she looked so pretty with her shining curls and pink cheeks that he had half a mind to run away with her himself.

'Bring them back here,' Lord Hanley said. 'Mark can borrow my car to drive to Moorend. After such a late night I shall not expect you until midday Marie, Mark can return the car then.' Marie thanked him, her eyes luminous with joy and gratitude. If he had not been her employer, and her father's landlord, she would have hugged him.

When they had the house to themselves Lord Hanley added more coal to the fire and refilled their brandy glasses. They were now on Christian name terms of Fordyce and Adrian.

'I know Marie is young in years,' Lord Tannahill mused, 'but she is sensible and practical. She proved very capable the way she kept house for her uncle and brother at Bonnybrae, as well as caring for their little girl. I hope her parents will agree to let her marry Mark sooner rather than later. We all know the temptations when a couple in love are forced to be apart.'

'I agree but I understand there will be a problem of a place for them to live if Mark is selling the Manor House and has yet to build a home somewhere else. Apart from feeling Marie is too young to marry, William Sinclair doesn't want his daughter to begin married life living with her aunt and uncle. I understand that, although I believe they are kind and mean well, but all young couples are better on their own.'

'I agree. I noticed how readily Marie volunteered to help your maid make up the beds,' Lord Tannahill remarked, 'so I don't think she would be offended if I offered them the use of the flat I am renovating at Stavondale Tower with a view to employing a housekeeper eventually. I need someone to live on the premises to keep an eye on my own residence in my absence, as well as the west wing where we accommodate guests who come for the shooting. There would be nothing onerous for Marie and Mark to do if they accept my offer of the flat as a temporary home. They could be together while they build the house they want.' He smiled whimsically. 'I like Mark. I always have, ever since he came to stay with Rupert for the school holidays when they were about nine or ten years old. I had no idea then that he was my own young cousin. Most families seem to have some dirty linen in the closet,' he added wryly.

'You're right there. I am very fond of Marie. She was a wonderful companion to my wife. I would have been proud to have her as a daughter. I might ride over to Moorend tomorrow and have a word with her father, William Sinclair. Although he and his wife tried hard to keep their past a secret, things have a way of leaking out and rumour has it that Jamie was born before they married. I think Jamie discovered the truth and it unsettled him and caused him to run away to Scotland. I don't think Sinclair will want anything like that to happen with Marie and Mark.'

'No indeed.' Lord Tannahill stared reflectively into his brandy glass, then he looked up and met his new friend's dark gaze. 'Did it ever occur to you that Thea Winkworth might have had little option but to marry in haste after your son's death?'

'Little option?'

'Her child was supposedly born prematurely. Two months early we were led to believe, although he was never a weakling boy. She was married to Whitelea for seven years but she has never had any more children. There are stories that he was unable to father a child himself.' He paused, allowing his words to sink in. 'Rupert can be a brash young puppy, but he is right. Young Dicky Whitelea is extraordinarily like the photograph of your son. Is it possible he could be Richard's child? Your grandson?'

'My grandson!' Lord Hanley came to his feet. He began to pace the room. 'A grandson? My God! I suppose it is possible. We never considered such a possibility. Surely Thea would have told us? We seemed to get on well. We liked her very much.'

'Thea was widowed last year. Whitelea had taken to travelling alone. He was on one of those river boats on the Mississippi. It was said he had fallen overboard. He has not left his wife and son well provided for so she has returned to live with her parents.'

'I see . . .'

'It would give me great pleasure to repay your hospitality, Adrian. Why don't you come up and stay with us before too long. Think about it,' he added hastily as they heard the sound of the car returning.

* * *

The three young people came in amidst some teasing from Rupert because Mark had his arm around Marie's shoulders.

'He's afraid she might escape,' he chuckled. 'I thought he would never stop hugging and kissing our little Marie when he saw her at the station. Even the ticket collector waved them by with a big grin.'

'Stop teasing. Did you have a good journey, Mark?' Lord Tannahill enquired.

'Yes, I did, thank you.'

'Cook has left sandwiches and some apple pie,' Lord Hanley said. 'She remembered how much you enjoy her apple pies, Mark. Come and sit here my boy and eat while you tell us your news.'

'I will make tea for everyone, shall I?' Marie offered.

'Just for the three of you,' Lord Hanley said smiling, indicating their brandy glasses.

Mark told them he had called in at the MacQuades' offices on his way to the station and told the lawyer to go ahead with the sale of Stavondale Manor to the industrialist who was buying the mill and business from Mr Courton and Joe Greig.

'I left my bicycle there for safe keeping too and Mr MacQuade gave me a lift to the station. He seemed pleased we had managed to come to an arrangement over the land. Now both the mill and the house sale can go ahead.'

'He will be pleased. It will be good business for his firm,' Lord Tannahill said drily.

'Gosh, I didn't realise I was so hungry,' Mark said, reaching for another sandwich.

'Love makes you hungry, does it?' Rupert asked, with an irrepressible chuckle.

Mark had finished the sandwiches, with assistance from Rupert, when Lord Tannahill made his suggestion about the new housekeeper's flat at Stavondale Tower.

'You could live there until you have built a house where you want it. It has a large bedroom and sitting room, plus a kitchen and bathroom so you would be entirely private.' Mark looked at Marie. She was very tired but she was so happy she felt she must be dreaming.

'It sounds a perfect temporary solution, doesn't it, Mark?'

'Anywhere will be wonderful so long as we can be together,' Mark said. 'I really appreciate your offer and all your help, but will you tell me why we were almost parted? I know now it was not Marie's wish, but she will not tell me anything. Rupert also refused to tell me, except it was something about a letter.' He looked at Lord Tannahill.

'It was a poisonous letter,' he said with a grimace. 'I burned it. I'm sorry the woman who acted as your mother could be so cruel, Mark. My advice is to forget about her. I doubt if she will trouble you in future. I shall speak to her about it. Marie was trying to protect your good name and character by submitting to Sybil's blackmail.'

'I should have guessed! I have endured her censure all my life.' Mark reached for Marie's hand and squeezed her fingers reassuringly. 'We should go now or your parents will wonder where we are.'

'They will if you linger on the way, stealing more kisses,' Rupert grinned.

'Marie, if your parents give their consent to let you marry, tell them it would give me the greatest pleasure to hold your wedding here after the church service,' Lord Hanley said. 'You can regard it as my joint wedding gift to you both.' Marie wondered how much brandy he had drunk and if he would remember his suggestion in the morning. She looked at Lord Tannahill. He had high colour in his cheeks too. He winked at her.

'Go home to bed, the pair of you. And Mark, good luck with winning over Mr Sinclair in the morning. Remember a man's daughter is very precious to him.'

'Not as precious as Marie is to me.' Mark beamed and put an arm around her shoulders as they made their way outside to the car.

Mark couldn't resist stopping the car to tell Marie how much he loved her and to steal several kisses. It was well after midnight when they crept into the silent house, not wanting to waken anyone. They need not have worried. The kitchen fire had burned low but was still offering a cosy warmth. Emma was dozing in the wooden armchair with a woollen rug around her. She stirred when she heard the sneck of the door. She stood up and smiled in welcome. She saw the joy in Marie's eyes and the tenderness in Mark's and hugged them.

'It is a relief to see you back to your usual happy self, Marie. And you too Mark? Is everything going to be all right between you now?' she asked anxiously.

'Mrs Sinclair, I can't tell you how wretched I have been, believing Marie no longer loved me. Now I know she does and I am the happiest man on earth.' They had not meant to share the news of the flat or Lord Hanley's offer until morning but Emma could see they were longing to tell her all that had occurred.

'It is very generous of Lord Tannahill to offer you his flat. It would solve the problem of where to live,' Emma said.

'All we need now is Father's permission to marry.' Marie said uncertainly. Emma hugged her again.

'We have been so worried about you neither eating nor sleeping, Marie. I reckon William will be as relieved as I am that Mark has brought the colour back to your cheeks and banished the shadows from your eyes. Take my advice Mark and wait until he has eaten his breakfast before you mention weddings.'

'At this rate it will be milking time before we even get to bed,' Marie said stifling a yawn. 'We didn't expect you to wait up for us Mam. I'm so sorry . . .'

'I wouldn't have missed seeing your happy young faces for the world,' Emma said. 'We shall miss you, Marie. You will be living so far away, but so long as you are both happy, and Mark promises to bring you to visit us as often as he can, I am thankful.'

William gave his consent to Mark's earnest request to marry his daughter, but pride prevented him from accepting Lord Hanley's offer to hold the wedding reception at Silverbeck Hall. Lord Hanley had guessed this might be the case so as soon as his guests had left for their journey to Gloucestershire, he saddled his horse and rode to Moorend.

'I guessed your proud Scottish spirit might make you refuse my offer, William Sinclair, but to hold the wedding of two fine young people would give me the greatest pleasure. Also,' he held up his hand to silence William's protest, 'also, you should know me well enough by now to know I usually want something in return,' he grinned provocatively, 'as well as their happiness of course.'

'I see. But a daughter's wedding is her parents' responsibility and . . .'

'And I don't have a daughter for whom I can make a wedding. I know you and your wife can keep a secret and I entreat you to keep mine now?'

'Of course we would keep your secret,' William said with a puzzled frown, while Emma nodded.

'I would like to invite two guests of my own who are unknown to you. A wedding reception would be an ideal excuse. Lord Tannahill believes I have a grandson.'

'A grandson!' Emma echoed, clasping her hands in delight. 'That's wonderful news.'

'I don't understand,' William frowned.

'Well, you should. It never occurred to me, or my wife, that our son, Richard would yield to temptation even though we knew he and Thea were very much in love and intended to marry as soon as he returned from the war. As you know, both he and Douglas were killed. We were extremely hurt when Thea did not return to Silverbeck for Richard's memorial service, and more so when she married someone else so soon after his death. According to Lord Tannahill she gave birth to a son barely seven months after the marriage. Lord Tannahill is convinced the boy is Richard's son. A grandson! I can scarce believe it. Both he and Rupert saw a strong resemblance to Richard in photographs of him as a boy, and as a young man. The boy's name is Ricky. Why, oh why did the poor girl not confide in us? We would have taken her in, given her a home . . .'

'Shame,' Emma whispered, her face pale. 'People condemn more easily than they forgive.'

William crossed to his wife then and put a protective arm around her.

'Emma understands because I was as weak, or as selfish, as your son, Lord Hanley, and her parents sent her away. I can thank God I was not killed in the dreadful carnage they called war. We both have much to be thankful for.'

'You have indeed, and if Lord Tannahill is correct and the boy is my grandson, I shall do my best to recompense him and Thea. So you will allow me to hold the wedding reception and invite them?'

'I am sure you will invite them with or without a wedding reception,' William said wryly.

'Probably,' Lord Hanley acknowledged with a tilt of his head, and a half smile, 'but I have another proposition for you too. You will have heard rumours that Mountcliff will be coming to let?'

'We heard, but we didn't believe it. Is Gerry Wilkins really leaving his wife?'

'Yes, he and Miss Coby are moving to Scarborough. The farm will be to let from the end of March. I would like you and your sons to take on the tenancy. You can use the money for the wedding reception towards extra cattle, or sheep. Presumably you will have another wedding in the family then, even if Tindall will be paying. Oh yes, Bob Rowbottom keeps me informed, and I might add he is certain you and your sons will improve the Mountcliff land with your rotations, and the hill land if you keep sheep there as you do on the Common. Think about it and let me know by the end of the week.'

* * *

The wedding at Silverbeck Hall was declared the biggest and happiest wedding anyone in the village could remember. Lord Tannahill arrived with Sylvia, and his sister, Rupert's mother. Lord Hanley seemed to enjoy having so many guests and he had personally invited Mrs Thea Whitelea and her son, Dicky. Privately, Bob Rowbottom and his wife marvelled at the boy's resemblance to the young Richard they had known. They were convinced the boy had to be Lord Hanley's grandson.

Almost all the tenants, and most of the villagers, turned up and Marie and Mark were overwhelmed by their generous wedding gifts. Mark had driven Aunt Maggie and Uncle Joe down from Scotland, with Marguerite, two days before the big day. Rina, Jamie and the twins travelled by train.

Emma insisted Mr and Mrs Blackford should be invited as Mark's parents. She didn't know Sybil Blackford's atrocious letter had almost succeeded in parting Marie and Mark. When an acceptance arrived both Mark and Marie were surprised and uneasy, but they were too happy to worry for long. They were astonished when a subdued Sybil offered a faltering apology to Marie. Mr Blackford sincerely wished them happiness.

Rupert was best man, and several of his, and Mark's, mutual friends from school and university had come to wish Mark and his young bride every happiness. Marie was radiant as only a happy young bride can be and Marguerite was the prettiest little flower girl. Meg was matron of honour and Fiona a bridesmaid, smiling shyly at everyone. Several of the locals declared it was the loveliest wedding they had seen and Lord Hanley told William Sinclair he should be the proudest man on earth to have three pretty daughters as well as a delightful granddaughter.

At last Marie and Mark stealthily made their escape, through the kitchens and out of the back door of Silverbeck Hall. Joe was waiting with the car engine already running. He understood Mark wanted to avoid Rupert and the outrageous pranks he and his friends would play on them. Joe's wedding gift was two nights in a small hotel recommended by Lord Hanley and run by a widow who used to be cook at Silverbeck.

'It was a wonderful wedding,' Mark said drawing Marie into his arms as soon as they were alone. They were delighted and a little overwhelmed to discover they had the top floor of the three-storey house to themselves with a tiny bathroom, a bedroom and a small sitting room, complete with a bowl of fruit and a large vase of flowers. 'I never expected anything like this.' Mark sighed happily. 'I thought I would never get you all to myself.'

'And now that you have?' Marie asked mischievously, her blue eyes sparkling as she snuggled into his embrace.

'Now,' Mark smiled tenderly down at her, 'all I want is to make you truly my wife, my darling Marie.'

THE END

THE JOFFE BOOKS STORY

We began in 2014 when Jasper agreed to publish his mum's much-rejected romance novel and it became a bestseller.

Since then we've grown into the largest independent publisher in the UK. We're extremely proud to publish some of the very best writers in the world, including Joy Ellis, Faith Martin, Caro Ramsay, Helen Forrester, Simon Brett and Robert Goddard. Everyone at Joffe Books loves reading and we never forget that it all begins with the magic of an author telling a story.

We are proud to publish talented first-time authors, as well as established writers whose books we love introducing to a new generation of readers.

We have been shortlisted for Independent Publisher of the Year at the British Book Awards three times, in 2020, 2021 and 2022, and for the Diversity and Inclusivity Award at the Independent Publishing Awards in 2022.

We built this company with your help, and we love to hear from you, so please email us about absolutely anything bookish at feedback@joffebooks.com

If you want to receive free books every Friday and hear about all our new releases, join our mailing list: www.joffebooks.com/contact

And when you tell your friends about us, just remember: it's pronounced Joffe as in coffee or toffee!

ALSO BY GWEN KIRKWOOD

THE MAXWELL FAMILY QUARTET
Book 1: AN ORPHAN OF SCOTLAND
Book 2: THE SECRETS THAT BIND US
Book 3: DREAMS OF THE VALLEY
Book 4: SOMEWHERE TO CALL HOME

THE SINCLAIR FAMILY SAGAS
Book 1: MOORLAND MIST
Book 2: MOOREND FARM
Book 3: RETURN TO BONNYBRAE
Book 4: A SCOTTISH DESTINY
Book 5: LOVE HAS NO BORDERS

Printed in Great Britain
by Amazon

28251170R00158